DEDICATION

This novel is dedicated to those courageous people who came out before Stonewall, post DOMA bi-national gay and lesbian couples unable to return to the US, and child survivors of World War II in Germany, whose traumas wait to be healed.

DUPLICITY'S DAUGHTER

A NOVEL

NAOMI STEPHAN

ISBN: 0-9631262-9-6

Book cover design by Mary Austin Speaker,
www.maryaustinspeaker.com

Book design and production by Maureen Cutajar,
www.gopublished.com

Photo of Berlin Wall by Jen Westmoreland Bouchard,
www.luciditewriting.com

Editing and proofreading by Sarah Gallogly,
sjgallogly@gmail.com

Author photograph by Monika Braun.

All translations are by the author.

ACKNOWLEDGEMENTS

Duplicity's Daughter (DD) would have been impossible to complete without the help of three women who gave me immeasurable counsel on my novel. Each played a distinct and indispensible role based on her individual expertise.

The first, Sue Carroll Moore, ever my co-conspirator, mentor and friend, agreed to peruse DD with me line-by-line, paragraph-by-paragraph. For at least three years, we met every day via the Internet. Sue became my severest critic, and demanded only the best from me. I learned from her more about the power of the pen than I ever thought possible. Her psychological insights and knowledge of literature, poetry and writing skills proved invaluable. Without her unfailing support, DD would have been unthinkable.

I can only say, humbly, thank you Sue for standing by me in times of illness, delay, despair and discouragement. We made it to the end of my – really our – novel, and I am grateful for your love and faithful suiting up and showing up. You are my *sine qua non*.

The second woman is my dear partner Julie. While she faced tenacious physical challenges, Julie took precious time from her work and treatments to read my manuscript more than once. She offered me an elegant way out of a knotty linguistic problem, gave valuable suggestions on how best to formulate some of the novel's German words and phrases into English, pointed out any repetitions I had overlooked, and raised plot questions for me to solve.

Julie's emotional support gave me strength through the nadirs and zeniths of my days on DD. She gave me encouragement when I needed it, toasted to the end of the manuscript, only to learn that I had decided to take another look. "Love alters not when it alteration finds," as the Bard wrote.

Before she publishes, any writer knows a manuscript needs fresh eyes. And for this purpose, Sarah Gallogly, a professional editor, took on my manuscript several years ago. Sarah guided me through the technical, grammatical and formal intricacies of this novel, never losing patience with my missed deadlines. With the keen eye of a hawk, she detected every remaining error, typo, discrepancy, inconsistency, repetitive phrase and downright silly goof. (She is not responsible for any rewrites after that!) I thank Sarah moreover for graciously answering in detail all the countless emails I sent, and for providing me, unasked for, with a style sheet and glossary. Well done!

Thanks also to so many others who provided support and suggestions. I hope you, the reader, will benefit from the prior scrutiny of these fine people. If you catch anything else, all I can say is "mea culpa". To err is human, but it feels divine, as I once noted on a California bumper sticker.

PREFACE

The path to *Duplicity's Daughter* has been long and winding. I grew up in a campus parsonage at Indiana University (IU) with my clergyman father and church musician mother. Their expectations were high. After graduating from High School in the National Honor Society, I earned my BA, Phi Beta Kappa, from IU, and my MA with a Fellowship from the University of Illinois.

Thanks to back-to-back Fulbright scholarships I went on to study voice at the College of Music in Berlin – a seminal time in my life. During those Cold War years, I visited East Berlin hundreds of times for museums, concerts – even church – and occasionally the German Democratic Republic, in spite of the hassle of paperwork and visas.

After receiving a second BA in voice, I was at loose ends, not able to envision my dream to perform early music. And, I had developed severe vocal problems, which I now know were due to stress and anxiety about the future, as well as my sexual orientation.

With a heavy heart, I returned to IU to focus on a doctorate in German literature and music history. I completed my coursework and accepted a position as Instructor of German at Valparaiso University near Chicago. Four years of teaching passed with little progress on my dissertation topic: The Interpretation of Heine's lyrics in the Songs of Robert Schumann.

I took two years off from a heavy teaching load – bolstered with a German government grant (DAAD) – and chose to live in Düsseldorf,

Heinrich Heine's hometown, where Robert Schumann spent his later years as Musical Director. After completing my dissertation, I returned to my post as Assistant Professor of German in Valparaiso and also performed vocally both in Valpo and the Chicago area. DD was not yet even a glimmer in my eye. A further year abroad in Düsseldorf in the mid-seventies was a thrilling turn unfettered by academics or studies; I began to sing early music both as a soloist and in a Kantorei.

Yet doubts arose in my mind that I could manage this type of artistic life full time. Once again, I went back to my teaching post. By the early eighties I finally had had enough of academe, and resigned from my academic post at VU one year short of a full professorship – with nothing in place. What was my next step? Where was I headed? What was my mission in life? For almost six months in my new home state, California, I did intense soul searching and life review. I knew my life had witnessed far too many stops and starts with my passions and discovered that the search for a mission was a field largely untouched in life planning. With the help of my partner Sue, I founded Life Mission Associates (LMA), a life mission consulting and psychotherapy firm.

In my role as co-owner of Life Mission Associates, I used my own experience as a basis for working with clients on their abandoned missions, and their grief confirmed I was not alone in having jumped ship. I worked long hours developing seminars, lectures and workshop tours to help others find their mission. That was a necessary step. I began to heal myself alongside my clients.

To support our LMA cause, I wrote a groundbreaking book, *Finding Your Life Mission* (FYLM), in which I detailed how clients can identify, develop and live their mission based on my own insights. During the writing process – cathartic, valuable, and necessary – I constantly had to face my past, particularly my four adventurous and musical years in Berlin. These painful reminders awakened a desire to integrate music more fully into my life, in just what form I didn't know yet. I eased back into my music by revisiting my musical roots: choral and vocal music and started to compose, often to settings of my own lyrics or lyrics mostly by women. The acceptance and commissions I received demonstrated to me that I was on the right track. The twenty-first century arrived. Musical grants rolled in, particularly for *Mater in Memoriam* MIMI*)*, a 45-minute requiem dedicated to my mother.

Despite all the success of LMA and my music, I still felt the need to take the concept of mission to a deeper, soul level. I wrote a fourth edition of FYLM and entitled it Fulfill Your Soul's Purpose (FYSP).

But my old dream of DD would not release its hold on me. Those thoughts about Berlin fueled the idea to write a novel with a Cold War backdrop. As I had told multi-talented clients over and over, when passions beg to be heard, treat them with love, care, and attention.

From the beginning, the title of the novel had been clear, as well as the basic plot and many of the characters. Like a butterfly emerging from a cocoon, my novel was about to take new shape. More than "just" a cold war tale, DD was now in the first person along with new structures, themes, plots, genres and literary devices. But how to find time for it?

Providence stepped in. Mission and soul had become part of common parlance. In contrast to responses from publishers 15 years previous who sniffed that the word "mission" smacked of militarism or religion, new copycat books sprouted forth, and it was time to close that chapter.

One thing I hadn't counted on: meeting a musically gifted Brit, who had come from Europe to attend one of LMA's weeklong soul's purpose seminars. I visited her in Europe afterwards, and the following year, she returned to the States to assist me in the production and performance of my requiem. It was that experience that sealed our bond and desire to live together in Ojai.

A year later, as the "gay marriage" topic was heating up in the US, we drove 500 miles though the night to San Francisco and stood eight hours in line, joining some 4000+ gay and lesbian couples that married there in 2004 – to no avail, ultimately. Our marriage was annulled. In the end, love lost and US bigotry and injustice won. A five-year attempt to maintain our home in Ojai exhausted all our finances, legal resources, and time. In 2007, we left for England for a last good bye to my partner's dying mother. One day longer in California with an expired visa would have turned Julie into a felon in the eyes of the law, unless she would have gone underground, which was not an option.

I underwent the most wrenching experience of my life, choosing exile to Germany. In 2008, we gave possessions away, took our two dogs, the grand piano, and moved abroad to the tune of $20,000. I think about the morning we had to leave Ojai, and the grief of saying goodbye to our little home before it was put up for sale.

In Germany, we lived in a one-bedroom apartment with my friend Sue and her partner, also a binational couple – and the dogs – a tight squeeze. While Julie worked at a small computer station, I stood in a corner and tapped away on the novel until we could afford to be on our own. The stress robbed time from my pen, and no doubt contributed to a life threatening illness two years later. But a small house in Northeast Germany has since given me the serenity and opportunity to finish what I had started more than twenty years ago. For us, a return to the states would be expensive and emotionally draining despite some changes in DOMA. We can only hope a day will come when heterosexuals no longer decide the future of us all, and justice and the right to love another person freely and responsibly without fear of separation will prevail.

Naomi Irene Stephan 2014

DUPLICITY'S DAUGHTER

1

∞

My hand slipped from hers as I heard the final call for my flight to Frankfurt. I dashed to the gate with my ticket, walked down the ramp – more like a gangplank – and turned around to wave once again. Laura's beautiful smile would have to last me a long time.

At the entrance to the plane, I wanted to say, "Stop!" and reclaim my baggage. But I couldn't turn back now. I had to follow through with my plans and put aside my fears of going this alone.

Time and aging have soothed the pain of that perilous Cold War year in Berlin. But the hold of memory gives me little respite.

* * *

It was the fall of 1962, the beginning of my fourth year as assistant professor of German at Ryan College in Wisconsin, when a grant application from DAAD – the German Academic Exchange Service in Bonn – crossed my desk, offering a year's stipend. In just three years, I would be up for tenure, which required a PhD. The DAAD would provide an unencumbered opportunity to finish my dissertation on the interpretation of German Romantic poetry in the Third Reich.

Competition would be stiff, but after mulling things over, I decided to apply. Several trump cards were in my favor: I spoke the language fluently, and my access to primary sources in Germany would build a good case. Howard Laemmert, my department chair, agreed to my leave. His wife Frieda, a native speaker, was only too eager to take over my classes. Moreover, Dr. Blume, my dissertation advisor, wrote a compelling one-sentence recommendation that German Romantic poetry was "Renate Seiler's daily bread."

Winter wore on. No response from Bonn yet. At the spring break, I was in the process of selecting poems for my fall poetry class when, to my delight, a letter awarding me the grant arrived.

I went down the hall to Howard's office to give him the news.

"Wonderful!" He shook my hand. "You'll finally get to connect with your old hometown. I'll prepare your leave papers and mail a letter and introduce you to Dr. Bautsch at the German State Library in East Berlin."

"Thank you."

Howard motioned for me to sit down. "Apropos the GSL: The library keeps rather short hours, compared to what we're used to in the US – so no overnights in the library for our department workaholic."

The fellow does possess a wry sense of humor, I thought.

After leaving Howard's office I phoned my mother in Chicago.

"Mama, DAAD gave me the grant." I tried to keep my voice from trembling.

"Oh, Reni, I'm so happy for you!"

Over dinner that evening, Laura Sanchez, a friend in the Spanish department, told me:

"Let's face it, Renita, you'll get a break from hearing your students slaughter those awful German verbs."

"The four-year itch."

We laughed and toasted to my success.

*   *   *

When my mother's frail health worsened in early June, my elation about the grant dampened. Her next-door neighbor called to tell me that Mama had suffered a massive heart attack and had been admitted to Presbyterian-St. Luke's in Chicago. Laura dropped everything and drove me the seventy miles to the hospital.

The doctors did all they could to keep Mama alive. She looked terrible with all those tubes stuck in her. I couldn't bring myself to have them removed, even though she didn't want artificial support and was slipping in and out of consciousness.

I went back and forth from Mama's place to her bedside at Presbyterian. In those final days, I held her hands – how slender and beautiful they were, I realized, with their perfectly manicured nails and cuticles. When I sang her favorite lullaby, her head turned toward me.

I notified Pastor Gunter to come as quickly as possible and give Mama communion. Mama barely recognized him. As she was too weak to hold the chalice, the Pastor asked me to take Mama's hand, dip her index finger into the chalice and place it on her lips. I put my other hand behind my back and pressed the thumbnail underneath my index finger to keep from crying. I knew Mama did not want tears at this time.

Several days later, a nurse called just before dawn to tell me Mama had passed away. I arrived at the hospital too late even to say goodbye. Her body – willed to the Indiana University Medical Center – was already gone. Her only reminder was a book of devotions on the nightstand opened to the lesson for the day. Edda always wanted to be theologically prepared.

Ten years before, my mother had announced her decision to donate her body to IUMC, avoiding what she considered "that dreadful ritual, the American funeral."

Any protest was useless.

"All that makeup and for what? I'll be glad to see my Savior, and he won't care how I look."

The nurses wrapped Mama in a fresh sheet before the medical school wards removed her. I was numb, and barely knew what to think or feel. I was only certain that my absence in her final moments would haunt me forever.

*   *   *

I called Pastor Gunter at home to tell him Mama had passed away. He understood Mama's wishes, but we set a date for a memorial service,

3

allowing time for Hildegard – Edda's older sister and my only living relative – to attend if she wished.

For sixteen years, Mama and her sister had corresponded, and occasionally I added a note. On our last visit before emigrating to the US, Mama tried to persuade Hildegard to come as well, but she declined.

"Abandon the farm, where I've lived my entire adult life? Forsake Millie and the other animals? No! And Detlev won't go. I know that for certain. Besides, I don't much care for that soldier husband of yours, Edda. He'll never replace Kurt."

I looked through Mama's address book for Hildegard's number.

The phone rang several times.

"The Rehberg residence."

In spite of my excitement, hearing her voice – weaker and more fragile than I expected – sent sadness swirling through me.

"Hello, Auntie, this is your niece, Reni."

"My goodness," she said, "what a surprise to hear your voice! How are you?"

"*Ach*, Auntie, I'm so sorry to tell you that Mama died of a heart attack the day before yesterday."

"What, Edda's passed away? Oh no!" Her voice trembled. "Reni, what happened?"

I told her about Edda's heart problems, the call from her neighbor, my trips to the hospital and Edda's last days.

"I'm in shock," she said. "I never knew. Edda didn't let on how she was doing."

I could not control my tears.

"Reni, are you all right?"

"Yes, I'm holding up as best I can. A colleague from Ryan is helping me out. And Pastor Gunter has been very kind and paid me a visit."

"Edda wrote several times he was a wonderful man."

"Auntie, how are you doing?"

"As well as can be expected."

"There is a memorial service on June 27. Would you be able to come?"

Hildegard paused. "No, I'm afraid not. I wish more than anything to be with you at Edda's memorial, but unfortunately, I've got hip problems."

"Oh dear. But perhaps I can visit you, Auntie. I'm coming to Germany in a few months."

"You are? Well, yes, of course I'd love to see you – but I plan on a spa visit for three weeks in August, so it would have to be after that."

"Perfect. I'm leaving in September. I'll give you advance notice about my arrival."

"Reni, I shall be with you in spirit at Edda's memorial, and light a candle for her."

"Thank you, Aunt Hildegard, I'm sad you won't be here, but I look forward to seeing you after all these years."

"My blessings to you. May God grant you strength and solace at this difficult time."

*   *   *

My conversation with Hildegard relieved me greatly. Maybe the time apart had softened her from the person I'd known when we left.

For the music at my mother's Lutheran church, I wanted Oscar, our organist, to play her favorite Bach chorale, "O Sacred Head, Now Wounded." I selected a poem from Friedrich Rückert's cycle *Songs on my Children's Death* – "Oft denk' ich, sie sind nur ausgegangen" (Sometimes I think they have just gone out for a while).

Like Rückert struggling with the loss of his children, I couldn't believe Mama was really gone. Reading the poem assuaged my grief. I also printed a strophe of Hildegard's poem, "Solace in God," by Ernst Moritz Arndt, in Edda's memorial bulletin.

> *Dahin! Da ist dein Himmel,*
> *Da ist dein Heimatland,*
> *Das dir im Erdgewimmel*
> *Verdunkeln Leid und Tand,*
> *Da klingen Wunderklänge,*

Die machen frisch und neu,
Da klingen die Gesänge
Von Gottes Lieb' und Treu'.

Over there, that is your heaven,
Your homeland,
Where suffering and baubles
Cloud life on
Our hectic earth.
There miraculous strains
Will make you fresh and renewed,
There songs proclaim
God's constant love and fidelity.

I wondered if the pastor approved of the poem, since it wasn't "religious" in any proper sense – but if not, he kept his objections to himself.

After the congregational dinner to commemorate Mama, I returned home to sort through Mama's effects. I looked into her clothes closet, took a blouse or dress and pressed it close to my face to smell her presence once more. Old family photos dotted the kitchen table, sweet memories of my childhood and the later harsh realities of the Third Reich.

In the attic, I found Edda's old steamer trunk. Mama and I had departed from Germany in 1947 with just two suitcases and that very trunk. I pulled over a rickety footstool, sat down and looked inside. A few pairs of forties shoes with low heels were on the top, with aprons, embroidered pillowcases, housedresses with florid patterns and ties behind their backs, and what looked like a baby blanket neatly folded underneath.

At the bottom, I found two envelopes, each containing a letter. One came from a government office in Berlin and looked as if someone had crumpled and smoothed it out again. Stamped with a swastika, it announced the demise of an Oberstleutnant Kurt Seiler. The other, typed and dated 1951, was from an Eberhardt Westerheim, who sent belated regrets to Mama about Kurt's "tragic death in 1945."

Who was this man? Why hadn't Mama ever mentioned these letters about my father – and his being an army officer? Puzzled – even stunned – I needed to investigate. Perhaps Hildegard would be able to help explain. I began to see the significance of my grant in a new light. Answers to any questions I might ask, however, would have to wait until my arrival abroad.

*   *   *

For days, Laura helped me through the hot Wisconsin August preparing for my trip. We packed up books, stored personal papers and threw out tons of old student exams and dissertation drafts from my office to make room for Frieda.

"I know you'll take good care of my ficus tree," I said to Laura as we set it down in a corner of her office. "You're much better in the green thumb department."

"Come, let's relax at my place," she said when we were finished.

While I lay on her chaise longue on the balcony, Laura fetched wine and nibblies. I reflected on our friendship, which had begun at a department reception when I arrived at Ryan in 1959. Now, four years later, it would be wrenching to bid her goodbye.

Laura attributed our instant friendship to "propinquity," since we had offices only two doors apart. She'd helped me get adjusted to campus life and listened to my hopes and fears about completing my PhD. In spite of the fact that Laura had taught at Ryan a year longer than me, she hadn't yet completed her doctoral exams at Columbia. My tales of woe about the dissertation made her wince a bit – but not enough apparently to rush her through the process.

"I don't know if I have the gumption to work like a dog for the next three years and hang out my shingle as Dr. Sanchez."

For relief from the small-town atmosphere, Laura and I drove to hear the Chicago Philharmonic subscription concerts together – and often stopped to visit my mother for coffee and pastry beforehand. On snowy winter weekends, we made fires in Laura's cozy fireplace, watched TV on her grainy little console model or gossiped about our students.

I remembered the frigid January in 1961 when Friday mid-day classes were canceled so that the students and faculty could watch President Kennedy's inauguration. Laura and I viewed the entire ceremony at my apartment – appropriately, with wieners and Boston baked beans. Both of us were taken by Kennedy's new vision and compass for the nation.

"What an inspirational speech," Laura said. "Imagine, ask what you can do for your country."

"I agree. It's original and so simple – just turn the notion of citizenship around and put the responsibility on our shoulders."

Not long thereafter, Kennedy established the Peace Corps. One evening, over dinner at Laura's, she said, "You know, I'd like to join the Corps sometime. Seriously! It'd be something new after these years at Ryan. How about you, Renita – would you be interested?"

I was in a different place, with Mama not faring so well physically. "I'd consider it, once my doctorate is finished."

Laura looked down at her glass.

"Just for fun, Laura, what country would you pick for the Corps?"

"Somewhere in South America, maybe near the coast, I guess. And you? The Austrian Alps?" Laura let out a yodel.

"I kind of hoped we might go to the same country."

"Okay. What's halfway between Chile and Austria?"

"The Canary Islands?"

We both chuckled.

And now I was about to leave on my own. How would I manage my year abroad without Laura's compassionate soul to offer me support? In Germany, I wouldn't be able to afford phone calls to the US. I'd miss her comforting voice.

At the end of August, Laura once again pitched in. With the help of two students staying over the summer break, we vacated my campus apartment and put my books, clothes, kitchenware and furniture into storage.

"Maybe with that PhD in hand you'll be able to afford the Ridge apartments next year." Laura poked me in the rib.

"Yes, with my salary raise, an upscale new pad with tennis courts and a swimming pool will be just the thing to set me apart from the MA faculty," I said in a mock British accent.

After we'd delivered the last plastic bag to Goodwill, Laura and I took my suitcases and duffel bag to her apartment.

My original idea had been to spend my final night in the US with Mama in Hyde Park. Sadly, that was no longer an option. Edda, so enthusiastic about my grant, had insisted on paying for a plane ticket to Germany with funds from her small savings account. "I don't want you to drag luggage from some harbor to a train station like we did when we came to the States."

On our last night together, Laura poured me a flute of Spanish Cava. "I know you're still in grief about the loss of your mother. But you have to go through with this grant. Edda would be proud of you, wherever she may be."

I could barely contain my tears. I feared a future that was falling into place. Soon enough, I'd be on my own, much like the lonely wanderer in the first line of Schubert's song cycle *The Winter's Journey*: "I came as a stranger, and I depart a stranger."

Laura and I left early for O'Hare airport. Even at that time, the sky was absurdly blue – so characteristic of Midwestern fall weather. We traveled the hour in silence. At the airport she carried my two suitcases, while I took my duffel and carry-on bag.

On the way to the terminal, people rushed by while I struggled with my private sadness.

"Let's stop here." Laura set down my two bags to the side of the corridor within view of boarding. She reached into her purse and handed me a gold-plated fountain pen: "Use this to record your experiences – and to drop me a line or two."

"Laura, you're so thoughtful. How could I not write you? Without you, I don't know how I could have managed Ryan."

"And this is something to open on the plane." She slipped a wrapped present into my duffel bag.

"Don't forget to keep me posted, no? Take good care of yourself, Renita."

I reached into my pocket for a hanky.

Laura took my other hand. "What if I flew to Spain for a couple of weeks next summer for a rendezvous? You'd have your own personal guide and translator."

"Wonderful idea, Laura. I can hardly wait!"

2

∞

I stood in the aisle with my suitcase. My seat was next to a mother and her infant. When the announcements for taking seats began, the child started to fuss. Her mother sat by and appeared clueless. A stewardess asked me if everything was all right. She must have sensed my distress. Another row was available, she told me – my best bet would be in the rear – in the smoking section.

Ugh! But it beats an unruly kid. I hoped they wouldn't be on to-morrow's flight from JFK to Frankfurt.

The entire last row was unoccupied, providing a chance for some shut-eye, perhaps. The night before, Laura and I had stayed up late.

I put my carry-on bag under the seat next to me and fastened my seat belt. When the captain switched off the seat belt sign, I went across the aisle to peer out the window.

The plane angled to the left and was passing over an emerald-green Lake Michigan. We flew on past northern Indiana with the trees still in their lush green summer attire. In seven or eight weeks at my alma mater, they'd be bathed in red, yellow and gold. How Mama and I had reveled in their beauty on her autumn visits to campus – until the year she was unable to come anymore.

After lunch, the passengers quieted down and I made myself a place to stretch out on the three empty seats. After an hour of restless tossing and turning, I reached under the seat next to me, pulled out Laura's present and unwrapped a diary! Blue clothbound, it had an inset watercolor of willow branches that bent downward toward an uneven hillside terrain, dotted with pink flowers and green leaves. So delicate, wistful, lacy they were – revealing a hidden spot that seemed to beckon private thoughts.

I opened the diary and discovered a dedication:

Cara Renita:

A blank page is always daunting. Browsing in the bookstore for your diary, I ran across this poem by a friend of mine, Sue March – and knew a few of her lines would be perfect:

Write anything
on a piece of paper
blankness blossoms into meaning
words float forth from silence

*

distinct specificity
with felicity

Have fun with your journal, and don't be too hard on yourself if words fail you (though you know and I know that rarely happens)! The important thing is, connect with yourself this year, as you and I have connected with felicity at Ryan.

Love, Laura

In spite of my weariness, I searched through my purse for Laura's pen.

September 4, 1963 – on the plane to New York
I can't sleep, and figure maybe I can get a few thoughts penned. Here goes – I haven't a clue how to keep a diary, but I bet Laura thought a grown woman just turned twenty-nine could figure it out. Why did I decide to undertake this crazy idea of a dissertation year in Germany when I was so settled at Ryan – when I had my

year all in place, and my subscription renewed for the Chicago Phil with Laura?

A few hours after my goodbye to her, my heart is as empty as the row I'm in – like Gretchen in Goethe's Faust: *"My poor head is awhirl, my thoughts in shreds, my peace is gone, my heart is heavy. I'll never find that peace again."*

Everyone should be lucky enough to have a friend like you, Laura. You helped me weather my teaching debut, and let me cry on your shoulder when Mama died. I wonder where you are about now – near the outskirts of Ryan in time for the first faculty meeting? Poor you!

And then there is Mama. Honestly, would I have taken this year off if she were still alive? How would she have fared in my absence? Would she have been happy with me gone so long? I'll never know.

What does fate have in store for me? Papi always told me to be brave, and Mama was elated when she heard I was awarded the DAAD. So I guess I've got a green light from both of them. I can't let them down now.

What my parents couldn't tell me was that I was about to embark on a journey through a house of mirrors. With each new room I entered, I'd see a new self staring back at me – and by the time I exited, I wouldn't recognize myself.

3

∞

Jet-lagged, I settled into my hotel in Frankfurt after an overnight in New York and the transatlantic leg to Europe. With a day in town ahead to help me adjust to the six-hour difference, I would be rested for my trip to Hildegard's.

The next morning, I took a tour bus to Goethe's birth house, a stately five-story wooden structure located in the old town with the former Jewish ghetto and the Jewish cemetery nearby. I wondered how old Goethe would have rated his Frankfurt now, with its dull banks, commercial high-rises and traffic. No matter. After all, his poetry had gotten me going on my dissertation topic.

At the hotel over lunch, I looked through some travel brochures. One caught my eye – a special trip up the Rhine to Cologne, with connections from my hotel to the embarkation point at Bingen.

Still exhausted from the long flight, and blessed with predicted gorgeous weather to enjoy, I decided to alter my tentative arrival plans in Hanover. I asked the concierge to look into a seat on the Rhine cruise for the next day, connections from the landing pier in Cologne to a hotel, and train reservations from Cologne to Hanover two days later. She verified that the cruise, connections and accommodations in Cologne were available, and got me a special deal on the transfer of my luggage to the cruise ship, my hotel in Cologne, and the next day to the train. Armed with several arrival options in Hanover, I went to a telephone booth off the lobby and called Hildegard.

The phone rang several times.

"Rehberg."

"Hello, Aunt Hildegard, it's Reni!"

"So you've landed safely in Frankfurt?"

"Yes, but still recovering from the long trip. Would you mind if I came in two days – instead of late afternoon tomorrow as planned – say on the 2:43 P.M. train?"

"In that case, I can pick you up at the station. I can't manage the commuter traffic anymore after three o'clock on weekdays."

"All right. See you on Monday the eighth, then."

"I'll see you soon, Reni."

The phone clicked.

*   *   *

The cruise proved to be what my soul needed. The majestic river, with its cradling hills resplendent in fall colors, soothed my anxious mood – and temporarily stemmed my memory of the harsh German winter to come.

The Rhine had a long history of inspiring music, poetry and folk legend, the most well-known example of which was the Lorelei. Located at a treacherous navigation point, the mermaid Lorelei was said to sit high above the Rhine on a cliff. A powerful female force, her siren song, so the tale went, lured boatmen to gaze upward. Disoriented by the dangerous currents, the men would dash their vessels upon the rocky shore beneath her. I was familiar with another Lorelei tale as well, from a Schumann song my father Kurt used to sing. The poet Joseph Eichendorff portrayed her as a witch disguised as a lovely bride. As a man rode through the forest alone, she seduced him to his doom. What was it about the seductive female, I wondered, that had fascinated men over the centuries?

For several hours, the boat passed by romantic medieval castles interspersed with steep vineyards. As we neared Bonn, the terrain flattened and awakened me out of my romantic reverie.

Rested and invigorated by the Rhine journey, I settled in at my hotel in the shadows of the Cologne Cathedral. What good fortune it was to be in the city on a Sunday! I discovered on a walk the next morning that the Cathedral music for Mass was the Gloria from Mozart's Coronation Mass in C Major. What an exuberant performance! After mass, I strolled around inside and stopped in front of a lovely portrait of the Virgin by Stephan Lochner. Was this the Virgin who conjured up Heinrich Heine's description of his beloved? No matter, her likeness in the poet's comparison stood on its own:

> Flowers and cherubs float
> about Our dear Lady.
> Her eyes, her lips, her cheeks
> resemble those of my beloved exactly.

The next morning the hotel deployed my luggage to the purser at the nearby Hauptbahnhof, or main train station, where I boarded at 11 A.M. for the trip to Hanover.

I treated myself to lunch in the dining car, which provided an excellent view of the scenery. After we left the industrial area of the Ruhr, the train traversed the rich farmlands of Westphalia and entered Lower Saxony with its characteristic towns dotted in clusters of half-timbered houses and red roofs.

Caught up in the nostalgia of this once familiar rural landscape, I lingered as long as possible over cup after cup of coffee, and welcomed the remembrances of "Bird's Repose" – or Vogelweide, as Hildegard called her farm – that flashed by vividly in my mind.

I was below school age when my parents and I first went on summer holiday to visit my aunt and uncle. For two weeks in advance I packed and repacked my little suitcase. Summer vacation had begun prior to our arrival; in the local villages, most children were occupied with Hitler Youth summer camps. Just as well – my parents didn't approve of my exposure to all that Nazi propaganda.

The farm was a child's paradise. I loved going with Detlev to the barn to watch him milk Millie, a big Brown Swiss, who happily supplied the cats with warm squirts from her udder. Outside, manure piles steamed; an unforgettable smell wafted through the early dawn haze. After breakfast, I helped feed the animals; afternoons, I swam in a nearby lake; and in the evening, all five of us ate dinner together. Now and then, my parents and I would go on a day's trip to the nearby Harz Mountains or the Lüneburg Heath, or enjoy a Sunday dinner with Hildie and Detlev at a neighboring *Gasthaus* known in the area for its savory venison.

After supper, the parlor was filled with music (but only after all the dishes were done). Hildegard played the piano and Papi sang German lieder. Afterwards, Hildie and my father would declaim poetry while Detlev puffed on cigars in the study off the parlor. I was allowed to stay up and listen well past my regular bedtime. Not surprisingly, it was on those evenings at Vogelweide that I first fell in love with German poetry.

Once at a soiree my father and I acted out Goethe's poem "The Erlking," which describes a father's futile efforts to prevent a supernatural being from assailing his child. "My father, my father, now the Erlking is grabbing me!" I cried. A struggle between the Erlking and the child's father ended with the anguished father carrying the limp, "dead" child out of the room. The audience sat in hushed silence as we returned to the parlor for a bow.

After Germany invaded Poland in 1939, my parents rarely took vacations to the farm. The next year, when my father took a research post at Charles University in Prague, Mama and I remained in Berlin. I never understood exactly why. I only knew that Papi was busier than ever and couldn't get away. I especially missed the music, the poetry and the animals.

On one occasion, Papi, Mama and I did manage a visit in the summer of 1942. My father and I went on a walk in the woods to gather mushrooms, and he showed me how to tell the difference between the poisonous ones and the safe ones.

"When you go on your own twelve or so years from now," Papi said as he adjusted his green felt hunter's hat, "you'll know precisely which mushrooms to pick for your husband's supper!"

On that visit, a courier arrived at the farm to deliver a telegram to my father. Papi went into the bedroom with Mama, and I heard him pace back and forth, talking in a loud voice. Mama came to me afterwards, saying that Papi had to drive away with the courier. "Professorial duties must always come first with your father."

Papi packed, kissed me softly on the cheek and said to do him proud with my school marks. Then he climbed into the courier's vehicle, and with a faint smile, waved goodbye. I watched until the car rounded the bend. When Papi left, a part of my heart went with him. Little did I know this would be the last time I would ever see him.

Mama decided to return us to Berlin. It all went so fast – we left the next day, and I didn't have a chance to say a proper goodbye. All I could do was tell Hildegard I loved her through my tears.

In 1943, with the increase in Allied attacks on Berlin, life became a matter of pure survival. I rarely saw Mama cry – except when she learned that her mother and father had died in the night bombings of Berlin. Trapped by the flames in their bedroom, they couldn't make it down the stairs in time to get to a bomb shelter.

A formal funeral was impossible, as so many perished beyond description from those dreaded nights. Our Pastor Schmidt ran from one end of the city to the other with condolences for the survivors.

At our house, Mama improvised a service with candles reserved for blackouts and displayed family pictures, taken from an album grandma had stored away. *Would any of us survive this horrible war?*

It was at this point that Mama insisted I evacuate to Hildegard in the country. Terrified to leave my mother alone, I begged to stay on. What would happen to her, I fretted, while we were separated?

"I am only doing this for your protection, Reni. God be with you." Mama stroked my forehead. With a heavy heart, I waved goodbye to her from the train.

Without the safety of Vogelweide, I might not have survived. Our house in Berlin was damaged in a nighttime raid as well – and if Mama hadn't been volunteering at the German Red Cross Center that night – I might have lost her, too.

The fact that I was safe didn't ease my painful loneliness. The atmosphere was different without Mama and Papi. Hildegard, who had always entertained us with music and song, had changed. She seemed unable to deal with a girl in my stage of adolescence when I needed someone to talk to. The war dragged on with no end to the fighting in sight. Many nights I lay awake, terrified I would never see my parents again.

One bright spot, perhaps, was that Hildegard gave me piano lessons. It seemed that was her way to communicate with me. Practicing filled the void of Mama's absence. Although I enjoyed the piano, as I made some progress Hildegard would comment on my every mistake.

"Tsk, that should be an F instead of an F#," she said from the kitchen, as I made my way through a Bach invention. My only option was to practice during Hildegard's morning errands. Finally, I gave up my lessons in frustration and anger.

One day, in early 1945, my aunt called me into the parlor. She could barely speak. Her face as white as a sheet, she told me that Papi had died in a plane crash. It was only later I found out the plane had lost its way in the fog in North Bohemia – a remote region of Czechoslovakia annexed by the Germans.

In tears, I ran to my bedroom and didn't emerge for hours. How could this have happened? Mama had assured me that being a professor would keep Papi safe. My grief over my father's sudden death never completely subsided.

In Papi's honor we sang some hymns with Hildegard accompanying us, and her pastor came by to deliver a eulogy. It was small comfort. How could God allow this to happen? I thought.

Through her boss at the German Red Cross Center, Mama was able to secure a tiny loft apartment on the outskirts of Berlin after the cease-fire – which meant I could reunite with her by the end of summer. I think Hildegard was glad not to be responsible for a budding teenager anymore.

*   *   *

A voice over the loudspeaker announced our arrival in Hanover in ten minutes. I joined the passengers detraining at the same stop. Only a few people remained for the trip east to Braunschweig.

At 2:43 we pulled into the station. I peered out the window. Would I recognize my aunt, frozen in my visual memory for all these years? There, to my relief, by the escalator stood a woman in her sixties, propped on a cane, with an unmistakable Roman nose and narrow, high-cheekboned face.

As I put down my luggage cart and walked toward her, Hildegard's expression changed from a squint to a smile of recognition.

"Hello, Reni." She extended her hand to me. "Welcome back."

"Auntie, I am so glad to see you!" She tensed when I hugged her. Did no one embrace her now?

We proceeded slowly through the lot to an older-model Opel. "Your uncle bought me this automobile a few years before he died," she said, running her hand down the side of the door.

She'll probably never buy another one.

To get to the farm, Hildegard took a route that circumvented the city. There was a cozy familiarity about this landscape, where farmhouses nestled among undulating hills, and cows, pigs and sheep grazed peacefully.

Hildegard at the wheel brought me back to the day I'd evacuated to Vogelweide. The lush fields and intact houses looked as beautiful as ever.

"Auntie, has the city rebuilt that fourteenth-century church in Hanover – the one near the marketplace?"

"The Aegidenkirche, you mean? No, only the tower and the *Glockenspiel* remain. They were left to stand as a memorial," she said, negotiating the off-ramp to Altendorf, the nearest town to the farm.

We drove through several villages and reached Altendorf, which consisted of one long street with a church in the center. I was in a time warp; the village was exactly as I remembered it, as if I had never left.

At the end of the village Hildegard headed up a narrow country lane. "There's where you used to swim." She pointed to a lake visible beyond the forest line. "It won't be long now before we'll be at Vogelweide."

My throat lumped up.

A farmhouse with half timbers came into view; a large barn was set further back. I remembered this view as the last I'd seen of Vogelweide before we departed for the States. When we left, I'd craned my neck from here to see Hildie and Detlev wave goodbye.

We pulled into a large courtyard, where Uncle Detlev used to let the chickens roam.

"I'll be just a minute, Auntie." I hopped out of the car, walked down to the dilapidated barn and peered in. The cows and chickens were gone; just old farm equipment and a few sacks of potatoes for the winter remained.

Hildegard joined me for the short walk to the house. "I couldn't manage all the animals after Detlev passed on."

"And Millie?"

"We'd kept her almost as a pet, well beyond her milking years. When Detlev took ill, I made the decision to ship her to the slaughterhouse. We cried our eyes out. I think saying goodbye to her contributed to his rapid demise. I'm lucky I still have the farm, with taxes and upkeep so expensive."

We entered through the back door into the kitchen. It was the same door I'd run through every day as a child on holiday; after a swim in the lake, I'd always found a cookie and a glass of milk waiting for me on the table.

I took the old path through the house to the parlor. The grand piano still occupied a place of honor by the big front window. I tried to imagine seeing Papi standing here with his music in one hand and gesticulating with the other.

From the layer of dust, I knew the Steinweg had not been used for a while. I lifted up the lid to play a scale or two, but stopped and walked across the room to the fireplace. The mantle still displayed the framed photo of my Grandma Ruthie, Grandpa Theo, Hildegard, Detlev, Mama, Papi and me standing in this very room on Easter day in 1939. We all looked so innocent, so blissfully unaware of the events about to unfold later that year.

Continuing to the front door and out onto the lawn, I remembered standing at the edge of the road and waiting for Papi's black

Mercedes to make its way up the hill. To an excited youngster, it had seemed to take an eternity for the car to reach the driveway.

That evening, I was touched that after all the years Hildegard remembered my favorite foods: venison tenderloin with fresh noodles and red cabbage, served in her treasured Dresden china pot, one I knew she used only on special occasions.

"If we had had one of these dinners right after the war," she said, sipping the red wine I'd brought for her, "we'd have thought we were in heaven. We were skin and bones then, almost the way you and your mother looked when you emigrated."

"Mama didn't see much future in Germany, but I know she was sad to part from you."

"I never did understand what Edda saw in that American soldier."

A ticket to the United States.

In the days that followed, Hildegard and I walked the meadow path from the barn leading to the back of the property. "I need the exercise, and I'm glad you're along, Reni. My hip is not what it used to be," she said, using a cane for balance.

When she napped, I seized the opportunity to write in my diary.

September 15 – Vogelweide

Returning to Vogelweide has given me a lot to digest, and I wonder if I'm up to the task on a regular basis. Goethe's diaries, for example, filled 13 volumes of observations, insights and impressions. I'll be lucky if I'm able to fill one book. But I wonder if a diary person is who I am. I've never found it easy to write. Maybe that's why I haven't brought myself to crack open my diary here at Hildegard's.

My dissertation, too, seems more like a mountain climb. I can't wait until the thing is done, but haven't touched so much as a page while I've been here – so there, DAAD!

It's hard to describe what Vogelweide means to me now, without Papi and Mama, Detlev – or Millie. I've kept it in my memory as a piece of my past, a place I loved – and later, when I came back alone during the war, a place where I felt the loneliest I'd ever been.

When he was here with me, Papi seemed unburdened by cares

and had time to take walks with me. But then I have the painful remembrance of Vogelweide without Papi. I never realized until now that these bittersweet experiences made me long to stay, and also created the need to go.

One thing's for certain: I'm concerned about Hildegard's health. It's odd to see her walk so slowly. She's always been so active. I can see how frail she is, and I sense bringing up the past with the documents might upset her. I'll need to work up my gumption, nevertheless – but when?

I put my pen aside and thought about Laura, and how she must be feeling with me gone. Did she miss me already, as I missed her?

*   *   *

One afternoon, Hildegard and I enjoyed that venerable German institution, *Kaffee und Kuchen* – coffee and cake – outside on a deck Detlev had put together from wood scraps. She showed me photos of Mama and her in the garden of our Charlottenburg house in Berlin, along with Papi and Claus and Reiner, two of my uncles from the Rhineland whom I had never met. Such handsome boys they were, their innocent eyes belying what lay ahead for them during the Third Reich.

Later, we sat on the front porch swing and Hildegard braced her cane against the railing, pushing us back and forth. I told her about Chicago – my high school, undergraduate days at Indiana, graduate studies, and my teaching position at Ryan College. She listened, then posed a few questions about Edda, her church life and friends, but inquired little about my life.

After dinner, we moved to a tea table in the parlor for another glass of wine. While Hildegard lit her tiled stove, I went to my bedroom to fetch my briefcase. When I returned, I took out the letters.

"As I wrote you from the States, I found these in Mama's steamer trunk." I placed the envelopes on the tea table.

Hildegard adjusted her shawl, added a small log to the fire and walked over to an etui lying on an armchair table nearby. She returned with her glasses, perused the first letter, sighed and handed it back to me.

Dear Frau Seiler,

This is to notify you that it has been determined your husband, Oberstleutnant Dr. Kurt Seiler, perished in a plane crash somewhere in Bohemia on January 28, 1945, due to inclement weather conditions. No effects were found after a search was made.

Heil Hitler!
WASt Berlin, February 3, 1945

"Edda did advise me of Kurt's death. You remember I had the unhappy task of telling you the news."

"Yes. Were you aware that Papi had served in the military?"

"No. All I knew was that he was a professor of mathematics at the Charles University in Prague. I guess in retrospect I'm not surprised to learn about his officer status. Hardly any male was able to avoid the Wehrmacht in some way or another. Even Detlev was forced into civil duty, although he was well beyond conscription age."

"I wonder why Edda never mentioned this to me."

"I'm afraid it's too late to know the answer to that question. I only know that your mother wrote me to say she'd received official news that Kurt had died in a plane crash. We were all in grief, of course. Detlev and I decided to place a stone cross in his honor alongside the house. You had left for the States by then."

My worst fears were confirmed. Despite what I had always been told, Papi was a professor, but with officer status under Hitler, and thus part of a shameful regime. How could this be? I could barely contain my feelings of despair and remorse. I reached into my pocket for a handkerchief and gazed into the fire until I was able to speak.

"Do you remember the memorial service your Pastor Felter officiated for us here? You played *Now Rest Beneath Night's Shadow* – you know, the one with Paul Gerhardt's beautiful poem as its text? Papi loved Gerhardt's poetry."

Hildegard nodded and touched my forearm. I was taken aback by the break in her usual reserve.

Despite my feelings, I had to discuss the other letter I had brought along. "Hildegard, who is this Herr Westerheim?"

"Eberhardt is an old family friend – a boyhood chum of your father."

"A boyhood chum?"

"Yes. After Kurt got married, as I learned from Edda, he didn't see his friend much, because Eberhardt had a demanding job in Leipzig. After I married Detlev, I started holding summer musicales at the farm, and your father asked me to invite Eberhardt to Vogelweide. I observed that he and Kurt enjoyed catching up on each other's lives. Eberhardt did pay one other visit to Vogelweide when you were very young, so you wouldn't remember him with so many people in attendance."

"That's correct, I don't."

"After that visit, I lost track of him. I heard he had been conscripted to the Russian front, and feared the worst. Imagine my surprise – and relief – when a card from him arrived in the mail years later, saying he had moved to Berlin, and asking how I was. We remained in contact but mostly via Christmas cards. Since Detlev not in good health, I had no inclination to invite Eberhardt to the farm. After Detlev passed away in 1957, I invited Eberhardt to come visit me. We met for an afternoon, but he declined to spend the night, saying he was on his way to Hildesheim for a hunting trip. I sensed his shyness at being in my company without anyone else present."

Hildegard placed Westerheim's letter neatly on top of the other one.

"Do you think Herr Westerheim might be able to tell me anything more about Papi? Should I visit him?"

"Perhaps it might be helpful if I sent him a letter in advance."

"Thank you, Hildegard, that's kind of you. I'd prefer not to phone out of the blue."

"I think he will certainly recall you from Vogelweide, and I may have mentioned in a note to him that you and Edda had left for the US." Hildegard went to the secretaire opposite the piano, paged through her address book, and jotted down Westerheim's address and number on a piece of paper and handed it to me.

That night I tossed and turned as all these new revelations raced through my head. No matter, I arose early. Following an old family tradition, I placed a remembrance before I departed. In the past, Mama and Papi had left a card, a plant or a trinket. Just after sunup, I planted a potted rose at Papi's cross.

Hildegard and I remained silent as she drove me to the train station. She pulled into a parking spot near the terminal, reached into her bag and gave me a small wrapped package. "You may open it now, if you like."

I was stunned. It was the framed family photo from her mantelpiece!

"Aunt Hildie, are you sure you want to part with this?"

"Yes, my dear, I am certain you don't possess many photos of your family. It was taken in 1938, and now I want you to have it."

Hildegard got out of the car. "I must bid you goodbye here. It's difficult for me to manage that upper level. I wish you well and hope you may return someday. And, as the embroidered cloth hanging in my bedroom says, 'Take care, but do not be full of care. Everything transpires as God wishes.' I never forgot you, Reni."

"I know, Auntie. Even though I didn't write you as much as I'd have liked, I do love you."

From the platform, I turned around to wave goodbye again.

But Hildegard had already left.

4

∞

Almost empty, my train to Berlin seemed like a ghost ride to nowhere, or at least nowhere anyone would want to visit. Within the space of a week, I had been reintroduced into my family, and now, just as suddenly, I was on my own. Would I see Hildegard again?

I had mixed emotions, uneasy about the train ride and my rendezvous with Westerheim, yet hopeful about my grant. What would await me when I arrived, I wondered? Was this trip worth the reentry?

I took my seat in a row behind a middle-aged businessman in a trim blue suit, a plump woman wearing a boxy beige hat, and a young man who jiggled his gangly legs.

The train approached the East German border and slowed to a crawl. We passed through a narrow no-man's-land with double walls, barbed wire, a death strip, and floodlights. A series of watchtowers provided dismal accompaniment. Guards with machine guns patrolled along a narrow, well-trodden path; if anyone managed to get past all of that, they'd still get picked off. I shivered at the thought of an escape attempt here.

A Grepo, or border patrol officer, entered our car and shouted, "Passports!" clipping the "ss" sharply. He checked our documents, inquired about my intended length of stay and the currency I carried, and stamped my transit visa for a one-way passage.

I wondered if the authorities had planned the rail route to go through barren landscapes. Compared with the colorful countryside of Lower Saxony, the view from the window resembled a film noir – occasional bicyclists, a couple of people on a country road, and empty fields. In the distance, the twin spires of the Magdeburg Cathedral briefly broke the relentless monotony. There wasn't much to do but take a nap with one eye open.

After an hour, the train began to slow at Drewitz, a small village that served as a border crossing outside the city limits. Tall, spindly pines loomed ahead.

I flashed on the fir trees I'd seen exploding like twigs in a freshly lit stove ignited by the Royal Air Force's incendiary bombs. Sirens used to warn us to take cover. Mama and I would huddle in the neighbor's cellar when the planes approached at night. I'd clutch my dog, Nora, and massage her floppy ears. She'd put her paw on my knee, as if to assure me we'd be all right. Animals know. I wished Nora were snuggled next to me now.

Another Grepo boarded the train, reexamined my documents and noted in my visa the time of my entry into the GDR.

After a change to Western personnel, the train eased past a final maze of barbed wire lining the tracks. When the train crossed the border the scenery resembled a revolving set from a Bertolt Brecht play. First, we passed a series of lakes straddling posh suburbs with dilapidated villas only retaining a hint of their former elegance – like old ladies too tired to keep up appearances. The train then skirted the lush urban forest of Grunewald, approached the tall RIAS tower – short for Radio in the American Sector – and passed through the commuter stations of Westkreuz paralleling the Kaiserdamm, a cross-town shopping street.

The autumn sky, the characteristic color of damp cardboard, was just as I remembered it. The surrounding architecture seemed to follow suit, stretching out in a grayish-white mantle of massive *Altbauhäuser*, or prewar apartment houses, most now battle-scarred and disfigured with pockmarks and twisted bits of metal.

Melancholia crept through me. I was a stranger returning to familiar and beloved places, but without the familiar or beloved faces I ached to see.

The locomotive thrust us into a curve leading toward our final stop. With a piercing screech, it halted under the steel-domed canopy of the Bahnhof Zoo, West Berlin's main train station.

In spite of my sadness and fears, I was glad to be back home again.

5

∞

It was early afternoon when I stepped off the train, and the air had turned chilly. I stood on the platform and got my bearings. A small clutch of people with briefcases dashed past me, headed downstairs in a determined Teutonic manner.

What's the rush, Ren? I walked my luggage cart to a kiosk, ordered coffee and picked up the *Berliner Morgenpost*. At a small table, I read the front-page headline article, which reported a tragic incident at the East Berlin border. A grisly photo showed the lifeless body of a man who had attempted to climb over the Wall and escape by swimming the Spree River to freedom.

My whole body trembled, as it had on the day when I heard the East Germans were building a concrete wall through the heart of Berlin. Camping with Laura, I had just bought some provisions for our supper, and now pulled my VW off the road to hear every detail. In my mental disarray, I don't know how I found my way back to the campsite.

"What's wrong? You look like you've seen a ghost," Laura said when she saw me.

"I'll tell you later." I made a beeline to the tent and crawled onto my cot.

At the campfire at night, I revealed the news on the radio.

Laura put another log on the fire. "I can only imagine how you feel." She listened as I poured out my grief over my old hometown.

The story got worse as the days rolled by. The wall not only separated East from West Berlin, but surrounded the entirety of the city. West Berlin became an island within East Germany. Angry and feeling helpless, I couldn't recover the carefree tone of our vacation.

I'm sure Laura cursed the East Germans for ruining the trip we had so looked forward to.

*   *   *

I finished my coffee and stood up to find the next train to my pension.

"Potsdam," the voice intoned. My commuter train, the Friedrichstrasse-Potsdam line, had just rounded the curve, precisely on schedule.

This line symbolized one of divided Berlin's sad ironies. As my guidebook warned, the City Railway, or S-Bahn, was controlled by the East German regime. Since the Wall, the German Democratic Republic or GDR had effectively cut off East Germans from access to the S-Bahn within West Berlin. The train traversed the East-West axis from Friedrichstrasse in East Berlin, through West Berlin, and continued without passengers to Potsdam in East German territory. I noted a final irony: the S-Bahn had "DR" – for Deutsche Reichsbahn – the Nazi German Reich Railway, emblazoned on each car.

To add to the mix, Berlin also had a U-Bahn, or underground local railway, which covered all of Berlin and was run by the West. If you wanted to go to East Berlin, you needed to ride on the Eastern-owned S-Bahn, since the U-Bahn was not available for Westerners to ride to the East.

Insane or what? The whole transportation system was schizophrenic – and laughable – if it weren't for the deadly seriousness of the East German regime. The whole ridiculous setup confused and disgusted me.

A gentleman helped me on the train with my luggage, and carried it off again for my stop at Savigny Square. After a mercifully short walk, I reached the pension, a massive four-story prewar effort. The façade was adorned with fake Greek columns, which seemed to offset the effects of railway soot. Artillery fire had left gashes in the walls; the balconies, stripped bare to their concrete foundations, looked like envelopes with their labels torn off. No matter, I'd booked a room here.

I opened the heavy entrance door into the foyer. A cool draft wafted from the courtyard or *Hinterhof*, so typical of old apartment structures in Berlin, a welcome relief after the heat of the trip. A workman in paint-spattered overalls sat on a bench over his *Brot* and wurst with a bottle of Berliner Kindl beer. He nodded and greeted me with *"Mahlzeit,"* a typical German workman's noonday greeting. Off the entranceway, behind a massive set of double doors, I heard muffled voices and footsteps – probably an office or business of some kind. A sign warned visitors about the newly polished floors. German efficiency.

The cage elevator creaked to a halt; I stacked my luggage and squeezed in. When I stepped off on the fourth floor, a man in a drab, ill-fitting suit stood at the door.

"Guten Tag. Schulz." He shook my hand. "Please I take your baggage, Fräulein Seiler."

"Danke schön. Ich spreche Deutsch."

"Ach gut." Schulz made a sigh of relief and motioned me into an office with a view of the brick street below. Windows, partially covered by thin, cobweb-like curtains, further diffused the thin afternoon sun. A line from a poem drifted up in my memory: "Despair is not darkness, but weak light."

"Fräulein, there's something for you from the States." He handed me a card from a stack of mail on a table behind his desk. "You can't believe how many pieces I throw away, addressed to guests who never show."

It was from Laura! On the front was a photo of the Chicago skyline and Lake Michigan. The back read:

Cara Renita,

I timed this to arrive the same day as you. Just to let you know I miss you but am making the best of it. Last week was the first full week of school. Ugh! Sixteen more to come! I walked by your old apartment house and remembered how you used to wave from the window when I came by. Take good care of yourself, and drop me a line when you can – and make it before the first pop quizzes!

Con todo mi amor,

Laura

How sweet, and how sad it makes me to see her lovely handwriting.

"How many days do you want to stay?" Schulz said, tapping a pen on his desk.

"For now, I'd like to book for at least a week, provided I like the room, of course."

Registration was tedious. I had to fill out hotel and police forms; Schultz reviewed my passport and added the room information. By the time the paperwork was done, I was mentally drained and ready for a rest.

Down a long hall on the way to my room, we passed a door with a sign reading *"Frühstückszimmer."*

"Breakfast is daily from seven to ten," Schulz said. "We converted this house to a pension in 1948. Only the very rich could afford to own space with ten rooms on each floor. We weren't in that category. The rest is rented out." Further down the hall he opened a door with a brass number nine on the front and handed me the key.

I set down my bags. Number nine faced the back courtyard, away from the traffic on Bleibtreustrasse, and had a high vaulted ceiling with a tiny light fixture hanging from a cord in the center. Two night tables flanked a bed covered with down comforters and oversized pillows. In the corner stood a white washbasin with thin towels draped on rungs to the side.

"Please follow me." Schulz rounded a corner to show me several cubicles with W.C. on the door, unmarked for gender.

Charming.

"If you want to make a call, you may use the pay phone in the office or the phone booth across the street."

Okay, it isn't the Hotel Kempinski, but the price is right.

"Is there a bathroom nearby?"

Beyond the toilets was a room marked *"Bad."* Schulz reached in his pocket and unlocked the door with a key that looked more appropriate to a medieval castle. A long tub filled almost the entire length of the small room; overhead, a large water heater jutted out from the wall.

When they say "bath," they mean it! You can stretch out and enjoy – no way I'll run out of hot water.

"The bath costs one mark, and the key is available until 9 P.M. each day. Your mail can be picked up at the office from Monday to Saturday. Is everything satisfactory?"

"Yes."

Schulz wished me a pleasant afternoon.

I returned to my room, flopped down onto the pillows and placed my sore feet on the wedge. My mind, out of phase with the calm courtyard, had raced furiously for the last month with travel details.

The courtyard won, lulling me to sleep.

6

∞

Nearby church bells tolled six times. If I wanted to have snacks later, I'd better get to the neighborhood grocery store – listed on a pension flyer – before they closed in a half hour. I zipped down the stairs and just made it in time to buy cheese, crackers, wine and sausage – and a Swiss knife with corkscrew – enough to keep me afloat, at least until breakfast.

Too early to call it a day, I figured. After a hasty *Abendbrot* in my room, I decided on a stroll downtown. Turning up my coat collar against the damp air, I walked along Kantstrasse, at this hour quiet, empty and devoid of pedestrians. At the next intersection, I headed to the Kurfürstendamm, or Ku-Damm as the Berliners called it.

The boulevard, with its broad cobblestone sidewalks and glassed-in window displays, was still a-bustle with strollers admiring the chic displays of Asian art and the latest fashions in furs or women's leather boots. I walked toward the Kaiser Wilhelm Memorial Churches, both Berlin landmarks – the one bombed out and the other modern and sleek.

The older structure now gutted and charred, had one lone jagged tower, or "hollow tooth," as the Berliners irreverently dubbed it, a reminder of Berlin's destruction from 1943 to 1945. The postwar church consisted of a freestanding six-sided bell tower and a squat octagonal sanctuary, erected on either side of their somber companion.

According to my guidebook, the modern church had been dedicated on the anniversary of the day in 1941 when Coventry

Cathedral in England had been destroyed by German Luftwaffe air raids. The radiant illuminated blue glass, a gift from France, symbolized a brighter future of reconciliation and peace.

The juxtaposition of the old and new made a powerful impression on me. I crossed over the street and walked up the sanctuary steps, which served as a popular gathering place for tourists, students, and *Halbstarke*, Germany's term for teenagers. Tiered in groups, they smoked cigarettes, strummed guitars or watched people stroll by.

How sad. Did any of these carefree adolescents even know the beauty of the prewar church? Did they appreciate the symbolic significance of the new one?

Posted on the sanctuary door was a notice about an organ recital scheduled for Saturday evening at six thirty. The program included selections from Bach's *Orgelbüchlein*, or Little Organ Book. As the sanctuary was now closed, I went down a few steps and sat down. I recalled a walk on the Ku-Damm with my mother in April of 1939. It was Eastertide, and the atmosphere felt electric with women in bright hats and the latest fashions parading up and down the boulevard.

At that time, Papi was gone a lot. I wasn't sure why. I could barely wait for a trinket or two upon his return. He seemed to know what Mama and I liked. For Edda, he brought Russian caviar, lace from Belgium and crystal from Prague. Once, he bought me a cute Moravian doll, a *Moravske panenka*, he told me, in Czech, a language he spoke fluently. That Christmas he'd given Mama and me a tin of *Moravske Vano ni Kukyse*, or homemade Moravian Christmas cookies, "a specialty of my hometown of Stramberg."

My memory of the gifts evoked a stanza from a Brecht poem in which he enumerated all the gifts the soldier had brought back from abroad.

But, for me, Papi's return to Mama and me was always the best gift of all.

Ooo-EEE, ooo-EEE! The blare of the police sirens returned me to this nippy autumn night. I shook a tingle from my spine, walked down to the square and crossed over to the Schultheiss Restaurant for a drink.

I spied an empty oval table toward the front – the perfect spot to review my plans in peace and quiet. After ordering a Brause, a mixture of carbonated water and white wine, I opened my pocket calendar. "WESTERHEIM" was written at the top of today's date.

A smartly dressed woman entered the restaurant and inspected the fruit tortes on display at a polished, gleaming front counter.

"*Guten Tag*, Frau Thiele," said the waitress from behind the counter.

Frau Thiele appeared to be about Mama's age and height. Her stylish fur cap and black leather coat were visual evidence of Germany's economic recovery.

I wondered how she had survived in Germany. Had she stacked rubble into piles as a *Trümmerfrau*? How had she braved the lean postwar years before the German economic miracle in the 1950s?

Frau Thiele ordered a blackberry cobbler at the counter and proceeded to a table near the window, directly in my field of vision. She made brief eye contact with me. Unnerved, I lowered my head, only to look up a moment later to convince myself she could not be Mama.

I pulled out my diary.

Berlin, September 20 – Schultheiss Restaurant downtown
So here I am, glad to be back, but anxious about Westerheim and sad to have left Hildegard. So many losses – my mother, Papi, and, last but not least, Laura. Tonight's chill makes me lonely for the warmth of her laughter. I hope she's okay with her heavy load this semester. If I were there we'd hunker down for the long winter over a glass of California red wine, no doubt. Argh, just when my friendship with Laura was rock solid, I had to put it on hold. What if she left Ryan herself – to return to the East Coast, perhaps? After all, she was born and raised in the east and might like to be closer to her parents.

All the same, spending a paid year on my own in Germany without the pressure of college duties still feels like a big gift from the universe. This year gives me a chance to reconnect with a place long forsaken. Had I ever really left Berlin in my heart? After all, it was Mama's decision to emigrate, and Papi was whisked away. I was too young for any say in the matter.

I looked up. The woman with the fur hat was gone.

The waiter brought the check. I paid for my drink and bundled myself against the cold before I stepped out. The Ku-Damm pedestrian traffic had dwindled to a few strollers. I stopped in front of a cabaret theater called Die Stachelschweine, or Porcupines, named for the theater's famously pointed political satire. *Hmm. Here's a show I could check out.*

Resuming my walk, I glanced at the boulevard shop windows: children's Christmas toys too early for the season, hand-blown stemware from Italy, slender candles in elegant silver holders – nothing I could persuade myself I needed.

Down the street, I could make out the darkened Café Kranzler, an unmistakable landmark this evening, even without the sun reflected on its golden roof.

More than twenty years had passed since my first trip there with Mama. I must take her there with me – if only in my heart – on a visit soon.

A block from the pension, I turned onto the deserted Bleibtreustrasse. Now, I too, was left with a suitcase in Berlin – the one Mama had taken with us when we left.

7

∞

Forward to the Past

Unsettled and restless, I kept thinking back to the woman at the restaurant. It appeared I hadn't gone out just to see beautiful churches and luxury shops, but had been unconsciously guided to places that awakened intense memories. Even now the back garden of Pension Schulz reminded me of summer socials with relatives, and a glimpse of Café Kranzler made me flash on drinking chocolate there with Mama.

I took out a gift of gorgeous photos of prewar Berlin my mother had given me for my college graduation in 1955. I'd been thrilled with my book, even if I didn't yet have a coffee table with which to grace it! Despite its size and weight, I'd never seriously considered leaving this treasure behind while packing for the flight.

In Chicago, over coffee in her kitchen, Mama pointed out all her favorite places in the book: the Pergamon Museum; the Spree River; the magnificent downtown cathedral; and Grunewald forest, with its sandy paths through the pines, elegant villas in the suburbs and Lake Müggelsee in the east, where the family had enjoyed picnics with Grandpa Theo and Grandma Ruthie.

"Reni . . ." (Mama used to lean over her cup when she wanted to make a point), "why don't we take a trip back to Berlin together?"

"I don't know. I need to concentrate on college applications."

"And on dates with boys, too?"

Mama rarely broached that topic. *Why now? Is she afraid I'll end up a wizened old maid? Do I worry about it? Look, I'm a big girl now, Mama.*

I regretted not taking Mama up on her suggestion about Berlin, however. Each time she got a big idea in her head, it had turned out for the good. With her German tenacity, Edda had vowed to get us out of a bombed-out city with its female population ravaged by the Russians. Her goal was to get us to the United States as soon as possible. She enrolled in accelerated courses in English, secured a job with the US Army and began to date American soldiers. I didn't much care for them, but I understood Mama's plan depended on snagging one of them. Thanks to the War Bride Act of 1947, Edda engineered her goal through a younger American soldier named Luke, who proposed to her almost on the spot.

Edda and Luke married at the base in Germany. Mama said it wasn't the elegant ceremony she had had with Papi, but "it got the job done."

Luke would never take my father's place – and I could tell from the nicknames Edda used when Luke was away at work ("fluke Luke" was her favorite) – that she felt the same way. In July of that same year Mama and I packed up; I shed tears when we gave Nora to the director of the Red Cross Center. In the few days that followed, my life changed forever. We sailed off on a freighter from Rotterdam to Montreal, and took the night train to Chicago, Luke's hometown, where he met us in a shiny late-model car. I learned later it was called a Studebaker. *Funny names these Americans give their cars.*

*   *   *

I had come from a city of rubble and empty lots. Now Chicago, with its tall skyscrapers, huge houses, expansive lawns and enormous lake, overwhelmed me. Those impressions proved minor in comparison to school.

Within weeks of our move into Luke's tiny suburban bungalow, I entered Central High School, or CHS, as everyone called it. My first year was torture. With only limited English skills, I was terrified to speak in class. Mama and I practiced new vocabulary words, which she wrote on cards.

One word I learned right away was "scapegoat." My classmates found it convenient to blame me for all the evil Germans had perpetrated upon the world. For some of my classmates, I was part of "them," not "us." Debbie Frangipani called me a "Luthern." "In spite of what they say around here." she insisted, "the only important folks in Chicago are Catholics – and Italian," pronounced "EYEtalian." Amy Johnson threw barbs at our first-hour assembly. "Krauts – all they can do is make war, sausages – and lampshades," she said, arms folded.

My face flushed with shame.

Larry Hartmann, the school clown, loved to impersonate Hollywood's version of Nazi generals. Propping a lens over his eye, he strutted up and down the aisle: "The Tcherrrman RRReich vill rrise again!" For the full effect, he wore black boots and his father's dark raincoat.

I sat there, my stomach tied up in knots. I had seen boots like those before ...

"Superiority does not breed good taste," Mama said when she heard my tearful stories from school. "Americans have no idea how we civilians suffered. But remember, we've got a roof over our heads, enough to eat, and my job at the pharmacy. None of it would've been possible in Berlin." She consoled me with hot chocolate.

As usual, Mama was right. Nevertheless, being called a "Kraut" and a "Luthern" hurt. What kind of Lutheran was I anyway? Hard to say. I'd been confirmed before we left Germany, in our half-bombed-out church, and for my "trip abroad," as our Pastor Schmidt called it, he gave me a German bible. He probably wanted to make sure I wouldn't forget my baptismal vows. Good thing I had that bible – in Chicago there were few people with whom I could share Luther's exquisite and poetic command of the German language.

Mama's congregation, Trinity Lutheran, offered me cold comfort for friends. On Saturdays, I helped clean the sanctuary with other teens, but most of them attended the area Lutheran parochial high school, which we couldn't afford. The kids were clannish and too churchy for me anyway. And musically, an out-of-tune choir singing "A Mighty Fortress Is Our God" was worse than no hymn at all.

I wasn't much of a rah-rah Christian, unused as I was to the social nature of American church life. In Germany, Mama and Papi had been private when it came to religious practice. Here in the US, my stepfather Luke was a nominal Catholic, and went to mass only for the usual Christmas and Easter festivities.

*   *   *

My outsider self fought for acceptance with new tactics. I asked our drama teacher for help. She demonstrated how to smooth out my German-accented English. After school, I spent hours in front of the mirror practicing the American "R"; my tongue reared up in my throat like a stubborn horse, but I succeeded. People no longer asked where I was from.

Just before school started in the fall of 1949, Mama and I were both granted citizenship after two years of residency, thanks to the War Bride's Act.

I proudly announced my new status at home room and kids actually cheered! It was wonderful to be a regular US citizen just like everyone else. I started to wear bobby socks and pleated skirts, and – to my surprise – I got the part of Emily Webb in the quintessential American play, *Our Town*.

Mama was overjoyed at my achievement.

In the same year, I joined the high school band. Mr. Doty, our director, suggested I play bass drum – an honor for me – since he felt I kept the beat better than anyone else. I loved our spiffy band uniform with its bright red tie, dark jacket and pants with a stripe down the side. I never would have had all this in Germany.

Mama showed me how Papi had tied his Sunday tie. "If only your father could see you now, he'd be so proud!"

Luke remained uninvolved in my high school activities. Once he attended a CHS football game with Edda, when we played his old high school's team, or "Polski High," as Central called it. Edda told me later that at halftime, when the band performed, Luke had gone out for a smoke behind the bleachers with his high school buddies "to discuss the game." Apparently, this meant they'd talked about the girls in the stands they could proposition.

In the summer of 1950, between my junior and senior year, Mama gave me a book of poetry that had belonged to Papi, which she had saved in her trunk. Once a week, we read a poem to each other and discussed it. I enjoyed our Saturday salons and was impressed with Edda's insights.

Mama seemed taken by my flair for the German Romantic idiom. "These poems are really in your blood, aren't they? It's a shame CHS doesn't offer our language. Why don't you enroll in a German literature class at the local college?"

"The school administration probably won't allow it, Mama."

"Unsinn!" ("Nonsense!") Edda called Mrs. Foote, a fellow church member and German instructor at City College, and told her about me. An interview ensued, and I was thrilled to be accepted into her poetry class.

Mama and I prepared my first class with Goethe's early poetry, written before he left Frankfurt for a position in Weimar. I marveled at the bard's energetic descriptions of nature and the human spirit, and loved Eichendorff and Heine, who touched me with their weltschmerz and romantic irony.

Luke wasn't thrilled with our German poetry sessions. The only German he knew was *"Willst Du tanzen, Fraulein?"* He even frowned when Mama and I chatted in German when he was home.

I looked forward to Luke's night shifts. During that time Mama and I had the house to ourselves. When Luke worked days, he'd walk in the door, grab a liquor bottle from the pantry, light a cigarette and disappear to "his" armchair in the TV room.

*　　*　　*

At the start of my senior year at CHS, Mama filed for divorce. "Luke's roving eye and the booze clinched it," she said.

Mama got an immigration lawyer to handle the details, which were settled with dispatch, and she returned from court two weeks later waving the divorce papers.

I was glad to leave. At least I'd be spared the embarrassment of a high school graduation with Luke present in the audience reeking of alcohol and Pall Malls.

Mama and I moved into a duplex in Hyde Park, near the University of Chicago, or U of C, as it was called.

In November, Wellesley, an all-women's school in Massachusetts, awarded me a one-year tuition scholarship. But when I attended a reception for prospective students at a suburban villa in North Chicago, I knew I couldn't survive at that institution for even one year on scholarship. I didn't fit in.

When she got wind of my plight, Mrs. Foote, who had received her MA from Indiana University, encouraged me to apply for the IU Foundation Little 500 Scholarship for needy students. I asked Mrs. Foote if the money for tuition and board would be enough to keep me afloat for an entire year.

She peered over her half rim glasses. "You can work alongside your studies for pocket money. Keep up your grades, and the work-study program will be automatically renewed. If anyone is diligent and dedicated, it is you, Renate." (Mrs. Foote took care to pronounce my name "Renateh," in the German way.) "As for grades, they don't come any better than A+. Here," she said, handing me an application, "fill out the form. I've even got a stamped envelope to mail it in."

I sent the letter off. Based on Mrs. Foote's recommendations, Edda's low income and my excellent high school grade average, IU offered me a Little 500 Scholarship. Together with two sorority scholarships, I would be set for the first year.

I could hardly believe my good fortune: not only would I get my university education, but I also would have access to a renowned German department and music school. Was there a better deal anywhere else?

Our high school spring break coincided with the break at the IU campus in Bloomington. Wanting to make sure I'd be happy there, Edda suggested we visit the campus. Through Mrs. Foote I arranged a meeting with a Professor Fuerstenberg in the German department to discuss my undergraduate program.

*   *   *

On our way to Bloomington, Mama and I traversed the flat moraine of northern Indiana that gave way to soft undulating hills and limestone outcroppings in the south. Almost immediately, I felt cradled, safe, grounded.

"Mama, don't the hills and forests remind you of the countryside around Vogelweide?"

She nodded.

After we registered for our room at the student union, Mama and I took a late afternoon walk on campus and admired the numerous limestone edifices built in the nineteenth and twentieth centuries – including University Lutheran, a church situated across from Dunn Meadow on Seventh Street.

Mrs. Foote had mentioned the wonderful music program at U Lutheran and their talented and somewhat "unconventional" choir director and organist, Martha Mueller.

We viewed the sanctuary and noted from a flyer that there would be a solo aria, "Hear My Prayer," by Mendelssohn, performed by IU Professor of Voice Madame Dorothee Manski, on Sunday.

We exited the church and looked at an outside bulletin board.

"Sunday services are at nine thirty and ten forty-five. By all means, let's attend," Mama said.

Stopping at the university auditorium, we picked up concert brochures. I was fascinated by the WPA frescoes on the wall, and by the three-tiered concert hall, which held three thousand people. And this in a small town of twenty-five thousand! It certainly was not, as one of my CHS classmates had said, a Podunk town in the middle of nowhere.

In the morning, while Mama rested, I set off to Kirkwood Hall for my appointment with Dr. Fuerstenberg. I fell instantly in love with the building, one of the oldest limestone structures lining a broad sidewalk on the edge of the university woods.

After climbing the stairs to the professor's office, I straightened out my vest and knocked. A rotund man in a casual shirt and slacks came to the door.

"Guten Tag, Herr Dr. Furstenberg." I extended my hand. "Renate Seiler."

"Willkommen, Renate. Bitte setzten Sie sich." He pulled a chair over to his desk, and sat down across from me.

"Wo haben Sie Deutsch gelernt?"

"I was born in Berlin. When I was fourteen, my mother and I emigrated to Chicago. My mother and I still converse in German."

"What prompted you to consider us here in the boonies?"

"My German teacher told me about your fantastic department – and the music school."

"The music school. What is your training in music?"

"When I was eleven my aunt gave me piano lessons on her wonderful Steinweg. But the destruction of Germany in 1945 put an end to any further piano playing."

Unable to control my sadness, I stopped for a moment.

"I understand," Dr. Fuerstenberg said, shifting in his chair. "Do you sing?"

"I took part in our *Hausmusik* concerts and when we sang together as a family. But I've never considered formal voice lessons in that sense. My father used to perform German lieder at *Hausmusik* concerts when I was young. His singing affected me so deeply. I realized while listening to him how much I loved German art songs. I don't know how I could ever recreate the performances my father gave."

"Hmm. So you've chosen the academic route."

My throat tightened.

Perhaps sensing my discomfort, the professor said, "Renate, we can't accomplish everything we'd like to in life – at least not all at once."

"I suppose not, sir."

"Now," Dr. Fuerstenberg reached for a note pad on his desk, "tell me more about your goals."

For about half an hour I outlined my special interest in Romantic poetry and the German composers who had set those poems to music, while Dr. Fuerstenberg took notes.

"Given the stiff competition I observe in our music school, I think your plan might well be a wise choice. Your enthusiasm, love of German culture and obvious language skills are wonderful prerequisites for combining a major in German literature and music history. And you may be interested to know that the music school hired a number of German speaking professors – most of them Jewish refugees from Nazi Germany."

*   *   *

Getting that strong nod of approval from Dr. Fuerstenberg, I left his office on cloud nine. How different was my reception at IU than at Central High! I could barely contain my excitement as I told Mama all about the interview.

She was tickled pink. "Reni, shall we continue your wonderful day and look at some dorms this afternoon?"

We picked Memorial Hall, a limestone dorm blanketed in ivy, with a beautiful rear courtyard. At the office, we inquired if we might see a student's room.

Upstairs, Edda walked to the window. "Look, Reni, you can see the music school right from here! And your German classes will be barely a five-minute walk away."

It all seemed so perfect, yet a commitment to IU proved a tough decision for me. To leave Mama would tear me apart. Since Papi's death, there had been just Edda and me on a survival trip to a new country and new customs. That night at the union, I stared out the window, scared to embrace the "yes" I wanted to give IU.

*   *   *

On Sunday we attended U Lutheran, and arrived to find the church almost full. Mama and I took the only pew left in the front. The service was remarkable, from the choral prelude by Buxtehude to Pastor Mueller's intelligent sermon and the postlude by Samuel Scheidt. But most indelible in my mind were the moments after the first hymn, when a murmur arose toward the back of the nave. I turned and saw a statuesque woman stride down the aisle, her pungent perfume wafting through the church. She glided by us, then, via a side archway, entered the pulpit and adjusted her fox boa.

"That must be Professor Manski," Edda whispered to me.

When Mrs. Mueller began the organ introduction to the aria, Madame Manski, as I soon learned to address her, took a step forward. Standing erect, she began in a soft, lyrical, reverent, voice: "Heerr my prayer, O Gott incline Syne ear. Syself from my peteetion, do naught hide . . ."

The choir joined in for a vigorous "The enemy shouteth . . ." with precision and dramatic flair as Mrs. Mueller skillfully directed from the organ.

As Manski reached the familiar second part of the aria, she raised her palms to the heavens with a look worthy of the Pietà: "O for the vinks, for the vinks of a duff . . . In the vildernesss, built me a nesst . . . ant remain sair forever to resst."

I didn't move a muscle, stunned as I was by Manksi's outpouring of fervor that in a concert hall would surely have resulted in giggles. This U Lutheran church came across to me as way ahead of its time in music, gospel and simpatico, as Laura might have phrased it. *Bravo Madame Manski and Mrs. Mueller!*

After the service Mama walked right up to Manski and waved me over to shake her hand. In the future, whenever Mama came to visit me, Dorothee, as Mama called her, was part of Sunday dinner after church.

As we prepared to leave, Mrs. Mueller stopped us in our tracks with a bellow from the organ bench. "Wait a minute, young lady!" She climbed down off the bench with bulletin and a pen in hand, and rushed over to us. "I heard your voice, and am always on the prowl for new choir members! Are you a Lutheran? We don't approve of proselytizing." Her ample midriff shook with laughter.

"Yes she is," Mama said.

"Good. What's your name?" Mrs. Mueller stood with poised expectancy.

"Renate Seiler."

"Well, then, Renate, I'd like to invite you to choir practice on Thursday evenings. We begin punctually at seven fifteen." She wrote the time on the bulletin and handed it to me.

Before I had a chance to reply, Mama said, "This is an such honor for my daughter."

I said yes.

With the rich and wonderful service at U Lutheran on Sunday, Doctor Fuerstenberg's kind words, a chance to sing in a student church choir, and the magical beauty of the campus, the scales were tipped for me. The next day, Edda accompanied me to the dean's office, where I accepted their scholarship offer.

"I know you will miss me," Edda said as we drove back to Chicago, "and I'll miss you, too. But everything works out as God wishes. Besides, we'll see each other on holidays and in the summer. I know how to take care of myself, don't you worry. No one gets through World War II in Berlin without being tough."

*   *   *

The second week of September, Mama and I set out for Bloomington with three pieces of luggage, a new portable Olivetti typewriter (Mama's gift to me) and my favorite books: *Buddenbrooks*, by Thomas Mann, Goethe's *Faust* and Papi's book of poetry.

My first year at IU provided the stimulation my soul longed for. I loved singing in the U Lutheran choir. We performed hundreds of anthems I had never heard of, such as Randall Thompson's *Alleluia* and works by F. Melius Christiansen from St. Olaf. Mrs. Mueller, however, favored German Lutheran repertoire: Bach, Brahms, Buxtehude, Telemann, Luther and many others. Although we sang them in English, they reminded me of our church choir in Berlin.

I also was fortunate to be paired with a nice roommate, Carol "don't forget the T" Schwartzentruber (always a name to joke about between us) with whom I went to concerts and university events. We would stay up for hours discussing anything and everything, but mostly our classes or the latest foreign flicks at the local movie theater, the Von Lee. I think Carol was fascinated by my past (as I was by hers), since she'd grown up amongst Amish and Mennonites in the northeastern part of Indiana and was eager to broaden her horizons from her clannish upbringing.

A swimmer, Carol spent long hours at afternoon team practice, and I attended the team's Big Ten swim meets as often as I could on those weekends. Not much of a churchgoer now, Carol did come to U Lutheran when Mrs. Mueller had planned a major work at the church, like a Bach cantata.

In our senior year, Carol got a position as dorm counselor, which meant she had her own room and was busy counseling students. I was sad about living alone, but Carol was just down the hall, and I could still drop by when I wanted to talk.

During those first years of college, Mama visited twice a year – once in mid-October, when we took trips to Brown County twenty miles away to see the brilliant red, orange and yellow leaves reflected across Lake Ogle – and once in the spring, when the cherry trees were in bloom.

Mama promptly invited Madame Manski to have dinner with us at the Brown County Inn. The two women, although they had little in common on the surface, seemed to connect particularly through their mutual love of Berlin, and speaking German with one another.

Madame Manski told us hilarious stories about her concert days in the US. One time at a rest stop, she'd missed her tour bus. Emerging from the loo, she'd seen the bus heading down the road and emitted such a Valkyrian shriek that the driver had actually heard her and come back. We nearly fell off our chairs with laughter, raising a few eyebrows in the quiet dining room.

*   *   *

Academics were no problem and I mapped out the class schedule to complete a double major in four years. In my sophomore year, Dr. Fuerstenberg allowed me to take his upper-level *Faust* course. Within two years, I completed all the advanced undergraduate courses the department offered. I was able to devote my senior year to graduate seminars in German and undergraduate music history courses.

I decided to continue with graduate work at IU and applied for a teaching fellowship. My only worry was Mama's health. She hadn't felt up to her usual fall visit that year, and on my Christmas break I discovered heart medication on her nightstand. Mama brushed my questions off, saying the pills were just "precautionary." I called the doctor and learned Edda's heart had weakened. The doctor recommended she go on disability.

"Don't worry, Reni," Mama reassured me. "I was given a part-time secretarial job at church."

My mother's frailty and finances overruled my plan to stay on for graduate work at IU. Her church job and tiny disability were sufficient only for herself. With a heavy heart, I decided my only option was to return to Chicago. I think Mama was relieved I wanted to move in with her. Maybe I was relieved, as well.

Dr. Fuerstenberg suggested I apply to the U of C for my doctoral studies, and wrote me a strong recommendation for a stipend.

The stars were with me. The German department awarded me a full teaching fellowship.

*   *   *

The day before my commencement ceremony, Mama called to say she couldn't attend. "Dr. Cantola advised me not to go given the heat wave you've got down south."

I was disappointed and alarmed, as I knew how Edda had looked forward to seeing me in my commencement gown and cap.

Madame Manski attended the ceremony in Mama's stead; I was touched, as she hated crowds and the Bloomington heat. Pastor Mueller delivered the moving invocation on the power of making one's life work as a prayer – *ora et labora*. I went up to the podium to receive my magna cum laude BA, fighting back tears as I nodded to him. Mrs. Mueller came up after the ceremony and said in a voice loud enough to reach New York: "There goes my loyal soprano."

In my last days at Indiana, I visited the people who had made Bloomington home for me. I said goodbye to Carol, who was being picked up by her folks before traveling in August to UCLA. She looked so tan and fit from spring outdoor swimming – and would no doubt soak up the sun in Southern California.

In retrospect, I learned a lot about being an outsider from Carol, although she was not someone I'd have picked as a close friend under other circumstances. Maybe that was why saying goodbye was painful, but seemed to be right for both of us.

I knew it would be hard to find another music program like U Lutheran. Maybe that's why I never connected with choirs after that. When I learned to my surprise that the Muellers left for a campus church in Los Angeles the next year, I realized how fortunate I had been to be in the right place at the right time.

In the afternoon, I dropped in to see Madame Manski for a glass of lemonade out in the garden – with her poodle underfoot.

"Sanks gott for a lovely young woman like you, Renate. Please give Edda my best wishes."

We agreed to stay in contact. I felt far from sure of ever seeing her again.

At the entrance to Kirkwood Hall, I ran my hand across the rugged limestone block before going upstairs to Dr. Fuerstenberg's office.

"Hello, Renate," he greeted me with a warm handshake.

"Professor, I've come to say *Auf Wiedersehen*, and to thank you for these unforgettable four years here at IU."

"You proved to be the excellent student I had you pegged for." From his library, Fuerstenberg pulled out a leather-bound book, then penned a few lines on the title page and handed the volume to me.

It was a book of Heine's early poetry. I read the dedication, a first line from one of his poems: "*Du bist wie eine Blume, so hold so schön so rein.'* (Thou art like a flower, so graceful, so beautiful, so pure.) Stay the lovely woman this poem describes."

"Doctor, this book will be my companion wherever I go."

"Please come back to visit – perhaps when you've finished your PhD? Then I can address you as Dr. Seiler."

"I'd be delighted."

"Best of luck, then. We wish you could stay on. Nevertheless, I know the U of C German department will take you under their wing."

As I walked through the woods back to the dorm, I hoped I'd find the support I needed in Chicago. IU would be tough to match.

*   *   *

Bloomington got its share of cold weather, to be sure, but not like the long, brutal winters of the Windy City, as locals referred to Chicago. On my way to classes, I fought the harsh storms, icy sidewalks and snowdrifts. By the time I walked into my Middle High German seminar, the color of my legs matched my lipstick.

But the weather was not my greatest problem. After my first year of graduate school it became clear Edda's heart ailment was even more serious than I ever realized. When Luke was still living with us, he'd taken Edda to her appointments – I wasn't allowed behind the wheel. Even after her divorce, Mama had never learned to drive, as she felt it wasn't worth the trouble. Now, trips to the doctor by bus weren't an option anymore. In 1956 I got my license, and Edda negotiated a deal on a used red sedan through a church member.

Within two and a half years, because of my many graduate classes at IU, I finished my coursework and written exams for the PhD and searched for positions in the area. When Dr. Blume, the chair of the German department alerted me to an instructorship at Ryan College in Wisconsin, I drove up with Mama for the interview. An offer for the post of Assistant Professor of German arrived in the mail within a week.

I accepted the position, although with some trepidation. Mama encouraged me as always to move forward. "*Ach*, Reni, Ryan is right on Lake Michigan, and the position's a feather in your professional cap. We'll visit on holidays, and can always phone each other."

*   *   *

The traffic had died down to a trickle, and the night air smelled of fallen leaves. Yes, this was my old hometown, but what was home for me now? Where did I belong – in Berlin, a walled-in city, or in Ryan, where I knew my way around, even if my past kept me somehow a stranger anyway? Was I an Americanized German, or a German-American? Whom could I call my family? I went down the hall, opened the window and leaned out to look at the majestic linden tree in the courtyard. My future, like a plane in preparation for its descent, was searching for a place to land.

*   *   *

I was jolted out of my nostalgia when Schulz came by to say a small apartment down the hall would become available at the end of the month.

Schulz's unexpected offer gave me an affordable place – my own little pad near the downtown – and rescued me from the prospect of a drafty student room in some *Altbau* without elevators. Into the bargain, I could continue to have breakfast and peruse the newspaper before braving the city each morning.

I inspected the apartment just to make sure. What luck! There was a desk, an easy chair, a kitchenette and a tiny balcony looking onto the courtyard. Now I was relieved of one less worry – and one less distraction – from getting on with my grant project.

To celebrate my joy and relief, I took in a concert by the Berlin Philharmonic under the direction of Herbert von Karajan. Mahler's Fourth Symphony, with its lovely soprano solo in the final movement, was on the program.

Once, when Laura was ill, I had persuaded Mama – who favored mostly piano music and lieder – to accompany me to the symphony. The Chicago Phil had performed the identical symphony – Mahler's Fourth – then under the direction of Carlo Maria Giulini. Mama was so thrilled to hear German sung!

Now my heart ached for Mama next to me. While Karajan and the concert hall seemed to embody the recovered, new Berlin, Nonetheless, certain memories of my former hometown remained like an old friend.

It was time to share a visit to the Kranzler with Mama.

8

∞

Standing in my best slacks, silk blouse and scarf, leather jacket and boots – with a new purse I had slipped out to buy – I looked at myself in the mirror and sensed Mama's approval.

Diary in hand, I set out for the Ku-Damm, green-lined with tall, thick sycamore trees. On every block I passed sidewalk cafés filled with patrons, and shops galore for any palate, offering pastry, ice cream or scrumptious lunchtime treats.

The Kranzler was situated on a prime corner of the Ku-Damm. Mama and I had first come here for a treat on my sixth birthday, and had taken a window table to watch the fashionable crowd parade their latest outfits, or couples out on romantic strolls.

A waitress in a white apron over a black uniform took my order, returned soon with a *Kirsch torte* and a pot of coffee. She wished me a pleasant afternoon.

I reached opened my diary and flattened out the spine.

September 26 – at the Kranzler
It's a resplendent fall day and I'm enjoying my leisure time. These days, I'm tempted to write instead of taking my usual lazy route – staring out the window. I'm sure I'll thank this journal in years to come for having kept me posted on what happened to me – both in-side and outside.

Only a few customers are inside. Most everyone else has opted

for the outside terrace – people with kids and dogs especially. So I've
got the place just about to myself except for two elderly gents with
newspapers and pipes and several ladies with friends. How this
calm atmosphere contrasts with my hectic schedule at Ryan, where a
few gulps of coffee was all I could sneak in between classes.

On the subject of coffee . . . you hear people reminisce about the
pleasure of their first kiss. For me, it was my first taste of coffee at age
seventeen. Mama and I sat on her terrace – the weather was much like
today. Mama had made a plum torte with fruit picked from a local or-
chard. She'd always had coffee with her afternoon pastry, and up until
then, I'd drunk milk. Now, what would life be without caffeine?

I put down my diary and had to smile. I could hear Mama announce to me that it was time to introduce the magical effect of
coffee into my life. I'd be at the university before I knew it and that
meant social events with friends and late-night studies. I saw her
return from the hallway cabinet with two cups from her treasured
Meissen porcelain service – and matching pot. As I picked up my
steaming cup, she advised me to sip at first, to get used to the stimu-
lants. I'd soon be up to several cups a day. How right she was! In this
short time, I had already finished my pot!

As I looked at the empty chair across from me, I tried to imagine
what it would be like if Mama were sitting there. If her premature
passing was meant to be, as Christians say, then what was I destined
to learn with Mama gone?

The waitress came by to see if I wanted anything further. I ordered a glass of California Shiraz, and with pen set aside, stared out
the window. The wine helped draw me back again to my conversation with Edda on the terrace.

I remembered watching how caffeine worked on Mama, the chat-
tiness that seemed to come over her. I decided then to ask her to tell
me about her girlhood in Dresden.

"There was a melancholy beauty to the 'other Paris' – that's the
way natives referred to Dresden. It was an architect's dream. Did you
know your great-great grandfather designed the *Gewandhaus* – the

cloth hall? Papa would take me to sit outside the building, and I'd sit on a bench drawing on empty pages from Grandpa's old sketchbooks. But I gave up on that sort of thing after my coming of age. Girls simply didn't consider a higher education then."

You were born too soon, Mama!

"How did you meet Papi?" I asked. She got up, poured herself a second cup and moved to her comfy rocker near the window box.

"One summer afternoon, we attended a local horse show. Your father looked so stately, all decked out in proper equestrian attire on his shiny chestnut-colored mare! I sat with Oma and Opa in the review stand. When Kurt passed by, he looked over at me and tipped his black hat. Doesn't it sound like those romantic novels they used to run in the women's section of the newspaper each week?"

"How old were you then?"

"I'd just turned twenty-one, and it was time to get me 'on my way,' as my father put it. He arranged to have Kurt come to dinner and pass muster. When I found out your father had completed his PhD in mathematics, I asked him a question about proportions on Gothic cathedrals. His eyebrow went up as he answered. When he went off to the stables with Papa, Mama Ruthie cautioned me to discuss 'more general' subjects. Scientific matters 'were the provinces of other circles.'"

"Mama, I think I suddenly understand your concern about my 'overly mental' life."

"How so, Reni?" Edda adjusted the sleeve on her blouse.

"It's what Freud called projection: you ascribe to another your own thoughts or attitudes."

It was the first time I'd seen Edda blush.

"I don't put much stock in all that Freudian business. Dissertations and research are fine, but remember, even great poetry isn't a replacement for romantic love with a man."

*   *   *

I gazed around the Kranzler – still the only woman alone.

"Would Madam care to place another order?"

"No, thank you. Would you bring me the check, please?"

Just outside the Kranzler, people rushed to catch nearly full buses. How long had I been in this reverie, I wondered?

Grief and relief welled up. In Berlin, I was fated to forge my future, while compelled to revive my family's past.

I finished up with a last entry:

Closing time at the Kranzler

I've spent an afternoon with Mama, as if she were next to me, and achieved some measure of closure. I've got so much to thank her for, but most of all for our emigration to the US. It gave me the answer to the first line of a song set by Johannes Brahms: "Oh, if I only knew the way back, the sweet way back into the land of childhood." America gave me my childhood back, my youth again, however painful the road.

This return to my old hometown, in contrast my relocation to Chicago seems to be about coming full circle – back to my lost childhood – and forward to shape my own future. Mama, your departure frees me to be who I am. Don't take it the wrong way, Mama. I'd dearly love to have you here, but it's in my hands now. Thank you for the marvelous time we spent together.

9

∞

I awoke refreshed from my afternoon at the Kranzler – yet with little urge to be productive. The DAAD supervisors in Bonn required a progress report twice a year, but otherwise, I was left to my own devices – so long as my diss. was done by the summer. Nevertheless, before getting under way in earnest, I decided to take a daylong bus tour of East and West Berlin.

When I reached the street at our pickup time, ten fifteen, the bus driver had just pulled up to the curb. A group of chatty Americans with southern drawls had gathered to board. I walked past them, climbed into the bus and snagged a window seat. Along came a hunk replete with cowboy hat, leather jacket and boots. He nodded to an Italian bombshell across the aisle and took the seat next to me.

"Name's Clyde," he said, and tipped his hat. "From Dallas. Pleased to meet 'cha."

"I'm Renate. Glad to make your acquaintance. I'm from – Chicago."

"Hey, the Windy City," he grinned.

I looked out the window.

Over the course of several downtown hotel stops, a mixture of European and Asian tourists, to judge by the languages spoken, joined us for the tour. Clyde began a conversation with Gina across the aisle, which gave me the opportunity to relax and have something from the day.

The bus tour began with a visit to the Strasse des 17. Juni, which honored the East Germans' revolt against their regime on that date in 1953. At the Brandenburg Gate, we viewed the border area from an observation tower. As a child, I'd walked through that very gate with Papi to see the *Gendarmenmarkt*, with its two magnificent cathedrals and stately concert house. Now, I stared in horror at the grotesque reality before me: a concrete wall three and a half meters high cut through the middle of Berlin. Behind it, armed Grepos patrolled an open strip lined with iron crossbars to stop anyone from ramming a car through to the West, as our guide explained.

It all felt like a knife through my heart.

On the way to our border crossing, Clyde explained to Gina that the Wall couldn't possibly happen in the States.

Checkpoint Charlie – the crossing's official American Sector name – was run by the US military and consisted of a rectangular timber hut with sandbags stacked facing the East Berlin side. With the motor idling, the driver checked in at the window, and then eased the bus into Soviet territory past two armed Vopos.

"We should've used our tanks to blast into their friggin' Wall, Texas style." Clyde clenched his fist.

Gina nodded in approval.

Too bad Clyde hasn't suggested his tank plan to President Kennedy.

In East Berlin a new GDR guide came on board, together with two officious Vopos who checked passports and counted money and passengers.

On Unter den Linden, East Berlin's answer to the Ku-Damm, we alighted from the bus to view the changing of the guard, which consisted of soldiers goose-stepping in metal helmets and black boots at the Tomb of the Unknown Soldier. The sight chilled my blood.

As we drove off, the guide continued with his script, making no mention of the Wall, although we could see it at the far end of the boulevard. The tour moved on past the showcase cultural spots: the State Opera House, the Brecht Theater am Schiffbauerdamm and the Komische Oper. I planned to return to each of them on my own. At the Pergamon Museum, we disembarked for an hour's visit – enough time to see a fraction of the magnificent antiquities collection.

No modicum of color enlivened the remainder of the tour. Department stores and shops were nonexistent, except for a few state-owned stores on Karl Marx Allee, a boulevard with garishly white wedding-cake-style apartment houses.

The bus proceeded to Alexanderplatz, a train and traffic connection to points east and south. Today, at least, the scene was depressing, reminding me of some old daguerreotype prints I had seen at the Art Institute in Chicago, where a few people stood motionless amidst a gray backdrop of empty streets.

*   *   *

After lunch, we stopped to pay our respects to the Red Army's liberation of Berlin at the Soviet Memorial in Treptower Park, commemorated with an immense statue of a Soviet soldier and child. Before leaving the East, we passed deserted lots witnessing the final battles near Potsdamer Platz.

Back across the border, we drove by scaffolding stretched over damaged *Altbauhäuser* with workers sandblasting grit and soot away from facades. Still, for me a deep sadness hovered in the air. As they dug out sand for new foundations, baggers turned bombed-out structures into gaping holes without memories. The city was now divided, but the war hadn't taken sides.

On the bright side, the transition to downtown West Berlin demonstrated how much the West Berliners had toiled to remove their scars of war. In less than a decade, much of the inner city had been cleared of rubble from air raid attacks and replaced with office structures, churches and shops – an "economic miracle," our Western guide reminded us.

Behind the memorial church, a new Europa Center was under construction, scheduled for completion in two years. Somewhere in this area, the famous Berlin literary institution Das Romantische Café had been located. Mama took me there to a matinee of German Romantic poetry when I was eight. A half-dozen men in brown shirts attended, standing in the back of the room with their arms folded.

*   *   *

The remainder of the day took us to the posh suburban areas of Berlin's southeast. We drove by a series of lakes. Here, the rich in their elegant villas had been spared some of the Allied attacks the rest of Berlin was subjected to – although, as Mama used to say –"No one came out of the war intact."

The bus stopped at a café in Grunewald, a large forested area that provided expansive paths for the otherwise caged-in Berliners. Such lovely woods were worthy of a longer visit.

September 27 – at the pension, after a tour of Berlin
Today was a beautiful if somber day, and full of contrasts: the East dismal, the West still in search of its way. I have an overview of what my new home is all about – a resilient city, but difficult to relax in, given you can't venture far without a reminder of oppression.

Much as I'd like to continue sightseeing, a voice inside me says enough dillydallying, time to knuckle down on those dissertation plans – which means a visit to the German State Library. (Maybe I'll sneak in a longer visit to the Pergamon museum!)

"Cheers for the poetry collection, boos for East Berlin," Howard said when he described his visits to the GSL last summer and the persnickety things the Vopos did at the East-West Berlin crossing. I gather I'll have to put up with delays and watch my exchange of money.

But the idea of any kind of research straight off appeals to me about as much as blood sausage for breakfast. This is new. Leisure sure is not a word in my vocabulary, as Laura teased more than once. Okay, girl, so I'm used to cramming in coursework and teaching four courses a semester at Ryan. For the first time in seven years, there's no need to rush off to pre-dawn classes. Maybe I'm more burned out from academe and class prep than I care to admit.

The next morning at breakfast, I perused the *Berliner Morgenpost* for cultural events; Schiller's drama *Wallenstein* was scheduled for tomorrow at the Schiller Theater. Wallenstein, a general in the Thirty Years War, shared a dual heritage from Moravia and Bohemia, and, just like Papi, spoke Czech and German. No doubt such similarities gave this drama particular appeal. I decided to catch the matinee performance.

The taste of Schulz's strong Eduscho coffee began to revive me.

I glanced at my calendar: as I turned the pages, "WESTERHEIM" reproached me with its block letters. I hadn't yet mustered the courage to follow my own admonition. What if I drew a blank again, as I had with Aunt Hildegard? Still, her comment that Westerheim might shed light on my father's death nagged at me.

On the way to my room, I glanced out of the stairwell window and saw the empty telephone booth below. I gathered my courage, checked for change in my purse and raced down the four flights, suddenly afraid to miss this chance. Good – still empty. I dropped two ten-pfennig coins into the slot and dialed.

A woman answered the phone. "The Westerheim residence, Olbers speaking."

"*Guten Tag*, Renate Seiler is my name. May I speak to Herr Westerheim, please?"

"I'm sorry, Doctor Westerheim is out of town."

"Oh, what a shame. I believe you may have received a note from Frau Rehburg – my aunt – to explain that I'd be coming to Berlin."

Frau Olbers' formal tone softened. "*Ach*, yes, we did receive a letter of introduction from a Frau Rehburg."

"Yes." *Thank you, Hildie. You followed through!*

"Would you care to leave a message, Fräulein Seiler? I'm sure the doctor will return your call the minute he gets back."

I gave Frau Olbers the phone number at the pension, relieved I had made the attempt to arrange a visit. Was I ready to talk so soon to the gentleman anyway? I wasn't sure.

The next day, after breakfast, with the help of Schulz and another employee, I got my clothes, toiletries, books, luggage, dissertation materials and snacks transferred with dispatch, and settled into my new abode down the hallway.

"No need to clean your room," Schulz said. "We'll take care of it. Enjoy your new quarters."

I inspected my new place – at first glance it had everything I needed – including a firm bed, shelving for books, an easy chair and a generous-sized wooden desk, with sideboards for papers and manuscripts. I was touched by Schulz's present of a bottle of German red wine. What fun it was to spruce up the place over the next few days – flowers, candlesticks and a bedspread helped do the final trick, and of course goodies for the little fridge.

I treated myself to the Sunday afternoon performance of Friedrich Schiller's *Wallenstein*, and came back to sit on my small balcony over wine, listening to the birdies warble and coo. *I can award myself a few of these days, surely.*

The next morning, after a quick errand to the department stores for a few knickknacks to put on my dresser, I actually settled down to address my introduction. I knew several rewrites would be necessary. *What else is new?* All beginnings are difficult, as the Germans say.

For several days, I agonized over my intro. Somehow it wasn't quite right. Changing my approach, I compared the Nazi perception of Heine before and after he left Germany. Finally by Friday, I had something solid to show Dr. Bautsch.

I went down for a mail break. A card had arrived in the morning from Laura! I stashed it in my purse and headed out for some exercise and fresh air. Rome wasn't built in day, *nicht wahr?*

After a half-hour walk, I checked out a *Kiez* (a Berlin word for a distinct neighborhood) located in the district of Charlottenburg that boasted alternative shops, hippie coffee houses and fresh vegetables on outside racks.

Tasty-looking rolls in the window of a small bakery promised a cozy atmosphere. I walked in and picked out a marble cheesecake.

At the nearest table, two elegantly dressed older women discussed in animated fashion the latest klatsch in their apartment house – and how many single women lived there.

Some days have their themes, I mused. Today, I decided, it was being alone. Laura must have intuited my state of mind, with her sweet postcard of the Wisconsin Dells. In the background, the fall palette of reds and oranges in the nearby woods made me ache with homesickness.

The telephone number of a Robert Bennett was on the back.

Dear Renita,

I don't want you to forget your beloved Wisconsin. Things just aren't the same without you here. Even the Cava doesn't taste as good as before! I hope you've adjusted well to your new environs. Have you connected with anyone yet? I know it's got to be tough to be a complete stranger. Last week, I thumbed through my alumni newsletter from Columbia University and discovered that Robert Bennett, a student I knew there, has a teaching fellowship in sociology at the Free University in Berlin. I called the alumni office and got his phone number at the FU. I always thought Robert was a nice fellow – not my type, but hey, maybe yours? Give him a call! Got to get to class – and this in the mail before the weekend. I miss you!

Love,

Laura

I put Laura's postcard back in my purse and ordered another cup of coffee.

October 4 – Konditorei Petersen, late morning
What a difference a few days can make! Last week at the Kranzler, I came to terms with moving on without Mama. Somehow, there must be a good fairy watching over me, (Mama in disguise?), because an important concern – an apartment – has fallen into my lap. Yay!

A Sunday afternoon to see Wallenstein – whew! What a long play – full of action to the end. The setting of the play in Bohemia in wartime, and the importance of conscience made me think of Papi. The play contains such an elegant maxim: "The curse of every evil deed is that, if continued, it must of necessity bear further evil." I felt a shudder go down my spine when Octavio Piccolomini betrayed

Wallenstein, his own friend and confidant, dismissing the plea of his very own son! An honest conscience is no match for an evil deed, Piccolomini tells him. Can this be true? Is this Schiller, the idealist, capitulating to realism or political exigencies? Deep stuff.

And now, here I am, doing the coffee and pastry bit again, this time at a small place not far from the Charlottenburg castle. I've never seen so many kinds of rolls – from my beloved Schrippen to six-inch pretzels sprinkled with salt or dark efforts such as rye in every shape and size. All in all, more comfort food than I ought to consider at this hour. By the looks of the clientele, it attracts a local crowd – the waitress greets almost everybody by name.

Was it a mistake to accept Schulz's offer and sequester myself? I certainly don't need to confine connections here to the likes of yak-king Americans on my tour. I've figured how to avoid such tourist types in the mornings, anyway – I just need to have breakfast after nine thirty, when most guests will be gone and I won't have to share a table.

I wonder if visitors really understand how we Germans were treated like chess pieces after the war. Those of us who ended up in one of the three Western zones are the lucky ones, while the rest, the East Germans, became victims of Soviet control. If you ask me, just change the uniform slightly and presto, a Vopo looks like a reincarnated Nazi.

I ate another morsel and mulled over Robert's phone number. *Should I contact this guy Robert out of the blue? Well why not? We're both foreigners abroad. Better get a hold of him before I get too bogged down with my dissertation. I wonder who would be Laura's type? Well if he puts the make on me, some girls might use headaches, but I can lean on my diss.*

I discovered a pay phone at the rear part of the *Konditorei*, next to the toilets, tastefully set off by a half-wall partition. Eleven thirty A.M. was as good a time to call as any. I grabbed the card and dialed. I was about to hang up when a pleasant-sounding voice answered.

"Bennett."

He's learned the correct way to answer the phone in German.

"Hello, Robert, I'm Renate Seiler, a colleague of Laura Sanchez from Ryan College. She told me about you in a letter and suggested I call."

"Hello, Renate, what brings you to town? Laura said you might be in touch, but she didn't really fill me in."

Except to mention I was single, I'll bet.

"I'm on a German government grant to complete my dissertation. How about you, Robert?"

"I have a Fulbright teaching fellowship at the Free University in sociology. This semester, my courses include a class in American postwar social patterns."

"Sounds innovative."

Robert chuckled. "I guess you could say so. But ironically, I've been more focused on *German* social patterns. Berlin is a fertile place to observe all manner of them. Would you be interested in some exposure to the infamous Berlin nightlife? My first lecture isn't for a few days, so I've got some free time."

"It's a good time for me, too. I just got an apartment, and have been fixing it up. I'd enjoy a bit of diversion."

"Good. There's a nifty small club near the downtown with great atmosphere and a terrific singer who does old standards and love songs."

"Love songs?"

"You know, music from the thirties and forties."

I hope this isn't some hack German schmaltz.

"Okay, I'm game."

"How about eight o'clock this coming Monday, then?"

I gave him directions to the pension.

"Looking forward to it, Renate."

10

On Monday evening I put on a dark blouse and vest with my corduroy jacket, hoping they'd be right for the occasion. At 7:50 I began to pace the hallway, peering out now and then to see if Robert had arrived. I'd forgotten to tell him it was verboten to park in front of the pension. When I saw a red VW Bug heading away from the pension, I knew it had to be his car. I buttoned my jacket, stepped outside to the curb and waited.

Two minutes later, the red VW pulled up again and Robert hopped out to open my door. A slight man in his early thirties, he was dressed in dark slacks, a beige pullover and a blazer.

"Allow me, Gnädiges Fräulein – or is it Frau Professorin?" Robert shook my hand with a bow and opened the door.

"You flatter me." *Or is he confirming my marital status?*

I got into the VW – brand-new, to judge by the smell. A fox with the initials LH on it hung from the rearview mirror.

"What does LH stand for?"

"Lincoln High! The best doggone football team in the whole state!"

"When did you come to Berlin, Robert?"

"In August, to take advanced German language courses at the Goethe Institute."

"By the way, your German pronunciation is excellent."

His face reddened. "Gosh, what a nice compliment! I hear you're a native speaker."

"I'm glad I didn't need to learn it. German's not an easy language to master."

"For sure! Can you imagine being a farm boy like me from Ohio and finding yourself lecturing in Germany?" Robert turned onto Hardenbergstrasse and drove past the university.

"This is a perfect time to head downtown," he said. "The theater traffic's died down, and the clubs aren't open yet."

"Have you seen much of the city, Renate?"

"Yes. It'll take me time to get used to the bright lights and commercialism of this area now. The former downtown was so beautiful and elegant."

"Oh, what a dumb question – you were born here, right? How did you feel when you first looked around?"

"I must admit that ugly Wall is a shock to my system."

"I can imagine. It was a shock for me, and I'd never been here before."

"Have you ventured to the other side yet, Robert?"

"Yeah, but I didn't get much beyond Friedrichstrasse. I walked along Unter den Linden and watched the changing of the guard near the opera house. It's weird; the soldiers dress with steel helmets and all – they looked like Nazi SS types. The whole setup in East Berlin made me uncomfortable, frankly. Creepy! Maybe that's why I haven't gone back."

"We saw those same guards on the tour. Puts the fear of God into you. Still, I'll be going back to see some of the museums and theaters – especially the Theater am Schiffbauerdamm."

"Wasn't that Bertolt Brecht's old hangout? We had to read his *Mutter Courage* in fourth-year German class."

"Right you are. The actress Helena Weigel – Brecht's widow – still uses her late husband's staging. I've heard that you won't find a better performance of Mother Courage than hers."

"Such comments probably wouldn't win you any popularity contests in the States." Robert turned the corner behind the memorial church and headed down Tauenzienstrasse. "Renate, are you familiar with KaDeWe – the tall building on our right? It's short for

Kaufhaus des Westens. They've got a fabulous international department with peanut butter and other goodies from the US – even if their prices are double what they'd be in Ohio. That store's saved me from homesickness more than once."

I flashed on a December visit to KaDeWe with Mama to buy German stollen and candies from England. As for the peanut butter, the Americans used to include it in the care packages they sent us after the war. Mama and I thought the stuff tasted like toothpaste. In spite of our hunger, we threw the jars away.

At a dimly lit street sign Robert slowed down and craned his neck.

"Where are we headed?"

"Augsburger Strasse. Drat, I missed it."

After driving around the block, Robert turned into a narrow, dark street, which brightened as rows of small nightclubs, cabarets, and striptease clubs with neon lights came into view.

"Let's keep our eyes peeled – in this area, it's a real battle to get a spot."

"There's a space up ahead." I said.

Robert looked in the rearview mirror. "And just get that Ford Taunus on the left trying to nab our spot with an illegal U-turn!" With a swift jerk of the wheel, Robert pulled in before the Taunus.

The driver shook his fist at us. "You Amis – first you take our country and now our parking spaces!"

"How did he know you're an American?"

"I've got international plates and a USA sticker on the rear window. Comes in handy when I make a mistake. They can write me off as a dumb *Ami*."

Robert opened my door and offered his arm. We walked past several clubs where men milled out front.

"Do any women go to these clubs?"

"Some. But many of the places like this one" – Robert pointed to poster of a Pink Lady and a tilted champagne glass – "feature drag shows."

"Drag shows?"

"Don't worry, our program calls for golden oldies."

We crossed the street. Just ahead, a colored neon sign flashed "Der Schwarze Panther." Robert handed the bouncer two marks. With a flick of his head, the guy motioned us in.

The smell of stale smoke assaulted me as I entered the club. Fighting off nausea, I followed Robert down the steps into a cramped rectangular basement room with concrete walls and floors.

Robert turned toward me. "The Panther is all the rage now. You can usually get a good seat before nine. Later, it's filled to the gills."

I paused to check the space out. Unfinished wooden tables were supplied with Cinzano ashtrays darkened from cigarette butts; handwritten menus propped against Chianti bottles with candles in them. Along the middle of the left wall was an elevated stage with a barstool, mike stand and beat-up piano. A black cloth served as the stage backdrop, partially covering ugly concrete blocks. To our immediate left, a painted panther crouched in readiness.

I could see barely a handful of women – one pair at the U-shaped bar, dressed in overalls and jeans, and two others smoking cigarettes at a table near the side wall. The rest of the patrons clustered at the bar stage right were guys in spattered pants and work shirts, or young men dressed in casual slacks and leather jackets. Smoke swirled around grimy triangular ceiling lamps above them.

Stale and new smoke together – ugh! Here you need a facemask.

"Renate, look over stage left. Let's grab the two empty chairs at the table where the two guys are sitting."

As we approached, the two young men glanced up.

"Nice to see you, Olaf," Robert said. They shook hands.

"Olaf, meet Renate." He touched my arm.

I shook Olaf's hand, nodded to his companion and took a seat with a view of the stage. Robert sat down next to Olaf.

"So how was the first act?"

"Terrible – fellow's name was Conrad Dierk. He should change his name to jerk."

"Maybe the next act will make up for it," Robert said.

"The guy canceled – flu or whatever." Olaf reached for the candle to light his next cigarette.

"What do you think, Robert – should we go somewhere else, maybe to the Porcupines?"

"They're closed Mondays. Anyway, Christine's the one I wanted you to hear."

A husky fellow in a sweatshirt with "Ohio State Football" printed on it walked up to our table and patted Robert on the shoulder.

"Hey, guy, how are things?"

"Hi, Dick. Meet Renate from Chicago."

"Jeez, three Americans in one place. Like old home week," Dick said.

I smiled and said hello.

Dick turned to Robert. "Got a minute?"

"Do you mind?" Robert asked me, his face flushed. "We went to the same high school."

"Go ahead," I said.

While Robert chatted with his classmate about their high school football team, I surveyed the place.

"Rosie, how about those Pils? I've got six impatient customers," a waiter shouted over the din to an attractive redhead in her early forties, with a cigarette, tending the bar.

All the mixed drink glasses were lined to Rosie's left, while the bottles for liquor, beer and wine stood spread out to her right. From what I could tell, most of the tables had beer glasses, but the mixed drink glasses I guessed added a touch of a traditional bar scene.

"Take it easy, pal," she said. After taking a couple of final drags from her cigarette, she stuffed the butt into an overfilled ashtray.

A murmur rippled through the audience as a slender, dark-haired woman with a plastic bag slung over her shoulder ambled up to the bar.

"'N Abend, Rosie."

"'N Abend, Chris. The usual, darlin'?" Rosie smiled and plunked a beer on the counter. Chris scooped up the bottle and headed backstage.

"Ok, time to get to my seat. Nice to meet you," Dick said to me over his shoulder and sauntered off to a table with three men and a half dozen beer bottles.

"The woman in the leather jacket and tights at the bar, is she the performer you mentioned?" I asked Robert.

"You got it. Renate. May I buy you a beer?"

"What do you recommend?"

"Zwei Berliner Kindl," Robert called to the waiter, who relayed our order to Rosie. After removing two glasses from an overhead rack, she opened the tap and filled them, then skimmed off the excess with a straight edge. She topped off each glass with a squirt, whirled around, took two paper coasters from a stack and placed them over the stems.

The waiter added the glasses to his almost-full tray and came over to us first. He set two down on coasters, took a pencil from behind his ear and marked our round cardboard coaster with two lines.

"He'll settle up with us later. By then, most coasters will be full of hatch marks."

What would Laura say if I told her I'd gone with Robert to a dive full of smokers and drunks?

"So *Prost!*" Robert lifted his glass toward me.

"Prost." I tapped his glass.

Robert took a long draught. "Once the semester gets under way in earnest, there won't be time for too many club visits." He glanced over to stage left. "Hey, we're ready to roll."

Christine had just emerged through the back door, dressed in a black tuxedo with a carnation in her lapel and a cigarette behind her ear. Carrying a white-tipped cane and a slender black cigarette holder she strode across the stage, sat down, and crossed her legs. When the audience grew silent, Christine reached for the cigarette. Tapping it on her thumb, she inserted it into the long holder and waited for a few latecomers to scramble for a seat before nodding to the pianist to begin.

Using a stage prop telephone and with legs entwined,, she sang in a low voice to her imaginary lover. Unheard of, a woman called to entice her lover for an afternoon tryst? The audience loved it. At the repeat, Christine uncrossed her legs, propped one on the chair and lit her cigarette, tossing the match on the floor. The final plea she crooned in a husky low-voiced register. Would he come by or not? I didn't care. What mattered was listening to Christine's irresistible wooing. A chorus of male whistles followed as soon as the song ended.

What a classy singer! Too bad she has to put up with this kind of audience.

Christine transitioned from one song into another, changed the tempo and varied the mood with subtle gestures. Her pianist was right on cue. Toward the end of the set, she left the mike on its stand, sauntered forward to the edge of the stage and with a barely audible voice, serenaded a young man in the first row. Descending the steps, Christine paused at the bar in front of Rosie, swung her leg onto the bar stool, half facing the audience to place an order. Rosie obliged with another bottle of beer. Christine took several sips, sent the bottle skimming back to her along the countertop, dashed up the stairs and retook the stage.

My insides felt like butterflies fluttering about, trying to find an exit. I didn't dare look at Robert.

The pianist played the introduction to "Falling in Love Again," a Marlene Dietrich song from the movie *The Blue Angel*. At the end, Christine sat with spread legs on a chair turned backward, and with utter indifference, dismissed her largely male audience by lighting a candle with a match struck against the sole of her shoe. Laughing as she blew the candle out, she stood up, glanced over the audience and shrugged.

The crowd roared. Christine bowed with a kiss our way.

"Terrific!" Robert said. "I've heard bar sales are twice as good when Christine performs. What did you think of her, Renate?"

"She's got stage presence all right – and her voice is ..."

"Seductive? You bet. It's a relief to experience openness in a culture that restricts you at each turn: the hours children can play in public parks, the correct time for a social call, and when you can practice piano at home."

Robert seemed to enjoy his role as the bar sociologist. But he's got a point. Christine's approach came across as alluring, natural, and direct.

Two friends dropped by to chat with Olaf at our table, and Robert joined in. For the next ten minutes, I listened to male gossip about the female patrons at the Black Panther – and who might be approachable for a date after the show. They glanced furtively at me to read my reaction.

I excused myself and hurried to the WC. The cold water from the tap felt good on my hot face. A place like this took a while to get used to. My heart raced. Why couldn't I just relax and let go?

A fresh Pils awaited me at the table, with foam running down the sides. I wiped off the errant beer with the paper coaster. In the meantime, Olaf's two friends had scooped up their drinks and moved to the bar.

"Sounds like you come here often, Robert."

"I've been to the Black Panther a couple of times to hear Christine."

"How come you didn't tell me all this on the phone?"

"I didn't want you to turn me down, Renate – the performer being a chanteuse and all."

*   *   *

The audience scrambled for their seats as Christine, dressed in a black sequined dress slit up the side, began her second set at the back of the stage with lowered lights. Sweeping one end of a red boa over her shoulder, Christine leaned against a wall under a dim light, and sang her first song, Lili Marlene, a popular song during the war.

Gradually, she moved to center stage and pressed the mike close to her mouth. Like a dancer, she moved gracefully in a sideward walk and looked off into space, as if to conjure up a soldier boy she had met long ago under that very lamp.

For the remainder of the set, Christine invoked scenes and images from a nostalgic, romantic, irretrievable time in which the pain, gain and loss of love seemed to drench the landscape. I felt overwhelmed by the melancholy that hung in the air.

For her last song of the set, a tribute 'to the ailing Edith Piaf,' Christine offered "Je ne regrette rien" (I have no regrets). Removing her boa, she took stage center next to the microphone stand, and nodded to the pianist. With her head held high, Christine captured the unrepentant temerity of the lyrics. If I had closed my eyes, I would have thought Piaf was the chanteuse.

As she approached the climactic last line, Christine glanced briefly at me, and summoned a voice that melted away all defiance into an unabashed declaration of love. Amidst thunderous applause, she bowed to different parts of the stage, gestured to the clock above the bar, smiled and then exited.

"We sure got a winner tonight!" Robert said. "Did you see how she sang to us? I thought I'd pop!"

Minutes later, Christine wound her way through the crowd to my side. "How'd you like the show?" She leaned one hand on the table.

"Oh, I loved your choice of songs, especially Lili Marlene, and Je ne regrette rien."

"Please come again. I perform here on Mondays. You won't regret it." She tossed a flyer about her next show on the table. "Bye now."

After a few paces, Christine did an about face.

"What did you say your name was?"

"Renate Seiler."

"Next time you visit, I'll dedicate one of my songs to you, Fräulein Seiler."

*   *   *

Robert started the car. "How about a nightcap, Renate? There's a great place near your pension." He eased into the club traffic. "Christine seemed intrigued by you. I've never seen her stop to chat with anyone from the audience. It looked like you enjoyed the attention." On the Ku-Damm, Robert slowed down and looked left and right for a parking spot.

I sat riveted to the seat. Did he mean to imply I was turned on to a woman? Was he trying to catch me off guard to see what I would say? It was an awful moment. Tightness spread across my chest like a freshly washed sheet stretching to fit a new mattress. How was I supposed to bow out gracefully?

I resorted to the old grad student excuse. "Look, Robert, I'll take a rain check. I'm not much of a night owl and am meeting my dissertation adviser early tomorrow." I must have sounded about as convincing as a Fuller Brush salesman on his last round.

"Gosh, what a shame, Renate. The club was too loud for much conversation. I thought we could chat a little more easily at a different location. Okay, well, I guess it is a little late. I look forward to my rain check."

On the way to Pension Schulz, my buttocks began to ache, and my arms grew weak and limp. I used to hear the girls in the CHS locker room describe similar sensations after dates. It was a relief to get out of the car.

11

That night in bed I tossed and turned like a fish struggling to break loose from a hook. I was afraid to look too closely at the events of the evening, but a strange excitement wouldn't let me rest. Finally, in spite of the cold, I turned on the lamp and propped myself up with the wedge.

October 8 – at home after a date with Robert
It's 3:44 A.M. – and I'm wide-awake in bed. I tried to make it through the night, but I can't get Christine out of my head. A char-ismatic figure, there's no doubt about it. She really nailed me with that smile of hers. But what is it about her that affected me so strongly – maybe a certain fascination with her voice?

After the show, Robert just had to mention Christine. I think he sensed what was churning inside my head. When he invited me to hear a nightclub singer, I had to fight off the impulse to turn him down. The last thing I wanted after Mahler's Fourth was some schmaltzy chanteuse. Boy, did I get that wrong. I didn't expect a siren – or, perhaps better, a modern Lorelei. (!)

Does my agitation have to do with some sort of déjà vu? Laura and I once saw an avant-garde play in Chicago that featured a sexy performance by an up-and-coming actress. And what did we do afterwards? Spent half an hour carrying on about how the men in the audience had responded to her torch act: they'd looked ready to fly through the roof like some sort of Sputnik. Probably a hundred males stampeded the stage door for autographs. We speculated whether she'd actually agree to a date with one of them. Blah!

Why were we reluctant to talk about our own reaction to her? Maybe we were just impressionable grad students. I'd put the whole incident out of my mind until now. In retrospect, did I secretly want to be one of those admirers who queued up? I bet Laura wanted to stand in line, too. Neither of us could admit it to the other.

I woke up; the diary slipped to my side. Nine forty-five. Rats! Not worth the scramble to get dressed. And this fussing over women cost me my breakfast?

I lay in bed, my brain on overdrive trying to understand these new sensations. Another excursion to the Black Panther on my own was in order, I concluded.

For now, though, I had to get cracking. In just a few weeks I'd need to send the first installment of my dissertation to Dr. Blume. And the time drew near for that first meeting with Dr. Bautsch.

Before I left Ryan, Howard had suggested it would be easier to communicate with Dr. Bautsch on official Ryan stationery than from West Berlin. The doctor replied promptly to Howard's letter and confirmed a meeting with me at the GSL in early October. Armed with that letter – which would facilitate my entrance through the guard station – I was scheduled to see Dr. Bautsch the following afternoon at his office.

Fortified with hard rolls and pastry from a small bakery on Knesebeckstrasse, I assembled my research materials to make an outline for the meeting, alternating between exhaustion from last night and anticipation about hearing Christine again.

The next morning, I downed a bite in my apartment (after oversleeping yesterday I'd been careful to stock the fridge), dressed in my best academic outfit – heels, a beige corduroy pantsuit, dark blouse – and, briefcase in hand, made my first train trip over to East Berlin at ten thirty. The route itself was as easy as pie from Savignyplatz. No need to transfer. Nevertheless, I was on edge.

As we entered the ghostly Anhalter Bahnhof – with only the middle façade still extant in an otherwise bombed out station – an announcement came over the loudspeaker: "Last stop before Friedrichstrasse. All West Berliners must exit." Nobody left the train. The S-Bahn angled past the famous Charité Hospital on the left; and at the sign "State Border of the German Democratic Republic," the train slowed and screeched as the cars pitched from side to side like boats on a lake.

Below, Vopos, no more than eighteen years old, made their rounds on a meticulously raked open surface. With submachine guns casually slung over their shoulders, like coats in warm weather, they chatted and laughed. To the right, guards in a watchtower observed us with binoculars. *Nerve-racking.*

A minute later, we pulled into the Friedrichstrasse station – dubbed Tränenpalast, or palace of tears, Schulz had told me – the last place friends and relatives from East and West had been able to say goodbye before the Wall was erected.

"Last stop, everyone must exit," a female voice announced over the loudspeaker. Above us rusty steel girders and windows streaked with dirt provided a drab stage for the walk downstairs to border control.

A Vopo in a dull green uniform shouted, "Papiere!" In spite of State Department instructions to keep passports in sight, I handed him mine, and tried to look indifferent despite my nervousness. He pushed it through a slot to a shadowy figure behind a milk glass window.

A few minutes later, a hand returned my passport through the slot to the Vopo, who asked me to expose my left ear. He determined my face and medium blond pageboy matched the photo in his hand, stamped my visa and said, "Pay at the window and leave through the door on your right."

Along with the five marks for the visa, I bought five East German marks at the official one-to-one exchange rate. In the West the exchange rate would have netted me four times that much, but I didn't want the added stress of hiding illegally obtained East German cash. Although, to judge by the outrageously cheap books and records the guests at the pension talked about over breakfast, I guessed the Vopos could turn a blind eye to a sale when it suited them.

A siren wailed twelve o'clock.

At the lower level, the HO, or *Handelsorgansation*, the state-owned food store, displayed cans of beans and baskets of potatoes and cabbages.

The area along Friedrichstrasse, though busy with pedestrians, felt different from the capitalist hustle and bustle of West Berlin. People walked to fill up space, it seemed. The German proverb "At night all cats are gray" applied any time here. Even the sky looked like dishwater.

Harsh sounds assaulted me through the somber atmosphere: the rumble of trains over creaky trestles mingled with the rattle of trucks bouncing on potholes. A nauseous stench billowed from scooters and two-cylinder Trabis, an East German car.

There was far more evidence of a military state than I'd seen from the tour bus. Soldiers were everywhere, along with border guards and the ever-present Vopos in grey-green uniforms. I couldn't shake my uneasiness, a subcutaneous tension that refused to abate.

In spite of the noxious surroundings, I pulled myself together and walked up Unter den Linden to the GSL, sequestered behind iron gates. I stopped at the guardhouse to show Dr. Bautsch's confirmation letter and my passport. After a quick clearance, I proceeded up some steps and entered a foyer, eerily quiet at this time of day. The photos on the wall showed a once stately GSL, now humbled by the effects of air raids. The great domed reading room – located in what had once been an enclosed atrium – was in ruins. They probably lacked hard currency for rebuilding, I imagined. Such are the ironies of Cold War politics.

I was early for my meeting, so I went to the collections area. Just wandering amidst all the marvelous manuscripts lifted my soul. Particularly impressive was a special room with handwritten works of J. S. Bach. On the last penned page in Bach's life the ink shot downward. As the story went, he'd slumped over with a stroke.

I looked, willy-nilly, at other manuscripts of interest – like Mozart's *The Magic Flute* – and some lovely poems by nineteenth-century women I hadn't even heard of. I wrote several of them into my notebook for transfer to my diary later.

At twelve fifteen, I ate lunch in the canteen. No one said a word when I entered. It was a depressing place, with no lights on and only two choices on the menu – prune soup or a bockwurst with bread. The staff reminded me of the two depressed figures in *The Absinthe Drinker* by Edgar Degas.

When it was nearly 1 P.M., I went down an immense hallway and knocked on a door marked simply "Prof. Dr. Bautsch." A stodgy man in a baggy suit – more appropriate to a workman dressed for a special occasion – greeted me at the door. Bautsch shook my hand and motioned to me to sit across from him at his desk – already piled high on my side with at least a half dozen books and several manuscripts. As I discovered, the professor was not one to waste time.

While Dr. Bautsch spoke briefly on the phone about a cracked ceiling, I thumbed through several volumes from the library's Romantic poetry collection. Wow, here I had hit the jackpot. Sources I could not have obtained anywhere else were lying there ready to be plumbed, including some rare handwritten manuscripts and publications that related directly to my dissertation topic. I couldn't check any of these books out, of course, but Dr. Bautsch told me I could store them in his office, for use in the reading room down the hall.

Today, however, much of my first session consisted of listening while the professor expounded. All the Third Reich scholarship on Romantic poetry, he contended, was ideological (what else was new?). However, he opined, no traces of Nazi Germany remained in the GDR outside the library's collection – a curious position in view of the countless military uniforms, goose-steps, flags, and other reminders of that dictatorship I had encountered on the way from the train. When I told him about my introduction and Heine, he paused, stroked his chin, and changed the subject.

For deciphering the older manuscripts, Dr. Bautsch urged me to get more proficient in the elaborate German script alphabet, which I had first encountered as a child on Christmas cards from Grandpa Theo and Gramma Ruthie. I remembered how Mama had helped me wade through them. Still, I was rusty.

The professor agreed to meet the next day to get me an official

Ausweis, or identification card to show at the front guard post, and to set up a tentative schedule for future meetings.

After the Vopos inspected my briefcase and wallet for East German money, I took the short ride back in an almost empty train to West Berlin.

October 9 – at my desk, after the GSL
I'm exhausted, even if the day went smoothly – dampened some by gloomy weather in an already depressing East Berlin. I can feel this cold snap in my bones. Ugh! Even a hint of winter makes me want to crawl under the covers and reemerge in April. I thought this trip would be a breeze, and here I sit, as depleted as if I were at the end of a semester! The stress of meeting Bautsch and presenting my ideas took me back to my orals. I wish I could wave a magic wand and the diss would be over. Imagine, a year of going to the theater and sleeping till nine! Sigh, no such luxury.

I used the evening and a couple of hours in the morning to practice the German script alphabet. Then I copied some handwritten script from a page Bautsch had reproduced. At least the tedium took my mind off Christine.

Dr. Bautsch seemed impressed with my seriousness when I returned the next day with the assignment done. He nodded as I wrote out for him all fifty-four-alphabet letters (upper and lower case) without a mistake. I tested my knowledge by reading from a doctoral candidate's handwritten treatise from 1940. His point? Heinrich Heine's poetry was without a doubt inferior, trivial and simplistic. I thought better of any extended exchange on these views with the Herr Doktor.

Nevertheless, our meetings promised to be productive. A generous man, Bautsch would offer me scholarly opinions and resources, as well as provide a sounding board to help me firm my own convictions about my focus.

We would meet, usually twice a week, until such time as I finished plumbing my library loans from the GSL, or when I had no further questions or topics to discuss. In short, our work together would be focused yet flexible, which I liked, and with no strings attached.

So, as long as I either steered clear of controversial political issues, or simply refrained from a counterattack, I could safely look forward to a cordial relationship as well the chance for an insider view of GDR scholarship. Maybe this was fodder for a scholarly book in the future?

12

October 11 – in bed
What a week – my first meeting with Robert, a visit to the Pan-
ther – and two sessions with Bautsch under my belt. A busy month
and I'm less than halfway through it. Tempus fugit.

I put down my pen and struggled to dismiss a sudden melancholy.
A problem dawned on me as I sank back in bed. What was I going to wear to the Black Panther on Monday? After some of Schulz's
wicked strong coffee, and his waffle to end all waffles, I returned to my
apartment and dragged out my entire "better" wardrobe, laid it across
the bed and inspected what I had worn the last few years at Ryan –
beige sweaters, red-and-white pullovers, some dark blouses, a leather
jacket and a dark green pantsuit. None of them would work, except in
a college town in small town Wisconsin. Here, everyone seemed to
wear black. I'd never been particularly interested in clothes, and hated
shopping for them. Nevertheless, I decided to splurge on a new outfit.

It was Laura, my trusted fashion consultant, who had usually
helped me pick out new stuff whenever I could feel motivated. Twice
a year, we drove to Chicago and made the rounds to Marshall Field's
and the Michigan Avenue stores. From the items Laura chose, we'd
repair to the dressing room and put together what I would wear for
dinner and the Philharmonic concert to follow, and stash the rest of
my purchases in the car.

Where to go for an outfit on my own in Berlin? Maybe I should check out the latest fashions at KaDeWe. Mama had always bought her things there. The guidebook on Berlin confirmed my choice: "As the leading department store in the country, KaDeWe sets new standards in service. The ladies' apparel selections will turn any visit into an extraordinary experience."

I figured it was worth a try, although I planned to skip the peanut butter.

*   *   *

The bus stopped directly in front of a magnificent block-long stone edifice still adorned with its original iron gate from 1907. To judge by the fashions on show in the windows, KaDeWe appeared to be gearing up for winter. Mannequins – a number oversized – were dressed in theater attire or for outdoor sporting events.

I walked through the revolving doors and entered the cosmetics department. There amidst the bright décor, smartly dressed women preened themselves before spotless mirrors and immaculate counters.

The directory offered seven floors of whatever one wanted – restaurants, cafés, a beauty salon, apparel, lounges, and a tailor – even a currency exchange. The collections in the women's apparel department were impressive and pricey. I removed my coat and inspected myself in front of a mirror: what a frumpy outfit! For ten minutes I wandered about, thinking this was silly and perhaps the wrong store.

I was about to flee to the escalator when a clerk sauntered by. I must have looked quite befuddled.

"My name is Suzanne Peters," she said in English. "I am a fashion specialist with the house. Please call me Suzanne."

Lest I forget, her name was affixed to her jacket lapel.

"Would you care for something in particular?" Suzanne asked with a winsome smile.

"I don't know, exactly . . ."

"Perhaps we should begin with a basic question. Would you like to see evening gowns, or apparel more for the daytime . . ." Suzanne looked me over from shoulder to knee, "or might it be for a special occasion?"

"Uh, yes, I'd say it should be appropriate for dinner and a movie, a lunch engagement with a friend – clothing I can combine with other pieces now and then."

"A layered look?"

I nodded in relief. "Yes, layered, that's it."

"Follow me!" Suzanne said. She led the way into an open area called "casual chic," with generous room and mirrors for perusal.

"Let's begin with a cardigan." Suzanne reached over to a pile of neatly stacked knits. "We could add, say, a sleeveless blouse" – she walked me to a section where mannequins modeled an assortment – "and a tailored skirt, or possibly a blazer." She took the cardigan over her arm, picked a grey wool skirt just below the knee, and laid them out on a table.

"Add textured stockings in herringbone and a scarf, and you'll look terrific for about any occasion. Would you like to try these items on? When you're dressed, feel free to view yourself outside in front of the full-length mirror."

The Dutch doors of my dressing room opened onto three wall mirrors. I removed my outerwear and looked at myself from all sides. *Straighten up those shoulders, Ren! Well, I'm not exactly Miss Twiggy.* I looked over my shoulder to see my backside. *Those legs are actually rather attractive. When we went swimming once, Laura remarked that I had a sweet butt. But my hair! The pageboy with bangs definitely must go.*

I tried on the skirt, blue silk blouse and light-grey blazer. *The combination really flatters me!* I turned around several times, envisioning myself at the club.

There was a tap on the door.

I opened the door.

"Let's have a look." Suzanne motioned me to the floor mirror. "I think the outfit suits you well, if you'll pardon the pun."

"Um, I wonder if you've perhaps got some slacks in . . . in addition to the skirt?"

"Certainly! The gentlemen customers are quite fond of our line of ladies' snug slacks. I'll bring you a pair in a jiffy."

Two women across the aisle were browsing together; one looked up briefly and eyed my attire. I made a hasty retreat back to the dressing room area and waited.

Suzanne came with slacks and a scarf and followed me into my dressing room. After some struggle, I managed to pull the zipper over a bulge from my steady diet of rolls.

"There! I think you look terrific," she said, adjusting the scarf around my neck. "Of course, you'll want different shoes than your sensible Oxfords. A pair of knee-high leather boots might be just the ticket."

"I already own black boots."

Luckily, Laura and I had bought them on sale at Tall Girls in Chicago.

I dressed and took my selections to the cash register.

Suzanne asked, "In addition to the blouse and skirt and blazer, shall we include the scarf, the slacks and the hose?"

"Certainly."

The register rang. "The total will be 525 marks and 87 pfennigs."

I reached into my purse. My heart sank. I had only 400 marks along.

Suzanne smiled. "We do take American Express, if you wish."

Sweat trickled down to my bra. I plunked my card onto the counter. Suzanne helped me to the elevator and handed me two large bags. On the main level, the concierge assisted me to the entrance and waved for a taxi.

Schulz was stepping outside as I fumbled with the entrance key.

"Good afternoon. Need help with your packages?"

"No, I'm okay."

I threw my purchases on the bed and collapsed next to them. What a relief it's over!

*   *   *

I was lucky to get a Saturday morning appointment at a small salon a few streets away, where I traded my pageboy for a bob! I can't count the number of times I checked it out in the mirror that weekend. A

89

whole new me! I'd have the weekend to get used to it, at least. The entire KaDeWe ordeal and the new haircut completely wiped me out.

On Sunday, I tried on a combo for the Black Panther and immediately dismissed the skirt. Didn't go with the bob. Slacks were it, with the blazer and short-sleeved blouse. I tried to arrange the scarf as Suzanne had, but it came out a tangled mess. I threw the scarf on the chair next to the bed to try again later.

In spite of my exhaustion, I spread out my notes from Bautsch on the bed and tried to come up with a plan for next week. I'd need a light and easy meeting after the Black Panther. How about just picking his brain for angles I hadn't thought of? I laid aside my notepad.

October 13 – on the couch at home

Okay, I've gotten a start with Bautsch, but I can't seem to sink my teeth into anything "German Romantic" right now. Could it be my topic no longer grabs me as it once did? Maybe I'm not PhD material. I watched how fellow students at U of C dived right into their dissertations and got the job done in a year. But most of them were married with a wifey-poo to shop, clean and cook. What do I want this doctorate for, anyway? So I can push students through their language requirement with a German verb or two?

I'll never forget the day when I instructed my intermediate students to pick a poem of their choice – not in the textbook – and comment on it. That smart aleck Rick Denver opened his flap and asked if he had to go to the library and READ something extra? I wanted to crumple up the sheet of paper with his selection on it and stuff it into his fat mouth. I was glad when he flunked out early – beating the rush.

Or have I just been thrown off track by a dark-haired diva in a dive? (Ooh, I've always loved alliterations!) Naja, Rome wasn't built in a day.

On Monday, I managed to collect some brief passages from a couple of Jewish poets in preparation for my third meeting with Bautsch, then fell asleep and woke with a jolt.

Four o'clock! I cleared off the bed, laid out the items I intended to wear, and showered.

I hadn't eaten since breakfast. Supper at the Café am Steinplatz would be perfect. I dressed in my Oxfords, shaggy sweater and leather jacket – didn't want to risk a stain on my new clothes. An hour before my taxi was scheduled to pick me up, I walked returned to apply my makeup and get dressed.

The cabbie dropped me off at the club with time to spare. Prominently displayed at the entrance was a slanted poster of Christine in a sequined gown and top hat, sitting cross-legged on a barstool. "All New Show," the flyer billed it.

Inside, a pianist entertained the almost full house with soft jazz. I walked down the stairs, nerves on edge. *Ren, you don't need to talk to anyone, just nurse a drink and take in Christine's performance.* I spied an empty seat at the far corner table off the stage, where two women, one with rolled-up sleeves and slicked-back James Dean hairdo, the other in full leather regalia and jewelry, were already seated.

"*Guten Abend.* Is this seat taken?"

"*'N Abend.* It's for you." The James Dean woman pulled back a chair and seated me. I put my handbag by the side of the table – and even though the place was warm, I left my blazer on over my blouse.

"I'm Greta, and this Ulli."

"Uh, I'm Renate – pleased to meet you. I hear our performer tonight is really great."

Greta took a cigarette from a pack in her sleeve and held it against the palm of her hand. "Care for a ciggie?"

"No, thanks."

Greta lit the cigarette and extinguished the match with a flick of her wrist.

I saw Christine enter in a black sequined décolleté dress with long gloves, her hair swept up in a forties style like Bette Davis. Good, the show was about to begin.

The new act featured a mixture of American songs from the thirties and forties, sprinkled with old German favorites by Kurt Weill. Christine made the most of the songs by Rodgers and Hart, tapping into their melancholic melodies and accessible lyrics. When she sang "My Funny Valentine," I nearly fell through the floor – her English pronunciation reminded me of the German chanteuse on the gramophone records my stepfather Luke had played when he and Mama danced. And the song? I hadn't ever been someone's sweetheart. What would that be like?

As she slowly crossed the stage toward our table, I saw Christine's eyes alight on me for a brief moment – but soon she moved to the far side where mostly men were seated.

As she'd done the previous week, she concluded with a song in French, this time "La Vie en Rose," dedicating it "to a special person in the audience who will remain anonymous." Ulli and Greta glanced at me. The audience clapped in rhythmic unison and pounded their feet until Christine reemerged with a guitar and sang several encores. The audience wanted more, but she tapped on her wrist.

*   *   *

Greta and Ulli had just stood up to go to the bar when Christine came down the steps and sidled up to us.

"*'N Abend*, Ulli, *'n Abend*, Greta, how's it going?"

They shrugged. Greta flicked the ashes from her Gauloise into the darkened Cinzano ashtray. She and Ulli left with a hasty good-bye.

"Hello, Fräulein Seiler," Christine shook my hand with a gentle squeeze.

She remembered me!

Christine pulled up a chair. "May I join you?" Without further ado, she called over to Rosie for a glass of wine and "one for the lady."

"So, Fräulein . . ." *Darn, I don't know her last name!*

"Just call me Christine." She raised her glass. "And you?"

"Renate."

We toasted.

"So what brings you back to the Panther, Renate?"

"I wanted to take in your next show."

"And?"

"Your selection of American songs reminded me of–"

"Anyone in particular? Your first time here last week was with a gentleman friend, as I recall. And tonight you weren't alone, either."

What did she mean?

"I shared the table with them."

"Sorry, that was nosy of me."

"Tell me, Christine, how you got your engagement here."

Christine smiled. "Connections – the way things work in the entertainment biz." She took off her black jacket and adjusted her scarf.

"My uncle Edgar is a schoolmate of the owner, Bernd Schwarz. Edgar arranged for an audition, and Bernd heard me the very next week. I've had this gig for six months, filling in now and then before I snagged this regular slot on Mondays. Herr Schwarz says he'll give me a solo evening when one of their regulars moves on – don't know if I believe it."

"It sounds like a step forward in your career. I'd love to attend!"

"I'd hoped we might see each other sooner. Can I make up for my probing question and invite you for coffee sometime?"

I tried to hide my trembling hands as I pulled a pen out of my purse and scribbled my address and phone number.

"Pension Schulz – over by Steinplatz, right?"

"Yes, on Bleibtreustrasse."

"I'm going to visit a friend for at least a week and also my brother in Saarbrücken, but I'll give you a call when I return."

"If I'm not in, tell Herr Schulz you're a cousin of mine."

October 15 – late at night after my second visit to the Panther

Wow! I'm jazzed, as Laura would say. Christine noticed me during her first song! Plus, I think she liked my outfit! It's great to have instant gratification from my frazzled spree at KaDeWe – not like the tense wait I can expect while Dr. Blume evaluates my chapters.

But the flip side of the coin is, the way Christine looked at me made me both uncomfortable and – what else to call it – aroused. The whole taxi ride back I obsessed about what I had done – and at the same time wondered whether she would call. Was going back to the Panther maybe an impulsive mistake?

13

The next few days were probably too soon to hope for any message from Christine, and I tried not to be disappointed she hadn't called. As long as I didn't hear from her or from Westerheim, there was no excuse for shirking. U of C doctoral candidates in the department had told me just how quickly the time could slip away. So I gathered up my pens and pencils and my notes from Bautsch and, miracle of miracles, addressed the first section of my dissertation. Over the course of several more visits to Dr. Bautsch, I completed two chapters, which I planned to get to Dr. Blume with a third by Thanksgiving at the latest. A relief I hadn't lost my touch. *And now down to the mail – it'll only take a sec, right?*

I found a letter from Laura, which took me by surprise when I tore it open and a $20 bill flew out.

Hi, Renita,

Thought I'd surprise you with a twenty spot. Allow yourself a special treat – like a fancy meal out! I understand from Howard the Hilton has a great penthouse restaurant.

Nothing much to report stateside, except – you remember Ryan was caught off guard when Homer Atkins in Geology quit – he never did like it at Ryan. They scrambled around and found Phil Bates, an ABD just out of Penn State. He's the proverbial tall, dark and handsome, in his late twenties, cute and unattached. Too bad you didn't decide to stay on!

Turns out, Phil loves to hike (you don't much care for hiking, I know). We drove over to the Wisconsin Dells one Saturday and explored the sandstone outcroppings along the Wisconsin River. Gorgeous!

Frieda seems happy to be in front of a class. It's the first time I've seen her laugh to any degree. She asked about you. I told her you were hard at work at the diss, and about your neat apartment near downtown Berlin.

Come to think of it, other than the German State Library and an occasional theater or shopping spree, I don't really know what you're up to. Is life still basically all work and no play? Robert did write to say you and he had gone to the Café Kranzler on some snazzy street – the Ku-Damm, or however it's spelled. That's what I really miss from my junior year in Europe: the cafés!

As usual, I'm swamped with work and faculty committees. And get this: a new one is supposed to oversee plans for a new foreign language building, with an atrium in the middle (a nod to our Latin colleague Janet Alexander).

Time to close. I'm meeting a couple of friends at the Circle Bar. Not great food we know, but a relief from my own Michelin three-star cuisine. (Ha!) By the way, could you pick me up Bach's French Suites the next time you pass by your music store? No rush – figure I'd practice them for sure with my own copy.

Love,
Laura

Even though Laura's request wasn't urgent, a trip downtown for sheet music sounded like the perfect way to keep my mind off Christine for another day. Plus, I'd been looking forward to visiting an information center for American culture, called Amerika Haus.

The next morning at breakfast, Schulz brought my favorite, a large waffle with a slab of butter and creamer of maple syrup. When he came around to clear the dishes, I asked him, "Can you recommend a downtown restaurant for locals? No tourist traps, please."

"Hmm. There is a Berlin institution – name's Aschinger – near the Bahnhof Zoo."

"I'll give it a try."

Schulz gave me directions.

*   *   *

It was unusually mild for late October. Before setting out for the downtown, I went out to buy some groceries for the next few days. On this Monday, Germans – scrambling from one and a half days of supermarkets being closed – were doing the same, while clerks ran around stocking shelves emptied on Saturday. Funny system.

I sure miss grocery shopping after 6:30 P.M. At Ryan I did have a few trump cards.

Ladies in premature winter coats and their ubiquitous boxy hats sat on park benches at Savignyplatz with their shopping bags beside them. Students hurried by, jackets on their shoulders – a brief respite before the long months of study in cold, drafty rooms.

After filling my fridge, I went back out and passed by the Technical University and the College of Art, where the German Expressionist painter Schmidt-Rottluff had been director. Only a few steps beyond, at the corner of Fasanenstrasse, was the modest concert hall of the Berlin Philharmonic. The paper had just advertised all of Beethoven's symphonies conducted by Herbert von Karajan, and symphonies by Gustav Mahler were also scheduled – great programs to look to forward to! Adjacent to the concert hall was the Hochschule für Musik, or College of Music, which completed the cluster of institutions. What a thrill with so much culture and intellectual stimulation nearby!

Across the street was Amerika Haus, a bright, sleek, rectangular structure. To the right, I entered a library well stocked with American newspapers, magazines, records and books, and picked up the current *Time* magazine from a rack. President Kennedy was planning a trip to Texas in November. Would the president's presence there match his popular appearance in Berlin this past June?

On the way out, I stopped to look at the lobby exhibit on several major German emigrations to the US in the nineteenth century. I resonated with the fear, hope and pain expressed in the letters and occasional photos documenting their imminent journeys and recalled clutching Mama's hand on the ship as we watched our homeland slowly but inevitably fade from view.

I left and walked down Hardenbergstrasse, passing underneath the train trestle, and turned to my right. Midway down the block, I located Aschinger – easy to spot with its art nouveau façade and large picture window – and peered in. A crowd of students and pensioners stood around tall round tables over soup terrines and rolls. Self-service seemed to be the deal. You picked up your soup (with or without a sausage) from atop the glass counter, grabbed free *Schrippen* (Berliner for hard rolls) from a huge basket, and proceeded to the stand-up tables at the window.

Okay, not exactly the Hilton, but there must be a place to sit some-where. Or is this just a poor man's joint? Let's give it a try.

I entered through the revolving doors and was immediately greeted with the pungent smell of the pea soup. Was there anything else to eat?

Sensing my hesitancy, perhaps, a waiter motioned me to an empty table toward the rear in a separate, more "elegant" sit-down section. Most of the patrons looked to be blue-collar workers. I felt slightly out of place, but it beat a meal up front – and besides, I could bury myself in my diary. I ordered a beer and one of the house specialties.

Two men – one sandy-haired and stocky, and the other older, slightly shorter, with coarse, gray hair – approached the table.

"Are these seats taken?" the younger man asked.

"Please, sit down." Separate tables were not in the cards today.

The older man's hand had rough nails. A gold band fitted tightly on his ring finger. Both men sipped on beers and the sandy-haired fellow lit a cigarette. The silence felt awkward.

Thank goodness, the waiter appeared with my order of *Eisbein* – a hock of pork with generous mounds of sauerkraut and mashed potatoes.

"Bitte schön." With a turn of his wrist, he adjusted the "A" logo on my plate to face me. *"Guten Appetit,"* he said, and my new neighbors echoed the sentiment.

The two men discussed the work world and soccer, and reminisced about East Berlin. Try as I might, I couldn't help but overhear their story.

"Ja, Fred, it would be nice to visit Müggelsee again," the younger man said, smoothing out the beer-soaked runner at the base of his glass.

"You know, Heinz, I haven't been back to the lake since Martha and I picnicked there before the war." Fred quaffed down the rest of his Pils.

"Well, pal," Heinz poked him on the shoulder, "you could've stayed in East Berlin and celebrated the October 7 Revolution with red herring! Now you'll have to settle for Reformation Day – and church. It's coming up soon, by the way, on the thirty-first," he said, chuckling at his own joke.

Fred didn't look amused. "Karl needs a new prescription for his ticker. Those bastards in the GDR haven't got any decent drugs. It's easy enough to get meds on this side, of course, but what good is that if we're not allowed to take them over?"

As if the East isn't bad enough, you can't obtain proper medicine, either?

"Perhaps I can help. I'm a foreigner, and plan to visit East Berlin soon. Could I deliver the medicine to your friend?"

My tongue stuck to the roof of my mouth. *Miss Goody Two Shoes, what are you thinking?*

Fred's eyebrow arched.

"It's kind of you to offer, Fräulein – uh – Frau . . ."

"Fräulein Seiler."

"Pleased to meet you." Heinz extended his hand. "Baumert is my name. May I introduce my friend, Alfred Tenne?"

"Nice to make your acquaintance."

"Do you mind if I ask where you're from?" Heinz said.

"Originally from Berlin. My mother and I emigrated to the United States after the war, but we spoke German at home. I'm an American citizen now."

"*Ach so.* That explains your excellent command of the German language. Are you sure you wouldn't mind dropping off the medication?" Alfred asked.

"Not a problem, I should think. You mentioned Müggelsee. I'd like to visit that lake."

"You know about it?" Heinz said eagerly.

"I've read about it in the novels of Theodor Fontane."

"Without question our most beautiful body of water. And Karl lives nearby, in Friedrichshagen."

Alfred put his hand on Heinz's arm. "When exactly do you expect to visit East Berlin, Fräulein Seiler?"

"I haven't any firm plans. I want to see Felsenstein's production of Janáček's opera *The Cunning Little Vixen*. And I've been reading about the plays at Das Theater am Schiffbauerdamm. Brecht's wife, Helene Weigel, is still–"

"Brecht!" Heinz snorted. "He was a communist. You couldn't pay me to see one of his plays. As for opera, I can't stand all that screeching."

"Hmmm." Alfred cleared his throat, eyed the newly arrived patrons at the adjacent table and turned to me. "We'd like to get the medicine to Karl as soon as possible. Could you possibly arrange to go within the next few days?"

" I don't know, I guess so."

"Let me show you Friedrichshagen and the lake." Heinz pulled out a folded map and pointed to a suburb with an oyster-shaped body of water located in the southeast of Berlin.

Alfred motioned to the waiter.

"Separate checks?" The waiter frowned as he picked up my plate with its half-eaten hock.

"Add the lady's bill to ours." Alfred handed the waiter ten marks.

"That's not necessary."

"Consider the meal a welcome back to our mutual hometown."

"In that case, thank you."

We made our way past the pea soup section; Heinz pushed the door open for me as we exited onto the street. The sun had given way to clouds and a cold wind. I put on the beige wool cap Laura had bought me for the Wisconsin winters.

Alfred wrapped a scarf around his neck. "May we walk you to your hotel?"

A gentle soul, Alfred reminded me of my father. They'd have been about the same age. "Thanks, but Pension Schulz isn't far away, and I'm in the mood for a stroll."

"East Germans are touchy about their lack of medical supplies, so please don't mention our discussion to anyone. You never know who might be from the other side in this town," Alfred said. "We'll be in touch."

I watched the two men walk toward the zoo train station and disappear amidst pedestrians on their way to commuter trains. On the right, the Memorial Church stood bathed in blue light.

I guess when Berliners get dark days, at least they can enjoy the beautiful stained glass windows at night.

On my way I stopped at Bote und Bock, the largest sheet music store in Berlin, across from the university. The patrons, mostly students, browsed in sheet music bins. I looked for the Breitkopf und Härtel edition of the Bach piano suites Laura wanted. I was in luck: suites for the sweet, I chuckled to myself.

Happy with my purchase, I continued my walk – too early to call it a day just yet. At Steinplatz Square, I entered a café and found a table away from the smoke. Over beer or coffee, students read, chatted or worked on assignments, briefcases and books scattered around their seats.

Adjacent to the café was an art film house, which featured movies in their original languages. A theater and café all in one spot was a sensible arrangement. The discovery took me back to the Von Lee Theater in Bloomington, right across the street from the university library. The promise of relief from the daily study grind, and a love of

European film, lured me – and often roomie Carol – to the Lee. In my senior year, those nights included a beer at the popular Nick's English Hut down the hill.

Outside, the sycamore leaves scattered across the sidewalk reminded me of Southern Indiana, too. A pang of homesickness gripped me. I flashed on Dr. Fuerstenberg's poetry class and the first time I'd read Rilke's "Herbsttag" (Autumn Day), so exquisite in its interior vowel palette and rhyme. The poet's prayer for a respite from the bleak winter to come resonated with me as we braced for the season ahead.

> *Leg' Deinen Schatten auf die Sonnenuhren,*
> *Und auf den Fluren, lasst die Winde los,*
> *Gib' Ihnen noch zwei südlichere Tage*
> *Und jage die letzte Süsse in den schweren Wein.*

> Lay your shadow on the sundials,
> And on the meadows, unleash the winds,
> Give them a few more southerly days,
> And chase the last bit of sweetness into the heavy wine.

I drank my second Pils and perused the film program. Did I want to stay on for a French love story? I wasn't in the mood – at least not alone.

Darkness had set in and I decided to head back to the pension. When I arrived at my room, I found a note under my door: "Sorry I missed you. I'll phone first thing tomorrow. Alfred Tenne."

14

The radiator clanked faintly as I squinted at the alarm clock and groaned – 6:30 A.M. I threw my legs over the bed. Brr! My bare feet landed on a cold linoleum floor.

I made it to breakfast by seven fifteen. Luckily, the only guests were an English couple in sturdy hiking shoes.

Schulz looked surprised at my early appearance; he disappeared and returned with a basket of *Schrippen*, butter, marmalade and a bone china pot of coffee with matching creamer. As always, his brew tasted divine. It only took a minute before my head began to clear. I cracked open the roll and spread a little butter over it, skipping the marmalade.

Schulz poked his head around the corner. "Telephone for you, Fraülein Seiler – a Herr Tenne."

"Morgen," a clerk mumbled in the office, and handed me the phone.

"Guten Morgen, Fraülein Seiler. Alfred Tenne here. I'm calling to find out if you could deliver the medicine to Karl today."

Groan, not another obligation.

"Be assured it's urgent. I can't say more at this time." His voice sounded tense.

"I thought it would take a few days to get this organized."

"There's been a change of plans."

"I see."

"My nephew Walter has offered to pick you up at the Wedding S-Bahn Station around nine thirty. You'll need just twenty-five minutes for the S-Bahn from Savignyplatz."

"Very well." I closed, and hung up.

When I returned to the breakfast room, Schulz – always attentive - brought my egg perched on an eggcup and left to clear the English guests' table. Grateful for a brief lull, I gathered my thoughts for this day's unexpected docket.

*   *   *

"What's there to see in Wedding?" I asked Schulz in the hall on my way to the S-Bahn.

"It's not exactly a tourist attraction. But there's one place foreigners often visit – the Plötzensee Memorial."

"A memorial to whom?"

"It honors the officers executed after the 1944 plot against Hitler."

When Schulz offered a few gruesome details I cut him off in midstream, mentally striking the memorial off my list of things to see.

When I stepped off the train in Wedding, a young man with a map strode up to me.

"Hello, Fräulein Seiler. I'm Walter, Herr Tenne's nephew. Welcome to our wonderful district. My ersatz Mercedes is around the corner."

I climbed into an ancient VW with a tiny rear window and upholstery smelling of stale smoke.

On our way to Alfred's apartment, Walter filled me in on the area. "Wedding is notorious for tough teenagers, alcoholic men and low-income high rises – locals call them *Baracken*. It makes for an easy transition into East Berlin."

"Because we're so close by?"

"Because East Berlin looks so similar." Walter turned into a triangular complex and parked. "We're in luck. At the end of the weekday you can't find a spot to park your car anywhere near here."

We walked though the courtyard – a bare space dotted with scrawny trees – and a deserted playground – to three gray concrete apartment houses and entered the middle one, where someone had smeared in red paint *"Amis Raus!"* ("Yanks go home!") The stairwell walls, covered with greasy scuff marks, cracked paint and exposed plaster, emitted a smell of cheap antiseptic cleanser.

A hefty, ruddy-cheeked woman in a print smock greeted us at Alfred Tenne's apartment door.

"Welcome, Fräulein Seiler. My name is Lichtenmeier. I'm Herr Tenne's assistant." She straightened her shoulders and beckoned me to follow her into the living room. "Please take a seat. Herr Tenne will be with you in a moment. I'll bring the coffee." She turned to Walther. "Hurry up, now, you'll be late for your class."

"Ja, ja." Walter picked up a briefcase, then, shouting *"Tschüss!"* – "Bye!" – raced out the door and down the stairwell.

I sat down on the couch and placed my handbag on the floor. In front of me was a tea table stacked with napkins, and a notepad and pen. I heard the muffled tones of a man – probably Tenne – talking in an adjacent room. I looked around. Sunlight streamed through the curtain of a large picture window and fell onto a faded beige rug and an overstuffed armchair wedged in the corner. Prominently displayed on the mantle piece stood a framed bronze medal and a photo of a young man in a full-length army coat, rifle in hand.

"Willkommen, Fräulein Seiler," Alfred said, emerging from an adjacent room. He smoothed back the errant strands of his thinning hair and shook my hand. "Sorry I wasn't able to greet you."

Frau Lichtenmeier emerged with a platter of open-faced sandwiches made with butter and lunchmeat, which she laid on the tea table. She wrapped one of them in a sandwich bag and placed it to my side.

A snack for the way home, perhaps?

"This time," she said, putting her hand on her hip, "I bought peppered salami. It's not every day we get a visitor from America who speaks German." She smiled at Alfred. "Be sure you eat all of yours. You can't afford this too often on your pension."

104

Alfred sat down next to me. "Please help yourself to a *Stulle*."

I dutifully took a bite from my sandwich, and placed it on a napkin.

"Who'd have predicted I'd end up in one of these beehives? Manor Court, they dubbed it." Alfred gestured with a sweep of his hands. "What a joke! And *Drüben*" – "over there" – he pointed to the radio tower visible in the distance – "it's even worse."

"*Drüben, schmüben*, I must be on my way." Frau Lichtenmeier, said, putting on her coat. She left with a resounding *"Auf Wiedersehen!"*

Alfred ate the rest of his *Stulle* and settled back on the couch. "Fräulein Seiler, up to now we've used a West German contact in Berlin to take Karl his medication. Unfortunately, the man has just moved back to Hamburg. We're grateful you've agreed to step in especially at such short notice."

"I'm glad to be of help, Herr Tenne."

"You know, Karl and me go back a long time. We grew up in the suburbs, in Köpenick, went to school together and were both drafted in 1940. They sent me to the eastern front, and Karl to France. The Russians captured me after the battle of Stalingrad in 1941. Many of my comrades didn't survive the first year of imprisonment, wasting away before my very eyes. In 1948, they shoved me into a cattle car to Berlin with just the clothes on my back. At home, I searched everywhere for my wife and son and found out they both had died in air raid attacks. Our property was a heap of rubble. I couldn't find Karl, either."

"All that terrible loss you've had," I said.

Alfred nodded, but then his face brightened. "A month or so later I spotted Karl at the Pankow S-Bahn station and shouted, 'Hey buddy, I knew you'd show up!' I'll never forget that day. When the fighting ended, the French shipped him back to Berlin. He was lucky to land a job with the transportation department and married his high school sweetheart."

"Did Karl's marriage affect his relationship with you?"

"*Ach*, we remained close pals. But politics intervened in 1953, when I became involved in a workers' revolt against the East German regime. At the height of the Cold War, I decided I'd been tailed enough. By that time Karl had children and chose to stay in the East with his family. I took the S-Bahn to West Berlin – shivering in my boots – but I made it.

"Shortly thereafter I met Heinz at a Social Democratic Party meeting, and was relieved to find like-minded socialists who believed in the democratic process unlike the devilishly sham ideology of the *German Democratic Republic*."

The front door clicked open. Heinz came into the living room carrying a leather briefcase.

Alfred got up from the sofa. "Well, speak of the devil and he shall appear," Alfred laughed, and shook his friend's hand. "Did you get the maps photocopied?"

"You know Frau Krause is nosy, so I went over to the Tegel Airport – luckily the machine worked." He put his briefcase next to the tea table.

Alfred turned to me. "Fräulein Seiler, before we continue, would you excuse us for a moment? Please help yourself to another *Stulle*."

"Thank you."

The two men went down the hall and closed the door. After a few minutes, Alfred returned with a pack of cigarettes.

Heinz followed, pulled a chair over and sat across from me. He reached into his briefcase, pulled out the photocopies and placed them in front of me. "Fräulein Seiler, I'd like to review the route to East Berlin. Feel free to write directions down."

I picked up the pen and notepad.

"To get to Friedrichstrasse," Heinz said, "you'll have to take the U-Bahn from Reinickendorf to the Zoo, and then transfer to the Friedrichstrasse S-Bahn line. As you can see, it's not the most direct route, but the only way you can get there from these parts."

An unavoidable detour, thanks to our sweet neighbors from the East.

"Have you already visited East Berlin by train yet?" Heinz asked.

"Yes, but only on from Savignyplatz to Friedrichstrasse."

"So you're familiar with the passport and documents control."

"Yes."

"Good. When you get down to the street level, cross Friedrichstrasse to the Czechoslovakian Bookstore two hundred meters down the street to the right. Before the Wall went up, we used to buy our favorite music records there. Enter the store just before twelve thirty. You'll see a man with a briefcase embossed with the initials MJ. He's got your estimated time of arrival. When you walk into the store, he'll be browsing the classical records. Find the S section and search for Josef Suk's Serenade in E-flat Major, Op. 6; then go to the counter and ask whether they have Suk's piece in stock. That will signal to MJ that you are Renate Seiler."

"Do I have to buy the record?"

"It's sold out everywhere. MJ will leave the store at this point. Follow him, go about five to seven minutes to the bridge over the Spree River, and pause where the guardrail begins. MJ will stop and stand at the middle, and as you walk onto the bridge he'll light a Gauloise cigarette from a blue pack, like this one."

Nothing transpires without tobacco, I guess.

"While he smokes, take out the *Stulle* – the one Frau Lichtenmeier wrapped. Eat just two bites. MJ will turn around and pass you on his return to the Friedrichstrasse S-Bahn."

"This seems awfully complica–"

"We'll review the route when I've finished. Follow MJ back to the station." Heinz handed me two aluminum twenty-pfennig coins. "Buy a return ticket with these for the Erkner line, and detrain at Friedrichshagen. The trip lasts fourteen stops, or about half an hour. A sign above the door of each car shows its route. When you reach your final stop, descend the stairs onto the street."

Heinz turned to the photocopy of the map of Friedrichshagen. "MJ will walk down Bölschestrasse, the main drag. He'll turn left at the church, go down a short street, and turn right at the dead end into Möllenseestrasse, to number 17. It's a brick apartment house with a yellow sun protector on the upstairs balcony, and a boarded-up window at street level. Easy to spot."

"Left at the church and right onto Möllenseestrasse. Give me time to get this all down."

Heinz lit a cigarette before continuing. "When you see MJ go into the house, stay on your side of the street, turn right at the corner and go around the block. Lake Müggelsee will be to your right. After eight to ten minutes, circle back, cross the street and press the bell under Meier."

"So Karl's last name is Meier."

"No. Just call him Karl."

I was about to tuck my notes away into my handbag, when Alfred shook his head: "You've got to memorize the instructions."

"Memorize?" My face felt hot.

"Fräulein Seiler, you cannot carry any suspicious material. Please take a moment to look over our directions. You'll do just fine."

If I had learned complicated medieval German verb forms for a doctoral written exam, I supposed these details wouldn't cause a problem. Notes in hand, I outlined the scenario to Heinz, and then repeated it without my crib sheet.

"Wait until MJ goes on from the guardrail before you follow him. He may pause if there are police around."

"What if he doesn't appear?"

Alfred put his hand on my shoulder. "He'll be there, don't worry. Now," he reached into his pocket, "we've giving you some East German coins for the U-Bahn, a map of East Berlin – and the medicine." He filled an empty cigarette pack with tablets from a medicine bottle. "And then, of course, there is your *Stulle*."

Alfred went out to the balcony and returned with a handbag, a pair of shoes and a coat. "Last but not least, we have some items, which will make you look a little less Western or capitalist." The large handbag was made of some sort of reddish–brown synthetic material with two sturdy straps. The color of the low- healed shoes roughly matched the handbag. The doughty coat added a final touch, with huge buttons – on large cuffs.

To my surprise, both the shoes and the coat fit.

I certainly won't make a fashion statement, though.

I retrieved my purse and unzipped the GDR handbag, placing Heinz's things, the documents, and my coin purse, lipstick and opera ticket to an interior without compartments.

"Some East German eau de cologne will make the final touch." Alfred daubed a few drops behind my ears and handed me a small bottle for touching up later. "Good. Now you look and smell East German enough."

I added the bottle to my stash. *All that's missing now is the kitchen sink.*

"All right," Alfred said, "we need to get going. I'll accompany you to the train station and Heinz will walk ahead to buy your ticket."

"What about my things?"

"When you return, you'll find them under you name at Reinigung Clemens, a cleaners on Knesebeckstrasse around the corner from Pension Schulz."

As the Germans say, *Kleider machen Leute* – clothes make you what you are.

15

Ahead of us, near the station, I saw Heinz stop and go into a shop. Stuffing a pack of cigarettes into his breast pocket, he exited and disappeared around the corner.

"I thought Heinz was going t–"

"Fräulein Seiler, I've got an idea. You'll feel more secure with MJ if you practice tailing Heinz. Stay within eyesight of him. I'll drop behind and watch."

No time to protest. At the corner, I saw Heinz thirty yards ahead standing in front of a jewelry store. I feigned interest in a funeral parlor with two bronze urns on a velvet cloth: "From Ashes to Ashes. Tastefully Done at Oldendorf and Sons."

But Heinz didn't move on. I started to walk past him; then he made an about-face. I looked around at Alfred, who came up to assist.

"Keep far enough back to react." We paused in front of a department store sales window. "What other options did you have?"

"Maybe read a bus schedule, look at my watch, or . . ." I shrugged my shoulders.

"Asked someone for directions on the street or searched in your handbag," he said. "No mater. We've got half an hour to spare. Continue a bit longer."

On our left, Heinz darted past us to the intersection and crossed to the opposite side. When I reached the corner, the light had already changed. I walked parallel to him and waited for a break in the traffic.

Dammit! It seemed like all the trucks in Berlin had converged on Aroser Allee today. Heinz joined passengers waiting for the bus. By the time I made it across the street, the bus had pulled out.

At a taxi stand, I yanked open the door and scrambled in.

"Quick! Follow that bus."

"Shall I radio the cops?"

"No. I've had a spat with my boyfriend."

He grinned and stepped on it. At each bus stop the cabbie maneuvered behind the double-decker. "There's my guy!" I pressed five marks into the driver's palm. "Keep the change!"

The cabbie pulled over and kept the taxi idling.

I ran up to Heinz, winked to him and rolled my eyes in the direction of the cabbie. "*Schatz*, let's talk!" We feigned a brief argument that ended with a conciliatory hug.

The cabbie gave me a thumbs-up and roared off.

"Did you enjoy the small detour?" Alfred asked, after stepping out of a taxi behind us.

"In the future, I'd prefer more direct routes to my destination."

"Good work. See you shortly." Alfred said. He returned to his cab, got in, and the taxi drove off.

"All right," Heinz said, "to get you to East Berlin from this point, we'll be using the U-Bahn railway owned by the West. Let's practice *being* followed. Your objective is not to shake me, but not to let me get too close, either. You go on ahead."

I walked down the street in the direction Alfred's taxi had taken, using store windows to track Heinz, who now was three shops behind me. In one window, I watched a decorator on a ladder arrange a display of winter shoes. Reflected in the window, Heinz appeared to have a lady's boot perched on his head.

At a roundabout, the light turned yellow. I crossed to an island, feigned a stone in my shoe and waited until the light changed. For several blocks I wound my way through heavy pedestrian traffic to the underground entrance and saw Alfred waiting at the ticket counter.

Heinz came up behind me moments later. "Excellent work, Fräulein Seiler."

"No one would ever believe me if I told them about this."

Heinz pursed his lips. "I'd rather you did not mention it."

Alfred handed me my ticket. "It gave me pleasure to say 'Friedrichstrasse, please' – even if I can't ride there myself. This ticket will enable you to transfer to the S-Bahn at the Zoo without buying a separate ticket."

We ascended the stairs to the platform. A large rectangular sign hanging from the rafters warned: "Attention! This is the last stop before East Berlin. All West Berliners and citizens of the BRD without visas for East Berlin must exit here."

"Good luck," Heinz said, as my Zoo-bound train rounded the bend. "We'll check in with you tonight to see how your day went."

*   *   *

At the Zoo station, the S-Bahn held only a handful of passengers, including a small group speaking a Germanic language with pronounced guttural sounds. I guessed they were from the Netherlands. At Friedrichstrasse, I exited the train ahead of them and hurried downstairs to deal with grim-faced border guards and irritating formalities. Everything went without a hitch. I checked my watch: 12:18.

On my way to the Czechoslovakian Bookstore, I stopped at a nearby kiosk to peruse the theater and opera fare for the winter season, and jotted down performance dates for *Mother Courage*. A travel agency window advertised group trips: "Sun for your November" was the theme. The only place offered was Soviet Georgia.

Twelve twenty-seven. I paused at a window display featuring four Czech composers – Smetana, Dvořák, Janáček and Suk – and entered the store. A young girl with a small violin case stood at the register with a piece of sheet music, along with a distinguished-looking white-haired man – probably a Westerner – holding several books.

Half a dozen customers were browsing in the record section. A balding man in his mid forties, dressed in a rumpled grey suit, placed a leather briefcase next to him with the initials MI visible, and paused to inspect an album. I looked again. Were the initials actually MJ with the J worn away?

I rummaged through some classic LPs and found a live recording of Smetana's *Ma Vlast* with Vaclav Talich from 1939 – a bargain at fifty-five cents! Further down the aisle, I glanced briefly at the Stravinsky records before moving to Suk. No Serenade in E-flat. The man with the briefcase looked up as I went to the cashier.

"I can't find the Josef Suk E-flat Serenade. Is it in stock?"

"No. It's sold out."

I thanked the clerk and exited, following the man with the briefcase for about seven minutes to the Spree River across from the Theater am Schiffbauerdamm. Pedestrians hurried by in both directions.

Stopping at the middle of the bridge, he gazed over the river. As I approached, he pulled a Gauloise from a blue pack, lit it with a match and took a puff.

Trembling with relief, I reached into my handbag for the *Stulle* and ate a couple of bites. MJ paused to check something in his briefcase and continued to smoke.

My practice earlier in the day with Heinz had helped. I checked my map until MJ flicked his cigarette butt into the Spree, turned, and passed by me at a fast pace.

I turned and dashed to keep up, fishing out the two aluminum coins Heinz had given me. As I bought my round trip ticket to Friedrichshagen and back, MJ was on his way up the stairs. I heard a train arriving and raced up the escalator to spot MJ at a newspaper kiosk smoking a cigarette.

Two trains came and went. When the Erkner line train to Friedrichshagen rounded the bend, MJ moved forward toward the tracks and entered in the middle of the train. I took a seat in the car behind him near the glass partition doors separating us. MJ faced away from me, nose buried in a newspaper.

In contrast to my brief but nearly solitary train ride from West Berlin, the passengers were children, pensioners, shift laborers in dirty work clothes, and two women in smocks and bandanas. As Heinz explained, an infamous "right to work" policy in the *Arbeiter- und Bauernstaat* – or

Farmer and Worker's State – required each adult to have a job. So here I sat, a Florence Nightingale on a secret rescue mission, melding into the gray, brown and green attire of the proletariat.

In the row behind me across the isle, the two women just off work – to judge by their conversation – discussed in hushed tones the vacations they'd planned for next year.

"My husband and I have already applied to the authorities for a room to ourselves for next July," the one woman said in a Berlin accent, "if only for two weeks in Romania. You're so lucky you snagged a state apartment on the Baltic Sea."

"Well, yes, but for that privilege, we'll have to take our grandchildren along, while yours will go off to Pioneer Camp," her older companion countered in a thick Saxon accent.

"You can't have it all," the Berlin woman said, as they prepared to exit.

The train pulled into Ostkreuz Station, a multilevel transfer point for East Berlin and environs. The two women from the train proceeded arm in arm toward a lift to the upper level.

At this station, the S-Bahn stops lengthened from two minutes to almost three and the scenery changed from soot, factories and smokestacks to lush green forests and small towns. After four stops, the only passengers left were two gents with canes, MJ and me.

How do they spend their retirement years in this dismal place?

As our train pulled out of the Hirschgarten station a raspy male voice announced over the loudspeaker: "In a few minutes we will arrive at Friedrichshagen."

MJ stood up, stuffed the newspaper in his briefcase and stepped to the exit.

I mentally went over my instructions.

MJ got off, followed by the two gentlemen and me. The stationmaster watched as we walked by, got up from his lone desk in a cubicle and stood on the platform. As the train pulled out, he held up a large red-and-white sign shaped like a lollipop and said, "Stay back!" to a deserted platform.

The eerie silence gave me goose bumps. At the platform timetables, I stopped to confirm the departures to downtown East Berlin;

seventeen and forty-seven after the hour until five o'clock and then only at seventeen. Hurrying down the steps to the street level, I looked in the direction MJ was supposed to take, but he had disappeared from view.

16

I scanned the area just outside the train station again. The curious stare of the ticket agent behind iron bars made me cringe. I was tempted to scrap this frigging deal. No, a promise was a promise. I couldn't let Alfred and Karl down.

Bölschestrasse, the main thoroughfare, was devoid of cars. The clack of my heels echoed on down the empty corridor and my heart thumped in accompaniment. Exposed, vulnerable and tense, I'd arrived right at this damned *Mittagszeit*, a holy time from one to three when Germans are supposed to be quiet, children avoid playgrounds, and people go home for a hot meal. I rounded the corner of Möllenseestrasse, saw the yellow awning at number 17 and continued on toward Lake Müggelsee. At the water's edge, I paused to breathe in the moist air and enjoy the calm underneath billowy clouds.

Little seemed changed from Fontane's idyllic descriptions of picnics with family and friends. Two canoes and a platform rocked back and forth in the light wind. The sound of a nearby church bell echoed over the lake and followed a lone bicyclist and schoolchild on their way. An ache tugged at my chest. How I wished I could have come here with Mama, instead of making a trip alone to see a perfect stranger. The sound of a stroller behind me jolted me out of my melancholy. A woman had stopped to adjust her toddler's blanket.

At Möllenseestrasse, I looked over my shoulder, half expecting a

Vopo to round the corner. I walked up to the directory and rang the bell under the name Meier.

"*Bitte, kommen Sie herein!*" a man's voice crackled over the intercom.

He buzzed me into the house. As I made my way up the musty stairwell, I heard a pop tune blaring with monotonous, regular beats: "*La la la, Es ist heut' schön wenn Du bist da!*" (It's so nice today when you ain't far away). *Bad music, bad grammar.*

As I reached the fourth floor, the door opened. MJ pressed a finger to his lips and motioned me in.

"*Guten Tag*, Fräulein Seiler." He extended his hand. "Sorry we got separated. I decided to come here and wait for your arrival. I trusted you would find the house anyway."

Is this another one of your little tests?

MJ motioned me into a large loft room. "Fräulein Seiler, please meet Karl."

A man with the sallow complexion of a shut-in sat on a couch with a glass of water in front of him. Supporting himself with a cane, Karl rose to extend his hand. "Pleased to meet you, Fräulein Seiler. I'm so grateful for your help."

"My pleasure." I gave Karl the cigarette pack.

He opened the pack, took a tablet out, washed it down and eased down onto the couch.

"May I also introduce Alfred's nephew, Dieter Jacobi, from Leipzig?" MJ motioned to a young man with long crossed legs sitting askew in a corner armchair. Barely able to stand upright under the slanted ceiling, Dieter come over and greeted me with a smile. "Nice to meet you, Fräulein Seiler." Thick-lensed glasses magnified his reddened eyes. "Won't you please join us for *Kaffee und Kuchen*?" he said. "We hope you have a few minutes to spare, *ja*?"

In spite of my desire to leave, I could hardly refuse.

Dieter pulled up a chair for me opposite Karl at a table set with assorted colored cups and saucers, white plates, a variety of nondescript pieces of cake and an enameled coffee pot on a warmer.

MJ went over to the couch and took a seat next to Karl, while Dieter pulled his sofa chair to my left and sat down. He poured coffee for MJ, himself and me.

I selected a piece of cake sprinkled on top with poppy seeds. This was a cultural experience: dry cake, and coffee that tasted more like chicory.

"We hear you live in America. I've got a relative by the name of Aldo Braun in Pittsburgh. Have you been there, by any chance?" MJ asked.

"No, I'm from Chicago – in the central part of the country – about six or seven hours away by car."

"Oh, I see. When did you leave Germany?"

The men listened while I described my move from Berlin to Chicago and my life in the US with my mother.

With his index knuckle, Dieter pushed his glasses frames up to an indented spot. "Fascinating," he said eagerly. "What a big change from Berlin after the war. You know, we don't get much in the news about the USA here. It must be strange to be back. How does Berlin strike you after being gone so long?"

"Herr Jacobi, Berlin looks much different than it did after the war. I love the new concert hall, the restored Kaiser Wilhelm Memorial Church, and the Ku-Damm I knew as a child is back with beautiful shops and cafes. It helps me feel at home."

Silence.

"East Berlin has a rich cultural life, too, judging by the kiosk at Friedrichstrasse."

"We do have many theaters here." Dieter said. "The plays are carefully selected by the state. The GDR makes sure it feeds the soul before the body."

"Speaking of Brecht, didn't he opt for East Berlin instead of remaining in California?"

"Right. Brecht's views weren't popular with the US government, and he had to leave the US for fear of being arrested."

"I wonder what he would have thought about the Wall if he were living today," I said.

"A good question. Brecht believed capitalism manipulated the cultural landscape. I'm sure he'd have figured a barrier to protect an ideology was a necessary step."

"In reality, the communists decided to shut 'fascists' out, to keep *us* in – that's the official story they give for their 'Anti-fascist Protection Wall,'" MJ said. "It won't take long before the GDR will have anyone left who knows what freedom is."

Frank speech. But does everyone over here feel this way?

After we finished the pastry and coffee, MJ cleared away the dishes and took his seat again at the couch. Dieter got up to open a window and took his pipe and tobacco from a bookcase on the wall. He cleaned out the barrel with his thumb and index finger, took a pinch from a pouch labeled "Tobacco Cuba" and stuffed it into the barrel. With a wooden match, he lit the protruding strands; his cheeks hollowed as he sucked air through the stem. The fragrance of tobacco filled the entire room.

"May I ask why you didn't escape before the Wall?"

The three men looked at each other.

"Some people did split, as it's called here," MJ said. "Take Alfred. He lost his family in the war, so there was no one to hold him back."

Karl tapped his chest. "With my bad ticker, Wall or not, it was too late."

Dieter uncrossed his legs and leaned forward. "I considered *Republikflucht* – fleeing the country – a crime of high treason. Now it's almost impossible."

"Almost?"

"Like escape through a tunnel, or by car in a remote border area." He took a puff from his pipe.

The buzzer rang and MJ excused himself. "Probably the mail."

"Fräulein Seiler, how long do you plan to stay in Berlin?" Dieter asked.

"Until I finish my dissertation."

"Oh, I'd assumed you were . . . here as a tourist."

"Well, not exactly, But, thanks to Karl, I've done a bit of sightseeing today, visiting a suburb of Berlin I only knew from novels."

Dieter's eyebrow arched up. "By Theodor Fontane, perhaps?"

"Why, yes, as a matter of fact."

MJ emerged with two envelopes. "Would you please mail this letter for me in West Berlin? It's not yet sealed or stamped."

"Yes, I'd be glad to."

"Good. Please enclose it inside this second envelope and put a West German stamp on it. Heinz will reimburse you."

I nodded and placed the letter into the inner compartment of my purse. "Gentlemen, thank you so much for the *Kaffee und Kuchen*. I must be on my way now."

"Certainly." Dieter got up, extinguished his pipe and put it into a pouch. "Let me accompany you to the station. I'll go first, and you can leave a minute or so later. We can meet in front of the church about two blocks from here."

"All right."

"See you there."

The entrance door in the foyer shut with a dull thud.

Karl's eyes glistened as I reached down to shake his hand.

MJ walked me to the door. "I'm sorry we didn't have more time to talk. But Karl has the medicine and our mission is accomplished."

As I hurried down the narrow stairs I brushed past a woman with two nets full of groceries. I stopped to apologize.

"Ja, ja," she said. "People haven't got time for much nowadays. They should have bad ankles like me. Then they could see what they'd do."

The weather outside had turned cooler. Commuters in factory overalls trudged by, their heads braced against the wind. When I got to the church, Dieter was standing in front of a bulletin board.

"Excuse me, miss, can you tell me the time of Sunday's church service? Does it say eight thirty or nine thirty?"

"Nine thirty."

Dieter inspected his glasses. "This time of year, the wind kicks up a lot of dust." He puffed two breaths of air onto his thick lenses, held them up for reinspection and put them back on. "Let's head to the main street, cross over and turn left. We can talk freely on the way. The Vopos don't usually patrol along here, since it's not the standard route to the S-Bahn."

On the way, Dieter touched my jacket sleeve. "Fräulein Seiler, could you stay on for a walk at Lake Müggelsee? At this time the paths are almost deserted. It won't be like Goethe's line 'a thousand eyes are on me everywhere I go.' We'd have time to chat and still get you to your S-Bahn on time. In fact, I'm headed to the station myself."

We strolled toward the shore.

Dieter pulled out a large pocket watch, old-fashioned like my father's. Kurt always wore his shiny gold watch on a chain that hung in an arc from his vest pocket. I both loved and hated that watch. On walks together, my father would put his hand on my shoulder and say, "Let's see where we're at." With the thumb and forefinger of his left hand, he'd pull out the watch, cradle it in his hand and unclasp the cover with his thumb. I'd see the delicate dedication in German "At Your Confirmation, May 1, 1913. With love, Gramma." Papi never revealed the time he read inside. He'd simply purse his lips, nod, snap the watch shut and slide it into his vest pocket. My heart would sink when he pulled it out for the third time. It meant we had to head home.

*   *   *

"I hope I'm not interrupting something important by asking you to go for a walk."

"No, I have nothing in particular planned. I'm enjoying just being here at Müggelsee."

"Fräulein Seiler, we are university colleagues. Can we say *Du* to one other?"

"Yes, of course. In English, you know, we don't distinguish between the familiar and the formal 'you.'"

"In German, though, it matters." He extended his hand. "I'm Dieter."

"And I'm Renate."

Dieter pointed to a bench in a grassy area beyond the beach. "Could we stop there for a minute? The peace you experience here is hard to find in the city."

We sat down.

"Before, at the apartment," I said, "you mentioned Fontane. Have you read many of his novels?"

"Most of them – especially the ones that take place in and around

Berlin. I love the forests and lakes of Mark Brandenburg, and the atmospheric way Fontane describes them."

"So are you originally from this area? MJ said you were from Leipzig."

"I grew up near Fürstenwalde, to the south of Berlin, and visited my uncle MJ often in Köpenick, just nearby. I used to play on the beach close to this spot – when I didn't have my nose in a book. Philosophy and literature are the subjects I originally wanted to study. Chemistry was the only slot open at the University of Leipzig."

"So Dieter, did you manage to take any literature courses at all?"

"Yes, a few."

"What a shame," I said.

"I guess it worked out all right in the end."

"How so?"

"I soon found out that even at the university level, literature in the GDR is used for ideological purposes. The only 'safe' subject to study – and one I considered too narrow a field – would have been love poetry. Love rises above propaganda, because it's universal."

"I can't imagine a country that wouldn't allow me to major in a subject I liked."

"Which is what?"

"German literature and culture."

A gentle wind rippled across the water, moving the swings to and fro on the deserted playground.

"Dieter, you said that poetry was a narrow field of study, and I agree. But as for being ideologically safe, I don't know. The Third Reich, after all, glorified traditional values and found them mirrored in poetry. I bet the same is true for your country."

"So you see an affinity between German Romanticism and GDR ideology."

"Yes."

"But Renate, do you really believe the love poetry of great poets like Heine, Goethe, Novalis, Brentano, and Eichendorff fits into your theory? Not much you can distort in 'Du bist wie eine Blume.'"

I flashed on Dr. Fuerstenberg and his dedication of that line to me. A moment of sadness crept into this otherwise beautiful scene at the lake.

We got up and paused at the water's edge, watching in silence as expansive purple clouds drifted by to join gray-and-white puffy ones.

Dieter picked up a gnarled piece of wood and carved concentric circles into the sand. "Renate, as you can probably tell from these glasses, I have some vision problems – nearsightedness being one. I'll be going to the Charité hospital to undergo some tests at the beginning of next week."

"Oh, I'm sorry to hear that," I said. "What kind of tests?"

"I've inherited a condition called Marfan syndrome. It has to do with connective tissue, and I might need surgery for a retinal tear. The doctors tell me if I do, I'll need at least three weeks to recover – but after that, I should be able to be out and about. There's a lively café near Alexanderplatz called the Café Budapest. I checked their fall schedule, and on Sunday, November 24, they're featuring a gypsy band in the afternoon. Would you be interested in going there with me?"

I could hardly contain my surprise. "I'd like that very much."

"Shall we say at noon? I'll meet you at the Alexanderplatz S-Bahn at the newsstand on the main level."

As the sun dropped behind the trees, we retraced our steps toward the Friedrichshagen S-Bahn station. Before I ascended the stairs, I turned to Dieter.

"Thank you for the lovely afternoon."

"My pleasure. Goodbye until the twenty-fourth."

On the way up, I heard Dieter say "Alexanderplatz, round trip."

17

By the time I posted MJ's letter, it was dark. I deposited my "Eastern" coat and purse at the pension and collected my own things at Reinigung Clemens. Nothing was missing. Famished, but too tired to cook, I went out and picked up a roasted half chicken at the Savignyplatz station, and arrived at my apartment feeling like I'd just had my first job interview at Ryan College – dry lips, pounding heart and tensed shoulders. It seemed like I hadn't taken one full breath all day. *Even if the Queen of Sheba phoned – no dice for taking any calls.* I wanted to settle in for a hot bath.

Try as I might, I couldn't fall asleep.

October 29 – in bed, after my run
Today has been an emotional roller coaster. An unanticipated visit to Alfred and Heinz was stressful enough, followed by "impromptu" spy games through Wedding and a mission to East Berlin.

The minute I walked into Karl's apartment, I felt better. But when I described my life in the US, he and the others just stared at me. I might as well have been talking about the moon. How could they know what emigration to another country entails – or what a big American city feels like?

How ironic that I'd end up on a walk with Dieter at Lake Müggelsee, where Mama, Papi and I went on boat rides! Dieter seemed vulnerable, eager for company and relieved to find someone to talk to. I'm glad I joined him.

Our conversation reminded me of old times at graduate school or weekends with Laura. It was fun to learn about Dieter's background, his fondness for Fontane and especially his views on poetry. When he quoted from a poem by Goethe, I could hardly believe my ears! How many people in the States even know who Goethe is?

Our discussion of poetry got me fired up when it tied into my dissertation topic. As for Dieter's slant on love poetry – that pure love was somehow a "safe" subject not prone to ideology – I don't think I buy it. Love by any definition is a problematic issue, and isn't immune from distortion. What about Polly's love song in Brecht's Threepenny Opera? *How long love lasts or how you view it can change for sure. No, the Third Reich used Romantic poetry for its own selfish purposes, and you can't tell me the East Germans don't do the same!*

I miss intellectual stimulation of IU and the U of C. I never seemed to chew the fat with colleagues at Ryan – Howard was so bogged down with department chair stuff, and Frieda kept her distance. Laura doesn't know much about German culture and I don't know beans about Spanish culture, either, so we're even-steven.

Should I have just kept my mouth shut when I disagreed with Dieter about poetic love being immutable, or apolitical in the GDR? I didn't scare him away, I guess, his asking if we could say Du and all. Nevertheless I felt uneasy – too much of Mama's German formality in my veins, I guess. How about that, though, a first invite from a German guy for a Sunday meal – and in a communist capital, no less. Should I be flattered?

Speaking of saying Du . . . if Christine doesn't call me after a few days, should I phone?

I climbed out of bed later than usual, but still in time for breakfast. On the way, I stopped at the office to check my mailbox. Not a peep from Laura. *It must be midterm time. She'll probably put off grading and end up with a marathon session on the weekend.*

I was about to leave the office when Schulz came in.

125

"*Guten Morgen*, Fräulein Seiler. Two phone messages for you came in yesterday afternoon." Schulz rifled through some papers on his desk. "Let's see, one is from your cousin Christine, and the other is from – a Herr Tenne." He handed me two slips.

So Christine had called!

"Hey, Renate, how about four thirty this Friday for *Kaffee und Kuchen*? I'm in town for a while and hoped we could get together. Call me to confirm. Cousin Christine." Her phone number followed.

Herr Tenne wanted me to contact him at my earliest convenience. *That isn't now, Fred.* I was OD'ed on medicine trips, and besides, I had to prepare for tomorrow's visit to Bautsch. On the last visit we'd covered new ground on East German poets influenced by the Romanticists, so I still had a lot to absorb. *How can one be romantic in a prison state? I'd better not ask him that.*

I ate breakfast and scoured the newspaper for a good concert, until Schulz politely signaled he needed to clear the tables.

In my room, I placed the two telephone messages in my purse – plus my diary – and put on my leather jacket. I stepped outside and was greeted by a chilly wind sweeping occasional leaves across my path. *Brr, maybe I should have worn my warm coat.* I saw that the phone booth was occupied, pulled up my collar and headed to Kantstrasse, where I'd seen another booth. Drat, the line was busy! I scooped my two coins out of the return and tried again.

"*Guten Tag*, Zeiler Accounting. Christine Kaufmann speaking."

I took a deep breath. "Hello, this is Renate."

"*Guten Tag*. Is our appointment on November 1 – that's Friday – at 4:30 P.M. convenient?"

"Yes. Where would you like to meet?"

Christine lowered her voice. "How about at the Café am Steinplatz – near your place?"

"Fine."

"Very well. I look forward to seeing you then."

The receiver clicked.

*　　*　　*

I could use some time before my call to Alfred, and walked down Kantstrasse, passing a café on the corner of a side street. The place looked perfect for a short stop.

No doubt a hangout for the business district, the café was loud, with aftershave lotion or cologne wafting from men in business suits, attaché cases propped against the table legs, and not a female patron in sight. And I'd popped in with my tennies and jeans on. I found a table off to the side, went to a newspaper rack and took a copy of the Berlin *Financial Times* and a magazine of exclusive restaurants in the area. I ordered a cup of coffee and pulled out my diary.

October 30 – Café Niemeyer, off Kantstrasse
WHEW! These weeks have kept me on pins and needles, wondering if Christine would call. Not that I haven't been occupied with work since the Panther – with a "slight" interruption for a courier run to the East. Thank heaven the meds are safely with Karl. A & H should be happy, and I can tackle my own agendas.

But what on earth does Alfred want now? Talk about pushy. I feel like I have to report to my father like a teenager who's stayed out late.

I'm tickled Christine called to get together. I guess it means she doesn't make empty promises – you never know, out of sight, out of mind. She must have tons of guys who want to date her. Why hang out with me?

Not feeling terribly comfortable in this all-male environment, I downed my coffee and continued my walk. After half an hour or so, I reached the phone booth across from the pension. *Too bad it's not occupied this time. Okay, get this over with.*

"Tenne."

"Renate Seiler here."

"*Guten Morgen*, Fräulein Seiler. I'm just checking on how your delivery in East Berlin went."

"Fine. Your descriptions and directions were clear enough for me to arrive pretty much on time."

"I'm glad everything worked out. Did you – um – get a chance to talk with Herr Jacobi, the tall fellow at Karl's?"

"Yes. When I was about to leave for my train, he offered to accompany me to the station."

A young man pulled up to the booth on his bike.

"Herr Tenne, I'm afraid there's someone outside waiting."

"All right. I'll phone you at another time, then."

What else might Alfred want to know? Or what more might he ask of me? Tired of trying to figure things out, I went upstairs and took a nap.

*   *   *

After a feeble attempt at my chapter on Rhine poets, I stopped and nibbled on some leftover chicken from the fridge. For dessert, I grabbed some chips from my cupboard stash and sipped a beer.

A hot bath sounded good about now – the next best thing to one of Laura's famous back rubs when I got stressed. "You know, Ren," she'd reminded me on our last evening together, "In Germany, I won't be around as your personal masseuse."

Schulz was still puttering with receipts in the office. I plunked down a mark for the bath.

"So late in the day?" he peered over his reading glasses.

"No competition."

Schulz wrote "Seiler" into his time sheet and gave me the large key. "Bring it to me in the morning. I wish you a pleasant evening."

I luxuriated in a lavender oil bath and began a reread of *Irrungen Wirrungen*, a novel by Fontane. Set in Berlin, it tells about the love of a young working-class woman, Jenny Nimptsch, for Botho von Rienäcker, a Prussian *Junker*, or landed gentry – a fated attraction, impossible to resist, but a relationship doomed from the outset.

After a few pages I put the book away in my duffel bag, sank down into the water – still warm – and finished my bath.

October 30 – At night, propped up in bed

This trip has sure turned out differently than planned. I thought my agenda was clear-cut. Instead, I find myself entangled with people and events I hadn't anticipated. If I'd come here with Mama, would I have met Tenne and Baumert? Would Christine ever have been in the picture? Or Dieter?

Christine's message made me laugh. Maybe it was silly, pretending she was my cousin. I'm flattered she contacted me, but I don't know what to think about the Café Steinplatz invite. Be careful what you wish for. Is this a chance for her to play with some woman's emotions? Don't know if I want to meet her. Was my encounter with her fated? Ren! Stop making a big deal about a coffee klatsch. My M.O. is to figure everything out: plan thoroughly and dictate how things are supposed to go. Ordnung muss sein – *order must prevail, as the Germans say. These past two days with Alfred and Karl have thrown me off schedule. And me – the one who always got papers done on time! Tomorrow is my day with Bautsch. Will I be too distracted?*

Weary from all my self-reflection, I fluffed up the pillows while listening to the church bells ring eleven times, and dozed off.

An ominous knock on the door of our house awakens me from sleep. A voice yells, "Aufmachen Gestapo!" My mother rushes me to the rear bedroom and tells me to hide under the bed. I can't understand the exact words the men are saying, but it's clear they've come for Papi. Nora, our dog, cowers under the bed with me; I take her into my arms. One of the Gestapo men looks under the bed. "Ha! You think you can escape." He pulls me out into the room and shouts, "You'll never see your father again!" He laughs and grabs a billy club. Nora retreats, her eyes full of terror and helplessness, as she watches the Gestapo drag me away.

Then I'm at the Wall on Bernauerstrasse I climb the observation tower and see a man on the other side. He moves out from an alleyway and waves with a white handkerchief. It's Papi! I take my scarf and wave to him; he touches his heart and blows me a kiss.

Across the way, a Vopo turns around to find out whom I'm signaling to, but Papi is gone.

I woke up, bathed in sweat. *No, it can't be true he's gone. Papi, why did you leave me?* I cried into my pillow.

*   *   *

The next day, Bautsch and I digressed from the GDR Romantic poets and, in spite of my best efforts, drifted over to Heine. I got the impression the professor wasn't so enthusiastic about my thesis that Heine was a Jewish rebel with an ironic take on life and love. Bautsch apparently preferred to side with those East German critics who saw Heine as a poet of convenience: had Heine lived today, they believed, he would have been an exemplary GDR citizen, given his friendship with Karl Marx and the bard's acerbic comments on Germany (to be understood as West Germany, of course). As far as Bautsch was concerned, Heine's love poetry didn't fit in with the Romantics, or at least Goethe, "their" man since he lived in Weimar. I thought the professor was off base with his views.

Later, I pulled out Dr. Fuerstenberg's Heine volume and reread some of the earlier poems – especially the ones Schumann set to music. I listened to my recording of Schumann's "Berg und Burgen Schauen Herunter" – "Hill and Castles Look Down Below," sung by Dietrich Fischer-Dieskau. As the singer gazes out upon the river, he links its sunlit beauty to the smiles of his beloved. In the fourth strophe, however, the mood and message darken; we learn of the treachery of the beloved, while the piano continues the undulating patterns of the Rhine. How well Schumann captured Heine's irony. Had Wagner gotten his leitmotiv idea from Schumann, perhaps?

October 31 – at home after a session with Schumann and Heine
A couple of hours' distance from Bautsch works wonders when it comes to Heine. As a Jew in Germany in the 1820s, how could he not distance himself from the turbulent times with caustic critique?

But did that make him a capitalist? And did that devalue his poetry? Actually, I'm going to skip Heine in our last few sessions. The GDR has its entrenched ideology and that's that. I'll bet Dieter would agree Heine was not a party-line man or some kind of hack.

Today is Reformation Day – a holiday. Guess I wasn't interested enough to celebrate the day in a service. The Lutheran Church has a lot more reforming to do, especially when it comes to women, although Lutheranism sure beats the "RCs" as Mama used to refer to Catholics. Tee hee.

Waking early the next morning, I slipped on my robe and stepped onto the balcony. The skies remained unrepentantly dismal in contrast to the tingle in my arms, as I anticipated an afternoon with someone who fascinated me.

What should I wear for coffee with Christine today? *Don't want to dress to kill or arrive looking like a schoolmarm.* I dashed over to the C&A department store and bought a new sweater to go with my slacks. A little lipstick, rouge and casual dress should do it.

All this fuss reminded me of my college days, when I'd avoided such anxieties by hanging out with female friends like Carol. What I'd seen of the Saturday night ritual made me uncomfortable: shave legs and underarms, followed by a shower and shampoo. Roll up your hair in curlers, apply a face masque, check for zits, remove curlers and style hair, put on makeup and get dressed. After final touches to your hairdo, plaster it with huge amounts of hairspray so as not to mar your perfect coiffure. Lastly, you wait for the magical moment when your date buzzes his arrival. My student life had been single-minded: slog through coursework and a dissertation for seven years, and get on with a career as a professor. I'd been happy to let this dating silliness pass me by entirely – at least until now.

*   *   *

I picked a table in the corner with a view of the street, so I'd see Christine approach from any direction. I held up my menu, peeking over it to spot anyone who resembled her. A crosstown bus pulled up, and then another, but no Christine. With the third bus I saw her exit, and immediately returned to the menu.

Christine made a beeline for my table.

"Hello, Renate, good to see you." Her handshake was warm and firm.

"Hi, Christine."

"I'm glad you made time for your relative."

I groaned inside. *Was she going to tease me about the cousin bit?*

Christine hung up her coat and sat down. "Well, who knows? They say only six people separate you from any other person in the world. Personally, when I think of some of the people I meet at the Panther it feels a little scary."

"I imagine you run into weird types there."

"Some are intriguing, like you."

"Intriguing?"

"I noticed you came with a fellow the first time – but the next time you were alone. Did you ditch your date, or what?"

"Well, not exactly." I tried to find the right words. "You might say he's a friend of a friend."

"Forgive me, I'm pretty direct – if a woman comes with a guy, then it could be serious."

"I suppose."

"Okay, glad we've got that topic out of the way. It's Friday, and time to shift gears." Christine settled back in her chair. "How about some hors d'oeuvres and a glass of wine?"

"Sure."

"White or red?"

"I don't mind. Your pick."

Christine hailed the waiter and ordered a bottle of chardonnay, chicken wings, a bowl of Greek olives and bread sticks.

Interesting. Is this Christine's version of the switcheroo, as the senior women in our dorm at IU used to describe it? "You go out for coffee with some guy and end having a beer."

"So how was your trip?"

"I went to visit Anne, an old friend from grade school in Trier, by car. From there we went to Saarbrücken for a couple of days and stayed with my brother Georg. But even after a day there, Anne and I got cabin fever. There wasn't much of a bar scene. Saarbrücken has a nice atmosphere, but it's rather smalltownish, if you know what I mean. I guess nothing compares to Berlin. We're spoiled here."

"I can imagine. The Panther is something else."

"How else?"

"Smoky, loud, cramped, but terrific entertainment."

"I hope you're referring to me."

"It wasn't that awful singer Dierk before you," I laughed.

The waiter brought our snacks and poured our wine. Christine told me about the entertainers at the club – most of them male – and some gossip about the weekend lead, whom everyone thought was gay.

"Would you like more wine, perhaps?"

"Sure, but just a glass. I don't drink too much before evening."

Christine ordered a carafe.

"So do you like performing at the Panther?" I asked.

"Yes, even if I've got just one set. But hey, it's a gig – Mondays are slow, so they lower the cover charge – and attract a younger crowd – mostly students."

"Except Robert and me." I said.

"That particular evening turned out to be a blessing in disguise. I got to sing an extra set, and had a beautiful woman in the audience I could serenade in the bargain."

My cheeks burned.

"So, Renate, you're still in town. Are you on business or something?" In November, Wellesley, an all-women's school in Massachusetts, awarded me a one-year tuition scholarship. But when I attended a reception for prospective students at a suburban villa in North Chicago, I knew I couldn't survive at that institution for even one year on scholarship. I didn't fit in.

"No – I'm just writing my dissertation."

"Just? About what?"

"How the Nazis viewed German Romantic poetry."

"You mean Heine & Co.?"

"Why, yes, as a matter of fact."

"You're surprised I know about him? Don't worry; I'm not in the mood to discuss poetry today. I'm a Berliner. We try to live and let live, have fun and drink our troubles away."

"It explains why the Panther seems a perfect place for you, I guess."

"Yes, the club is more family. You know, Renate, I can't detect any accent. Are you from West Germany?"

"No, from the USA. I was born in Berlin, but my mother and I left for the States after the war."

"When did you leave?"

"In 1947."

"So you've come full circle?"

"I suppose you could say so."

"How does it feel to be back after all those years? I'd bet weird."

"In what way?"

"Well, I mean when you moved with your mom, not much of this town was left standing – and where you moved there were no signs of war."

*   *   *

Around us, a waiter began to prepare the tables for dinner and asked if we wanted to order anything more.

Christine hesitated, so I spoke up. "I can tell you're tired."

"The week has been long, I guess you could say."

The waiter tallied the tab, and Christine paid.

"Perhaps we could get together again soon?" Christine helped me on with my coat.

"Sure." I tried to mask my excitement.

"Let me walk you to your place."

At the pension entrance, Christine drew close to me, but I pulled my head away.

134

"Good night, Renate. I'll be in touch."

"Thanks for the wine and appetizers."

Upstairs in my apartment, I crawled into bed with my diary.

November 1 – after meeting with Christine at the Café am Steinplatz
My mind is in turmoil. I got through my first face-to-face without
a faux pas or saying something dumb. I don't know if we spoke
about anything special, but I was so nervous when I sat down that
I just let her talk. Then, at the end, I couldn't let her kiss me – don't
know why. My reaction certainly didn't match my desire. Was I too
scared? Where is this heading? I hope I haven't driven Christine
away!

I reflected on the poem I had read at the German State Library by Else Galen-Gube, an unknown poetess from last century. I put down my diary, reached over to the nightstand for my research notepad and flipped to the page where I had copied a stanza.

Du botst mir deinen Mund zum Kusse dar
und ich sprach "Nein," zum Trotz den wilden Gluten,
die, seit der Stunde, wo ich dich gesehn,
mein ganzes Sein wie Lavastrom durchfluten.

[You offered me your mouth for a kiss,
and I said "No" in spite of my wild passions
which, since the hour I first saw you,
have flowed through my entire being like a stream of lava.]

18

Engagements were out and the dissertation in. I worked straight through Saturday and Sunday, trying to focus on nineteenth-century Germany. After all, when required, I could put on the steam. Mama used to shake her head at my term paper times in grad school.

"I can't pry you away from your studies just for a little *Kaffee und Kuchen?*" she would ask me in the late afternoon. Occasionally I relented, especially when the smell of her coffee wafted through the house.

I wasn't the only one caught in the grip of her java artistry. Even the strongest of wills could not resist the aroma, her friends used to say. I wondered if Mama's yummy temptations contributed to her trouncing them at bridge when they played at her house, especially after the coffee break.

As for me, it soon became apparent I had to remain on campus in the library stacks until after K&K time. It hurt me to think about Mama sitting on the balcony alone with her masterpieces. I sure could do with them now.

Another diversion, however, tempted my discipline. Robert phoned me out of the blue on Monday morning near the end of breakfast. Since our visit to the Black Panther, we hadn't been in contact until now.

"Hi, Renate. How're you doin'?"

"Working hard. What's up, Robert?"

"You promised me a rain check at the Café Kranzler. Is this a convenient time?"

"Sure. How about November 6, the day after tomorrow? It's sort of my down day between trips to East Berlin."

"You're on. I have a late morning seminar, so I can make it by four."

*   *   *

From my table at the Kranzler, I recognized Robert on the other side of the Ku-Damm jaywalking across the divider strip only to pause when a tour bus slowed traffic.

Dressed in a corduroy jacket with leather elbow guards, white shirt, brown tie, creased slacks and a couple of itinerant pens in his breast pocket, Robert looked the professorial image.

"Hi there, sorry I'm late." He swung his jacket onto a chair, took s seat opposite me and loosened his tie. "A student held me up after class with the silliest question about American dinner habits, and I couldn't get rid of her. To add insult to injury, I got caught in commuter traffic at Westkreuz and couldn't find the Kaiserdamm. I'll never get the hang of that intersection."

"Don't worry. It's nice to sit back and do some people watching."

"Boy, am I glad to be off campus. I've finally finished my November preps during fall break. These German students demand a lot from their instructors – certainly more than my undergrads in the States. Then when I thought I could take a breather, the department asked me to present a paper for a symposium later this month. The theme ties right in with my work: Sociological Implications of a Divided Germany on Intra-German Communication."

"Congratulations, Robert! That's an impressive subject."

"Thanks. Not much chance to see the light of day before the semester is over, though. I'm glad you had time to meet. We academic types can be lame when it comes to any kind of social life."

A waitress carrying two long slender menus approached our table and looked at Robert. Will the lady and gentleman like *Kaffeee und Kuchen* this afternoon?

"Certainly," Robert said, adjusting his tie. "What would you care for, Renate?"

"Black Forest cake and a pot of coffee, please."

"Fine choice Madam – our classic pastry. Would you prefer extra whipped cream on the side?"

I glanced at Robert.

"Yes, why of course," he said, smiling up at her. "I'll have the same."

The waitress glided off to a nearby pastry bar. Removing a glass lid from a matching domed cake stand, she placed it beneath the counter, cut two pieces and transferred them to porcelain plates lined with dollies. After arranging them on a tray with cups and saucers, she added two steaming coffee pots and a chilled creamer from a refrigerator, and paused over her creation before replacing the lid.

"So Renate, fill me in on what's new."

"The diss is moving along, and my social life has picked up. By the way, this afternoon's tab is on me."

"How so?" Robert asked.

"I'm grateful for your introducing me to Berlin's night life scene. I went back to the Black Panther on my own."

"Really" Robert's couldn't conceal his surprise. "Who was performing? I hear they just hired a new band on Wednesdays."

"Actually, I went on a Monday."

"You did?"

"I wanted to hear Christine again."

"Was the place crowded like before?" Robert stirred a dollop of whipped cream into his coffee.

"Absolutely. In fact, the only table I could find was with two women."

"Were they perhaps Ulli and Greta sitting to the side of the stage?"

"How did you know their names?"

"They're regulars."

Small world this Berlin is, even if you're a foreigner!

"So, what did Christine sing?"

"A mix of Berlin tunes and American oldies, and a few numbers at the end with guitar. It was great how she captured the pre-war atmosphere of nostalgia and melancholy. And after the show, Christine even dropped by our table. We had a chance to chat together briefly, since Ulli and Greta had to leave."

Robert fell silent.

Is he upset I didn't contact him to go with me? Better switch topics.

I compared notes with Robert about living in Berlin. For him, everything was a blank slate, with little to compare it to. *Drüben* seemed more formidable for him than for me – no surprise, given our conversation on the way to the Panther. My experience of Berlin was more difficult to convey – such as the blurring of lines between the past and the present due to the war, my emotions from having lived in Berlin with my parents – and the Wall. *How can I make that understood to someone from rural Ohio?*

I told Robert about Bautsch and his DDR ways of viewing literature. We determined the professor's name had to be pronounced "botch" or something similar in American English. Good for a laugh.

Meeting Dick at the bar prompted me to ask Robert about his high school days. I found out that, like me, he had felt out of place with all the dating hoo-hah, sock hops, and love notes handed back and forth in class to some crush who could be replaced in the next semester, depending on the sport of choice that season.

*   *   *

"Would you care for some wine and appetizers?" Robert asked. "My treat."

"I accept."

Robert ordered a carafe of house red wine and antipasto.

"Coming back to your visit to the Black Panther: what was your impression of Christine as a person?"

"Charming and suave, I'd say. She threw me a curve and asked me out for coffee last week."

"For a date?"

"I wouldn't call it a date. After all, I hardly know the woman. Casual, it sounded to me."

Robert sipped from his red wine. "You know, Renate, I have to say Christine is not exactly what you might think."

My throat felt dry. *What's he driving at, anyway? Why all these questions?*

"Was she perhaps a member of the Nazi *Bund Deutscher Mädchen* – Hitler's League of German Girls?"

"No, nothing like that."

"That was just a joke, Robert. Seriously, what do you mean?"

"Although she doesn't exactly broadcast it, it's common knowledge around the bar scene that Christine's – well – different. I didn't tell you before we went to hear her. I figured maybe you wouldn't go."

"Different?"

"A couple of my students have tried to invite her out after the show. She always declines."

This is making me uncomfortable. Maybe I need to ask the questions.

"Have *you* tried to ask her out?"

Robert turned beet red. "I don't relish rejections. I get enough of them when I submit to scholarly journals. But I'm fascinated by a sexy woman who seems to prefer women, that is from a sociological and psychological perspective, of course."

"In college when Dr. Wilson, my English professor, discussed a Gertrude Stein poem in class, she mentioned Stein was a lesbian. But I don't think I've ever met . . . one."

"Up to now, at least. Where would you have encountered a woman who admits she prefers someone of the same sex? Gertrude was bold and courageous in a world where lesbianism was a taboo subject. Hitler promoted women who devoted themselves to family and children. Deviation was not tolerated, and women who were found out faced certain internment in a concentration camp."

"How horrible!"

"The US wasn't so terrible as Germany, of course, but during World War II, a woman could be discharged from her job if it was found out she was a homosexual, especially if she served in the military."

"You seem to know a lot about the subject, Robert."

Robert paused to finish his wine. "A few years ago when I went to Chicago to visit Alice, my favorite aunt, she filled me in about her secret life. I was taken aback by what she told me, although Alice had always been the topic of gossip in my family."

"What kind of gossip?"

"Things like: she dressed a bit on the masculine side, hadn't gotten married yet, had joined the Women's Army Corps (WAC) and flew bombers during World War II."

"Bombers?"

"Yes, but not for combat. Her assignment was to fly every aircraft in the military's inventory, from biplanes to B-39s around the country. She also flew planes with balloons attached so the boys could use them as target practice."

"Noncombat missions with bullets flying every which way? Sounds like they were – I don't know – expendable."

"Renate, the woman did it for three years and her outfit was decorated for meritorious service – not that her family attended any official ceremony. But there was a bright spot. Early on during her stint as a WAC, a new pilot named Edith was relocated to the command post. The following weekend, they spotted each other at a women's bar off base and 'sparks flew,' as Alice put it."

"Didn't she know what Edith was right from the start?"

"No, the bar was where women found out for sure. It was too dangerous to talk about it on duty, she said. Anyway, they got involved."

"How did they keep their relationship going?"

"Both were pilots in the same unit, which gave them reason enough to be seen together on the base."

"Actually, I meant – um–"

"How did they keep things going sexually? According to Alice, they had to be careful. I didn't probe any further on that one. When the brass got wind that "those kinds of women" were among the troops, they threatened to discharge them. Trouble was, the military needed every able-bodied pilot, because the men were in combat abroad. But the real hard part of the relationship came after the war ended. Who wanted to hire female pilots after the war then? Without jobs, Alice told me with tears in her eyes, Edith and she had no way to build a life and were forced to separate. In the end, after their discharge, both had to move in with their respective parents, who expected them to marry and raise kids. Edith caved in to the pressure and got hitched."

"How did Alice survive such a loss?"

"My impression was, she never got over it. Alice didn't play the fit-in game and settle down as her folks wanted. Sometime in the late 40's she met a woman named Ginny at the Circle, a bar in Northwest Indiana about 30 miles south of Chicago. She and Ginny hit it off and it didn't take long before they'd moved in with one another."

"That seems daring. Two grown women living together?"

"Well . . . yes, and no, Renate. My aunt lived in Hammond, Indiana, and worked in a nearby steel mill. She and Ginny were afraid to live in conservative Indiana, so Alice moved to Ginny's place in Chicago. But even then, they had to pretend to be roommates."

"How did your aunt's family react to Ginny?"

"Alice's folks lived in a town four hundred miles from Illinois, so she was spared the parents around the corner number. But, there were the holidays. In our Bennett clan, everyone gathers at my grandparents' place in Ohio for Thanksgiving and Christmas – with spouses and children, of course – unless you're Alice. And as I found out later, she was forced at those times to make some serious compromises."

"Did she stay home?"

"No. I recall the time when Alice arrived for Thanksgiving without her 'roomie' as the family referred to Ginny. By then, since Alice was almost thirty, the relatives started to ask more pointedly about her romantic life. She said she hadn't yet found a suitable guy. They must have known Ginny existed, but of course none of them – me included – had any idea she and Alice were emotionally involved. Then, when Ginny took sick over the next holiday, Alice made up an excuse to skip Christmas – volunteer work in a Salvation Army soup kitchen in Chicago – so the story went. My parents thought she'd lost her mind. Unsuspecting little me thought it was a neat idea. I was bored silly at these events by then."

My mind drifted back to holidays with my family: Papi, Mama,

Hildegard and Detlev, Ruthie and Theo. Christmas without them seemed almost more than I could bear to think.

Robert touched my forearm. "Is everything all right, Renate? Shall I stop?"

"I'm sorry. I got a little emotional hearing about family and holidays. Please go on."

"One time, she told me, Ginny did finally decide to visit Ohio for Thanksgiving weekend. I was in grad school working on my dissertation. Alice told me that they both felt so excluded and uncomfortable from the endless palaver about relatives and family that they left early and drove back to Illinois. Alice called some like-minded friends and invited them over to celebrate a real Thanksgiving dinner. At least they were 'among family,' as she put it." I think that was the last of her visits with Ginny. Alice found out that a gay person becomes an 'automatic outsider,' as she put it. You stick with those who understand that."

Robert excused himself.

This demands another beer. It seemed Robert was somehow compelled to tell me all this. I wondered why.

Robert returned and adjusted his seat to face me. "Sorry to unload so much on you at once. You're actually the first person I've told about this since Alice broke the story to me. Maybe I wasn't ready or able to tell anyone about it before you."

"Robert, I just have to ask. How did this stuff from Alice impact you?"

"I felt terrible. My aunt had been in pain for years and I was unaware of it until she told me her secret that day? And did I speak up for her after that? No. It reminds me of a Dietrich Bonhoeffer quote: 'I did not speak out when they came for the Jews, and when they came for me, there was no one left to speak out for me.' You can rephrase that quote with 'homosexual.'"

I needed to freshen up at the loo.

*   *   *

I saw Robert look up as I reached the top of the stairs. *He looks eager to continue our talk.*

"Do you think that Alice's story prompted an interest in sociology?"

"Could be. For example, I do wonder what the social consequences of Christine's openness are for her – and Rosie at the club."

"She's in a relationship with *Rosie*?"

"No, that's over, although I hear they're still on good terms."

"I see."

"Is there something wrong, Renate?"

"No . . . I just need to digest what you told me. It gives me a lot to think about."

"Mind you, Renate, I'm not gay myself."

November 6 – home after meeting Robert at the Kranzler
It was good to see the Robert again. This time with him was sure different than the Panther. Life is full of surprises – now I learn Christine is gay, not to mention Robert's Aunt Alice. I don't know what to think or feel. Everyone seems to be keeping little secrets. How come I didn't see the handwriting on the wall with Christine – did I want to ignore it? Should I have said no to coffee with her? What will she think about me if I accept her dinner invite? Maybe I hope down deep she won't call so I can get on with my grant.

Life with a man – Robert, for example – might just be easier. I could imagine the predictable and comfortable life: no made-up stories about relationships at office parties, both of us professors with ample vacations and job security. And he's a nice fellow – but all the same, I'm not sure I'm attracted to him. Dieter, on the other hand, seems to be a great guy . . . but is under treatment that takes him in and out of the Charité in East Berlin. Is any man the perfect one?

I looked at myself in the mirror before turning in, and wondered who was staring back at me.

19

After a restless night, I awoke to a sun, hardly visible through the clouds, dashing all hope that it could fend off winter. The grayness matched my growing pensive mood after seeing Robert at the Kranzler. I lay there, not able to shake the story Robert had told me about Alice's secretive relationship and how she'd felt forced to lie about her partner. Why did Robert bring the subject up in the first place, anyway? Did he want to warn me, turn me off to Christine, air his heart, or what? I don't know Alice at all, but if even half of what Robert reported was true, then the world that awaits a lesbian was one filled with deception, despair, broken hearts, cruelty, and wrecked lives.

Maybe it would be better, as the bard used to say, not to know something rather than endure the slings and arrows of outrageous fortune, bear the whips and scorns of time, the oppressor's wrong, the pangs of *despised* love? Aye, that's the rub. I realize that many, if not most people despise the attraction I feel.

I remembered Marge Tierney from the U of C, who'd suffered with me through a soporific three-hour Friday afternoon seminar on Klopstock. One week, during our break, I noticed she looked distressed. She confided in me she'd just dumped her friend Sally to marry a man, because she found it too painful to keep up the charade. Of course I was dumbfounded, unaware Marge had been in a relationship with a woman. Up to now, I hadn't thought much about her story. If anyone had asked me about it, I might have said it seemed like she had come to her senses and gone on with her normal life. I don't know I feel that way now. That would be caving into the oppressors' bigotry. But does this mean I want to take what seems to be a masochistic, forbidden path?

*   *   *

There was a knock. Probably Schulz.

"Yes?"

"Frau Kaufmann is on the phone," he said.

I opened the door a crack.

"I'll return her call at the phone booth."

I threw on a coat and raced down to the street.

"Hello." Her deep, mellow voice sent my nervous system into an uproar.

"Hi there. How are things?"

"It's gotten crazy at the office. Two women took off on holiday, and my boss is insisting I stay on extra hours to make up for lost work. But we'll be at full force in a couple of days. I'm ready for a dinner out – say on Saturday?"

"Yes, that would be wonderful."

"Great! I'll phone you to firm up details."

November 7 – after Christine called
Now it looks like dinner with Christine is for real! I feel weird, but also excited. Gosh, I've gone out to eat with Laura, and enjoyed it – looked forward to it after a busy week. But a restaurant with Christine has a different ring somehow. She foots the bill – there's no Dutch treat. I guess you might call it . . . a date?

Was there room for my feelings somewhere in Heine's ironic take on *Liebe*, or love? Back in my apartment, I opened up his *Book of Songs* and reread the second verse from the poem entitled "Du bist wie eine Blume, so hold, so rein, so schön" – the one Dr. Fuerstenberg had chosen for my dedication.

Mir ist, als ob ich die Hände
Aufs Haupt dir legen sollt',
Betend, dass Gott dich erhalte
So rein und schön und hold.

I feel as if I ought to place
My hands upon your head,
Praying that God may keep you
So lovely, noble, and pure.

What a gorgeous little poem. Was Heine ever really in love? I wondered. What *is* love, anyway? Is it to touch a woman's hair and ask God to keep her pure? Where are there poems like this from one woman to another?

The next day an invitation came in the mail from the US Embassy to all grantees in Berlin to attend a reception on Friday evening, November 22.

It's time for a little chummy contact with the other Americans in town. Maybe Robert will be there.

When I went outside to mail the RSVP form, I phoned him at the office.

"Bennett."

"Hey, Robert, Renate here. It was good talking with you at the Kranzler the other day."

"I hope I didn't overwhelm you with all my family stuff – and about Christine. I didn't mean to upset you."

"Not to worry. I'm digesting it."

"So what's up, Renate?"

"I just received the embassy reception invitation. Did you get yours?"

"Uh, yes."

"Are you attending?"

"I wouldn't miss it."

"Good! Maybe we could connect there."

"Why, sure. Why don't we look for each other at the open bar?"

"Okay, then, see you on the twenty-second."

*   *   *

At breakfast, Schulz came to my table. "A Herr Westerheim is on the phone. Would you like to use the office while I finish up with breakfast? My assistant is on an errand."

"Okay." *I'd have a bit of privacy.*

I downed a last sip of coffee, hurried to the office and sat down next to the telephone stand. My heart pounded.

"Renate Seiler."

"Eberhardt Westerheim here."

"Thank you for returning my call."

"My pleasure. Are you settled in, I trust?"

"Yes. I feel quite at home."

"Good. I imagine you're finding Berlin looks much different than it did at the end of the war."

"Indeed it does."

"I'll be in Berlin for a brief period of time, and wonder if we could meet at my place for *Kaffee und Kuchen*, say tomorrow around three o'clock?"

Oh no, what about my dinner date with Christine?

Perhaps noting my hesitation, Westerheim said, "Early next week I'm off to England. If it's not convenient, we could wait, although it may be a while before I'll be in Berlin again."

Darn. I've got to strike while the iron is hot and reschedule with her.

"Dr. Westerheim, I'd be delighted to come tomorrow."

"Excellent." He gave me directions to his flat in Schöneberg.

I decided to take the streetcar to the Charlottenburg Palace and gather my wits. Diary and guidebook in hand, I set out for my trolley stop on Kantstrasse, and exited opposite the palace entrance. Destroyed in World War II, the royal residence was one of the first public structures rebuilt in 1945, at the initiative of architect Margarethe Kuhn. The enormous statue of Kaiser August on horseback provided a dramatic view of former Teutonic grandeur – but, sadly for me, in stark contrast to an ugly wall visible at almost every turn.

Passing a school class, two women with baby carriages, and an occasional tourist armed with a camera, I proceeded around the side wing to the formal gardens handsomely laid out with decorative plants, chalky white baroque statues and expansive lawns.

For contemplation, I recalled, nothing would surpass the restored Belvedere, or teahouse, a slender, proud, two-and-a-half-story baroque edifice at the very rear of the grounds. Not many visitors around here yet this morning. I took in the reflecting pond across from the Belvedere's elegant bronze cupola and walked over to a nearby bench.

November 8 – at the Belvedere in Charlottenburg
Just the smell of the pond on this beautiful day evokes my walks here with Papi after church on Sunday. We followed a regular routine: I took along a small bag of seeds to feed the birds, while Papi smoked a cigar. Then we'd take a different route home through the gardens, to Mama and dinner.

All this nostalgia – what's the point? With Berlin in the midst of a facelift, it isn't the place I left. I wrestle with the feeling that the shores of Lake Michigan, the Indiana Dunes to the south, or even the hills and farms of southern Wisconsin are where I really belong.

And re: the past – now that I've got the invite from Westerheim, do I really want to dredge up skeletons? Why not just let that rest, move on and finish the PhD! Do I need any more revelations about my father? Would they be of any use? Perhaps I should focus on the work I came here for and be done with it. Travel some – maybe visit Hildegard again, fly to Spain with Laura before my flight on to Chicago. I haven't heard from her about the trip, but it's probably too early to book a flight, anyway. As the Germans say, the one with the choices is the one with the torture.

I looked up as a pair of swans glided by. Such elegant birds, unruffled, as it were, enjoying their ride. Sitting at this pond settled my nerves. I knew I'd made the right decision: Westerheim was just too important for now, and I didn't want to postpone my need to talk with him any longer.

But wouldn't Christine be miffed if I canceled at short notice? What if I lost her friendship? Unfortunately, I had no way of knowing what would happen with Westerheim. What if I was late, or couldn't face a dinner and conversation after our talk? Stirring up the past, I didn't know what I might find. I needed to beg off the dinner date with a good story. That wouldn't be so hard, would it?

I walked to the café behind the palace, bought some postcards and, over coffee, wrote Laura on the back of the same view of the Belvedere I had just enjoyed. I told her about the diss and Bautsch. *Not an altogether inspired card this time.*

* * *

Under my door, I found a message that Christine had called. For sure that was to firm up the dinner arrangements. I sat on the bed and mulled the situation over. What story seemed plausible? A headache? A glance from the stairwell window showed no one was in the phone booth. I trudged out to the street; every step made my feet feel like lead.

"I'm so sorry, Ren," Christine said, after we exchanged hellos, "but I have to cancel our dinner for tomorrow. It's my mother's knee. She sprained it today, and I have to take her to the doctor and help her get around this weekend. I'll make it all up to you, I promise!"

"I understand, Christine."

"I'd rather spend time with you than playing nurse."

"Don't worry. Just take good care of your mom."

"I'm glad you aren't annoyed."

And I'm relieved I didn't have to make up a story after all.

* * *

Westerheim lived in the mid-city district of Schöneberg, full of avant-garde apartment complexes, neighborhood architectural delights and bustling squares. The district had been home to scientists Einstein and

Busoni, singer Billy Wilder, and writers Else Lasker-Schüler, Nelly Sachs and Christopher Isherwood. Last but not least, Schöneberg was the birthplace of Marlene Dietrich. Its cemetery afforded Marlene a final resting place, in spite of her long exile from Germany in Paris. At the end of Dietrich's life, her song "Ich hab' noch einen Koffer in Berlin" became prophetic.

Tucked in a narrow street, Westerheim's *Altbau* apartment house had a massive entrance door with an expansive foyer and wide wooden stairs. Out of breath after five flights, I paused in front of the bronze door plaque reading "Dr. Westerheim" and rang.

A trim man with graying hair and glasses, dressed in a beige sweater, brown corduroy slacks and jacket with leather elbow patches, opened the door.

"*Guten Tag*, Fräulein Seiler. Please come in." Westerheim took my coat and beckoned toward the living room.

"Please make yourself comfortable. I'll be just a moment."

I sat and placed my briefcase down beside me at a large oak tea table on which two place settings, a coffee warmer and an assortment of pastry on a silver tray shared space with an art book on English formal gardens, a silver candlestick and a carafe. From floor to ceiling, the wall opposite me was filled with neatly arranged books. A grand piano draped with an embroidered silk throw stood in an open area to the right, and a lamp stand flanked by two overstuffed chairs occupied the opposite wall. In a far corner a majestic green tiled stove stood with cut logs stacked underneath.

Westerheim appeared with a porcelain pot of coffee, placed it on the warmer and took a chair opposite me. He took a porcelain cup and filled it, handed it to me, and poured himself a matching cup. "I recall Edda loved her *Kaffee und Kuchen*."

"Yes, she certainly had a sweet tooth." *It warms my heart to hear Mama's name.*

"Please select a pastry you fancy," Westerheim said.

"The fruit torte looks wonderful."

He removed a slice and served it with the pointed part facing me. After helping himself to a portion, he settled into his chair.

"It's so nice to be able to entertain you at my place. Normally at this time, even on a Saturday, you'd find me working late at a research lab near Lake Krumme Lanke. A location near the water sounds lovely, but you don't get to see much of it during the day."

"So you're on vacation now, Herr Doktor?"

"A permanent one, actually. I've just retired, so I'm footloose and fancy-free. I'm glad I was able to invite you over for a visit before I travel to England – and then, after Christmas, a longer trip to 'down under,' as they say in Australia."

"Sounds wonderful – all those kangaroos and Aborigines."

"I've planned to see the sights, of course, but also to explore the country. Since the Wall, Berlin feels a little cramped."

After we finished our coffee and pastry, Westerheim showed me a few of his objets d'art in the living room: a silver hunter's knife; some rare commemorative coins, with the likeness of Heinrich Schütz, a Reformation composer; and an old book in English on climbing the Colorado mountains. "Would you care for a bit of peppermint schnapps?"

I nodded with a smile.

"All right then. Let's move to the overstuffed chairs. I had them shipped from England some years ago."

Westerheim moved a pipe holder to his side of the lamp stand and filled two tiny glasses from a carafe on a small oak table between us. He sat down and crossed his legs.

"So, Fräulein Seiler, what brings you to Berlin?"

"I received a DAAD stipend to complete my dissertation, and was granted a year's leave from my college position in Wisconsin."

"Congratulations. An academician! Great stuff."

"You flatter me, Herr Doktor."

"I'd be interested to know your focus."

"The interpretation of German Romantic poetry in the Third Reich."

Westerheim's eyebrow arched. "I'm intrigued. How did you settle on that topic?"

"Papi used to read me poems before bed, and also performed

them as lieder. How could I not have fallen in love with them? My Aunt Hildegard told me you had attended a couple of her soiree evenings, but I must admit I don't remember you."

"*Ach ja*, I think you were too young. I visited the time you and your father acted out Goethe's poem 'The Erlking,'" Westerheim said. "Unforgettable!"

"Papi and I rehearsed the poem many times. He wanted it to be just right."

Westerheim reached for his pipe. "Do you mind?"

"Please go ahead." *Is there anyone in Germany who doesn't smoke?*

Westerheim filled his bowl from a tobacco pouch on the table.

"Apropos of Goethe's poem, I should think 'The Erlking' could be interpreted as a parable of Nazi Germany."

"A parable?"

Westerheim paused to light his pipe. "Could it be your father sensed a connection between German Romanticism and Nazi idealism?"

"Absolutely!" I felt my excitement mount as we headed right into my dissertation topic. "Take the Nazi adoration of Wagner, especially the *Ring* – a double-edged sword that intoxicates but also destroys. I think Nazi ideology instilled a false idealism in the German soul. As Nietzsche said, '*Ja! Ich weiss woher ich stamme, ungesätigt gleich der Flamme, glühend verzehr' ich mich.*' (Yes! I know where I come from, insatiable, like the burning flame, I consume myself.)"

Westerheim pursed his lips. "How easily a dream can turn into a nightmare." He fell silent, then leaned forward in his chair. "I'm curious, Fräulein Seiler. May I ask why you contacted me?"

Oh, good. I don't have to beat around the bush.

"After Mama died, I found two letters in our old trunk. On my way to Berlin, I stopped to visit Aunt Hildegard and asked her about them. One of those letters was from you. She suggested I might contact you to find out more."

"Yes, I indeed received a note from Hildegard." Westerheim paused, rubbed his hands together, and folded them. "Fräulein Seiler, your father and I were such long time friends. May I call you Renate?"

"I'd be honored!"

"Let's drink to it." Westerheim removed the schnapps glasses and took two wine goblets from a cabinet. From a carafe of red wine on a cart, he poured us each a glass.

"*Zum Wohl*, Renate."

"Cheers, Eberhardt."

After a few sips of wine, I felt bold enough to ask, "Eberhardt, before we get to the letters, what can you tell me about my father?"

Westerheim looked up at the ceiling, then over at me. "Kurt was my boyhood pal in Stramberg, a Moravian village near Poland. The Seilers, as you must know, came from generations of weavers and horsemen. I shared Kurt's love of horses and worked with him in the Seiler family's local stable. Your grandparents, Jakub and Katherina, let me borrow tack and riding gear when Kurt and I took the stallions for a run. But this was nothing compared to the kindness they showed me as time went on.

"When I was twelve years old, two terrible things happened: my mother died of pneumonia, and Jakub and Katherina moved to Dresden with Kurt for the sake of his education. Perhaps you can imagine how adrift I felt without my mother and my best friend. A year later, when my father died in a riding accident, your grandparents came to my rescue. They invited me to live with them until a foster family took me in from amongst the congregation members at St. John's, the Seilers' parish in Dresden. Kurt and I were thus able to attend the same gymnasium.

"After our graduation, we were both accepted to the University of Leipzig – Kurt in mathematics, and I in physics – and roomed together during our studies there. But in our last year your father met a young woman named Edda Habermann on a summer's visit to Dresden. After Kurt received his PhD, he asked for your mother's hand in marriage, and I was his best man at their wedding. Edda and Kurt made a lovely pair. At the reception Hildegard, Detlev, Theo, Ruthie and of course your grandparents Jakub and Katharina shared our happiness with a toast to the newlyweds. Kurt and Edda bought a house in Berlin, where Kurt had received a professorship at the Humboldt University. I remained in Leipzig, so I didn't see him so often as before."

"Did you stay in touch with Jakub and Katharina after your graduation?"

"Yes, I visited them once before they emigrated to Sweden in 1935."

"Mama always spoke highly of Papi's father and mother. I'm so sad that I never got to meet them." *So many losses in my life. When will they ever end?*

"Fine people they were, indeed. Their departure was a blow to your father, but ultimately a wise choice for the two of them. At least in a neutral country they could live out their lives in peace."

Westerheim fell silent. "I think a fire would be in order." While he was busy preparing the stove, I turned to the book about climbing the Colorado Rockies. Several notes in German with almost illegible signatures were scattered on the inside cover of the book. Not wanting to appear nosy, I leafed on through the book itself, which featured pictures and portraits of the Rockies, with information on their height, weather conditions, and the proper gear for climbing them.

Westerheim walked toward the stove, selected another log and stepped back to survey his budding fire. Soon the whole room glowed from his creation.

"Did Papi ever talk to you about politics and the rise of the Nazi party?" I ventured.

"Before Hitler came to power, we had many discussions. It seemed to Kurt that most Germans responded to the Nazis like the frog in a pan of cold water."

"A frog in a pan of cold of water?"

"Yes. Throw a frog into a pan of hot water, and it will instantly jump out. But if you place a frog in a pan of *cold* water and heat the water slowly, the frog won't react until the water gets hot. By then, it's too late. Unlike the frog, Kurt sensed the ominous signs of war heating up, and felt the Nazis warranted close scrutiny."

"Did Papi ever consider emigration, as my grandparents did?"

"No. Kurt felt he should resist Nazi ideology from within, and by the mid thirties, the political scene had worsened, especially for full-blooded Jews or non-Aryans. In 1935 the Nuremburg racial laws removed basic civil rights from all Jews."

"I don't understand. What do the Jews have to do with Papi?"

"What I am about to tell you, no one knows except me. Do you know the name of your great-grandmother on your mother's side?"

"Sarah. She died two years after I was born."

Westerheim took a deep breath. "Your great-grandmother Sarah was a Jew."

"Jewish? No, that can't be. Oma Ruthie was my godmother!"

"In Jewish law, Jewishness is inherited through the mother, which would meant your grandmother Ruthie was a Jew as well. Ruthie was baptized and confirmed in the Lutheran church. On matters of faith, you can choose either to embrace it or not. For example, Felix Mendelssohn was a Jew but embraced Lutheranism."

"I had no idea that the definition of Jew was so complicated."

"The Nazis came up with their own definitions to determine whether you were Jewish or not. On your mother's side, Sarah and Ruthie were Jews by inheritance, and Lutheran by faith. But no one knew this because their identities remained a secret even to them."

My mind raced in confusion and disbelief. Ruthie and Sarah didn't know they were Jews?

"Often a Jewish heritage only came to light after Hitler's laws decreed people had to produce a 'clean' ancestry traced back to 1750. When Kurt examined both your family trees and church records, he discovered that Edda was descended from a Jewish grandmother and thus mother. Kurt knew Edda was out of danger for the time being, because she was married to an Aryan and had three Aryan grandparents. He feared it could only be a matter of time before the Nazis would reclassify your mother – and thus you – as Mischlinge, or mixed race Jews, which would have been enough to seal your fate."

"All this was going on and I knew nothing about it!"

Westerheim added two small logs to the fire and returned to his chair.

"I assume you knew your father had a professorship at the Charles University in Prague."

"I did. Why?"

"In December 1944, while I was on a short leave from duty to visit my foster parents in Dresden, I wrote Kurt that I would be in the area. When I arrived in Dresden there was a letter from him asking me to meet him at the Vyšehrad Cemetery Gate in Prague at ten thirty, two days later. A funeral was scheduled for eleven – and I was to be dressed in black. All this puzzled me, but I complied.

"At the entrance, I saw a man approach me from across the street. I hardly recognized Kurt – save for his smile. I was distressed to see the deep lines in his face and how haggard he looked. We walked around in the cemetery, far away from the funeral service, stopping at a memorial plaque for Jan Hus, the great Czech reformer. Kurt wept when he quoted Hus's last words, 'Truth will prevail.' At that moment he confessed to me that he had joined the Nazi party."

"Papi a Nazi? How could he do such a terrible thing?"

"Believe me, Renate, I asked myself the very same question. Your father's fears about reclassification proved to be justified. To protect you and your mother he made a deal with the Nazis. Kurt was commissioned an officer in the German army and agreed to ferret out Czech resistance for the Nazis in Prague. In turn, the Reich would not take actions against his family. The fact that Kurt spoke fluent Czech and had a research professorship provided perfect covers."

My mouth turned so dry I could barely speak. Westerheim brought me a glass of water.

"But things soon took an unexpected, and tragic turn. Kurt told me that two Czech patriots, Jan S. and Martina M., were caught and hanged as an unintended result of his undercover work. When your father realized the deaths he had caused, he joined forces with the Bohemian contingent of the plot against Hitler. Through a contact in England, he arranged to reveal German activities in Prague to the headquarters for Czech resistance in London. At the same time, he began feeding the Nazis false information about local resistance."

"My God!" Eberhardt's words sent shock waves down my spine. *Papi became a Nazi spy to save Mama and me? So that's why Mama and I had to stay behind in Berlin!*

"There's more to the story, Renate. It may shed light on the kind of man your father was. When the attempt on Hitler's life failed in 1944, the Führer, in a fit of rage, ordered everyone remotely involved in the plot to be rounded up. In the winter of 1944-45, someone found a diary that implicated a number of conspirators. Among them was a colleague of Kurt's. It was only a matter of time before the Nazis would catch up with your father, too. Kurt told me he'd hatched a plan to crash a plane in a mountainous region in northern Bohemia. On the day we spoke at the cemetery, your father was finalizing details for what would appear to be a routine flight to that area."

I felt my world crumbling before my very eyes. So my father had gone against his conscience for us, and then taken his life as penance. I struggled to regain my composure. "Eberhardt, here is a letter I found in Mama's trunk." I pulled the envelope out of my briefcase and handed it him.

Westerheim put on his reading glasses. "Oh so German, this letter, so matter of fact, sent by the official German government office, or WASt, which was responsible for notifying survivors of soldiers who were killed in action. At least Kurt was clever enough to make the authorities think his plane crash was an accident.

"When I was returned to Germany after the war, I combed the German and Czech aviation records and discovered that scattered pieces of Kurt's plane had been found by hikers trekking through the woods near the small town of Haber. I sent your mother a letter to that effect with my condolences. It provided Edda and me with some closure as to where Kurt lay."

I could not control my tears. That letter was the other document in Edda's trunk.

Westerheim handed me a handkerchief, and we sat for a while in silence, while I dried my eyes.

"When Kurt and I parted at the conclusion of the funeral service, we were careful not to shake hands, for fear of being watched. I knew this would be my final goodbye to him. At his departure, he entrusted me with his last thoughts. Up to now, I have abided by his wishes not to tell anyone in your family."

"Why did you decide to reveal all this to me now?"

"Because I thought you deserved to know the truth. Your father died a heroic death and hoped history would pardon his actions. I can only trust that history will teach us never to succumb to such evil again." Reaching into an inside coat pocket, Westerheim took out an envelope and removed a yellowed sheet of paper. "Please allow me to read aloud your father's goodbye, which I've done hundreds of times to myself over these eighteen years." Westerheim leaned forward.

My dearest ones, as my life draws to a close, I will leave with one piece of unfinished business: the chance to say to the families of Jan and Martina that I am sorry, and to ask for their forgiveness. Should they ever read this document, they might say it is justice being served. So be it.

Likewise, I cannot receive forgiveness from you, my own family. I grieve over the imminent separation from you, my faithful wife Edda, and my darling daughter Renate, whom I will never see grow into womanhood. After much thought, I recognize that it is I who must forgive myself for my evil deeds committed against my conscience.

I remember Jesus on the cross asking God – his father – to forgive the evildoers who had nailed him there. As an evildoer, responsible for the death of innocent people, I ask God for absolution. As a Christian, I know to take my own life is wrong, I cannot undo what I have done, but with death, my evil deed will end with me.

I depart with a heavy heart and entrust this letter to my longtime friend Dr. Eberhardt Westerheim for safekeeping, until such time that history is prepared to read it.

Keep me in your hearts dear Edda and Renate. God bless you.

Dr. Kurt Seiler

Prague, January 25, 1945

When Eberhardt handed me the letter, I could see, in spite of my tears, that Papi's beautiful penmanship had remained strong and firm, even in the face of death. My father's words transported me to a place beyond grief, remorse, and guilt.

Westerheim placed his hand on my shoulder.

"Eberhardt, please excuse me if I close our talk today. I'm exhausted."
"Shall I see you to the train?"
"I'll be fine."
He accompanied me to the foyer and helped me on with my coat.
"I hope this won't be our last visit."
"Of course not."
Now there were more questions than answers.

*   *   *

I spent a restless evening and night, then awoke early, numb, with no desire to get up. After an hour, I found myself pacing around my room like the panther in Rilke's poem of the same name – a curious irony.

At the last possible moment, I went down to Sunday breakfast to get a bit of sustenance. Everything tasted like sawdust. No amount of makeup could hide my puffy eyes. Schulz either didn't notice or refrained from comment. Safe again in my apartment, I propped myself up on my pillow and turned to my diary.

November 10 – almost noon, in bed
Yesterday I visited Eberhardt. Finally I had the key to the mystery about Papi. From his information, my father was a Nazi, a collaborator – and a member of the Czech resistance, who engineered his own death. It's almost more than I can grasp.

I was touched while Eberhardt described Papi – it seemed as if he had opened a buried treasure and found a rose. But how could my father, the rose, have joined the Nazi party? Didn't he tell me to act in accordance with my conscience, and be guided by a higher power? Can I forgive him for his collusion with the oppressors, especially when his wife – my mother – was a Jew? Could my father's involvement in the Stauffenburg plot against Hitler ever right such a wrong?

Nevertheless, his contrite letter means so much to me. I feel his presence, his love and bravery.

Most important, I can forgive him for wanting to save Mama and me.

I paused and looked out the window. The church bells rang twelve times. I flashed on an afternoon walk with my father. I must have been between five and six years old. We'd just come from a Lenten service in the memorial church, where the pastor had spoken about Christ's sacrifice and death for us. On the way home, we passed some charred ruins on Fasanenstrasse.

"Papi, what happened to this church?"

"Some mean people burned down the Jewish temple."

I recall he looked over his shoulder behind us.

"Why?"

"Sometimes people do hateful things to Jews, and hate is always wrong."

"Why don't people like the Jews?"

"Because they're afraid. They think Jews are different."

Papi stopped and took my hand. "You must promise me, Reni, to be brave and always say the truth, no matter what!"

At the time, I didn't fully understand what was happening in my country. Only later, when I began to study German history in college, did I comprehend the intense hatred Hitler and others had felt toward Jews, homosexuals, and people who deviated from the Aryan "norm." Papi knew it, too, if only too late.

I continued with my diary.

Eberhardt's revelations give me something else to fathom: my Jewish heritage. I wondered what to call myself – a Christian, a Jew, a doubter in search of answers? Is there a place for me in all of this? Where is my spiritual home – in a tarnished former homeland? No, important discoveries keep me here. Maybe it's fate – a journey I hadn't really planned on.

To commemorate the Papi I loved and remembered, I bought a potted red rose from the neighborhood florist and placed it on the windowsill.

20

With a long walk, followed by a nap and some cleaning, I tried to recover a sense of normalcy and sanity. My thoughts bounced between Westerheim and Christine, the former a repository of dark family secrets, and the latter a woman who loved women.

The revelation that my father had betrayed innocent people brought me to my knees with shame and anguish. I tried to picture Eberhardt's rendezvous with my father in the Prague Cemetery. I didn't dare imagine what had gone through Papi's mind as he prepared to crash his plane.

*   *   *

I had to get out of my four walls, and decided to see *The Deputy: A Christian Tragedy*, a play by the contemporary German playwright Rolf Hochhut. Some critics took the position that Hochhut's play attacked the Catholic Church for Pope Pius XII's ostensible failure to denounce the Holocaust. After the play, I didn't know what or whom to believe. But I questioned how the Pope could have withheld comment on such an important and tragic issue. Was silence in fact golden when it came to the Pontiff? Not if I understood the playwright correctly.

To whom, then, would the Pontiff turn for absolution? And, for us mortals, is there a deed so horrible it can't be forgiven? These questions plagued me, enough to distract me from thoughts of Christine.

*   *   *

I was checking for mail in the office on Monday morning when the phone rang. Schulz placed his hand over the mouthpiece. "It's your cousin, Fräulein Kaufmann."

My heart began to race. "I'll take the call here – it won't be a moment."

Schulz grunted and handed me the receiver.

"Hello Renate. I'd like to confirm our dinner invitation. Is Friday still good for you?"

"Sure. Where would you like to meet?"

"At the Piccola Italia – near my place, just across from the U-Bahn station at Gneissenaustrasse. Shall we say six thirty? I'll be coming directly from work."

"Fine. I look forward to seeing you."

I rushed to my room and shouted, "Yippee," tossing my pillows up in the air. I sat down over a bottle of wine and a box of Kleenex.

*   *   *

The rest of the week was quiet, full of work and thankfully uneventful. I got through two more afternoons with Bautsch. I don't know how I looked, but Bausch asked me repeatedly if everything was all right – uncharacteristic for a German – and an East one, at that. I told him I'd had a couple of rough spots in one chapter to clear up. It seemed to do the trick – better than to mention that my father was a Nazi – or that I'd accepted a date with a woman.

When Friday rolled around, I spent the better part of the day with chores, a walk and a bath. Then I had to pick out appropriate clothes, since Christine would be dressed up. *Okay, I can match her with heels and all.* Ugh. I had just two pairs to choose from: leather boots for the theater, but too fancy for tonight, or a somewhat clunky but comfortable pair for my German class. The clunky ones won out.

I took the U-Bahn and arrived across from Piccola Italia at 6:30 on the dot. By the looks of it, the restaurant was a neighborhood affair, tiny, with red-checked tablecloths, salt dishes on the table, a well-worn, plastic-encased menu, and the ever-ubiquitous Cinzano bottles with candle drippings. I was the first guest and picked a table at a side window away from the view of the U-Bahn station.

A rotund man appeared wearing a long apron dotted with various shades of red.

"*Buona sera.* I'm Giuseppe. Is it just you for dinner?"

"I'm expecting a friend."

Giuseppe nodded and went to the bar.

Maybe a glass of wine in advance would help calm my edgy self. I was about to order when a smartly dressed Christine in pointed high heels entered the restaurant with a bouquet of flowers.

"*Buona sera*, Giuseppe."

"*Buona sera*, Signorina."

They exchanged kisses on both cheeks.

"Bring me a vase with water for the table, *no?*"

"*Certamente.*" Giuseppe disappeared into the kitchen.

Christine handed me the bouquet. "Nice to see you." She kissed me on the cheek.

Her cologne flared my nostrils, and adrenaline raced through my body. "The roses are beautiful, but you didn't have to go t–"

"Oh, yes, I did. I stood you up, and besides, I can't resist buying flowers for a beautiful woman." Christine removed her coat and hung it on a wall peg. "Been here long?" She took a seat opposite me.

"No, I just got here."

"Glad I didn't keep you waiting." Christine slipped her high heels off and put her feet on the rung of the chair. "Eight hours of these idiotic shoes drive me up the wall. I'd planned to stop at my place to change, but instead just dropped into an *Apotheke* to pick up a pack of tissues." Reaching in her purse, Christine pulled out one and daubed her nose.

"Did you catch a cold?"

"Yeah, caught it from one of the women in the office, but not through direct contact, of course."

Giuseppe brought the filled vase to our table.

"May I?" Christine reached for the flowers, arranged them in the vase and set it in front of me.

The fragrance in this bleak wintry season lifted my spirits.

"Let's begin with drinks!" Christine turned in her chair to Giuseppe at the counter: *"Vorrei del vino rosso – una bottiglia."*

Giuseppe took a bottle of d'Abruzzo off the bar shelf, came to our table and uncorked it. He poured a small amount into Christine's glass.

"E bene?"

Christine held up her glass. *"Perfetto."*

"Allora un antipasto, per favore," she said to Giuseppe.

"Come al solito?"

"Si." She turned back to me. "Giuseppe knows I always order the usual."

Christine poured us our wine. *"Salute!"*

We toasted to our health.

"It seems like eons ago since we saw each other last. In my defense, I've got lots of work piled up at the office, and there's always my mom, as you know. I don't want you to think I was avoiding you."

"I've been busy, too."

Giuseppe brought a plate of marinated small peppers, olives, pepperoni, provolone and fresh mozzarella.

We talked about Christine's Monday gig and work stress, and my adjustment to Berlin life, including, with one notable exception, my trips to East Berlin.

"I can't imagine any need to go *Drüben* even once. Something must be awfully important to take you to that hellhole, pardon my language."

"Every week I meet with a Dr. Bautsch at the German State Library."

"Hmm."

Giuseppe picked up our antipasto plates and returned. *"Cosa vuole da mangiare, spaghetti bolognese come d'abitudine?"*

"Si, per favore."

"E la Signorina?"

"Would you care for anything in particular tonight, Renate?"

"Oh, surprise me."

"This restaurant features Roman cuisine. I think *saltimbocca alla Romana* would be just the ticket."

"And that is . . .?"

"Veal with prosciutto and sage. *Saltimbocca* means, 'jump in the mouth' in Italian. They prepare their food from scratch. Does that sound okay?"

"Heavenly!"

Giuseppe left with the order, humming with delight at our enthusiasm.

"Christine, I didn't know you could speak the language!"

"It comes from a trip to Italy. I learned the most important words. I love Italian cuisine – it's so simple and direct in contrast to German fare. See the sawdust? In Italian restaurants it's on the floor; in German ones, it's in the food."

I laughed. *Good sense of humor she has.*

After we finished our first glass of wine, Giuseppe brought us our entrees, and with a hearty *Buon appetito* went to the counter to meet three arriving patrons.

In spite of the Italian cuisine, I paid little attention to the food. Seeing Christine again had turned my brain to putty, and my senses took over. I was half afraid she'd want me to come up to her place, and kept the conversation away from that direction.

As we finished the meal, Christine, perhaps intuiting my thoughts, said, "I'd love to invite you up for a nightcap, but with this cold, it's a no go. I almost canceled again, but I couldn't bear to opt for bed rest."

"I understand." My heart sank as my body tightened up in disappointment.

The coffee and dessert tasted like the proverbial sawdust beneath us.

Christine put on her heels and signaled Giuseppe for the bill.

"I'll walk you to the train station."

At the station, she gave me a hug.

"Get well soon, Christine."

166

"I'm motivated."

From the bottom of the stairs, I looked up and waved goodbye.

November 15 – at home in bed, after dinner with Christine
I'm full of conflicted emotions. I was impressed by Christine's savoir-
faire. Giuseppe was certainly charmed by her (what man wouldn't
be?). But it seems either she goes away on a trip, is tired, or now gets
a cold. Is it all a game? If so, why does she want to get together? Can
I trust that she'll contact me again? I'd like a less topsy-turvy week.
When she pulled the cold number tonight I thought I'd sink through
that sawdust floor. How can I be disappointed and scared at the same
time? Couldn't stop my vagina from twitching, and all the while, I
tried to think of reasons not to go home with her. Would I actually
have gone to her apartment? My frustration level is through the roof,
and my confusion puzzles me.

On the positive side, I <u>love</u> the bouquet – smelled the roses again
and again during the ride home. Has anyone given me flowers before?

I put my diary away and went to the kitchen to make a cup of
Sleep and Nerve tea – a quaint German marketing term for valerian.
Why was I so on edge? Christine's roses, I realized, had triggered a
memory. It was a hot, humid June afternoon, the day of my graduation from IU, and the silly mortarboard kept sliding around my
sweaty brow. People were even carried off the field that day!

I was so relieved yet down that Mama hadn't come after all. How
thrilled I was when Madame Manksi came through with a bouquet of
roses after the ceremony! The next day, before I boarded the afternoon
Monon Railroad for Chicago, I brought the flowers over to Madame
Manski's house. It just seemed too much to carry with all my baggage.
We both cried when Manski set the bouquet on her piano.

*   *   *

On the train, the boisterous mood of grads shouting up and down
the corridors contrasted with my sad mood. The ride to Chicago felt

so different now than four years ago when Mama drove me back –
then a scared little freshman-to-be, maybe a little anxious about what
to expect in the coming fall – and now feeling like a young bird
nudged from my nest to take flight I knew not where. Maybe IU was
the first place I had thought of as home. Good bye my Alma Mater,
you will always have a special place in my heart.

I watched as the Southern Indiana hills gave way to the grain
fields and seemingly endless moraines of central and northern Indiana. Which is worse, to be the one who goes or the one who stays
behind? There are so many partings in Romantic poetry. Most often,
the woman remains, while the man takes off for parts unknown. This
day in Bloomington, I was a woman saying goodbye to another
woman, Dorothee Manski. I'd never thought about it that way until
now. Would Mama and I ever be able to visit her sometime in the
future?

21

C hristine phoned me at breakfast.
    "Hi, Renate."
"How's the cold?"
"Fair, but a long herbal bath and some rest are doing the trick."
"I had a good time last night."
"I did, too. You know, Ren, I forgot to mention yesterday that I've got a day off next Wednesday – a holiday here in Germany. I should be fine by then. Would you like to visit Grunewald for an afternoon?"
"That sounds like fun."
"Wonderful. How about I meet you outside Pension Schulz at noon?"
"Sure."
"See you on the twentieth."

November 16 – after a call from Christine
Another invite – to Grunewald with Christine – sounds just like what the doctor ordered. I haven't been on a walk with anyone except Dieter since Vogelweide. On the other hand, I can't say there's been a shortage of absorbing conversation. The description of Alice's clandestine life and Eberhardt's revelations were certainly not light fare. Maybe I should crawl into a hole, get on to my research and skip the social stuff. Laura told me often enough that Leos need people. What about the rest of my chart? What secrets does it contain? I'll ask her the next time I write.

The next morning, I asked Schulz what the holiday the following week was all about. He explained that *Buss und Bettag* was some Lutheran observance to do with repentance and prayer. Once a year seemed enough to do the trick.

While perusing the newspaper, I found an organ concert scheduled at the downtown memorial church the evening before the holiday. I decided to attend.

*   *   *

The illuminated memorial church immediately improved my stubbornly somber mood about Papi. The theme of the concert was repentance, and began with the chorale text by Michael Franck "*Ach wie flüchtig, ach wie nichtig*" (Ah, how fleeting, ah, how inconsequential is our time on earth), set by the baroque composer Georg Böhm. I was moved by a lovely alto solo, "Buss und Reu" from the Matthew Passion – which describes the soul, torn in two by guilt and repentance, offering the suffering Jesus a balm from its teardrops. The aria set the theme for three chorale variations on those words by Johann Sebastian Bach, Johannes Brahms and Max Reger.

In spite of the serious mood of the evening, I left soothed and renewed.

November 19 – after the Buss und Bettag *concert at the memorial church*

What is repentance, anyway? Do I have anything to repent? If so, what? Maybe Catholics have the advantage here. They can ask the priest in that little booth to absolve them of their wrongful thoughts and deeds. But does forgiveness avail me anything? I could go right out and sin again, and return to the confessional for a second helping. What sticks to the ribs after you confess and receive absolution?

I ate some chocolate – with no guilt – and looked up the origin of the verb "repent" in my German dictionary.

So "repent" has to do with being sorry. What am I sorry about? Should I be? I think the heart plays a big role in repentance – certainly more than actions or deeds. I remember the liturgy that I used to sing as a child, "Create in me a clean heart, O God, and renew a right spirit within me." But what does a clean heart mean – an about-face in life, a change of mind, a change of self? I wonder what a Lutheran pastor would say if I mentioned it. Does consorting with a lesbian jibe with a clean heart? Can she have an unclean heart because of the women she loves? And Papi, what would he think about me if he knew? Mama's take on the subject was clear – in so many words. That bit about having time for boys – she gets it from her upbringing, I guess. Then where do I get <u>my</u> take on love? Heredity? Environment? Fate?

The anticipation of my walk with Christine tomorrow, uncertainty about the path I was on, and my exposure to Lutheran repentance all flowed together in a cocktail of torn emotions and troubled sleep. My weeklong funk lifted at last, and excitement crept up and down my body.

I dressed in a variation of my Panther outfit, this time a more casual approach – jeans, a blouse and vest seemed right. I put on a wool jacket and left. Outside, the weather obliged for the day as the dirty clouds of Berlin ceded to a steel-blue sky. Christine was sitting on a park bench across from the pension. She had on stylish black slacks, a turtleneck sweater, a leather jacket and shades. As I approached, she rose to greet me, propping her sunglasses on her head.

"Hey there. It looks like a fine day for a walk."

"I'm all yours."

"Be careful what you promise, Renate."

Grunewald Forest proved to be a top choice for Berliner outdoor activity, since no stores were open for Christmas splurges. Our walk began amidst couples, families, and people with pooches in tow.

"I know a side path for more quiet." Christine steered me to the left. She picked up a pinecone and aimed for a tree. The cone struck the center of the trunk.

"Hey, how about that?" she said.

"Great shot, Christine!"

We walked on.

At a clearing, we stopped to soak up a brief burst of sunshine.

I got myself together to ask more about Christine's family without seeming too nosy.

"Have you got any sisters or brothers?"

"Just one, my brother Georg. And you?"

"No."

"A bright, single child, *nicht?*"

"What about your father?"

Christine's smiled faded.

"Dad died in the battle of Stalingrad in 1942. It came as a horrible shock, even though I went through many of my classmates losing their dads on the eastern front. You never get over it when it's your own father. And your pop?"

"Papi was a university professor in Prague. Because of his scientific work, he was exempted from the draft."

"How lucky!"

"Depends on how you look at it. Papi died in a plane crash in Bohemia a few months before the war ended."

"I bet that was tough."

"What do you mean?"

"Well, your pop avoided combat, but died during the war anyway. Ironic, wouldn't you say?"

"I suppose so." *No need to correct her impression.*

"We school kids prayed the war would end soon, so no more of our fathers would have to die."

I told Christine about my evacuation to Aunt Hildegard's farm in 1944, while Mama stayed in Berlin.

"Mutti and I didn't have anywhere to go," Christine said. "It was hard enough to survive the Allied attacks, but when you're a teenager, it makes life seem so crazy, confusing and unfair."

She went on to talk about the lack of food, the air raids, and the invasion of the Russians at the end of the war – rape, plunder, hunger and humiliation. Penniless and half starved, her mother had earned money as a *Trümmerfrau*.

So we'd both lost our fathers, and our mothers had lived through the bombings in Berlin. The war bound us together, as it had torn our families apart. But I'd been lucky to evacuate. I came away with the better deal.

We walked on to the end of the forest path, where the sun met us again.

"Do you mind?" Christine slipped her arm through mine. Her cologne, spicy and sweet, wafted through her jacket.

"How about we stop for a hot drink, Ren? There's a nice place just ahead."

"Okay."

"I'll lead the way."

We rounded a bend. As if by magic, a restaurant came into view with a wide flagstone patio. A cool breeze wafted over the lake as the sun prepared to slip beneath the water. Most of the patio furniture had been stacked and moved to the side. A few tables remained; patrons hovered under the eaves around heaters.

"We have our choice. Downstairs, you can still see the sun set. We could also go upstairs for a better view, or watch from the patio and enjoy a hot drink to stay warm. What'll it be? You're an outdoor girl, I'll bet."

We took the one empty table with a heater, next to the entrance. Christine ordered a hot chocolate and whipped cream, and I took tea and rum with lemon and cinnamon.

Our conversation picked up where we'd left off. We traded stories about life after the war: Chris had gone to a trade school to learn accounting, but also found work at the club. It didn't pay much. She'd saved money by living with her mother until she got her first real job at an accounting firm after the German economy began to recover in 1949.

I described the huge adjustment of emigration to America – my struggle in high school as a foreigner with rudimentary English skills at first.

Christine listened and nodded. "It's not easy to move so far away from home. It sounds like you felt scared and different from the others."

"You hit the nail on the head."

I began to feel comfortable in Christine's presence, as if we had known one another for years. My afternoon with her gave me a sense of home, and of *Geborgenheit* – so hard to translate: a sense of being supported, cradled, like a child in a bassinet.

"Christine, tell me about Rosie. From what I observed at the Panther, you seem to be good friends."

"Rosie?" Christine's eyebrow arched. "I met her in my mid twenties at a women's event – she was dressed a notch above everyone else. We got to chatting, and I learned she had a husband and a kid. Then she invited me to her place for coffee."

"She *invited* you?"

"You don't think normal women make passes?"

"I . . . I don't know."

"Of course I couldn't resist an offer from a beautiful woman like her. I'm not a nun, you know – haven't made it to age thirty-six without some fun. Tell me, have you ever known anyone . . . like me?"

"You mean –?"

"Different?"

Not unless I include my friend Marge. So she's as much as admitted it. Oh, my God, I'd hoped it wouldn't come up.

"You look surprised. Didn't Greta and Ulli tip you off? One minute next to them and there's no doubt where they stand. Many of us keep our alternative life to ourselves. But we're everywhere. Think of an 'old maid' aunt, a single woman, maybe two adult women who share an apartment – good chance they might be homosexual women."

Hmm. Phyllis and Edna were two women in their forties who'd attended Trinity Lutheran in Chicago. Edna lived in Missouri and came to visit Phyllis one weekend every month – which included church. It was touching the sweet way they interacted with each other, holding hands. It had never occurred to me they were . . . possibly homosexual until this moment.

"Some, like Rosie, get married and don't even know they prefer women. From the way she talked, I guessed her sex life wasn't great. I took the hint, and our attraction changed all that. Turned out her husband was away on some business trip or other. Things – well – just happened.

"Not that we were able to see much of each other – she had a house in Zehlendorf – you know, in the southwest corner of the city, super ritzy – and I lived an hour away in scruffy Kreuzberg. So we got a kind of long-distance affair under way. Rosie was afraid to drive her fancy Audi to see me. Couldn't blame her, actually. Besides, she couldn't leave her boy alone."

"So how did you manage to see Rosie?"

"Most times, I went to her place by subway and bus. She wouldn't pick me up at the train station out of fear that someone would see us together, so I'd take the bus to a stop that was close – but not *too* close – to her house.

"Now, her place was gorgeous – lots of rooms, veranda, garden – even a sauna. You name it, the works. We took long walks, made love all day when we wanted, when Michael – that's the husband – was gone."

"And how did you handle it with Rosie's son?"

"Timmy would spend the night at a school chum's. Sometimes Rosie's neighbor would babysit for our rendezvous. That made our life a lot easier. It's difficult to develop a relationship when a kid could burst in any moment."

"How did Rosie end up at the Panther?"

"You mean, how did she end up in a place like that?"

"Um, I didn't ..."

"It's a fair question, Renate. One day, hubby came home early from another of his trips, waltzed right into the bedroom and caught us in the act. You can imagine the furor. He kicked Rosie out that day. She slept at my place for a week before she could decide what to do next.

"Michael divorced Rosie and took custody of the kid. Rosie was out a house, child, and financial support. There are two standards for extramarital affairs in the eyes of the court: okay if you're making it with the opposite gender, no good if it's with the same. Funny, though, Rosie hung on to her marriage, even when she found out Michael had stepped out on her since almost the day they married.

"I got her the gig at the Panther, but our relationship fizzled after that. I think she blamed me for her troubles. I'd say she took the first step. But we are often seen as the bad guys."

"I'm sorry."

"Not necessary, Renate. But, you should read the price tag before deciding on the article, *nicht?*"

I was amazed at how easy it was for Christine to talk about her homosexual life, whether pleasurable or painful.

"Say, how about you come up to my place for a nightcap? The night is young, and it's still a holiday. My friends always refer to it as *Bus' und Bett Tag.*"

We laughed at Christine's clever pun – "Boob and Bed Day" was one I'd never be able to teach my students.

"Be right back, Ren. Nature calls."

Christine had that characteristic Berlin humor, poked fun at German cuisine, sexual mores – and the audiences at the Panther. Robert's assessment was right on: she was a charmer. But now I knew she was "different," and it unnerved me. If I responded, did that make me abnormal? I didn't know the rules.

* * *

Christine sat down and folded her hands. "So what's your answer, girl?"

What did I want to do – stare at a boring book in my room to-night? It offered no attraction. I couldn't pinpoint what drew me to Christine, and didn't want to figure it out – at least not for now.

"All right, but just for a nightcap. I'm kind of tired."

"You intellectuals need to let go and relax. Imagine, working stiffs like me don't get another day off for five weeks!"

22

We exited the U-Bahn in Kreuzberg – a funky district of Berlin near the Wall – and walked about ten minutes past gritty concrete apartment houses sprinkled with pockmarks. Trash blew across the street, oblivious to German demands for cleanliness.

"I'm at number 31 – just ahead."

We entered a dimly lit stairwell, and I held on to the railing as I followed Christine up the stairs.

"Trust me, there always some lights burnt out, but I know every step along the way. I grew up in this apartment house, and shared the place with my mother until she found herself a ground-floor flat in Reinickendorf."

Christine searched for her key to the lone apartment on the fourth floor and led the way into the foyer. On tiptoe, she hung my coat on the last available hook of a wooden rack draped with a long black trench coat, woolen scarves and a poncho, and tossed hers over mine.

"No need to wait for a cue." Christine opened the door to the living room. "Just go on in and make yourself at home."

Christine's place smelled of cigarette smoke. I sat down with my arms folded.

"It's cold, I know. I don't turn on the heat when I'm gone all day. It'll warm up soon – you'll see. Need a sweater?"

"No, I'll be all right."

With a toss of her head, Christine fluffed up her hair, just like in her nightclub act. *What a beautiful, shiny mane!*

I looked around. A far wall was covered with a huge oak buffet; beneath a slanted ceiling were a faded beige corduroy couch, a tea table with inlaid Oriental tiles and, to the side, a pine bookcase with one shelf missing.

"Not elegant, but it's home. Got most of my furniture from Georg after he finished his doctorate. He figured it wasn't suitable for a Herr Doktor. But I'm not proud. Objects aren't that important to me."

She emptied two Cinzano ashtrays filled with cigarette butts into a nearby wastebasket.

"I hope you don't mind if I smoke." Her raised eyebrow rendered any protest useless.

"Go right ahead."

I walked over to a pen-and-ink sketch of Christine in a strapless sequined dress. "Who's the artist?"

"Angelika's her name – studied at the College of Art here in Berlin. They had to do a project outside of class, and she asked me if I'd pose for her. It was hard to sit still so long – don't know how these models do it. It's a good likeness, don't you think?"

Christine's eyes appeared too big. But the artist had captured her soft look and graceful body. "Christine, you should get the drawing framed. It's too fine to be tacked up. The corners are curled!"

"I try to keep clear of shoulds. Maybe I'll get around to it sometime."

Christine led the way into the kitchen. Dishes were stacked in the sink; cups and magazines lay helter-skelter on the table, although the stove was clean. A beat-up black teakettle stood on one of the back burners.

"I guess you're not home much."

"You mean because the place is messy?"

"No, I ..."

"That's okay, no offense taken. I hate washing dishes, but I've got other qualities. Now, my mother – there's your typical German hausfrau. Couldn't sleep at night if there was a dirty dish in the sink, newspapers scattered around or furniture out of place. I take after my brother. We both used to litter, and Mutti could be counted on to pick up after us, even if she complained about it. I think it filled up her day."

"I know what you mean; my mother was the same way."

"Your mom's no longer alive?"

I nodded.

"When did she pass on?"

"It was last June."

"I'm sorry. How come you didn't mention this on our walk?"

"It didn't come up, I guess."

"Hmm."

"Could you tell me where the bathroom is?"

"Follow me." Christine escorted me down the hallway.

After Christine left, I daubed my face with cold water.

When I emerged, Christine was standing in a doorway. "This way for the tour. Come have a look at my pièce de resistance." She waved me into an oblong bedroom with high ceilings. Three bay windows, each with a thin lacy curtain, flanked a large bed covered with four fluffy pink pillows and a mauve woven Greek bedspread depicting nymphs playing a lyre and a flute. Maroon drapes hung gathered at either side.

"Where did you get this, um, unusual blanket?"

"In Crete on a trip with a friend. It was a present."

The walls were a matching deep maroon, with a large poster of Manet's *Blond Woman with Bare Breasts* displayed over one dresser.

Two candles in glass containers framed an ornate mirror with strands of beads cascading down the other dresser. A small Turkish rug covered the top, with several pieces of gold jewelry spread around – like some sort of shrine.

On the night table there was an old wooden radio with big knobs – the kind my parents had listened to in my childhood.

"So what's the verdict?"

"It's . . . unique! You have a knack for decoration."

"Knack!" Christine's shoulders shook as she laughed.

"I'm sorry," I stammered. "I like your eclectic style."

"You're right; not very German, for sure." Christine reached for some clothes piled on a chair. "Excuse me while I change. Why don't you have a seat in the living room? I'll be out in a minute. The couch is probably the most comfortable place to sit," Christine said over her shoulder.

Her voice reminded me of chocolate – rich, smooth, sweet and dark – the kind that nurses you through a difficult time.

*   *   *

The living room radiator began to clank.

Christine appeared in a polo shirt and blue jeans. *God, she must be impervious to her freezing temperatures at home.*

"My taste in wines is eclectic, too. I love French labels. Would you like some Alsatian Crémant? It's like champagne – quite elegant."

"Just a little, please."

Christine disappeared into the kitchen and returned with a bottle in an ice bucket and two flutes. She pulled out the cork, tilted the bottle and poured us each half a glass.

"Zum Wohl!"

I recalled how my mother had taught me how to toast – hold your glass by the stem, look your counterpart in the eye, toast, drink a sip, and then put down your glass.

The Crémant trickled across my tongue. "Tastes wonderful, Christine."

Christine lit a beeswax candle on the tea table, extinguished the match with a snap of her wrist and sat down on the couch with her feet stretched out on a footstool.

"There's a whole case of this stuff in the pantry – a gift from my esteemed brother. I cleaned his apartment while he defended his dissertation. So he's got the PhD – and me, the bubbly and the better deal."

Putting my glass on the tea table, I turned to face her. "So what do you do?"

"I work in an accounting firm. Mostly, I'm in charge of the payroll. It involves lots of detail work, which I hate, but it pays the bills.

How about you, Renate? How do you keep yourself afloat?"

"By teaching German at Ryan College, a four-year school in the US. It's like a German *Hochschule*."

"A teacher! I should have known."

"How's that?"

"Oh," she shrugged, "I guess it doesn't matter what a person does. I take folks where they're at." Christine's expression brightened as she walked over to a record player and rummaged through albums and covers scattered about. "Hey, this is a holiday. Time to celebrate. How about some music? Does *Light Classics on the Guitar* sound okay?" She held up an LP jacket for approval.

I nodded. The mixture of her Crémant and the quiet music calmed my nerves.

Christine reached for a soft pack of cigarettes on the lamp stand. "Dammit" – she turned the pack upside down – "don't desert me in my hour of need." She wagged her finger, and one last bent cigarette popped out onto the table. "All right," Christine put her hand on her hip. "Let's get straight who's boss here. I have another pack in my dresser drawer that's just as testy."

She sat down on the sofa, lit her cigarette and let the smoke out through her nose, arching her neck to blow the rest away from me.

"Did our discussion today make you uncomfortable?" She picked up the bottle and topped off my bubbly.

"The story about Rosie?"

"Look," Christine propped herself up against the armrest, "I grew up in the same world as you. But I turned out different. I know it bothers some people. Me, I'm okay with myself. But it's new territory for you, right?"

"Right, I guess." My tongue got stuck in my throat.

"I understand. Guess I forced your hand. Let's be honest, it's not often a woman comes to the club alone. I mean you weren't draped on the arm of your friend or whatever. And you accepted my invitation to go to Grunewald."

She reached for the bottle in the ice bucket. "Would you like some more?"

"Just a drop or two."

"I think the walk in Grunewald was special – cool, dry air, a blue sky, and the company of a nice woman." She moved closer to me on the couch and grazed my arm with her outstretched hand. The warmth of her touch flowed down into my back and chest.

"Look, I'd better . . ."

"Better what? Do you want me to stop?"

I tried to get up, but my body refused. I tucked my legs underneath me. Off in the distance, church bells rang nine times.

"You're shivering, Renate! Let yourself feel. Don't keep it in." She pressed me to her.

The lamp behind her head highlighted the reddish tinge of her hair, accenting her full lips and deep brown eyes through the glow. I hadn't ever looked a woman in the face so close up without feeling embarrassed.

"This is crazy, I need to go."

"Shh, shh, shh."

Was it wrong to be excited? *Please, let this conversation end right now.* At the same time, I felt trapped.

"Renate, you're a sweet person under that teacher's hide. I'll bet no one has been tender with you." Christine ran her hand through my hair and smoothed it back. "Your mother might have been preoccupied with the house, and your dad didn't know how to express his sweet side – least that's the way it often is with fathers."

I tensed up.

"Trouble is, Ren, what a woman needs, she doesn't always get – love, care, security – that kind of stuff. You're probably one of those softie teachers. You listen to students' problems after class and make sure they know where they're headed."

Better deflect where she's headed, Ren.

"I have a question for you, Christine. Did you know we'd already met before I encountered you on stage?"

Her eyes widened. "Where?"

I smiled. "In an ice cream store where I used to work in my teens."

"I don't follow."

"When business was slow I listened to records of Marlene Dietrich, especially 'Falling in Love Again.' So when you sang that very song, it took me back to those years. I was fascinated by your costumes, also."

Christine's face reddened.

"Which one appealed to you?"

"The tuxedo."

"You know, Ren, the first time you came to the Panther, I noticed you right away. And tonight, you seemed even more responsive to my singing."

I looked at my watch.

Christine got up. "Are you hungry?"

I didn't have to run away just yet – but did I want to find out what would happen after all this booze?

23

Christine emerged with Westphalian ham, cheese, pickles, Dijon mustard and a loaf of rye bread on a wooden platter. "Got these goodies at KaDeWe."

I sampled the mustard with the tip of my knife. "The Dijon is wonderful." I slathered it on my bread and added some ham.

After we finished, Christine looked through her albums and put on a record of forties slow dance music. She escorted me to the living room floor, cupped my left hand in hers, and slipped her right behind me.

I used to walk home from school to avoid dancing with my class-mates. In my freshman year, I'd go to the basement to watch the kids jitterbug to the jukebox at lunchtime. I must have looked like the school wallflower.

"Just listen to the beat," Christine whispered in my ear. She was a skilled lead, and after a few false starts, I got into the rhythm and steps.

"Where did you learn to dance so well, Christine?"

"*Ach*, I picked it up from Georg. He used to practice with me before he went with buddies to the local dance hall. He wanted to impress the girls. I never thought it'd be of much use to me until I met Rosie."

"Is she a good dancer?"

"You bet, but you have natural talent." With that, she swung me around, embracing me when the music slowed. A rush excitement coursed through my body. It was a lush moment, like before a Midwest rainstorm, when the sky was tinged with hues of magenta and grey.

Christine grazed my cheek with her mouth, and we danced until the music stopped. Short of breath, I sat down on the couch.

Christine joined me and caressed the nape of my neck. "I like to explore," she whispered. Her lips brushed my mouth. They felt soft and sensuous against mine, full of promise and resolve.

I had to admit I liked it with her in command.

"Ren," Christine pushed back my hair and whispered into my ear, "I want you to stay over tonight."

"I don't know – I'm not sure I should."

With a warm caress, Christine traced the edges of my lips with the tip of her tongue, and kissed me. I closed my eyes as Christine glided across the insides of my cheeks and the roof of my mouth. She thrust her tongue deep inside and pulled me into an embrace.

My tongue joined the dance in her mouth, reveled in the touch of her soft and vulnerable parts. I didn't want this moment to end; I felt moisture between my legs, and I ached to go on. We kissed and kissed again, until I couldn't count the times anymore.

Christine eased me onto the couch and cradled me. In slow motion, she removed my vest and put it on the arm of the couch. One by one, she loosened the buttons on my blouse, then reached behind my bra and unfastened it. "Your breasts are beautiful." She watched my nipples grow erect as she pressed them between her fingers.

She seemed to have all the road maps and guidebooks, just as she did on center stage. I tried to resist, but Christine responded by stroking me with her pelvic bone. A wave of desire flowed through my vagina as it began to throb.

"Stay right here, I'll be back." She walked down the hall to the bedroom.

My arms and legs felt like they'd turned to lead. *This is enough. What am I going to do?*

A few minutes later, Christine returned and took the needle off the record, switching the player off.

"Please come with me." She gathered up my clothes and took my hand.

A candle was lit on the dresser and the bed sheets turned back.

Motioning me to lie down, she took my vest, blouse and bra and put them on a wicker trunk. After removing my stockings, she turned me on my side. Her hand ran over my partial nakedness down to my feet and ankles. She unzipped my jeans, reached inside them and massaged my lower abdomen.

My whole body trembled when she stopped.

Christine took off my jeans and panties and added them to my clothes on the trunk. Still clothed, she lay down beside me. I could feel the heat of her body radiate through her shirt as she alternated between squeezing my labia and stroking my anus with her knee.

My vagina pulsated in response.

Christine followed along the crevices of my buttocks, shifted me onto my back and rubbed my pelvis.

I reached out to pull her closer to me, but she kissed me on my stomach and traced just above my pubic hair with her fingertips. Sliding alongside me, she inched up my torso with her nose and climbed on top of me. For what seemed like a delicious eternity, she kissed me. I groped to enter her mouth with my tongue, but she kissed me even harder. Spreading my knees apart, Christine touched the inside ridges of my vagina and increased the thrusts with the angle of her fingers deeper into my cervix.

The insides of my mouth became hot and dry. My body surged toward her. "Oh Christine, please don't stop, don't stop."

At times of great passion everything sounds so trite.

Christine continued to press in and out of my womb. "Fragrant," she said, smelling her fingers.

I wanted to touch her vagina, but she lifted my arm to my side. In one last furious vaginal thrust, she bit my nipple until I cried out in pain. A wave of passion washed over me and with a piercing snap rippled through my abdomen. Aftershocks followed. I began to shake and fell back on the sheets, drenched in sweat, followed by peaceful release.

Christine leaned over to wipe my eyes with the corner of the pillow. My whole body went limp as she put her arm under me and cradled my head and shoulders. Now prone, Christine reached beneath her panties and stroked herself in measured intervals. Seeming to sink into her own world, she moved down to massage my clitoris, and timed her strokes to mine in a rhythmical pas de deux.

"Oh, Christine, this feels so good, but . . ."

"You think somehow it's not quite right? I understand. It isn't easy to accept the emotions we have – at least at first. That's the way it was for me, at any rate."

The street had grown quiet. Christine lit an incense stick and placed it in a curved wooden holder on the dresser. I let her hold me as we listened to tolling from the nearby steeple reverberate eleven times through the night air.

"There were times at midnight I cursed those bells!"

A pang coursed through me as I imagined Christine in another's arms. I turned my head to the side.

"Oh, I'm sorry, sometimes I can be so insensitive."

Christine moved down my body, spread my labia apart, and inserted her finger into my vagina. Another surge of passion coursed through me.

My chest heaved as I clutched one of the soft pink pillows under my arm. My body went from a hot flow to a warm rinse.

"God, how I've missed you."

"And I've been waiting for you, too, *Schatz.*"

Christine opened her dresser drawer and pulled out a pack of cigarettes. We lay in the dark until the glow of her cigarette dwindled to an ember.

"Thirsty?"

"Yes. I'd like some water, please. But what about you?" I asked.

"Stay there and savor what happened."

Christine glided down the hallway to the kitchen. I heard the tap run, and the refrigerator door open and close. Draped in a knitted shawl, she came back with a bottle of water and two glasses still dripping, and placed them on the nightstand.

"Take off the shawl. Please. I want to see you in the candlelight."

Christine laid the shawl on a chair.

Her breasts were small, round and erect, her abdomen firm, like a singer's. I held the covers aside and welcomed her cool body next to mine. She sat up, and I leaned my head on her shoulder.

"How are you doing now?"

"Oh, Christine, I don't know what to say!" I lowered my head to her breast.

"Be right here with me." Christine removed her panties and began to undulate. Her chest grew hot and flushed, speckled with red dots. She took my hand and placed it over her clitoris. "This is where I'm most sensitive – it's in a different place than yours. Use just one finger, for now. Go into me slowly."

It was uncharted territory. I marveled at her warm liquid interior.

"Put another finger in me. Push in and out, hard!"

Her vagina shuddered.

Christine relaxed her body and focused her energy on herself. She billowed up inside, her breathing turning heavy and deep while she continued to masturbate. Her chest lifted as she approached orgasm.

I touched a nub at the end of her vagina.

"Yes, yes, yes, that's it, go on."

I felt her tremble with anticipation and penetrated her until she climaxed with a sharp cry.

Christine lay quietly for several minutes, then got up and covered us both with a soft blanket. As bells rang midnight, she turned out the light.

*   *   *

I woke to the smell of coffee wafting from the kitchen.

Christine poked her head through the door. "Ren, you're awake already! Stay right there." Dressed for work, she sat on my side of the bed and kissed me on the forehead. "I've bought you some goodies at the corner bakery."

"Don't tell me you've got to leave so soon!"

"*Schatz*, if ever I wanted to phone in sick, today would be the day. But I have payroll to get out, and I'm late already." She bounded down the stairs with a booming *"Guten Tag"* to someone below.

My brain was racing. Was I ready to accept the consequences of our night together? Did this mean I was – one of them?

A note was taped to the bathroom mirror.

Ren,

I had to get to work. You looked so peaceful – I thought it better not to wake you. See you soon – perhaps on Sunday? Give me a call.

Love,
Christine

She didn't know I had other plans.

24

Nine o'clock already! It felt odd being in Christine's sexy bedroom all alone. I walked through the house. Her cosmetics
piled up behind the basin, the fragrance of perfume and hairspray,
along with stale cigarette smell in the living room didn't contribute to
my staying there.

I threw on my clothes, downed one of the Danish rolls Christine
had bought, and gulped a mug of coffee from a thermos she'd left for
me. After making the bed, I penned a reply on the bathroom mirror:

"Thanks for your note and the breakfast! I'll phone you. Renate."

*   *   *

As I entered the pension foyer, Schulz stepped out of the elevator.

"*Ach, Guten Morgen*, Fräulein Seiler. Sorry, but breakfast is all
cleared away." He glanced down at my sturdy shoes and jeans.

"Not to worry. I had an early appointment with a colleague." *I bet
I look like a teenager facing a parent after a late-night binge.*

I stopped at my box in the office. A thick airmail envelope jutted
out of my box – from Laura, no doubt. I ripped it open and found a
photo of her, taken for the college yearbook. *Sweet face that Laura has,
intelligent eyes and curly red hair.* I turned the photo over.

"Renita, I miss you and our weekend chats around the fire. Love,
Laura."

In an attached letter, Laura lamented her new committee assignment – Special Events – probably one the administration would have slapped me with. *One reason to be relieved I accepted the grant.*

"There goes my Thursday night pizza and beer," she continued. Department gossip was juicy, involving Tanya, a Russian teacher who'd raised eyebrows with her sympathetic remarks about the Soviet Union. No mention of much else, except that Laura's father had undergone surgery for a slipped disk.

I stashed Laura's letter in my correspondence file, cleared away notepads and papers, put on my comfies and lay across the bed, thinking about my night with Christine. I put my fingers to my nose – even the faint fragrance of her vagina made mine throb in response. I imagined she was lying with me now, listening to guests head out to explore Berlin.

I showered, dressed and collected my notes for an afternoon stint at the GSL. I didn't relish the transition from Christine's erotic bedroom to a reading room, but Dr. Bautsch had promised to obtain some books on Aryan views of German Romantic archetypes for me from the university in Leipzig, and I knew he'd be miffed if I didn't show up. Thank goodness the library had later hours on Thursdays. I could use the trip over to East Berlin to regain my momentum.

*   *   *

The minute I boarded the train at Friedrichstrasse, thoughts of Christine emerged to plague me. I decided to relax with a bath. No need to cook – there were enough snacks, sausage and booze for tonight.

November 21 – Pension Schulz, on my bed
Just finished a lavender soak to help me absorb my overnight with Christine, I can't figure out what happened. Honest! I wanted to leave, but somehow it didn't turn out that way, not that I'm disappointed. Does one night with a woman mean I don't like men? I'm unsettled, excited, and puzzled. Do I dare admit how thrilled I was

to lie in someone's arms – especially a woman's – especially in Christine's? I'm not sure what this means. Has my life taken a sharp turn and all the preparation I've done to secure my future go poof in a few hours? I'd better not mention Christine for now, at any rate. Have I betrayed my very best friend? How can one be so conflicted about a night that left me tingling with passion?

Wake up, Ren. In no time flat there's too much on my docket: tomorrow a reception of US grantees at the American Consulate. Robert will be there. On Saturday I'll need to work ahead on my diss to make room for Sunday lunch with Dieter – at least I think it's still on; haven't heard a word to the contrary via Heinz. To top it all off, Christine wants to see me on Sunday as well – not possible, in spite of our night together. All these commitments drive me up the wall. Maybe men are better at the juggling act than women. How do writers and artists manage their numerous peccadilloes and still keep their creative life afloat? Somewhere I read about a musical director in LA who had so many affairs, he was able to book concerts in the act, so to speak.

PS – Christine's apartment – the state of the place! This woman really needs a housekeeper.

I dozed off and awoke to find the diary on my lap. It was close to nine o'clock. *What do I say to Christine? I dread turning her down for Sunday. Better phone her first before she tried.*

I threw on some jeans and a sweatshirt and headed to the booth on the street.

"Kaufmann."

"Hello, Christine."

"Hi there. Did you find everything okay after I left?"

"Yes. It was great to find your goodies, especially the coffee."

"So . . . how's it going today, Ren?"

"I don't know, I feel ..."

" Like you just went down a roller coaster?"

"I guess you might say so."

"Scared?"

"Yes – no – it's hard to describe. Kind of shaky, maybe."

"Maybe we should talk about it. Is Sunday all right with you?"

"Christine, I can't make it to see you this weekend, like you wanted. I've got a prior commitment."

Her silence unnerved me. Finally, she said, "I'm sorry. What did I do wrong?"

"Not a thing."

"Okay, I can read through the lines. You're hesitant."

"No, Christine. I want to see you again."

"Phone me when you're ready."

"Please don't be angry."

"I'm not. Talk to you soon, Renate."

Her receiver clicked.

After an almost sleepless night I still was wrestling with my frustrations and sensations about Christine. No matter, I had to knuckle down on the Thanksgiving deadline for Dr. Blume. After an hour I gave up. Too much went racing through my mind.

Maybe it would do me good to mix with a group of Americans for a change. I reached into my dresser and pulled out the tops I'd chosen for Christine's show; the embassy reception would be the perfect occasion to combine them with my plaid skirt and new scarf. I inspected my combo in the mirror. Not bad. A minor accomplishment: I'd assembled this without Laura!

25

November 22, 1963

When I walked into the large reception room, I spotted Robert talking with an Ivy League type at the open bar.

"Hello, Renate, good to see you. Meet Frank. He's a Fulbright scholar from Yale, studying at the Free University."

"Nice to meet you, Frank. How does the FU measure up to Yale?"

"Pretty good on academics and even better for the bars and night-life."

"Frank knows more of them than I do. In fact, after the reception, we want to hit a few nightspots – boys' night out, right, Frank?"

They laughed.

"Like to join us at that table near the podium? We've saved a seat for you," Frank said.

"I'd love to." I took an hors d'oeuvre from a passing waiter's tray.

We were milling about with drinks when a man pushed his way through the crowd to the podium and tapped on the mike. "Ladies and gentlemen, my name is Harold Fredricks. I regret to inform you that President Kennedy has been shot during a motorcade in Dallas and has been taken to a local hospital."

A gasp went through the hall.

"As yet, there is no further information," Fredricks said. "We ask you to remain for now in the reception area."

The sudden transition from a pleasant reception to utter disbelief sent shivers through my body. I took a seat next to Frank and Robert at our table. For a few minutes, I couldn't say anything. Thoughts raced through my head. Was the president badly injured? Who would do such a thing? I imagined mayhem in Dallas – a limo racing to the hospital – or a shootout as people ducked for cover.

"Only in Texas," Frank finally muttered through his teeth. "And I'm *from* Texas."

Waiters came by to offer us more finger food, but we all declined. My stomach growled at the smell of steak tartare on garlic bread. Attendees whispered to one another at their tables, but no one appeared to know what to do.

After what seemed an eternity, Fredricks came back and announced to us that Kennedy had just been pronounced dead.

At first, no one uttered a sound.

Then questions began to pour in, a cacophony of voices all trying to shout over one another, but the consul raised his palm. "The reception is officially canceled."

We stood up to leave.

"The Russians are behind it," Robert said, flinging his arms around me. "Renate, I hate to leave you at a time like this. Can we drive you home?"

"That's all right. I have a return ticket on the S-Bahn."

Outside on the way to my train, I watched Frank and Robert drive by in the direction of the university, and felt sad, numb, and alone.

*   *   *

The train ride to Savignyplatz was eerie. I wanted to stand up and shout, "President Kennedy has been assassinated!" – but my fellow passengers looked drawn and weary. I thought better of it. Kennedy's idealism had always resonated with me. Would Laura and I still want to join the Corps when Kennedy was no longer there to inspire us?

I walked – almost ran – to my apartment for any further news.

Tucked beneath my door was a condolence card from Schulz. He wrote warmly of the enthusiastic way Berliners had received Kennedy this past June. After JFK's death, he said, the world would not be the same. His kind words touched me.

On the radio, I listened to Berliners at Checkpoint Charlie comment on the assassination: "It hit me like a thunderbolt," "I was shattered," "It was terrible," they said. I was struck by their emotional depth and openness, which I found so uncharacteristic for Germans.

In a matter of an hour, a candlelight walk to Schöneberg City Hall was announced on the radio. I changed my clothes, took a candle from my pantry and joined the silent walk with other mourners. Soon the streets filled with people from every direction. We reached the city hall square where Kennedy had delivered his speech just five months before. As then, thousands were gathered, this time to hear Mayor Willi Brandt give a tearful speech in memory of JFK. Drenched with sorrow, the vigil was a momentous statement of the city's love for the American president.

I stayed until the last word was uttered, and found myself walking back with only a few stragglers, who left my path one by one for their homes. How eerie it felt to carry all this sadness alone Absorbed in my thoughts, I got back to the pension after midnight, exhausted.

A slip of paper had been slid under my door. Schulz, bless his soul, had extended breakfast an additional hour for the mourners. I flopped on the bed and fell into a troubled sleep, waking occasionally to be reminded of what had happened, and that it was not a dream, but a real nightmare.

* * *

At breakfast, I chatted with the guests who had been on the march.

"I'll never forget last night," Nancy, a young American student, said to me, zipping up her backpack. "I wanted to leave yesterday, but I'm glad I stayed." Newly weds on a grand European tour from New Zealand and an unshaven Dutch businessman with a briefcase and newspaper nodded. Sightseeing would undoubtedly be canceled today, and no business deals for cheese either, he remarked quietly.

After all the guests had left, I stayed on to devour any news I could find in the special edition of the *Herald Tribune*, which Schulz had placed in the breakfast room. The United States was paralyzed by grief as sympathy poured in from around the globe. The USSR issued only a factual sentence or two about the assassination. Schulz came with a TV set for guests to watch later in the day. I thanked him for his consideration, and for the card. He nodded and left, but returned shortly thereafter to tell me a Herr Baumert was on the phone.

I trudged to the office. Heinz wanted to know when we could meet. I told him I wasn't in the proper frame of mind now, but I'd get back to him. *Haven't I done enough for this guy?*

Surely Christine had heard. Best to check in with her.

I don't want to get into the topic of Sunday. No way out of that, I guess. So out into the cold to the phone booth.

"*Hallo*, Renate. I hoped you would call."

"How did you know it was me?"

"Who else would call me on a Saturday morning? My mom knows not to call before the P.M."

"Oh."

"Terrible, this shooting of Kennedy. I can't believe it."

"Yes, I'm wiped out."

"I can imagine. So I guess tomorrow is out – or not?"

"I'm afraid so. I'm staying put. But I'll call you in a couple of days to reschedule. I'm glad you understand."

"Yes, although I get pretty high marks for comforting, they tell me."

At this point all I need is to hear slushy stories about past lovers.

"Take care, Christine, I'm too bushed to talk any more."

*   *   *

Those demanding phone calls sapped any last bit of energy. I stepped out on the balcony and looked at the bare trees. The sad scene matched my mood. *Maybe I should just hunker down today. A time-out seems to be in order.*

I settled into the easy chair with a cup of chamomile tea, sequestering myself the rest of Saturday.

November 23 – at my window
Two historic dates a Berliner like me will certainly always remember: August 13, 1961, when the East Germans built the Wall, and November 22, 1963, John Kennedy's assassination. I can't believe he's dead. Please somebody say it was all a bad dream! Just yesterday I was choosing my clothes for the consulate reception, and today here I sit, bereft by the loss of such a fine man.

My private life has taken off at the same time as this terrible historic event – in a way that leaves me confounded. For starters, I spent an unintended night with Christine, a <u>woman</u>, charismatic, talented, down to earth, but almost a complete opposite to my introverted, mental, private self. Is she what I need or a potential disaster?

And then there's Dieter – the academic, well-read type, easy to talk to – more like me than not. I was struck by the way he warmed to me. If Laura were here she would probably say he was perfect. The only fly in the ointment is, a wall separates our worlds.

Finally, there's Robert, a boy-next-door type, maybe a bit homespun, but a nice guy – and an American. That's important (or is it?). When we agreed to meet at the embassy, did I hope he might ask me out again? And who is this Frank, anyway?

On the radio I heard that an American named Lee Harvey Oswald had been arrested late the night before in Dallas, though the news couldn't relieve my somber mood. I ventured to the breakfast room to watch the TV coverage, which consisted of a twenty-minute segment before the satellite signal faded out. Frustration!

Same day, before bed
Finally some news. It appears Oswald had lived in Minsk, and was married to a Russian. I'm not surprised, and frankly suspicious there is some communist connection. Here I go sounding like some

xenophobe. But let's get realistic. Is it smart for me, an American, to go Drüben *tomorrow, when the anti-Soviet mood of the world is mounting by the minute? If I go, should I feel guilty for keeping a prior engagement? No way to contact Dieter, though. Christine couldn't mask her disappointment that I turned her down. I don't blame her, but feel uncomfortable with the pressure she puts on me. Maybe I just need a couple of day's distance.*

Is it callous to look forward to Dieter at this terrible moment in history? Should I wear black and stay home instead, in respect? Truth is, I want to reconnect with Dieter and find out how his eye surgery went. Is that disrespectful to the President?? NO! Okay, enough. I'll go and see Dieter. End of discussion.

I put my diary away in my desk drawer. I wasn't going to take it with me for the East Germans, or anyone else, to find. I went to bed early and slept well. A good conscience is like a good pillow, as the Germans say.

26

Islipped into a grey wool skirt – a staple at Ryan – a blue cotton blouse Laura had picked out for me on one of our Chicago trips, and, to match, a grey and black vest I'd worn since college. I still had the East German purse and coat from Alfred and decided to use them again, plus the clunky shoes. For good measure, I added a drop of the eau de cologne Heinz had left with me, and, sans lipstick and rouge, set out for East Berlin.

The S-Bahn was nearly empty. I wasn't surprised. Was this stupid or what, traveling to East Berlin? I'd find out soon enough. Well, Ren, you could have spent this day with Christine.

*   *   *

Alexanderplatz, or "The Alex," as the Berliners dubbed it, was named after the Russian Czar Alexander the First. A multilevel train station, the Alex was still under repair after its total destruction by the Soviet army – a curious irony.

The station was eerily quiet this Sunday. I walked along past closed shops until I spotted Dieter's lanky frame bent over a paper at a newsstand. The official party rag, *Neues Deutschland*, lay stacked on the counter. The Saturday headline read: *ATTENTAT AUF KENNEDY!* – KENNEDY ASSASSINATED!

I walked up to Dieter's side and picked up a newspaper. A clerk was occupied with a customer at the end of the stand. Dieter, still bent low, whispered, "Before we head to the café, let's go to a water tower park about ten minutes from here, where we can talk. Follow me from a distance. If you lose sight of me, just go straight up Prenzlauer Allee on the left-hand side. Across from the church steeple on your right, turn left into Knaackstrasse until you see the tower on an elevated plot of land. Climb the stairs and wait for me on one of the benches. I'll approach from the rear."

"All right." I put the newspaper back on the stack.

Dieter ambled down the long concourse and paused at a column showing theater schedules. I went around to the other side, pulled out a pen and piece of paper from my purse, and jotted down concert dates until Dieter resumed his walk.

En route, I adjusted my scarf. Dieter must have crossed the street, although I couldn't see him. *Darn!* I'd just missed the light. When it turned green, I walked across to the other side, careful not to arouse suspicion. At Knaackstrasse I turned and saw Dieter headed down the street in the direction of the tower. I looked at several shop windows before ascending the tower stairs. *No one around. Now what?* I raised my hood over my head to guard against the faint drizzle.

These East German coats are doughty but practical, at least. After waiting a few minutes longer, I went to the other side and saw Dieter with an umbrella propped under his arm, wiping his glasses.

He looked up and smiled when I came nearer. "Renate, I was relieved you made it to the newspaper stand. Sorry, I must have sounded abrupt when you arrived."

"It's all right. I got the picture."

I looked at his eyes; some puffiness was still visible.

"How did your procedure go?"

"The docs determined I did have a detached retina, and they spent several hours operating on it. I kept my head down for over two weeks."

"I'm so sorry."

"It's all right. We can talk more about my situation later. I really want to ask you about Kennedy, if that's all right. I'm still in a state of disbelief over his assassination. What was the West's reaction?"

"At my pension, everybody seemed to be deeply affected – stunned might be the better word."

I described the radio interviews, the candlelight vigil and the somber, reverent mood of the crowd.

"You know, I'd have given my last pfennig to march along with you. Your president was our last hope for a united Germany. Now, if anything, I'm afraid his death will lead to military escalations between East and West Germany."

"A suspect's been arrested with possible ties to the Soviet Union."

"I can't understand how this could have happened in a free country like the United States."

I could offer no explanation.

Dieter pushed back his sleeve and glanced at an oversized watch. "I'd love to continue with our conversation, but we need to get to the Café Budapest – they open soon and tables go fast. The café is on a corner at Karl Marx Allee 91." He pinpointed the location on a well-worn map, and set out.

I walked past the massive apartment complexes on Karl Marx Allee – representatives of the "socialist classicism style of the Soviet Union," in the words of the tour guide, but to me, just plain ugly. I didn't see a soul around. No wonder – there were no places to shop – and not one chic window display for the benefit of tourists or Sunday strollers.

A half block ahead I spied Dieter crossing to the other side of the boulevard, and I dashed over to keep pace. Thankfully, the drizzle had stopped. After about five minutes, a white, boxy restaurant with a neon sign reading "Café Budapest" came into view. Patrons, mostly in their twenties and thirties, already stood lined up. I walked over to the end of the line, and Dieter took the spot behind me.

On the door a handwritten sign stated that the gypsy band had canceled for today because of the "illness of the violinist."

"Don't be fooled," Dieter said. "They're doing it because of Kennedy. We'll have to come another time for the music. I'd still like to stay for a meal, if that's all right."

"Of course. I'd love to."

We entered through a heavy cloth partition and offered the obligatory *"Guten Tag."* A few people looked up from their seats and nodded.

"We'll need to wait to be seated," Dieter said. "Maybe it's just as well. It'll give me time to adjust to the dim light."

The restaurant was about half full and already thick with smoke. At least a couple of dozen tables with red-checked tablecloths and matching vinyl seats were spaced close together on either side of a central aisle. A man in a tuxedo motioned us over to a side table. On the way past the bar, I noticed a man in his early forties hunched over a beer. His stiff posture and steel-blue eyes were a caricature of a Nazi officer in an American B film I'd caught once at the Princess Theater in Bloomington with Carol.

Dieter hung my coat and umbrella next to his on a nearby rack and helped me get seated. His slender wrists and long fingers protruded through an ill-fitting jacket. A few tables over, two men in suits chatted over coffee and cake. Probably headed to a matinee.

"This is the only restaurant I know where we can talk freely, but we'll need to be on our guard."

"Do you come here often?"

"Now and then on Saturdays for the entertainment. I sit at the bar and nurse a bottle of sparkling water. The Budapest is way above what my working-class family was used to. When I was young, we had to settle for grilled chicken at stand-up tables if we wanted to eat out."

A waiter came with a large rectangular menu, and asked us what we wanted to drink.

"We'll have Hungarian Zweigelt, please. Make it a half carafe with two glasses." The waiter grunted and dashed off.

If you miss smiles and friendly faces from Germans in the west, try the East Berlin variety.

"I can't sit by and let you drink alone. But I must watch my alcohol intake, according to my surgeon. One glass is my limit."

The waiter brought our carafe. *"Zum Wohl,"* he said, and left.

"Did your parents encourage you to attend the university?" I asked over our drinks.

"Actually, my dad wanted me to become a plumber. You've always got leaky pipes to fix, Papa figured. A practical trade seemed to him the only way to survive, but I was determined to have a higher education. One good thing about my father being a laborer: it guaranteed me a *Studienplatz*, a slot at the university. Forget admittance if you're a child of a clergyman or professor."

"But what happens to the next generation of university graduates? Your children won't qualify for higher education."

"Very astute. As you can imagine, it's not wise to make that observation in public." Dieter pursed his lips. "Anyway, I hope that won't be my problem much longer."

"Because you've already finished your studies?"

"You might put it that way."

With a swoop of his arm, an assistant making his rounds placed a red candle into a holder and lit the wick.

Stashed in my bra I had a few clandestine East Mark bills changed in West Berlin at the exchange rate of one dollar to sixteen East German marks. This meal would hardly cost me a couple of greenbacks to judge by the menu. I wondered whether I should offer to foot the bill.

Perhaps sensing my thoughts, Dieter said, "By the way, I'm paying for the meal." He removed his glasses and held the menu close to his face. After a few minutes, he looked up. "I'm sorry, it takes me a while to read small print."

The waiter came to our table. "Are you ready to order, sir? We recommend our house *gulyás mit csipetke* – goulash with potatoes and noodles – and our fresh rolls."

"Oh I can go for that. And how about you, Renate?"

"I'll have the same, please."

*   *   *

The waiter brought two terrines of steaming goulash and a basket of rolls.

The *gulyás mit csipetke* was cooked with onions, tomatoes, green pepper, potatoes and noodles, and spiced with Hungarian red paprika. But the surprise came when I ate the baked roll.

I reached for another one out of the basket. "Mmm. They're so fresh and tasty!"

"We're proud of our rolls. In GDR restaurants the chefs bake them from scratch. Café Budapest uses Hungarian lard and butter in them – ingredients we can't get locally."

"Lard and butter? Those don't sound too hard to get."

"All the good stuff in the GDR gets carted off to the Soviet Union," Dieter said in a lowered voice.

"So what do you do in Berlin?"

"Actually I'm on medical leave from a chemical lab in Leipzig."

"What did you do there before –?"

"I conducted theoretical research."

"That doesn't sound so awful to me."

Dieter moved forward in his seat. "If people knew scientists tossed hypotheses around all day, we'd have another peasants' revolt."

Wry sense of humor, this fellow.

I changed the subject and asked about the production of Brecht's *Mutter Courage* at the Berliner Ensemble.

"Helene Weigel, Brecht's wife, is the nonpareil actress as the lead, and she's a great director as well," Dieter said. "Nobody makes the Thirty Years' War more vivid than she does. I'll miss her productions, and the operas at the Komische Oper."

"But in Leipzig you've got Bach's music at St. Thomas Church and great symphonic concerts at the Gewandhaus Orchestra Hall."

"True, but I'm not ..."

"You're not what?"

"I don't plan to stay forever in Leipzig."

It must be the lure of Berlin.

After the waiter cleared away our dishes, Dieter ordered coffee.

I hadn't thought anyone could make a more tasteless brew than the Americans, but the Budapest's watered down effort took the prize. It turned out East Germans had little access to good beans.

"Do you mind if I smoke?" Dieter asked.

"No."

Dieter took out a pouch of tobacco from his jacket and a pipe from his breast pocket. After lighting up, he threw a tiny match into an ashtray, marked simply with VEB on the side.

"What does VEB stand for?" I asked.

"*Volkseigener Betrieb*, or the People's Own Company. Imagine, the state is ever present – even when you smoke!"

"In America we're bombarded with ads. I find the absence of commercialism in the GDR refreshing."

"Instead of commercial ads, we get propaganda at work, in school, on radio and TV, and especially at party meetings."

"Do you belong to the Communist Party?"

"No. But if we snub them, we can jeopardize travel plans, access to an automobile, and, most important, a decent apartment."

"You mentioned Bach's music in Leipzig, Renate. You know, there'll be a performance of his cantata *Wachet Auf* in the Advent service at the Marienkirche. And, Bishop Dibelius always speaks the first Sunday of the month. He's a radical – doesn't let himself be intimidated by anyone. Would you like to join me?"

"*Wake, Awake*? I love Bach's music, and especially his cantatas."

"Good. Let's meet in the church at about nine forty-five. Take the Alexanderplatz S-Bahn exit and walk up Karl-Liebknecht-Strasse to the tall brick church with a red roof and prominent spire. I'll keep a space for you in the seventh row to the right."

Dieter summoned the waiter and paid.

"Thank you for the wonderful time."

"My pleasure." He assisted me with my coat.

We walked separately to the station and arranged to stand on the platform next to one another.

As the U-Bahn pulled in, Dieter touched my arm lightly.

"Until next Sunday."

November 24 – at home after Café Budapest with Dieter
How bizarre. If I were in the US now, I'd be in a country at a standstill with a state funeral in the same week as Thanksgiving.

Here I spent a "normal" day with a nice guy at a Hungarian restaurant! The conversation flowed, no secret police to be seen, and the meal – although not turkey and all the trimmings – was yummy.

I put my pen down as sadness overcame me. This upcoming Thanksgiving would be the first for me without Mama or Laura. I wondered whom Laura would spend the day with. We usually prepared a big turkey and invited several of our stray foreign exchange students with nowhere to go. Then we'd take off for Chicago on Friday and hit the store bargains in the afternoon. Last year we'd even skipped the student bit and raced straight to Mama's on Wednesday night. After a good night's sleep, we'd joined in the preparations together with Mama.

This year however, I faced a full week of work to finish the next section of my dissertation, which mercifully, Dr. Blume postponed until the week after Thanksgiving. "Get your diss work to him in time, whatever you do," Tom Parkins had warned me after he tried to delay his submission on the history of diphthongs in East Freesia.

In spite of the looming deadline, I resolved that nothing was going to stop me from a concert next Sunday at the Marienkirche with Dieter. And what about Christine? Maybe I'll survive the Thanksgiving week after all.

After a full afternoon of gathering my materials and mapping out my agenda for Bloom, I was ready to contact Christine.

I picked suppertime to make the call – a wise choice – as the booth was empty.

"Hi, Ren."

"I'm phoning you as promised."

"So when would you like meet again?"

"Friday seems good, I've got a pile of work to complete this week."

"I'd love to hear about it all."

"Where do you want to go?" I asked.

"Why don't you come to my place?"

"Uh, okay. When?"

"Oh, say six thirty."

"Shall I bring something?"

"No. I'll make us dinner. I've got plenty of my Alsatian beauties to sample, as well."

"A home-cooked meal with white wine! Sounds great."

*　　*　　*

My writing for Blume went swimmingly – save for Thursday afternoon – when I had to fight off a few lumps in my throat. It always went better when I had cleared my desk and thought things through. My reward was to knock off the rest of the weekend. What a relief!

On my first visit to Christine's place, I'd had no idea what would happen. This time, if I stayed, I could predict the outcome. SEX! But with my period just starting, I didn't feel especially amorous. What did female homosexuals do in that case?

I rang Christine's bell, holding a bouquet of chrysanthemums behind me.

Christine opened the door in a long blue apron. I presented her with the bouquet.

"Thanks, Ren. I don't think I've ever received flowers from a woman. Please come in." She kissed me on both cheeks. "Learned that in Saarbrücken. People are so Frenchified down there."

I entered the living room. "You've been hard at work."

"Yes. I took a household day to get caught up. Been at it since 7 A.M. I didn't mention, though, *why* I needed to clean." Christine laughed. "Come, Renate, sit down on the couch. How about some wine?"

"I have to tell you, Christine, I've got my period today, and a bit of a stomachache."

"Hmm. I usually prescribe a shot of whisky for that. My mom always kept a bottle just for those times. Plus, you'll need something for your tummy."

Christine went to the hall cupboard, returned with a shot glass, a bottle of whisky and a hot water bottle, and sat down next to me.

"I need about ten more minutes to finish the meal, so why don't you just lie down for now?" Whistling, she went into the kitchen and let the tap run, then filled the bottle, returning to place it on my abdomen with a neatly folded blanket from the top of the couch. "There. After your tummy is warmed, take a sip or two of the whiskey. It should do the trick."

"Christine, don't go to all this trouble. I'm fine, really."

"No problem." She put on a record of Frank Sinatra at low volume and disappeared into the kitchen again.

The warmth did feel good, and I enjoyed listening to Frank croon with Christine humming along with him in the kitchen – an odd – but agreeable combination.

*   *   *

I must have dozed off. When I awoke, the table had been set with a tablecloth, lit candles, china and silver.

"You were out like a light, Ren. How are you now?"

"Better, thank you."

"Hungry?"

"Famished."

"Good, because I've cooked up a storm."

Christine served poached salmon, basmati rice with spices, and a beautiful mixed green salad tossed with olive oil, garlic and balsamic dressing.

"Mmm! What goodies did you put in the rice?"

"I sautéed the onions first, and later I added rosemary, tarragon, basil, *Herbes de Provence*, black pepper and garlic."

This woman really has a way with food. Too bad she's got so little time to cook.

While we ate, Christine sipped an Alsatian Riesling, regaling me with the love woes her female coworkers revealed during breaks.

"If people think female homosexuals don't like men, they should listen to our office gals sitting around coffee complain about how little their husbands or boyfriends do at home –'hausfrau work,' the guys call it. They'll go off to soccer games and leave their 'women-folk' to take care of the kids. And then, in bed . . . well . . . one co-worker says she lies and waits for hubby's four thrusts so 'it' will be over!"

"Not an idyllic picture."

"So far our front receptionist tells the best story. She took sick one day at work and had to leave early. On the way home in her car, she listened to a talk show where the station calls a random phone number to ask the listener a question. If you know the answer, you get free tickets for a concert. The station happened to call her house, and her husband answered! Imagine his surprise when she arrived and caught him in bed with another woman."

We both giggled.

"Do you talk with your colleagues about your intimate relationships with women?"

"No, Ren. I like to keep my private life to myself. It makes life easier."

Whew! At least that means I'm not a topic of discussion.

"Have any of the women at your office heard you perform at the Panther?"

"No. The club is way beyond their world."

"It must be tough to keep part of yourself hidden."

"I'm basically okay with being private, and that's all I care about. But you're right. If I had to be secretive with everyone, I think I'd jump out the window."

"Have you ever considered a man?"

"Oh, sure, you get tired of the struggle, and ask yourself what it'd be like to go on a regular date, hold hands, not worry about what people think. Honestly, Ren, I've got no objection to penises; it's just what they are attached to that's the problem. Let's go to the couch and I'll bring out the dessert."

While I positioned myself comfortably with the blanket, Christine went to the kitchen and fetched two bowls of ice cream topped with fresh raspberries and a faint swirl of hot chocolate.

"It was a scrumptious dinner, Christine."

"I'm glad to try out new recipes on such a charming woman."

"I mean you've gone to so much effort."

"Yeeess?" Christine looked at me out of the corner of her eye.

"Well, we barely know one another."

"Look, Renate, we've met at a restaurant, gone out for drinks and you've heard me twice at the Panther. Then, if you recall, we've spent an afternoon and a beautiful intimate night together. You're not exactly a stranger off the street."

"I guess I'm wondering . . . why have you picked me?"

"*Ach*, the *Gretchenfrage* – Gretchen's test of Faust after they slept with one another! To begin with, I love your blond pubic hair."

My mouth dropped open.

Christine chuckled.

"The question is serious, Christine."

"Look, Ren, I *am* serious. I love your blond curly hair – sound better? And what's more, you're intelligent and beautiful. Is that enough to begin with?"

"I'm just . . . not sure I'm at where *you're* at right now."

"Which is where?"

"I can't deny my erotic night with you. But I've mulled it over, and think maybe we should just be friends for now."

"Just friends? What's that supposed to mean?"

"Uh – well, I – I don't know."

Christine put her hand on mine. "People don't normally say 'let's just be friends' unless they want to lower the bar. Do you think tonight's dinner was some sort of 'just be friends' invite?"

"No, I thought our dinner was special. It's that – I don't know how else to characterize our relationship."

Christine looked down. "I'm very taken with you, Ren. I picked you out of the audience and sang in your direction."

"I was flattered."

"It wasn't flattery. Let's face it, I've crossed paths with a number of women in my life, but no one's affected me like you. To add to the list, you're sincere, work hard, have a way with language – and a sweet personality – a bit naïve, maybe, but refreshing. You should've seen

Giuseppe at the Piccola. He gave me a thumbs-up on you when you excused yourself."

"He did?"

"Giuseppe is *very* choosy. I think you don't realize what your qualities are. Okay, maybe we've gotten off to a ragged start with all our various commitments. So things may feel confusing right now, especially since this is new to you. But if you're worried I might try to seduce you tonight? No way. For me, our night together was real, intense, and honest. But when I feel a 'no' emanating from a woman, do you suppose I'd barrel on in spite of it?"

"No, I guess not."

"I'd seem like a brute. Listen, some of my relationships worked out longer than others, but they ended when they needed to. I didn't fight the inevitable or hang on when it was time to let go. Since Rosie, I've been single now for over two years. During my time alone, I saw a therapist and learned a lot about myself. For example if my life continues in the same pattern of mostly short-term liaisons, I'll have gone through a good five to ten lovers before I pass on."

Christine took a small ball from the bookcase and exercised her hands. "Right now I'm looking to change things. I'd *like* to have stability, continuity, and time to deepen a relationship. Most of my straight friends – the ones still married, at least – have at least one teenager and have been hitched a good fifteen years. I haven't even managed a *third* of those years with *one* woman.

"Anyway, I've ranted enough." She looked me directly in the eye. "Now let me pose *you* a question."

"Okay what is it?"

Good grief, what now?

"I'd like to know what *you* want in your life, Renate. You told me the night of *Buss und Bettag* that you had sensations you'd never felt before, and you'd been waiting for me." Christine got up suddenly. "Do you have a place for these sensations in your life?

"Think about it. Now I need to step outside for a smoke, okay?"

"Yes, go on. May I use your bathroom?"

"Would you like to take a hot bath? Feel free, if you'd like."

212

"Maybe so. It's been a stressful week."

"Towels are in the hall cupboard, and bath salts at the front of the bathtub. Take your time. I'll wash the dishes when I'm finished."

"Okay."

The door to the kitchen balcony closed.

*   *   *

I put my clothes on a stool and stepped into the tub. As the water ran, I slid down until it covered my breasts and placed a warm washcloth over my abdomen.

I hadn't experienced anything like the romantic relationships Christine had described. My path, the straight and narrow, so to speak, had led me from high school to the university and now my teaching job. Once I received the PhD, tenure would be a piece of cake, as the Americans said. Who could ask for a better deal? I'd have to do something horrible, like commit murder, not to get it.

What if I decided to be open about Christine at Ryan? Did I have enough room for those sensations, or enough room for her? Tough questions.

For ten to fifteen minutes I heard dishes clank and tap water running. Then Christine walked down the hall to the bedroom, and a few minutes later there was a gentle tap on the bathroom door.

"Renate? Are you still above water? May I come in?"

"Um – yes." I straightened up on my elbows and placed the washcloth over my breasts.

She entered, holding a bath towel over her naked body. "May I join you? I promise to behave."

She didn't, and neither did I.

*   *   *

Christine threw on her clothes and dashed out for *Schrippen* while I stayed in bed. During our night together, she hadn't pressured me; instead, she'd been tender, loving and aware of my physical needs,

213

giving me a rare sense of safety. Now, though, I felt on edge. How would I tell her about tomorrow? I dreaded slapping her with another Sunday rebuff.

Christine walked into the bedroom and waved a bag of donuts in front of me.

"They smell divine."

"See you at the table."

"I'll get my things on."

The kitchen table was set with cheese, rolls, boiled eggs, raspberry marmalade, butter – and coffee. It was a great breakfast to get my brain in gear.

"Most days, I'm into my second breakfast by this time."

"You are definitely the early bird," I said, cracking open my boiled egg.

"And you're the night owl – minus the screech." She laughed. "I guess we'd have to agree on when to be close. Afternoons? Well, then, I might have to quit my job."

"Are you serious?"

"Just kidding."

Over our second cup of coffee, Christine straightened up in her chair: "A propos Saturday afternoons, Mom and I always celebrate the first of Advent in Reinickendorf with her cousin and kids. I've got to go to her place and get it ready for the brood – they're a fussy bunch. Do you have plans for tomorrow?"

Oh God, the question – is this an invitation to visit her family? No way. I'm not ready "Yes. Professor Bautsch, the director of the German State Library where I've been doing research invited me for Sunday to meet his family. It's the last time I'll see him before he goes on a half-year leave to Romania. In fact, I need a thank you gift for him before the shops close today."

"Good, I'm glad you'll spend the afternoon alone in your apartment." Christine wagged her finger. "But you're not off the hook for future Saturday afternoons."

"I don't follow."

"Would you like to spend next weekend here?"

"Um, yes, I'll have to phone you this week to confirm . . ."

"Don't play too hard to get. Why don't we meet sometime this week so we can talk face to face? How about Wednesday? I could meet you at Café Steinplatz."

"All right." *She is not to be deterred.*

Christine washed the dishes and I dried. She showed me where everything went.

It seemed like old times with Laura.

27

I arose early, looking forward to the Marienkirche, relieved Christine needed to visit her mother, and hoping there wouldn't be any more collisions of this sort in the future. I trotted out my GDR outfit and accessories again, including a couple of drops of cologne.

After the usual border formalities, I changed to an almost empty U-Bahn, exited after two stops at Alexanderplatz, and walked along deserted streets named after radicals and communists. Hardly anyone was outside on this gloomy day. After a few minutes, I reached the stately thirteenth-century St. Mary's Church, which I was surprised to find already packed with worshipers. I walked down the side aisle toward Dieter's tall frame. As promised, he had saved me a seat. We greeted each other with a simple nod as I loosened my coat and scarf.

In the chancel, a large Advent wreath hung resplendent with red candles. The orchestra was tuning for the performance, and the choristers had taken their places on either side of the altar.

As Bishop Dibelius entered the church, the organist began Bach's regal prelude *Wachet auf* – an elegant, lacy musical rendering of the chorale cantata to come. The congregation turned and followed the bishop's stately procession through the nave with attendants carrying a cross and liturgical flags. At the altar, he sat and faced the congregation listening to the conclusion of the prelude.

Accompanied by the organ, the entire congregation then sang the same chorale. The thrilling sound of hundreds of people singing sent chills down my spine.

When the bishop read the Advent lesson from Matthew 25:1-3: "Watch therefore, for you do not know on what day the Lord is coming," I recalled Papi reciting the passage at our Sunday devotion before church. I was awash in mixed emotions as the cantata began – but in no time I was spellbound by Bach's joyful and vigorous treatment of Advent, putting a final stamp on the scriptural admonition in preparation for Christmas.

The bishop ascended to the pulpit, which towered over the congregation. His theme: vigilance in the face of danger. The call was to accept Christ in the midst of many who did not. There would be consequences for that acceptance, and I knew what he meant.

Dibelius thundered like Moses on the mountain and raised his fist defiantly: "Christ has not made life easy for me. On the contrary, it would have been more comfortable to be without Him than to live with Him. He lays burdens on the soul which one would rather let pass by unheeded."

A timely message.

As the choir sang at the collection after the sermon, I was reminded that since IU, I hadn't sung in a choir, and I missed the contact with vocal music. Of course, I'd hung on Christine's every note at the Panther. How would she have reacted to the cantata? No matter, it felt right to experience Bach and this service with Dieter.

We stood to the side as the parishioners filed out.

"Renate, isn't *Wake, Awake* so noble, especially the French Overture, with those stately, syncopated rhythms? It sets the stage for the watchmen on the ramparts, just like in a medieval castle. We listeners *become* the guards on the ramparts, in vigil for Christ's return. You almost expect to see a royal procession of angels proclaiming Jesus's birth," Dieter said.

Poor eyesight certainly does not detract from Dieter's musical experience. I've never heard anyone describe Bach's music so passionately.

"Renate, do you have time for coffee and a chat at the Budapest? I read that the Hungarian Gypsy musicians have rescheduled for today."

I couldn't refuse. "Yes, of course, thank you."

As before, I followed behind him at a distance.

We met up at the Café Budapest, and were seated at a table for two. Dieter ordered coffee and pastry.

A lively crowd had gathered to hear accordion music played by a stocky man with a mustache accompanied by a vigorous fiddler, both with open-necked shirts, broad pointed collars, embroidered vests and billowy black pants.

"The Budapest let's gypsies perform, even if the regime doesn't condone them. These fellows can't find regular jobs. They earn their money from tips or cash under the table from the café owners. The music is quite a contrast to the cantata, wouldn't you say?"

Now for a real *Gretchenfrage*, even though Dieter and I hadn't spent the night together. "Dieter, do you attend the Marienkirche often?"

"Yes, when they have a special event like today. And you, Renate, are you a churchgoer?"

"I used to go with my parents when I was young, and in the US I attended church during my university days, but I've gotten away from it. I'd characterize myself as a spiritual person who derives her theology from sacred music."

"Music is a good source. I get my inspiration from Bach and Brahms – and Einstein." Dieter smiled. "Did you know he was a violinist?"

"No, but I'm not surprised. Music and science seem to be good bedfellows."

A group of young men with identical soccer club jerseys arrived and stood at the bar over bottles of beer. They laughed and cheered about their team's win against a squad from Eisenach the day before.

"How long do you plan to stay in Berlin with your eye treatments?"

"I hope only until the end of this month."

"Oh." I could barely contain my disappointment.

Dieter leaned forward and touched my hand. "Renate, I need your help."

"Help?"

Dieter looked toward a nearby couple tapping their legs to the music. "I want to escape to West Berlin."

"Are you serious?"

"Yes."

"How?"

"By car."

"I can't believe this."

"We've gone through a number of plans and options, and decided you are the ideal person to help."

"Would 'we' include Heinz, Alfred and MJ?"

"Yes, and a few others, too."

"That explains the medicine." I tried to remain calm.

"Karl needed the pills."

"So it all was planned in advance?"

"When Alfred and Heinz met you at Aschinger, they seized the opportunity when you offered to take the meds to Karl. But they wanted to test you with a trial run to East Berlin. You can't know whom to trust around here."

"So now you trust me enough to ask me about an escape?"

"Renate, time is of the essence. The Charité has the only eye clinic in the GDR that can treat my condition. I have a temporary permit to stay in Berlin until my treatment is over. After that, any escape attempt will be impossible."

"How so?"

"After my release from the hospital, I must return to Leipzig, and I won't be allowed to visit Berlin. All GDR citizens need special papers to enter Berlin, or any area within five kilometers of the city limits."

Two Vopos in ankle-length capes sauntered in and took seats at a small table near us.

"Don't worry. Those two are regulars. They come to hear the music."

With rhythmic flair, the fiddlers and the accordionist began "Hava Nagila." We turned to listen. For a moment I was able to postpone a response to Dieter's request.

The strains of "Hava Nagila" brought back my father's solo dancing to the melody at the farm. I was not yet of school age when I first heard it, but picked up the tune instantly. Once, I hummed it on a walk with Papi in Berlin.

My father turned to me. "*Spatz*, we mustn't hum that in public."

"But why, Papi?"

"Some songs are for everybody and some not. We perform "Hava Nagila" only when we're at Aunt Hildegard's."

I swung my foot back and forth across the pavement. "But it's a happy song. It makes me want to skip. Don't you like it when I'm happy, Papi?"

"Of course, *Spatz*. Someday you'll understand what I told you."

*   *   *

"Is everything all right, Renate?"

"Sorry, what you just asked sets me back on my heels." Out of the corner of my eye, I caught the two Vopos staring at us.

Dieter reached for my hand again, this time squeezing it tenderly. "Please pretend we are an engaged couple," he said, sotto voce. He beckoned to the musicians. The men approached, grinning at us.

I had to play along.

"We're getting engaged soon," Dieter smiled back. "Could you play something traditional or romantic?"

"Our pleasure." The men conferred and one fiddler and a singer remained at the table, while the other musicians returned to their station.

The fiddler tapped his bow on the table for silence, and announced to the patrons that the group's next song was a duet in honor of our engagement. He launched into a beautifully lyrical introduction, and soon the singer joined him with a soulful melody: "O my lily of the valley, dear flower, a hope, the fire of love."

A hush fell over the entire restaurant.

When the two men finished, Dieter and I lifted our glasses in salute: "To us!"

The musicians turned and bowed, as the audience broke into spontaneous applause. The singer returned to the groups' station across the room, while the fiddler hovered, propping his instrument under his arm.

Dieter handed him a large coin.

"Thank you, and good fortune for your future years," he said.

The toast appeared to soften everyone's collective reserve, releasing the pressure in the room like the pop of a cork. The counter filled with empty beer bottles as the soccer fans began to shout their team's chants; other patrons chatted, laughed or came over to congratulate us.

If they only knew.

I reached for my handbag. "Dieter, can we discuss your request somewhere else? I can hardly hear myself think."

"Let's go back to the water tower. I'll follow you there."

The waiter came to add up the bill. Dieter handed him ten marks.

We slipped out. No one seemed to be sober enough to notice. Despite my fear that someone might follow me, I retraced the route to Knaackstrasse and mounted the steps. Away from view, I took seat on a far bench.

Minutes later, Dieter rounded the corner, looked around and joined me.

"I'm sorry if I upset you."

"To put it mildly."

"Renate, do you know the kind of life I'm facing here, and what would happen to me if the escape failed? I'd be hauled away to the dreaded Hohenschönhausen prison and subjected to unspeakable cruelties. You're my only chance for escape."

"I'm not just some naïve American, Dieter. I lived here in Germany under a government that controlled people through torture, intimidation and lies. I hear a knock on the door differently than my American friends. And it makes me all the more cautious. So why pick me?"

"We thought you'd be ideal *because* we knew you spent your youth in Nazi Germany. Your alibi is perfect, you're a native speaker, and you have professional reasons to travel between East and West."

When I saw the desperation in Dieter's cloudy eyes, I thought about Papi. There seemed to be no way out.

"I won't let you down, Dieter."

"Renate, I'm grateful. We haven't much time. Heinz will fill you in on the details."

As we parted at the train station, Dieter kissed my hand.

*   *   *

Outside the pension I stopped to call Heinz and arranged to meet him on Tuesday.

Shaking, I fumbled with the key to my apartment.

December 1 – late, in bed

What a day! Just turned on the radio, and the RIAS chorus is performing music for the first Sunday in Advent: "O come, O come, Emmanuel, and ransom captive Israel, that dwells in lowly exile here until the Son of God appear." Such a lovely, lilting melody it was, and fitting for that fervent text. Does "captive" refer to me, too? What does it mean to be in exile and wait for release? How could God have let down all those Jews, gypsies and homosexuals who suffered immeasurably, ripped away from their loved ones?

Dieter's plan hit me like a ton of bricks. Did I overlook some signal that should have prepared me? He seems to be such a sincere man. There must be other people Heinz and Alfred could choose. Why me? I don't know if it were possible to turn my back on Dieter and thereby seal his fate, as he claims would happen. What constitutes the limit of caritas and responsibility toward a person who wants to be freed from bondage – a person I hardly know?

Heinz and Alfred might not want my help if they knew I had slept with a woman or that my father was a Nazi. There are safer shores with Laura, my students and quiet Ryan. What would Papi think if I said no and played it safe? Perhaps I don't know care what Papi thinks. I pray for a resolution to my dilemma and haven't a clue what it is.

28

On Tuesday morning I paced outside the pension, waiting for Heinz. A brand new looking light blue VW Beetle with international plates pulled up.

Heinz hopped out and opened the door for me. "Sorry for the delay. Let's go to a small café I know, where we can chat."

It's nice to be in a VW again – I'd almost forgotten how much I miss my sweet car with its little Snoopy figure dangling from the rearview mirror. Maybe I should have kept it. Mama's covered parking spot would have been perfect.

Heinz drove past the RIAS tower and turned into a residential neighborhood dotted with single-family homes.

"I like this area," Heinz commented as we passed several narrow streets. "It's quiet here, but we're still close to major boulevards and the Avus, our only autobahn in Berlin." He pulled up in front of a two-story house with a five-foot hedge in front. A covered bus stop on the other side of the street blocked any view of the VW from the house opposite us.

"The café is right around the corner."

Maxi's, an old bungalow eatery, was open, but no customer was inside.

Heinz bent his head around into the rear of the café. "Hi there, Max, it's Heinz with a guest. We'll have the specialty of the house, please – two of them – and two coffees."

Max, a corpulent man in a spotless white apron, poked his head around the corner, accompanied by his equally white dog. "Comin' up." He disappeared into the kitchen and the dog followed.

"This eatery is usually empty around now. Max stays in his office and watches television until the first patrons arrive. We can converse freely here."

Max returned with two open-faced sandwiches consisting of a slice of rye bread topped with three or four thin slices of cured Black Forest smoked ham, a fried egg in olive oil, pickled gherkins, tomato and onion slices. By now I was hungry and dug in.

While we ate, Heinz kept the conversation light with banter about Wedding. Max left us alone and appeared just once to clear our plates and bring us coffee. When he retreated to the kitchen, I decided it was time to find out what Heinz had in mind.

"Dieter says he needs my help to escape to the West. What else can you tell me?"

Heinz wiped his mouth with a napkin.

"We want you to drive this Beetle with Dieter hidden in it."

"I can't quite envision it. Where?"

"Behind the trunk. I'll show you when we're back at the car."

"Drive with Dieter crammed into a space in front of me? You've not serious. Heinz, medicine is one matter, but smuggling an East German over the border with me at the wheel, if that's what you mean – it's crazy. If this fails, I risk terrible reprisal from the East Germans. I've read about *Republikflucht* – leaving the country illegally. That's worse than murder in their eyes."

"Consider this, Fräulein Seiler. You're a woman, a US citizen, and you'll have papers for a very popular make that Americans buy in Germany to ship back."

Oh fine. Will I get to keep theirs? Better not ask.

The first of several customers arrived and greeted Max, who had just moved from the kitchen to behind the counter.

Heinz lowered his voice. "We plan to have the escape the night before Christmas Eve. You'll be driving at night amongst Western autos from the Staatsoper. And, for the first time since the Berlin

Wall went up, thousands of West Berliners will be visiting relatives in East Berlin for one day at another East Berlin border crossing nearby. The East German manpower at Friedrichstrasse will be stretched thin."

Heinz went to the counter to pay the bill.

"Are you ready for a trial run?"

Do I really have a choice?

*   *   *

"For today" Heinz said, reaching in the car to unhook the trunk, "we've put sacks of sand approximating Dieter's weight in the trunk – minus your sixty-five kilos – to simulate the heavier load." He walked around to the front and unlatched the hood. "Think away the sacks – and that's what the Grepos will see when they lift the lid – an empty boot. We'll have a false compartment constructed beneath it at a garage that specializes in rebuilding cars. They're experienced – even if business has slowed since 1961," he said with a grim smile, closing the hood.

I paused to look at the VW before we got back in. "Heinz, I can't tell anything untoward from the appearance of the car except that it rode a bit rough on the way over."

"Before this practice session, we raised the tire pressure and eliminated any extra poundage: the spare tire, tools, and some insulation. Later, we'll also remove the first aid kit and floor mats and the tank will carry only a gallon of gasoline instead of a little over nine when it's full. We've reckoned the distance from the villa to Checkpoint Charlie, and will allow one quart of gasoline for extra measure. All told, it'll save about fifty pounds of weight."

"What happens if I get lost?"

"Not to worry. Tomorrow, Jack Baker, an English friend, will take you on a trial run to our contact house in Friedrichshagen. Will that be convenient?"

"I'd rather it be a later day."

"Fraülein Seiler, please. Dieter faces a critical deadline and we cannot delay it any further. In a matter of a few weeks the escape will be over and you'll have given a decent person a life of freedom."

I sighed. "When does Jack want to pick me up?"

"At 11 A.M."

Heinz motioned for me to go around to the driver's seat.

"Today our goal is for you to familiarize yourself with this vehicle."

I adjusted the mirror and seat, and practiced shifting with the clutch disengaged before restarting the motor. *Easy, just like my Beetle.* Traffic was light in Eichkamp; I maneuvered the narrow streets and slowed the car as we approached a few potholes.

Thank heavens it's winter, or I'd be in a puddle of sweat about now.

All of a sudden, Heinz yelled, "Gun the motor!"

I slammed the gas pedal to the floor.

"Now stop!"

The Bug screeched to a halt.

"Good. Just wanted to check your reflexes."

I drove for half an hour. Satisfied that I handled the VW easily with the extra weight in the front, Heinz instructed me to drive down the Kaiserdamm Boulevard, a broad commercial street. From the Kaiserdamm we continued on along Bismarck Strasse to Ernst-Reuter-Platz, and at the Steinplatz we turned into a side street near the pension.

"Good job, Fräulein Seiler. Now, this is the car registration." Heinz handed me a slim plastic case. "Keep it on your person at all times. Anyone in possession of this document is entitled to drive the car."

I glanced at it. The documents were made out to me!

"Surprised at getting a VW?"

I didn't know what to say.

"We've put it in your name to help explain why you're a woman alone driving across at the border, and to avoid registration questions. I suggest you take your car for a spin. When you finish, leave it at the upper level in the car park on Kantstrasse. Hide the registration and parking ticket under the mat for me so I can pick it up."

"But didn't you say–"

"Don't worry."

*   *   *

I dropped Heinz off at the Zoo station.

Why had I agreed to meet Christine for dinner on Wednesday? Now I was reeling: with Jack tomorrow and Bautsch on Thursday, I'd need Wednesday to myself. I must come up with something really good to tell her.

Where could I make a call in private? I recalled asking Schulz about the Tiergarten. He'd told me the park was a favorite of tourists and strollers by day, but warned me about staying after dark. "There's an infamous, secluded telephone booth in the Tiergarten that all the pimps use to make connections."

There was enough daylight left before any such activity began – and I wouldn't have to deal with Schulz's ears primed, or an impatient person tapping on the glass.

I maneuvered through downtown traffic and drove toward the Grosser Stern, or "Big Star," a central five-artery roundabout close to the Wall. Built in the seventeenth century, the Stern was set off in the middle by a victory column with the Goldelse, a golden sculpture of Victoria with a laurel wreath, on top.

As I pulled onto the cobblestone divider, the VW creaked with the extra weight. I paused a moment to calm my nerves. I was about to transport an escapee in this car, and had one chance to succeed or face terrible consequences.

My heart raced. Or was it in anticipation of hearing Christine's voice again? The passion and confusion she awakened in me were not helpful for the dangerous deal I had agreed to.

The rumble of pre–rush hour traffic in the distance competed with my reverie. Western drivers were forced to squeeze around the bulge in the Wall at the Brandenburg Gate in order to reach the eastern districts of Neukölln and Kreuzberg, where Christine lived – or the northern districts of Wedding and Reinickendorf – Alfred's home base.

After a wrong turn or two, I finally located the phone booth deep in the woods near a lone light pole. The scrawled numbers, graffiti, and tattered phone book indicated this place saw a lot of use. I tried to rub the window clear with my coat sleeve, but the glass remained smudgy and opaque. The smell of previous occupants' cigarettes began to nauseate me.

I gripped the door handle, propped my foot on a dirty ledge and pushed two coins into the slot. Busy! I slammed the phone down and waited for my ten-pfennig pieces. I tried several more times with no luck.

The light had dimmed except for the moist glow of the park lamp. The beams of headlights darted in and out of the trees to my left.

I tried the number again.

"Zeiler Accounting. *Guten Tag.* To whom do you wish to speak?"

"To Frau Kaufmann, please."

"Just one moment," the female voice answered.

"*Ja*, Kaufmann." Christine's voice went through me like a knife through butter.

"Christine—"

"*Guten Tag*, Fräulein Seiler. What is this regarding?"

"I want—"

"To set up an appointment?" She whispered, "Look, we're closing up for the day. Phone me later – you've got the number." Then, resuming her former tone, "*Auf Wiederhören*, Fräulein Seiler." The receiver clicked.

I hurried back to the car without encountering a soul. Safely inside, I pounded on the wheel. I was tearing at a fragile friendship, and for what? To smuggle someone I hardly knew over the border?

My life had broken into a thousand shards, a veritable prism of selves that wouldn't fit together now, no matter how I tried.

Later I phoned Christine again.

"Did you have a good time at your mother's on the First of Advent?" I asked.

"Yes, under the circumstances."

"I'd like to come for the weekend. I'm afraid any time before that is out – I just have too many commitments."

"Okay, then the weekend it is."

What a relief! She didn't even mention Wednesday. But I was apprehensive, all the same.

29

Outside the pension, I awaited Jack's arrival as calmly as I could. A trim man in his early forties, wearing a herringbone jacket and creased trousers, pulled his car over to the curb. He left the motor on and hopped out to greet me.

"Hello, Renate. I'm Jack." He smiled.

"Pleased to meet you, and thanks for the smile. They're scarce here."

"Don't mention it. Please get in."

The interior had cold leather seats and the smell of an ashtray not cleaned out.

"Brisk today, isn't it?"

"*Berliner Luft*, as they say here – Berlin air – which can whip you around on occasion."

Jack pulled out from the curb.

"Did you park in the Kantstrasse garage?"

"Yes."

"It's difficult to find a spot around here."

"So do you live nearby?"

"I know the area."

Jack drove up a series of narrow ramps to the still-deserted top level and pulled in next to the VW. "Perfect. Until noon the place is fairly empty."

Jack locked his car, took a few puffs on a cigarette, and then snuffed it out on the concrete, adding to a small scattering of squashed butts.

How many of these unsightly things do they sweep up a day?

I reached in my purse for the key.

"All right, let's head for Friedrichstrasse. Got the route there down pat, Renate?"

"Yes." *So nice to hear my first name!*

I negotiated the car down the arrow ramps to the exit at Kantstrasse.

"I've heard lots about you," Jack said.

"I trust it's all been positive."

"Indeed. You were born in Germany but moved to Chicago. Your American English, I must say, is flawless."

"Thank you. I was young enough to learn the language without an accent."

"Many Germans I know who moved to America have lost the fine touches with their mother tongue."

"My mother and I continued to speak German, though."

"Aha! A true bilingual lady!"

We passed the Theater des Westens, the Memorial Church, and the new Hilton Hotel. Jack had me skirt the south end of the Tierpark – for me a new route toward the Grosser Stern hub.

"German is not the easiest language to learn." Jack said.

"All you need to know is that the verb comes either first, second – or last. Everything else in between is filler."

Jack chuckled. "It's the first time anyone's made the German sentence structure so clear to me."

"Thanks."

A little humor helped settle the butterflies in my stomach.

At the Stern I turned right toward the Brandenburg Gate and was relieved to find the traffic light this time of day.

"Before we cross over the border, let's stop at Charlie's Restaurant. When you see the neon sign, pull in across the street. We'll only be minutes from the checkpoint then."

We entered an American fifties-style restaurant with high-backed plastic booths and a long counter with stools. A few patrons were lined up at the cashier to pay. As we walked by, the waitress greeted us without a trace of a smile.

"Rita's usually grumpy at this time. She's been on duty since 5 A.M., and on Wednesday, she's on her own between breakfast and lunchtime."

We took a rear booth and Jack sat next to me.

"Salami sandwiches and coffee okay?"

"Sure."

He hailed Rita and ordered.

She brought two steaming mugs. "Salamis will be just a sec."

"I assume you've not driven through Checkpoint Charlie before."

"No, I've only been on a tour bus."

"It's a bit more involved with cars. You'll need to have a close look at the setup."

Our sandwiches, piled open-faced on white bread, arrived with American swiftness.

"Let's eat before we look at our itinerary."

*   *   *

I raced through my food to keep up with Jack. We waited in silence until Rita cleared away our dishes. Jack spread out a map of the West–East border in front of us, and handed me some photos. "These were taken from the upper story of a building in the US zone."

"A bird's-eye view really helps," I said.

Jack used a pen to trace the layout of the East Berlin border area. "As you may remember, the Friedrichstrasse crossing consists of an elaborate series of concrete walls, crosshatched anti-tank barriers and tollgates. The actual border covers the length of an entire city block. The apartment houses with their windows filled in with concrete mark the far end."

"I'm amazed how they can make an ugly area look even uglier."

"They're masters at it." Jack bent over the map. "Okay, now for the particulars. From Checkpoint Charlie, you'll cross a white strip into

231

East Berlin through a no-man's-land of about fifty yards, clearly marked with a white border and a sign that says 'YOU ARE LEAVING THE AMERICAN SECTOR.' Because of a recent escape attempt near the checkpoint, all Western vehicles are now required to halt at the reinforced tollgate designed to prevent anyone from ramming his way through.

"The next checkpoint is a smaller tollgate" – Jack pointed to it with his pen – "manned by armed Vopos or Grepos. From there, cars from both directions stop at the rectangular hut for processing. After you park, exit and go through the passport control and visa purchase in the hut. The West-to-East leg ends with two offset tollgates; cars zigzag to the end point, where two Vopos stand watch."

"Not much chance of taking a wrong turn, is there?"

"No." Jack unfolded an enlarged map of East Berlin. "The trickiest part of our twenty-odd-kilometer route to Friedrichshagen occurs around a major connector train station, the Ostbahnhof, where railroad lines and the main road weave across the Spree River. From that point on, we follow the main drag, the Hauptstrasse, to Friedrichshagen. It's pretty simple."

When Jack excused himself, I moved the map in front of me to review it.

*   *   *

"Jack, is there anything particular I should know about the way back?" I asked.

"Yes. The Vopos can be more thorough at the hut. They wave each vehicle one by one through to the wider tollgate. When you see the sign 'YOU ARE LEAVING THE SOVIET SECTOR.' you'll be just seconds from Checkpoint Charlie. Continue to the cross street of Zimmer- and Friedrichstrasse." Jack pointed out the corner where Alfred and Heinz would wait to greet me.

"I know this is a lot to absorb, but you'll come through with flying colors. The trial run today should clear up any concerns. Questions?"

"No."

"All right," Jack folded up the map. "Let's give it a go, then."

In a depressing and desolate area near the border, where some of the worst hand-to-hand fighting had occurred during World War II, there were only a couple of pedestrians around. I turned into Friedrichstrasse toward Checkpoint Charlie.

"Are your knees feeling like putty?"

"I'm afraid so."

"When I drove over the first time I reacted the same way."

So why doesn't Jack to do this? Too late we're already at the border.

I slowed down and pulled up to the window at Checkpoint Charlie.

"Hello there," a US military policeman said. "Where are you headed?"

Jack leaned toward me. "We'd like to see the sights."

The MP looked at our passports. "Hmm, a Brit. Cheerio! Be sure to return before midnight." He handed back our documents and waved us on.

Jack smiled. "The officer must think I'm upper class."

I crossed over the white demarcation line into East Berlin in second gear. *What am I doing here?*

"My God, the guys with weapons, a no-man's-land, and enough barriers to keep out a tank. I had a lot of distracting Texans on the tour bus and didn't pay that much attention."

"Keep calm."

Shivering in the cold, two Grepos motioned us on through the tollgate; I eased through the opening lined with coarse, off-white concrete blocks, as ugly as a gap in cigarette-stained teeth. At the large reception hut, only a few cars waited to be processed. We parked, got out and paid for our visas. After one Vopo inspected the trunk, another motioned us on. It seemed to take forever to maneuver at a snail's pace through the offset barriers and deserted lot.

The air reeked of cheap gas and emissions from two-cylinder Trabis. I continued on to Unter den Linden and by the opera house, which I recognized from the bus tour, in the direction of the Ostbahnhof. Cars coming from other arteries added to the traffic. I followed the meandering main road through to the other side of the Spree River, and Jack had to remind me of a crucial turn over the river. I knew there'd be no room for error when I took this route alone.

*   *   *

In Friedrichshagen, I drove down the main street toward Lake Müggelsee, turned right, and parked just before entering our contact street. *No one around this cold day.*

On Emmerichstrasse, we walked alongside once majestic villas, now with shutters askew, and plaster chipped or cracked. Others were boarded up with scrap wood. About midway, across the street to the right, number 34, a stately and intact villa, graced the area.

"You'll rendezvous with Dieter and the crew in the villa opposite."

Jack tilted his head. Cupping his hands, he paused to light a cigarette. "Everything looks different when it's dark. Hardly any of these houses will have lights burning. As soon as you enter this street, switch off your head-lights and go up the driveway into the garage. Inside, a crew of three – Schneider, Helms, and Reinke – will make any last-minute adjustments."

I nodded and made mental notes.

Jack continued. "These fellows have worked together for a decade rebuilding Western cars. By day they're just ordinary GDR citizens – car mechanics – but by night they help desperate citizens who want to escape. Since the Wall, as you can imagine, their clandestine activi-ty has dwindled to a couple of successful attempts from the East German border to the West. They're eager to participate in this es-cape, and you can be confident you're in good hands."

Jack snuffed out his cigarette and put it into an empty hard pack. "Walk to the end of the street. When I pull up, get in on the passen-ger side. I'd like you to check out the reverse way to Friedrichstrasse."

Most of the way to the border was uneventful, and the spaghetti roads were much easier to follow in reverse.

"Think you've got a grip on the Ostbahnhof stretch?"

"Now that I've negotiated it, the way to Friedrichshagen seems less complicated."

"Plus, after sunset, the traffic dies down to a trickle."

We traveled down Unter den Linden. Jack pulled onto a divider strip across from the opera house.

I saw the traffic light and the road leading to the parking lot behind the opera house.

"*Der Rosenkavalier*, scheduled for December 23, lasts until roughly 11:10 at night. Then, when they reach their cars, the operagoers will need fifteen to twenty minutes to reach the border, depending on traffic."

"Got it." *I'd much rather attend the opera on that night than wander all over East Berlin.*

At Friedrichstrasse, we inched through the deserted area around the two offset concrete barriers, and parked at the hut control station for the vehicle inspection. The driver ahead of us waited for her car to be processed as another passed through the toll barrier ahead.

The Grepos looked under our car and shone flashlights into the interior. *"Weiterfahren"*– "Move on" – one of them ordered, and pointed toward the narrow passageway. After the final crossbar, we entered the fifty-yard gap separating the station from Checkpoint Charlie. Two young guards motioned us on with their rifles. Jack crossed the white line separating East from West Berlin, passed Checkpoint Charlie and slowed at the corner of Zimmerstrasse for my rendezvous with Heinz and Alfred.

*　　*　　*

At the Kantstrasse garage the upper level was about half full, but a Ford Taunus in the space next to Jack's was just pulling out.

Whew, glad this is over, although I'll need a couple of cups of calming tea to unwind. What will it be like on the target day?

Jack turned to me. "I'll give Heinz a full report. He'll drop by later to pick up your car and call you when everything is ready. You and I will make one final run before the target day."

"All right."

"By the way, here's a pocket pen flashlight and a fold-out map of East and West Berlin. After all, it'll be dark when you cross over."

"Thank you." I stuffed the map in the small glove compartment and the flashlight into my purse.

"Can I give you a lift home?"

"Not necessary, Jack. I can use the fresh air."

"All right, then, best of luck," Jack said with a toothy grin.

He waved goodbye as his car disappeared down the ramp.

Pension Schulz had never looked so welcoming. I propped myself up with pillows, and I took a nap. Could I really carry off this trip to East Berlin alone – or rather, with a secret passenger?

No time for further pondering. Tomorrow was my last session with Bautsch.

30

The train to the GSL was a piece of cake compared to the day before with Jack: no worries for the moment about routes, traffic or errors. Nevertheless, I was consumed with angst about the escape plan with Dieter. What would take more courage: to phone Heinz and say it was all off, or to carry out the plan for some reason I couldn't articulate. Maybe the weekend with Christine would bring a modicum of clarity into my taxed brain.

At the library, there was no chance of holiday fever. The atmosphere in the stacks and the canteen was dismal. Outside, a lone red star atop the Marienkirche served as the only subdued reminder of Christmas.

Dr. Bautsch and I ended our sessions on good terms. He was satisfied I came away with a correct (=GDR) grasp of Romantic poetry and had used, but not abused, the great collection in the GSL. In other words Heine remained in the shadows for now; I kept mum about my plan to bring him back when I revised my approach for Dr. Blume. We shook hands, and the professor gave me his latest book, *Die Romantische Seele*. I thumbed through the table of contents as the professor retrieved my coat from the tree at the far wall. From the looks of it, the book was a treatise on the "soul" of Romantic poets who had any connection with the geographic area of the GDR.

So Goethe and Eichendorff are now sons of the GDR. Oh well. At least they had souls.

On my way home, I reflected on our sessions together. Bautsch's exacting, lopsided scholarship, and the way he'd pushed me to take an ideological stance (in his corner, of course) on Romantic poetry, had amused me even as they'd frustrated me. Though I didn't agree with his views, they'd helped me define my own.

Goodbye, East Berlin, for now. Will Bautsch and I ever cross paths again? Probably not. I felt sad in some way I couldn't quite define.

*   *   *

It was good to be back in West Berlin. I celebrated my return from the East with a stroll on the festive Ku-Damm toward the equally festive Kaiser Memorial Church adorned with a white star at the top of the tower. After a strong cup of coffee at the Schultheiss Restaurant, I rejoined the hustle and bustle of shoppers and gathered gift ideas for the season. I got nostalgic thinking about what I might have bought Mama and Papi, or could pick up for Hildegard, Laura – and other ones near to me – but not in my midst.

I returned to my trusty desk piled with bags of crackers and chips sans any gifts for now. I dived in to revamp what I'd written at the GSL, essentially to appease Bautsch's negative view of Heine for my dissertation. Tricky business.

December 5 – home with Advent music on the radio
Just finished this day's work on my dissertation and ironed out the Bautsch Quatsch. *It's the eve of St. Nicholas. I remember Mama used to remind me to place my prettiest shoes outside the front door. Saint Nick would fill them at night, she assured me. I got fun presents, like chocolates and toys. And when I was six, Papi gave me a puppy. I found a dog's tag in my shoes, and when I went to the kitchen, there Nora sat, tail wagging. I was in heaven!*

I loved the way Mama made sure to find some trinket to put in my worn shoes, even if it came secondhand. I miss her so much, and Laura, too. I wonder how the St. Nick party in Ryan will be. All the German-Americans will contribute carloads of used toys for underprivileged kids. Enough charity racked up until next year. How cynical I've become.

I'm relishing the quiet of this night before Christine's tomorrow. What will things be like after another stay over? Will this weekend stamp me as her new girlfriend?

Tomorrow I want to pick out some lines from Hymnen an die Nacht *to show Christine. I'm curious as to how she will respond. My desk looks a fright. Oh, well no reason to straighten it up just now.*

Friday night, Christine met me at the door.

"Hi, Ren, how are you?"

"Fine, and you?"

"What've you got there in the shopping bag?"

"A pizza."

"Pizza? I though we were–"

"Christine, let me take some of the pressure off your week. I know it's been rough at work, and you've got to be tired."

I walked into the kitchen and put the pizza in the almost empty fridge. I wondered what she had planned for supper. Frozen stuff?

We sat on the couch over beer and nibblies, and talked about her week and mine. As I suspected, Christine's office had the yearly books to prepare, so everyone was frazzled and grumpy. I told her about my research on the poet Novalis, who epitomized the German Romantic pursuit of the elusive blue flower. I quoted to her by heart from the sixth poem of his cycle *Hymns to the Night.*

> *Gelobt sey uns die ewge Nacht,*
> *Gelobt der ewge Schlummer.*
> *Wohl hat der Tag uns warm gemacht,*
> *Und welk der lange Kummer.*
> *Die Lust der Fremde ging uns aus,*
> *Zum Vater wollen wir nach Haus.*

Blessed be the everlasting night,
And blessed the endless slumber.
We are heated by the day too bright,
And withered up with care.
We're weary of a life abroad,
And we now want our Father's home.

"I guess these Romantics really loved darkness, huh?" Christine said.

"Yes, Novalis especially adored the night."

"Could you be a person of the night, too, Ren?"

"Perhaps so." *I'm not going to pursue her bait.*

I jumped up from the couch. "Okay, enough of dark talk for now. Time to heat up the pizza." In the pantry, I poked around and found a tin sheet for the pizza, and set the oven timer for twenty minutes.

*   *   *

After supper, Christine returned to the questions she had posed the last time I'd stayed over. I tried to put her off, but she persisted.

"Renate, I asked you whether you have room for someone in your life. You've been somewhat unavailable – at least it's been my impression the past few weeks."

"Perhaps, like Novalis, I'm searching for the unattainable, that blue flower."

"What does this elusive search mean for your life, Ren?"

"The Romantics were constantly on the way home – *immer nach Hause* – but never quite there."

"And do you have room in your heart for a lover on this never-quite-there journey?"

"I admit it's uncomfortable for me. I don't know if I can label myself as anything yet. Yes, I've felt passion with you I'd never experienced before. But it confuses me."

Christine searched in her pocket for a hanky and gave it to me. "I'm a patient person, Ren, believe me. By the same token, I need you to find a way to accept who you are with me, for the sake of our relationship. I can't imagine a huge question mark hanging out there as to who you are."

"All I can say is, I need time. This is all so sudden."

"Don't expect me to hang around like a marionette on a string, though."

"I don't." *At least I think I don't.*

We aired our issues as far as we could that night, and ended with a hug.

Christine went off to the bedroom while I unpacked my bag for a soak in the bathtub. When I finished, I walked into a candlelit room. The bed was freshly made, but Christine had fallen asleep.

After breakfast in bed on Saturday (prepared by hers truly), I took a long walk along the Spree. Christine, in the meantime, had gone to pick up a few items for supper before the shops closed at 2 P.M.

The aroma of food wafting from the kitchen woke me up from my nap. Christine had evidently done a lot of shopping. She'd prepared steak, mashed potatoes, a cucumber salad, and freshly made crème brûlée for desert. If she wanted to spoil me, she did a good job.

On Sunday, we decided to take the train to an outlying lake Krumme Lanke for coffee and pastry. The setting was magical. An overnight snow had turned to ice on the nearby forest branches, glistening like a premature Christmas tree.

Christine was not especially talkative this weekend, so I chatted about my teaching experiences and my German students' dumb grammar mistakes, waiting for an opening to return to our postponed topic.

Finally, the neutral setting and relaxed atmosphere loosened my reservations. *Summa summarum:* I tried to assure Christine there was space for her in my life, and to let her know how important she was to me. For her part, Christine told me she wouldn't demand what I couldn't give, but that she wanted me to be open and extend myself to her. It felt good to have such a candid – if brief – conversation.

It felt so difficult separating from Christine and her bed early Monday.

*　　*　　*

Back home I hopped into my shower. At least there were no more preps for Bautsch – and no more gloomy meals at the DSL!

December 11 – at home
I've had my first complete weekend with Christine. Not sure if I'm ecstatic or wary. It's not just anyone she's interested in - it's ME. I don't know if I believe that. Why do I doubt my eyes and ears, and my insides? Then why am I so happy to be home? I'm lounging around, chapters organized in piles on the table. What a pleasure to hole up in my own apartment and snuggle up in my blankets to eat chips, drink beer and listen to whatever I want on the radio – no one to answer to, and I can come and go as I like. Christine's hunch might be right when she asked if I had room or time for her.

Preoccupied with these questions, I moved to my easy chair and continued to write.

Sharing Christine's space even for a couple of days was a challenge. Her domestic self unsettles me. It's not as if she hangs around my neck – she's got her job and the Monday gig at the Panther. Am I an ingrate?

I feel conflicted, seeking solitude on the one hand, but on the other, wondering whether I'm included in Christine's holiday plans! Will we be together for Christmas? If she spends it with her mother, will I be welcome? Is Christine out to her or not?

This relationship with Christine – from my perspective – am I in it for the candy? Is it physical passion, love, or just to explore? Why did she have to play psychologist and place demands on me? It seems almost like an entrance exam (pardon the pun) I have to pass. What do I want out of life, she wants to know. Isn't it clear I'm on track toward a career?

Meanwhile, thoughts of Dieter and the escape won't let me rest. I can't get the two Sundays with him out of my mind. Would Laura approve of his plea for help? What will happen when Dieter's in the West and becomes "available"?

I'm still in a sweat from a dream about Dieter getting stuck in a refugee camp – now is that prophetic or wishful thinking?

Christine was also in the dream as part of the staff that assigned bed numbers for the refugees. What's that supposed to mean? I never should have agreed to Dieter's plan. God, I must have a screw loose. Heinz has to find someone else. I don't know how to tell Christine about my involvement with Dieter, or for that matter reveal to either of them the terrible secret of my father's past! So many secrets to harbor. I'm stymied as to how to proceed – and could use some answers. From whom, though?

The next day, I took a break from my ruminations to work on my diss. I pulled myself together and wrote until late to capture any new insights from my last talk with Bautsch. Finally, I was ready to send Dr. Blume my promised chapters, due to arrive by December 21, in time for his semester break. *Merry Christmas, Professor!*

*   *   *

After sending the chapters off, I phoned Christine on a whim and proposed we celebrate the next day with a trip to Peacock Island, a nature reserve in the River Havel in southwest Berlin. Never mind that we'd had another snowfall and I had only bought one gift for Christine thus far.

"Friday's out, *Schatz*. No way I can call in sick. Let's go on Saturday right from my place. We'll have the place to ourselves. Everyone will be out shopping."

I was disappointed and hurt, with no desire to work on the diss and no one to talk to. Robert, his semester over, was on his way to Ohio, Westerheim was in Merry Old England, and the moon would have been easier to reach than Dieter.

There was nothing left to do but go Christmas shopping. Lucky I did! Bote und Bock had a special on an Amadeus Quartet recording of Schubert's Death and the Maiden – not exactly everyone's kind of Christmas present – but one of Laura's favorite string quartets, and the store even shipped.

For Hildegard I found it more of problem deciding on the right gift, but I finally settled on Fischer-Dieskau's recording of Schubert's *Die Schöne Müllerin* with Gerald Moore. I knew she had a gramophone, and loved the work. The LP, however, was not on special. No matter!

I arrived Friday night schlepping an extra bag, a daring final purchase after Bote und Bock. It was my first attempt at buying a nice casual chic outfit on my own, in case Christine decided to dress up for our excursion. After her stir-fry of rice and al dente vegetables, we sat over wine while Christine went over her shopping list.

That night, Christine had laid out on her dresser a classy wool outfit with a matching scarf, leaving my choice (designer slacks, a silk patterned blouse under a V-neck sweater, together with sturdy but handsome boots) to pale in comparison.

Nevertheless, the next morning, I carried on with my plan, marched to the bathroom and emerged fully dressed for breakfast as a surprise.

"Hey lovely lady," Christine said as she looked up from arranging hard rolls in a wicker basket. 'Let me have a look at you. What a neat combo you picked. Turn around."

She liked it! I obliged, putting my hands on my hips.

"You look really terrific!" She patted my behind.

"Hey watch where you put your hand."

*   *   *

On the weekend, the weather cooperated with blue skies. After a quick breakfast we hopped on the S-Bahn to catching the morning ferry to Peacock Island, tucked away on the Havel River near Potsdam. There was hardly a soul around. I enjoyed the peace and quiet as we strolled for several hours passing by the Luise Temple, the ruins of an abbey and the huge neo-Gothic Cavalier's House, an imposing building designed by the Berlin architect Schinkel and intended for the children of the Prussian Royal House. But mostly we watched the free roaming peacocks display their proud and magnificent multi-colored wingspreads that contrasted with the white midwinter mantle around us. Peahens hovered together looking for whatever seeds they could find, not paying much attention to their puffy, self-absorbed male counterparts.

After returning on the 4 P.M. ferry to the mainland, we stopped for a hot chocolate at a Gasthaus in the neighboring suburb of Wannsee.

"Do you miss Rosie?" I asked after we finished our drinks.

"It takes time to recover from the blow of a breakup. You always compare the next woman to the last. Some things are totally different with the new woman, and some remind you of a former lover – or lovers."

I don't have the guts to ask how I compare with her earlier amours.

Christine reached across the table and touched my hand. "It's been a while since I've shared a space with anyone – even if it's just for a couple of nights."

When we returned to her apartment, Christine prepared supper while I settled on the couch to read the *Berliner Morgenpost*. I was glad the conversation from last week didn't come up. For me, at least, Advent was a time in which you looked forward to Christmas. Between holidays I'd use my downtime to address her questions.

*   *   *

I went home on Sunday after an *Abendbrot* of boiled ham and cheese on dark bread with tangy mustard and pickles. The next day, at a specialty gift shop on the Ku-Damm, I bought cards in English and addressed them at a little coffee bar table set up for just such purposes. I wrote Laura, Mama's neighbor Eleanor, Pastor Schmidt, Howard and Frieda, my college roommate Carol in California and Dr. Blume, and mailed everything at the post office just to make sure.

Aunt Hildegard had told me in her last letter that she intended to visit her dear nephew Willi – *"mein lieber Willi"*– whom I'd never met, for Christmas. Nevertheless, I felt sadness well up in me. Under normal circumstances would I have skipped my only relative at Christmas? On the other hand, did Hildegard want to see me? With all that was on my plate with Dieter and Christine, no way I could have visited her even if she were at home.

As solace for my dilemmas, I invited Christine to accompany me to a concert of Renaissance music with ancient instruments. She seemed to enjoy the lively rhythms and tempos – and to her own surprise found the music upbeat. Hooray!

"I've just got to learn the recorder some day," she said.

The next day, I snapped up the last album of ancient Christmas carols with baroque instruments at Bote und Bock to give her as a present. Problem solved!

Meanwhile the dreaded call from Heinz lurked in my mind, and my need to clarify where I would spend Christmas.

31

On Thursday, December 19, Heinz called.

"Hello, Fräulein Seiler. Your VW has been rebuilt and is ready to go. Jack will pick you up tomorrow for the final run. Alfred and I will meet you on Monday night at the corner of Zimmer and Friedrichstrasse."

How did I get myself into this mess?

The next day, Jack drove up, and ceded me the wheel. With light traffic and decent weather, we made it to the villa and back to the pension without a hitch.

The entire weekend with Christine, my stomach was tied in knots. When we parted on Sunday, she suggested we meet to get last-minute gifts on Tuesday morning, the twenty-fourth. Monday night she planned to be up until all hours at a Panther holiday party, which I begged off from, saying I was going to see *Der Rosenkavalier* with a professor on my dissertation committee.

I still hadn't mustered the courage to broach where Christine wanted to spend Christmas Day. *Maybe I don't want to know.*

Should I have booked a flight to Chicago to spend time with Laura? *What a silly idea, Ren. Laura plans to visit her parents the week between Christmas and New Year's.* Had I painted myself into a corner and set myself up to spend the holidays alone?

Late Sunday afternoon, I left Christine's to rendezvous with Jack at the Kantstrasse garage. He had taken the VW through its final weight check, supervised the precise allotment of gasoline, and handed me the keys, registration, plus an opera ticket.

Frazzled, I tossed and turned all night listening to the bells peal each hour until three o'clock, when I finally fell asleep until the alarm buzzed.

*   *   *

Today was D-Day, Dieter's Day – albeit with less than seven hours of light. I made an even later appearance than normal in the breakfast room. An assistant was clearing the table of an Australian couple in town for the holidays. Schulz must be out on errands. Good – I'd have space to gather my wits.

No reason to hurry through my roll with Black Forest ham and cheese. There were another five or so hours before I had to be ready. For once, I had nothing planned to fill them, and my favorite time-waster, the newspaper, was saturated with ads to entice last-minute shoppers. Looking at my watch didn't make the time go any faster, either.

In my room, I was able to find only one radio station with any kind of appropriate seasonal programming – ancient carols, which calmed my nerves – and fortified me for venturing out. Unable to resist a visit to the Kantstrasse garage, I looked at the car once again from every angle. I couldn't spot anything unusual.

After a walk and a nap, I got around to finalizing my outfit for tonight – not an easy choice to make, under the circumstances. I had to look the part for the opera. After all, my seat was in the mezzanine, and it was the holidays when, as far as I observed this Advent season, women did "trot out their duds," as Laura would say. I was willing to bet for an evening at the Staatsoper the ladies would do it in spades. Would the Vopos know or care? You never know. Thank heavens I didn't have to dress like an *Ossie*.

My mental torture dragged on for at least an hour. Okay not exactly escape clothing, but I can't just dress in my usual theater pants suit outfit, or skirt jacket combo. Only one choice made me look believable: my black, long-sleeved dress Laura and I had bought for a performance of *Tosca* at the Lyric Opera in Chicago, plus a lined, three-quarter-length coat and boots to match. All right! I tucked my opera ticket, passport and car papers into my theater purse along with a hanky, lipstick and a few coins.

Five nineteen. Time to set off. Not a soul was around as I descended the four flights of stairs to the street. It was a relief not to attract undue attention to myself.

It took about twenty minutes to drive with holiday traffic from the Kantstrasse garage to Charlie's Restaurant. I phoned Heinz outside before placing my order.

"Remember," he said, "stick to the main road – Hauptstrasse – after Ostkreuz. Follow the yellow right-of-way sign; the street will funnel you north over the Spree River toward Friedrichshagen."

When I entered the restaurant, the waitress looked me over. "Going to a holiday party?"

"Um no, to the opera."

"Our prices sure beat theirs, I bet."

My face felt hot.

I finished my order of a ham sandwich and milk shake and paid. In the car, I sat glued to the seat and gave myself five minutes to settle my nerves before continuing on.

*   *   *

Clutching the wheel, I turned east onto Potsdammerstrasse. Through the mist, the white sentry hut with "US ARMY CHECKPOINT" on the roof loomed ahead. The Americans perched inside their guard post while two West Berlin policemen stood nearby rubbing their hands together in the chill. I pulled over for some deep breaths.

The American control was routine, the steps familiar now after my trips with Jack. I crossed the white painted strip at "YOU ARE LEAVING THE AMERICAN SECTOR," and inched through the narrow concrete blocks toward the rectangular hut. Two green-uniformed Vopos waved me toward a parking spot. From a watchtower above men with binoculars watched an American tour bus on its way to West Berlin.

On the hut roof, a clock with bare hatch marks indicated it was six fifteen. I paid for the day visa, handed over my passport and watched it slip through a slit in the wall. Then I joined the visitors – stiff in formal theater attire – gathered around in silence. Ten minutes later, a bundle of passports dropped into the bin on our side; a Vopo handed them to each person one by one, comparing faces and photos.

Arms folded, a Vopo waited at my car.

"*Pass* and *Zulassung*," he said.

My heart pounded as I handed him the documents.

The Vopo paged through my passport, checked the registration and, after a brief glance into the interior with his flashlight, motioned me to drive on. Behind the wheel, I put my purse on the passenger seat and the passport on the dashboard in readiness. Under the scrutiny of two more Vopos, I moved at a snail's pace around the offset barriers and showed my documents a final time. I took a moment to secure them in my purse, and then joined a couple of Western cars moving in the direction of Unter den Linden and the theater district.

Glad to be out of that dismal border area!

When I reached the old shell-shocked Ostkreuz station, stragglers at a bus stop looked up as they heard the sound of a Western engine. Wasn't it taking a long time to reach Friedrichshagen? What happened to Hauptstrasse?

It appeared I had wandered into an industrial area. At the end of the next block the street dead-ended into a long gray wall. *Damn!* It was no ordinary factory wall, but the Berlin Wall, separating the district of Treptow from Neukölln in West Berlin!

I pulled over on a deserted side street to pinpoint my exact location on my accordion map. I reached down into my purse for the pocket flashlight and searched through packs of tissue and car papers until my fingers located the cool metal cylinder. The Treptow area was buried in a crease and the street names were difficult to read.

While the motor idled, I paused to wipe my forehead and checked the map again. The only thing to do was retrace my route, which meant a U-turn back toward the main road. My instructions had been to arrive in Emmerichstrasse around six forty-five. I'd be late. No way I could rush, however. Heinz had warned me to observe the speed laws strictly. "Those Vopos like to pocket Western money if they see the least infraction. Better you be a little late than give those bastards any hard currency."

Out of nowhere, a green van pulled up behind me. Its headlights glared into my rearview mirror.

Polizei! A Vopo in a heavy, calf-length green winter coat got out, glanced at the license plate and walked toward the driver's side.

"*Guten Abend,*" he said, without a trace of a smile.

"*Guten Abend.*" The sweat trickled down between my breasts.

"*Papiere!*"

When I fumbled for my documents, the flashlight clanked on the floor. I handed the officer my passport, leaned over for the flashlight and slipped it into my pocket.

"'Friedrikstrasse' – control?" I shrugged my shoulders.

With a flashlight, the Vopo compared my face to the photo in my passport. After a moment's hesitation, he returned the passport to me.

"*Ach so, Amerikanerin. Dahin.*" He pointed straight ahead.

"Dankuh," I said in my best American accent.

"*Weiterfahren!*" The Vopo got in his car and waited for me to drive off. There was no alternative but to head the way he had indicated. Down the street I looked in my rearview mirror and saw the police car turn the corner.

After waiting several minutes, I made a U-turn, driving again past the grey outlines of factory walls. In the distance I could make out a few cars crossing Johanissthalerstrasse. Finally, with a cry of relief, I saw the street sign for Hauptstrasse to my right. It was only ten minutes to Friedrichshagen. By now it was 7:16.

Schneider, Helms and Reinke, don't give up on me!

*   *   *

Passing the train station at Friedrichshagen, I took Müggelseedamm, which paralleled the lake. As instructed, I slowed, negotiated the turn

251

at Emmerichstrasse and switched off my lights. A lone street lamp halfway down the block provided the only illumination. As the engine sound ricocheted off the cobblestone street, a light went on in a corner window of number 34.

I turned into the entranceway and a squatty muscular man stationed at the garage with a flashlight waved me down a long driveway. With a flick of his head, a second male, wiry and tall, motioned me in at the entrance. Dressed in a work jacket and overalls, a third man opened my door, whispered that I should get out, and placed his hands over the ignition. I exited, and the tall man got in and drove the VW up a small metal ramp onto a platform.

I looked around. Rolls of soundproof pads covered the walls, and open toolboxes, saws, hammers and wooden planks lay on a makeshift table next to the ramp. A small overhead bulb connected to an extension cord provided an improvised lighting system.

At least two cars like mine could have fit comfortably into the garage – probably a carriage house at one time. In Fontane's novels, aristocrats went for rides around Lake Müggelsee. Never did I imagine I'd end up at the same lake under these circumstances.

The man in shirt and slacks who had motioned me into the garage came over, wiped his hand on a towel and shook mine. "*Guten Abend*, Fräulein Seiler. Schneider's my name. Please proceed over to the house." He pointed to a breezeway leading to the villa. "Herr Reinke will summon you when we're ready."

Reinke nodded to me; then, as Helms leaned a ladder against the platform, he scrambled up it with a tool and reached through the driver's window to open the hood.

If this car has a screw loose somewhere he'll locate it. After he's finished, maybe he can try my head.

To judge by the plaster patches and different paint colors, the breezeway had seen better days. The door to the house opened and Dieter, wearing a long-sleeved flannel top and an old pair of pants, stepped out onto the breezeway.

I hurried to greet him.

Dieter bent down to hug me, his shirt damp from sweat.

"I'm a little shaky without my glasses. It's all a blur."

"Why can't you wear them now?"

"They're in a case." Dieter bit his upper lip. "Let's go inside."

We entered an unheated parlor with closed drapes – the only objects a few chairs, a small satchel, a lamp, several cups and mugs, and a table with a pitcher of water, some bread and an immersion heater. On a far wall, cardboard boxes were stacked helter-skelter.

My gown and coat felt like thin sheets on a winter's night. I laid my gloves down on the lamp stand and put my hands under my armpits for warmth.

"Would you care for some chamomile tea?"

"I could use some, thanks." I put my hand on his arm. "Dieter, are you sure you want to go through with this?"

"Yes."

I flashed on my encounter with Heinz and Alfred at Aschinger. *Fate operates just like words in well-crafted poems – unexpected – but inevitable in their forward motion.*

I prayed the men would finish in time to get us through the border and sat down to warm my hands with the mug Dieter handed me.

"Don't worry, Renate." Dieter reached for one of the stacked boxes, sat down on a chair and propped his legs up.

*   *   *

The noise in the garage stopped.

"Herr Jacobi, kommen Sie bitte!" a voice whispered from behind the door. It was Reinke.

Dieter and I both jumped up.

"God be with you," I said.

Dieter bent down to hug me and I kissed him on the cheek. He picked up his satchel and disappeared into the darkened garage. A hand closed the door behind him.

I paced around the two chairs. The scene reminded me of one time early in the war when we expected Papi to appear any minute from Prague. For at least an hour, I watched Mama walk through the house straightening up or adjusting books on the wall-to-wall mahogany shelves.

Helms returned, his clothes covered with sawdust. He took a slice of bread and poured himself a cup of water. Rocking to and fro on his short legs, he tore the bread into smaller pieces, popped each bite into his mouth and washed it down with a sip of water. He left, closing the door with barely a sound.

I covered my ears with my coat collar and checked my watch. Nine o'clock already! What was taking so long?

Out of nowhere I imagined Christine stretched over me, her small breast resting on my mouth. I took her nipple in my hands, kissed it and watched it become erect. A surge of desire coursed down my neck and arms. What would she say if she could see me now?

I heard something rustle. Herr Schneider stood at the door holding a piece of paper.

"Fräulein Seiler, I want to review the trip. You've got your route memorized, *nicht wahr?*"

"Yes."

To make sure, I repeated the route to Schneider and he nodded with approval.

"We estimate you should reach the opera house close to five minutes before eleven, just after the performance ends. In all, it should take Western operagoers a maximum of twenty minutes to reach Friedrichstrasse, depending on the traffic. One more important item: When you reach the checkpoint hut, get out. It will help make the chassis look a little higher. You should clear inspection in roughly a quarter of an hour."

Schneider paused at the door. "I'll summon you after we've assisted Herr Jacobi into his compartment and made our final check."

*   *   *

I was close to the end of my rope, when Reinke reappeared. I reached for my gloves on the lamp stand and walked into the garage. Down off the blocks, the vehicle faced the garage door. I went around to the driver's

254

side, and was relieved to see the VW stood about the same as when I had driven it with Heinz.

Schneider waited at the driver's side. "All set?"

"Is Dieter already –?"

"We just positioned him beneath the trunk. It took some work angling him around the gas tank." Schneider signaled for me to take the wheel. Any bumps you go over will hit Dieter with full force, like a rough road on a bicycle. Any brick or cobblestone street, such as Kempnerstrasse, will be painful, especially if you break or shift gears suddenly. Dieter has one towel for under his knees and um–"

"I understand." My face flushed.

"Be sure you meld into the line of cars as they appear from behind the *Staatsoper* – it will arouse less suspicion."

Reinke and Helms cleared the area around the garage door; then Schneider motioned them to the back of the vehicle.

I checked the mirrors and adjusted my seat. My shoe bumped against something metal. I pulled out an aluminum can.

"What's this?"

"Comes in handy in the event of a flat tire. Sorry, I forgot to mention it," Schneider said.

You've got to be kidding. "How do I work this thing?"

"Don't worry. Just pull the pin, stick the nozzle into the valve and press here." He demonstrated with his finger.

I slipped the can under the seat and reached for my key.

"Wait." Schneider put his hand across mine. "Do *not* start the engine. When we give you the signal, keep the clutch depressed. As the VW gains momentum, shift into second and release the clutch quickly to jumpstart the engine. Turn right at the end of the driveway and switch on your lights only after you pass the street lamp."

The garage door opened. Schneider whispered "Now!" to Reinke and Helms at the rear. I heard them grunting as they pushed the rear of the VW onto the driveway. It picked up speed; I shifted into second, felt the car jolt and the ignition fire. With the added weigh up front, I had to maneuver with caution into Emmerichstrasse. After the lone streetlamp, I turned on the lights.

Thank heavens the streets are empty.

It had begun to drizzle lightly. Droplets gathered on the windshield and the wipers smeared my vision. I pulled a lever toward me, but only a faint stream of water squirted out. Damn! Somebody overlooked topping off the tank. I pulled over at the end of the street to clear the windshield with my coat sleeve.

On the Frankfurter Allee, the VW bounced and shuddered as I drove across a short section under repair. "Dieter, I'm so sorry!" *Can he even hear me?*

So far so good – I'd guess about fifteen kilometers to go. It unnerved me to see the fuel at zero. Did we really have enough gasoline to reach Zimmerstrasse? Nothing can be done about it now. I continued on the main road and passed the Ostbahnhof, nearly deserted at this time of night.

Up ahead, the street lamps were few and far between – something I hadn't noticed when with Jack. The drizzle had turned to light rain, but the wipers continued to streak the windshield. I slowed down to wipe them, and then accelerated. Suddenly, I saw a pothole and swerved to avoid it. WHAM! The car wobbled and veered to the right. I managed to land at the curb and got out to take a look. The right rear wheel was flat!

I scrambled back into the car, rolled to a spot away from the street lamp, and checked the time: 10:27. The opera would be over in less than half an hour. Reaching for the air can, I took my flashlight, got out, rolled my evening dress up, and then, praying no police would drive by, knelt down to inspect the damage. For several minutes I fumbled with the valve. Though I managed to pump some air into the tire, I couldn't get it to inflate fully with just one hand.

One East German Trabant slowed down but didn't stop. *Wessies* were off limits.

I went around to my side and got in. My brain scrambled to find a solution, but what? I debated using Dieter to help. No, too risky. After ten minutes, beams from a headlight approached. I wiped the rearview mirror and saw a Mercedes with foreign tags pull up alongside me.

A man in a tuxedo opened the passenger window. *"Guten Abend. Huegli ist mein Name. Kann ich helfen?"*

"Oh, thank you. My rear right tire is flat."

The man parked his Mercedes ahead of me and walked back to my side.

"Have you got a spare? Frau ..."

"Johnson. No. I'm afraid not. I do have this pressurized can." I handed it to him.

"Hmm." Huegli pulled up his coat collar.

I showed him the tire valve with the flashlight.

"All right, then," Huegli said. "I'll give it a try."

While I continued to aim the flashlight – craning my neck for further traffic – Huegli applied the pressurized can to the value. After several attempts, he managed to fill the tire, then stood up and wiped his hands with his breast pocket handkerchief.

"I'd say the air should hold for about twenty-five kilometers, or half an hour. It's lucky you're just about eight from Friedrichstrasse. I'm just coming from the theater," he said, looking at my outfit. "I'm surprised I didn't see you there. It's the only theater in the area, so I would have thought ..."

"No, I attended ... a private party."

"Ach so."

"I'm so grateful to you, Herr Huegli."

Huegli nodded. "You can follow me. *Ade.*"

I waited for Huegli to pull out, and shifted into second to keep up with him, cursing the uneven roads.

No further Vopos appeared. When the *Staatsoper* came into view on my left, I slowed and turned onto the middle strip opposite the traffic light. I spotted Huegli in his Mercedes moving slowly, but when autos began to appear from the opera parking lot, he moved on.

It was five minutes past eleven. I gritted my teeth. When the light changed, I eased out just ahead of the first car, but my windshield smudged again. I paused at the curb to wipe it. Mercifully, the rain was slowing, but it wasn't going to be so easy to slip among the next group before the light changed. I waited and moved into line behind the last two automobiles, thank goodness with Western plates.

You still have enough time, Ren. Just take it easy.

At Friedrichstrasse, I wended my way around the two offset concrete barriers under the watchful eyes of a Grepo. At the Quonset hut, a lone Vopo directed me into a space adjoining the two remaining cars. As I opened the door to exit, he signaled with raised palms to wait. He then walked over and scrutinized the interior and trunk of an Opel next to me.

I watched with feigned indifference, my body racing with adrenaline. His search seemed to take forever. I opened my coat. Now it was my turn. He came over to me and looked down at my exposed evening gown. "You're the last vehicle in the theater traffic to cross. Did you attend the opera this evening?" His face looked wan and tired.

"Yes. It was *Der Rosenkavalier* – a superb performance!"

Smiling, I stared ahead as he shone his flashlight throughout the interior.

"Alles in Ordnung!" He moved to the side and waved me on.

He didn't even look underneath!

Slowly, I drove towards the final tollgate, where just two Vopos were standing between Checkpoint Charlie and me.

Dear God, let this be over as quickly as possible.

One of the Vopos in a long rain cape approached me and stood at my door, staring at me with blank eyes. He motioned for me to open the luggage compartment.

I shrugged my shoulders.

With lips curled, the Vopo walked to my side and pointed under the dashboard.

I yanked the lever. The hood unhinged with a clank.

The Vopo lifted up the trunk, pulled out a cloth and a tool – it looked like some sort of a screwdriver – and inspected it. He waved the other officer over and conferred with him.

I stared straight ahead. *Dieter, don't move a muscle!*

The officer tossed the tool and cloth back into the trunk, slammed down the hood and stepped aside. The second Vopo waved me on as the last heavy toll bar inched upward. I turned the key, but in my nervousness caused the VW to stall.

There was a sight jiggle at the front of the car. I restarted the engine. Oh no, I was in third gear! I released the clutch, and the car lurched forward through the upright tollgate. In my rearview mirror I saw two Vopos running behind me. "*He da Halt!*" one of them shouted, as shots rang out.

32

A voice whispered something, but I could only manage a groan. What happened to me? I tried to piece together where I was. My mind whirled like a microfilm on a spool; images raced by, but none stopped long enough for me to grasp them.

I heard a mature woman's voice say, "How are you?" into my ear. Her hand gently squeezed my right forearm. I tried to lift myself up, but I was too weak. Her features were still a blur.

"Your pulse is stronger now." She eased my mussed hair over my forehead.

Parched, I asked for a drink. She poured a cup of juice and brought it to my lips. The cool liquid soothed my throat.

"The doctor will come to see you on his round soon. Please get some rest. We've instructed your roommate, Frau Nippe, to refrain from engaging you in any conversation."

I must have dozed off.

*   *   *

A jab of pain shot through my left arm. Oh no! A rough bandage was wrapped around my left shoulder. I looked down to see a cast on my left wrist, and another bandage – sore to the touch – was wrapped around my forehead. My right arm, although bruised, seemed okay.

A plastic identification band on my right wrist read "Krankenhaus am Urban." How ironic. This was the hospital where I'd got my TB X-ray, a requirement for a student residence permit.

"*Ja, ja,* there was a real commotion in this room," Frau Nippe said. An older woman with her hair dyed red, she sat upright with a stack of *Klatsch* and movie star magazines strewn across her bed.

"I've been laid up the past week with gallstones. What a scene. The doctor explained you'd had surgery. I'd just turned out the light to go to sleep – my first real rest in two weeks – and suddenly my room turned into a double again. Can't imagine what you were up to at that hour in this area to end up in your condition, Fräulein . . ."

God, a busybody. I groaned and turned on my good side; searing jabs racked my shoulder blade, driving all other thoughts from my mind.

I awoke again when a nurse in uniform and cap entered the room. As she took my temperature I could read "Krankenschwester Heike" on her nametag. I registered her bright smile as she said, "Welcome back."

"Can you tell me what happened?"

"You were involved in an automobile accident at Checkpoint Charlie. Paramedics brought you to us by ambulance. Do you know what day it is?"

"I don't know . . . Christmas Eve?"

"It's the morning of December 26."

Oh no! How can that be?

"I'll let the doctor know you're awake. *Auf Wiedersehen,*" she said, and returned my chart to a chain at end of the bed.

So I had made it to the West! My memory came in erratic pieces, like vignettes. I could hear the shots, the roar of the motor as we raced into the no-man's strip, and the screech of the automobile spinning around. I pictured the villa, felt the car jerk on the rough streets, and panicked when it skidded. I could even smell the blood on my clothes.

But what had happened to Dieter?

*   *   *

It was morning. The even-paced steps of Schwester Heike were now replaced by a heavy tread. A pudgy man entered the room, his receding hair combed sideways over a bald spot. He shook my hand: "*Guten Tag.* Prof. Dr. Arnold."

Sure wouldn't want to miss out on a prof for a doctor.

Dr. Arnold pulled a pair of half glasses from his white smock. He glanced at my chart, pushing his lower lip up against the upper one. "*Ja.* Your vital signs look good."

Dr. Arnold took a seat next to my bed. "Tell me your name, and what you remember about your accident."

"My name is Renate Seiler. I remember passing the last tollgate in East Berlin on my way west. The VW stalled, and I must have gunned the motor. I felt the car jerk, and heard shouts from behind us. A bullet hit me . . . and then I don't recall much else."

"You were shot in the shoulder," Dr. Arnold said. "Your head and arms hit the window, which caused both a concussion and a fracture of your left wrist. We think the bullet wound in your shoulder came from a rifle in the guard tower. The bullet lodged at a fortunate angle and no further damage was done." Dr. Arnold indicated the entry spot on his jacket. "We removed it and also set your wrist." He took off his half glasses and stuck them in his breast pocket. "You'll need some time to recover before we can discharge you."

I groaned inside.

"Because you were first in intensive care before the orderlies brought you here early this morning, we took the liberty of looking in your purse and found your passport. We attempted to notify the American consulate but it was closed for the holidays," the doctor added. "As soon as you are able, however, the authorities will want to speak with you."

"What authorities?"

"I don't know the gentlemen's names."

"Has anyone else asked for me?"

"Two people, actually, inquired about you. One was a tall young man – the uh, companion in your vehicle – as far as I understand it."

My pulse quickened.

"I told the gentleman he was not permitted to stay until I had cleared you for visitors. And today, a nice-looking woman with dark hair – I'd say in her mid thirties – wanted to see you. The nurses at admittance sent her home but not before she put up a big fuss."

It sounds like Christine! At least she knows I'm here. I bet she's a basket case by now.

The doctor finished his notes on my chart. "All right," he looked at his watch. "I make my usual *Visite* each day around 7:30 A.M."

"I'll arrange to be here."

Dr. Arnold laughed nervously and glanced over at Frau Nippe, who immediately grabbed for a new magazine on her stack. He gathered his notes and wished me a pleasant night's rest.

By now, my neighbor must have picked up something of my situation, and I'd wager was eager to ask me all the gory details. I closed my eyes and didn't move a muscle. With all my pain, sleep was out of the question. Frau Nippe annoyed me with the constant rustling of her magazines and an occasional gravelly cough only added to my misery. What an awful way to spend this holiday.

I'll need to invent a good story for Laura if she asks how my holidays went!

A wave of depression washed over me. I was flat on my back in my former hometown, with neither Christine nor Dieter allowed in. Tears trickled down my cheeks. Fortunately, Frau Nippe, who was engrossed in one of her gossip rags, couldn't see me.

I tried again to lie on my left side. Every attempt hurt; I was doomed to stare straight ahead and could have used Laura's humor at this moment. She could turn any negative situation into a positive, even funny one. I could just hear her quip: "Hey, Ren, I know you like to keep guys in their place, but stuff them in the bowels of a car?" Or: "You said you'd give your right arm for tenure, but this is ridiculous!" Then I heard the sound of her laugh, shoulders shaking with devilish glee.

But it wasn't humorous that I couldn't be open about my situation with anyone – not even Laura.

Next morning, after a relatively good night's sleep, I prevailed upon Schwester Regina – the first nurse who checked on me – to scrounge up some paper and a pen. She came through with a notepad used by the docs: with "Krankenhaus am Urban" written at the top and a ballpoint pen with blue ink. After I finished breakfast, she raised my bed and handed me my writing materials.

December 27 – Krankenhaus am Urban, in my hospital bed
I'm supporting my left arm with a pillow and have my right hand on a notebook. My scribble may look funny, but the circumstances sure are no joke. First of all, a belated Merry Christmas to you, Ren! It's not the day you feared – whether at home alone or with Christine and her mom – and certainly not the one you wanted.

Today is dreadfully dull with a short staff on hand. At least I can recover in peace, though I still need to ward off Nippe, who sits there bored to tears on her bed looking for someone (i.e., me) to keep her occupied.

I already managed the few steps to the loo. Just peeing was a major effort. Thank heavens I was able to use my right arm to pull myself up. Grr!

I've got to speak to Christine as soon as possible. But I'm too weak to make it to a pay phone. What must she have thought when I didn't show on the twenty-fourth?

Actually, I'm apprehensive about seeing Christine. She'll demand to know what happened, and there's no explanation that will escape her scrutiny. She'll probably give old Nippe enough to gossip about for months to come. Maybe I ought to say I'm in too much pain to talk.

I remember when Robert took me to the Panther. Christine sang directly to me. Given my feelings for her, how can I push her away? What will this new turn mean for my friendship with her? I'd like to wring that Heinz's neck.

And what do I say to Dieter when he comes in? No doubt he's grateful to be in the West, but without a support system. I'm the only one he knows. The thought unnerves me.

Since arriving here in Germany, my clear path envisioned at Ryan has turned into a series of fateful encounters in different guises. Before, I was Professor Renate Seiler, faculty member on the road to my PhD. Now I don't quite know who I've become. And my father's history – a professor out of danger, above the war – has developed from that fairy tale into a frightening nightmare. What would I have done had I known about Papi's real activities? Maybe fate allowed me to table these issues until Mama and Papi were gone.

I put my notepad and pen aside, overwhelmed with pain and despair.

33

A nurse awoke me to check my stats. She noted the results, frowned slightly and looked at me. "I'm Schwester Anna. Are you all right?"

"Yes, why?"

"Your blood pressure is still high, and we need you to take this medication." She handed me a tablet. "I know you're upset and don't want to be here. But I think you'll feel better if you try to stay calm."

I looked up at her. She was different from the others. Her attentive and kind bedside manner reminded me of my father. Or maybe it was her soft Saxon accent. Perhaps she was just naturally intuitive.

Anna entered some notes into my chart. "If you need anything, just press this." She showed me a buzzer hanging by a chord at the back of my bed. "Please, get some rest." She patted my right shoulder and left.

Frau Nippe was called out for an emergency test – something about her blood values. At least now I had some peace and quiet to reflect. My thoughts drifted to Papi.

When I got sick as a child, Papi was usually the one to come in and comfort me – not that Mama wasn't there for me – but Papi was the one who massaged my forehead when I had a fever. On a Sunday outing before I reached school age, Papi and I went to the botanic gardens. I just had to sniff some petunias. Ouch! A bee had stung me! When I yelled, Papi rushed over to discover that my eye had swelled up, and I had begun to cry.

"What's this? No reason for tears." Papi took out his white embroidered handkerchief and handed it to me. "You can poke your nose in a book, *meine Kleine*, but don't try flowers," he smiled. "Come on, we'll put a cold towel on it. You'll be just fine." Papi taught me to be stoic about pain, though what really hurt was not the sting, but my fear our idyllic day together would end soon.

I remembered the episode so vividly because the next day Mama was scheduled to visit a school friend in Seefeld, a village near the North Sea, for some important reason or other. Tante Hildegard was due to arrive that night, and would take good care of me, my parents told me. I wasn't too happy about being left alone with my aunt, though Mama and Papi assured me Hildegard knew how to do fun things. Around noon, however, a telegram arrived. Hildegard would be delayed. Because of the war, trains were not always available for civilians. Troops came first, so Auntie was forced to put off her plans for a day.

My parents found another solution. Papi drove Mama to the train station as planned, but he returned with a surprise: He'd decided to stay home with me today. I skipped up and down the sidewalk. It was like a miracle.

"You really aren't going to work, Papi?"

"No, *Spatz*." He pushed my hair back over my ears. I loved it when he did that.

"We'll spend the day together. Tell me what you'd like to do."

It was a delicious day. I got all my wishes. Papi read me stories, we made *Pfannkuchen*, and he brought me more cold presses for my puffy eye. I felt like a princess in some castle on the Rhine, with my knight in attendance.

One flashback led to another. I was at Ryan, in the library, preparing for a lecture on Romantic imagery – knights on their steeds, castles, green valleys, sunshine – and happy-go-lucky fellows singing songs down country lanes.

Almost late for class, I dashed across campus to my office at Mason Hall. Folders lay scattered on the desk with committee reports, which I usually read minutes before a faculty meeting. I grabbed our textbook from a stack piled on the lower shelf and searched for my green attendance and grade book but couldn't find it! Whew, there it lay under a pile of corrected assignments!

*   *   *

Frau Nippe returned to the room to wait for her next test. I tried to look busy. Thank heavens my notepad and pen were at hand.

> *December 27 – around noon*
> *I'm never comfortable where I am. But who could be at ease in this place? Laid up, can't go anywhere, a prisoner. How long must I be cooped up here?*
>
> *The worst is, I feel like such a fool for jeopardizing my leave. If the college were to find out, I'd be in deep trouble. Blume will be in my face, so to speak, about the next group of chapters. I can push him off some, but not as much as I'd like. Here I lie – can't even begin to think about the next part of the dissertation.*
>
> *You've mastered every situation you've encountered, Ren, but this is a real challenge – and don't ever let me catch you at Aschinger again – not to mention with a dumb offer to assist some guy's medical needs.*
>
> *Hey, I just wanted to help. But best I stick to German verbs and Romantic poetry. At home is where I belong, not carting Ossies across the border!*

A woman – another hospital clerk I guess – dashed in. I put the pad and pen aside.

"*Guten Tag*, Fräulein Seiler. I'm here to take down your medical history." She crossed her fat legs; her nylons sounded like a fingernail running across a rough surface.

"Not much to report. Let's see, a broken ankle falling from my Aunt Hildegard's tree, tonsillitis, and menstrual cramps."

"I've noted them," the clerk said, and hurried off.

"Awfully nosy, that woman," Frau Nippe said, looking over my way for any indication of a conversation.

I lay facing away from her bed and fretted, interrupted only by a nurse who administered pain medication and a sedative.

*   *   *

Later that afternoon, I awoke to familiar footsteps.

"What's going on here and why was I supposed to wait?" Christine said, carrying a vase of red roses. She nodded hello to Frau Nippe, set the vase down on my night table, and adjusted the stems before coming around the bed to give me a peck on the cheek.

My eyes shot around to Frau Nippe, who for the moment at least was busy with her nails.

"Christine, the roses are beautiful." The pain in my arm mingled with the sad thought that I couldn't kiss her.

"I got them from the hospital florist and the vase from a cart in the hallway." Christine inspected my head bandage. "What on earth happened to you? Why didn't anyone contact me? My God, I'm so glad you're okay! You *are* okay, aren't you?"

"As well as can be expected. How did you find me?"

"When you didn't show up to shop on Christmas Eve morning, I called Schulz. He went to your room, but reported that you didn't answer the door. I waited an hour or so, tried Schulz one more time with no luck, and then figured something must have happened. I'd confirmed for three that afternoon at my mom's so there was time to phone some hospitals after my half day at work, but no one would give me any information, since I was not next of kin. Ditto for the police. No accident reported. I wondered if you'd decided to spend Christmas with your advisor, but I figured you would've notified me about any change of plans. A person just doesn't disappear into thin air! By then I was frantic, and couldn't let on anything to my mom how I felt."

Christine pulled out a stick of chewing gum from a pack in her purse.

"It sounds like I really mucked up your Christmas, Christine."

"Well, on Dec. 25th, I did come here to the front desk. Your family had to be located and notified, they said. When I returned yesterday, all the nurses were willing to reveal, after I pounded on the counter and said you were my roommate, that a woman about my age had been admitted late at night on the 24th after an accident. I should come back today when the hospital administrative offices were open."

I reached to touch Christine's hand.

"The wait has been like an eternity. I'll probably have to go in early tomorrow to correct any ledger errors I made." Her eyes moved back and forth as if she were trying to penetrate my soul. "The intake nurse told me you'll likely be out of here in early January, but only if you have someone at home to assist you, so it's settled. The moment you're released, I'll escort you to my place."

"What?"

"Don't worry, I called Schulz the minute I heard. He understood the problem – won't even take extra money for the time you weren't there. Yesterday, I phoned a couple of guys from the Panther. Good thing they had the day off. One's got a van he uses to transport props, and the three of us went to the pension to clear out your stuff in short order. Everything is safe and sound at my place. Do you need anything?"

I can't believe it. My apartment, my privacy, my space is gone?

"Could – could you bring me my diary? It's the one with a blue cover and Chinese print on it. I'd also like my address book, if you don't mind."

"I'm way ahead of you. I'd already discovered both in your desk drawer. Nifty-looking items. I've got your mail, too." She rummaged through her handbag and pulled out some letters, the diary and the address book, and put them on my nightstand.

An orderly poked his head in the door. "Your fifteen minutes are up, Fräulein Kaufmann."

"All right. I'm on my way." Christine turned to me. "I hear there might be other people who want to see you. Now, who would they be, I asked myself. See you later tomorrow." The hospital might let me visit longer then."

Frau Nippe had nipped off to the W.C. Christine grazed my cheek with her hand and bade me a cheery *"Tschüss!"*

Not ten minutes later a ruddy-faced clerk came by.

"*Guten Tag*, Fräulein Seiler. We need to take care of some personal information before the end of the year." She paged through a file entitled "Patient Details," scanned each column with her stubby index finger and looked up. "Now, let's see. Your address in Berlin?"

"Um – in care of Christine Kaufmann, Werther Strasse 31, Kreuzberg."

"The reason for your stay in Berlin?"

"To complete research on my dissertation."

She repeated my answer under her breath as she wrote it on the form.

My heart pounded, as I clenched my teeth.

"Any next of kin?"

"An aunt living in West Germany."

'Father and mother are dead,' as the Schumann song goes, 'no one knows me here anymore.' But you wouldn't know Schumann from a hole in the ground.

"Would you like us to notify your aunt of your hospitalization and expected release?"

"I'll write her personally."

The clerk juggled her papers, wished me "Happy New Year" and left.

*   *   *

I had just finished our dreadfully boring 5 P.M supper of bread and lunch meat, when there was a tap on the door.

Dieter poked his head through the door.

"*Guten Abend*, Renate."

"Dieter! I'm relieved to see you."

Holding a bouquet of spray carnations, Dieter hesitated when he saw the roses on the windowsill.

I stashed my notepad, diary and address book into the nightstand drawer.

"The flowers are from Alfred, Heinz and me. They send their best wishes."

"How thoughtful of you."

I motioned for Dieter to approach the bed, and whispered: "Two American officers dropped by and left the roses and a card with intake on the first floor. They're from the fellows who pulled me out on a stretcher. Please set your flowers on the windowsill and move the others further away."

Dieter nodded. He pulled a small vase from his rucksack and filled it with water from the bathroom sink. Pushing Christine's flowers towards the end of the sill, Dieter arranged his carnations and placed the vase within easy view. He pulled up a chair and sat down at the right side of the bed.

"How are you?" Dieter eyed my cast, bandaged shoulder and head.

"As well as can be expected. And you, Dieter?"

"I've got a sore rib cage, and some scrapes, but otherwise, I'm okay. I'm so sorry to have involved you in an accident. It wasn't supposed to turn out like this."

"I'm just glad we made it across the border."

"After the car stopped, I assumed we'd made it to the West. What happened, exactly?"

"In fact, the auto stalled. When I heard shots ring out, I turned the wheels to aim for Checkpoint Charlie but got hit and passed out. The doctor tells me I must have tried to brace myself to keep from hitting the windshield and wound up with a concussion and fractured wrist."

"How long will you be laid up here?"

"As far as I know, I'll be released the first or second week in January, with physical therapy to follow."

"It wasn't meant to be this way." Dieter folded his hands and rubbed his right thumb across the other.

"What happened when they discovered you?" I asked.

"I heard a man open the driver's door and say something in English to another person, so I assumed we'd reached West Berlin. I shouted and two men opened the hood. It took some engineering to get me out. To judge by the guys' facial expressions, they seemed surprised at how much of me unfolded out of the compartment below. When I pointed to the driver's seat and shrugged, they used their hands and arms to indicate you had been taken to the hospital – at least they knew the word *Krankenhaus*."

"Did you meet Heinz and Alfred?"

"No. The military took me to a detention center for medical attention and interrogation. The officers let me phone Alfred from the camp to tell him where I was."

"How long will you be staying –?"

An announcement came over the loudspeaker: "All visitors must leave." Dieter stood up. "I don't want to overtax you. Can we talk more tomorrow?"

"Yes."

Christine will be tied up during the day, thank heavens.

"Goodbye for now, then." Dieter touched my free hand, and left.

"Well! We certainly had a trainload of visitors all in one day! I'd be lucky if my good-for-nothing husband would even show," Frau Nippe said, looking up from her magazines. "My, the flowers are beautiful. If you've got an ordinary gallstone condition like me, you don't get much attention." She completed the sentence by blowing her nose loudly.

Perhaps it was time to be civil to the poor woman. She hadn't asked to have me as a roommate.

"So, what is it like with gallstones?"

"I just feel stopped up."

"Not pleasant at all, I guess."

"No, especially when so much is happening."

"Sorry for the commotion – especially during the holidays."

"Oh well, my stay here is about over," she said, with a faint smile.

"Oh?"

"Yes, the doctors feel I've made sufficient progress. I expect to be released on Monday, December 30 – "just in time," she said ruefully – "to replace my husband in the kitchen."

December 28 – evening in bed
Glad to have you back, diary friend! My foggy state over Christmas was probably a blessing in disguise. At Christine's, a holiday without Mama's Glühwein, decorated cookies and neatly trimmed tree would

have made me terribly sad. On the other hand, if Mama had been here, I know the entire scene would have shocked her: my injuries, Christine's storming in, and then Dieter's arrival. No way I could have explained that.

As for Dieter, if he'd arrived an hour earlier, I would've had an embarrassing encounter to deal with. I feel awful making up the story about Christine's flowers. These near misses, and even the idea of my new address, give me a headache. I'd like to use my good fist to pound on something. And, I wonder where Dieter is staying at the moment – at the Marienfelde Refugee Center? How could I forget to ask?

I was relieved to see Christine although it was a shock to find she'd arranged my life for me in my absence. (Psst! It doesn't feel like she opened my diary!) Oh shoot, Ren be thankful she brought it. When the clerk inquired about my address after the discharge, I felt invaded and exposed.

Okay, she had a perfectly reasonable request, but it all happened so fast and took me off guard.

Sigh. Now I have a number of people to notify about my new location, especially Hildegard and Laura – and for that matter – the college. But I have no extra reserve of energy to take care of any of that right now.

Speaking of probing questions from everywhere: the clerk who asked about my next of kin and the reason for my stay in Berlin – I wonder how she would have reacted had she known I was researching my father's Nazi past?

Frau Nippe, primo prober of all, isn't so bad, really. She's a simple woman with no kind of family life – and I'd bet a bad diet. Too bad she's stuck with a no-show husband. Just as well, with all the traffic in and out of here! Poor woman, she's heading home to resume her unhappy life and home chores. Which is better, leaving with a fractured wrist for a new apartment, or going home with a healed gall bladder to an unhappy marriage? Count your blessings, Papi used to say.

I wasn't prepared for Dieter's arrival so early on Sunday, and cinched my bathrobe. A young woman, who looked to be about his age, accompanied him.

"Hello again, Renate. I want to introduce you to Karin Tenne, my – fiancée." He shifted his weight from one foot to the other.

"Pleased to meet you, Fräulein Seiler."

My mind raced. So I'd helped a guy escape so he could unite with his girlfriend? Her wide innocent eyes told me she had no clue Dieter and I had shared anything personal.

"Won't you both sit down?"

Dieter pulled over chairs for Karin and himself from the table.

Now that I've helped Dieter escape, he appears with this Karin person. Why did he even bother to drag her along? Why not just disappear with her?

"Karin and I met several years ago in Leipzig. On the very day the Wall was built, she was visiting her uncle Alfred in West Berlin."

"I decided to stay on with my uncle," Karin chimed in, "and hoped Dieter might somehow find a way to escape. Through couriers, we arranged to wave to each other at the Wall, even though I knew he could only see my profile. But I stopped when friends warned me Dieter could be hauled off to prison. And now, he's here!"

Karin got up and touched my hand. "God bless you for your kindness to perfect strangers. I wish you a speedy recovery. Today we fly to West Germany; I've set up a medical appointment for Dieter this coming Wednesday at the university's eye clinic in Heidelberg. We'll send our address as soon as we can."

"Yes, please, I'd like to know how Dieter is faring."

Karin got up. "I'll wait down the hall."

Dieter sat with his head bowed. "Renate, the Advent service in the Marienkirche was special. I'll always remember it."

"Take good care of yourself" was all I could manage.

Dieter stood up and cupped his hand around my right hand. "My very best to you always, Renate."

*　　*　　*

I took my first sortie down the hallway to a stand where flowers for patients are disposed of, and got rid of Dieter's carnations. Nosy Nippe made some wry comment about the carnations being so pretty, and didn't I want to enjoy them a bit longer? NO! I wanted to shout over to her.

December 29 – late morning
I feel as if a truck just dumped a pile of sand on my chest. So Dieter slips out of my life as seamlessly as he came into it. How naïve of me to believe his story! I'll admit, something touched me about him – the fellow was intelligent, easy to talk to, and vulnerable to the extreme. And even if we didn't stroll down the street like a normal couple, we acted like one at the Café Budapest. That moment was special when the guy sang to us. I got to taste what a traditional passage was like, instead of looking on from the sideline, like at Marge's wedding at the U of C chapel. A weird situation. I knew she was nervous her ex-friend might show up at the ceremony just to make the bride squirm. I'd never muster that amount of sadism, but have I ever been in such a crazy position of having a female friend ditch me for a man? Can't even imagine what might have gone on in Marge's spurned girlfriend on that day. Ach, but I digress. Dieter is gone and that's that.

*   *   *

Christine came in the afternoon, gave a quick *Guten Tag* to Frau Nippe and sat down. "Bummer! I had to get the key from my boss and traipse over to the office this morning. Those are the liabilities of an accounting office at year's end. Everything's got to be perfect."

I know another bummer – ending up in a hospital in Germany over the holidays.

"Tomorrow is New Year's Eve, of course, she said, "and there's a cast party at the Panther. Can I stop by around six o'clock in the evening?"

"Sure." *No midnight celebration this year, I guess.*

"See you then. Lots to do around the apartment before you're released." Christine ran her hand across my cheek, and left.

Feeling very alone, I transferred the notepad entries into my diary.

I must have dozed off, and awoke to the sound of cupboard doors opening and closing. A medium sized suitcase lay closed on the bed. Frau Nippe, dressed in street clothes, stood with her coat over her arm.

"I'm about ready to go, Fräulein Seiler," she said, as she gathered up her night table articles to put in an overnight case. "I'm sure my hubby will be waiting for me with chocolates and a warm meal."

"Take good care of yourself." I got up to shake her frail-looking hand.

After Frau Nippe parted, I felt a pang of remorse and sadness. Did I treat her right? Should I have talked to her more? If I had lived in her neighborhood, would I have been likely to make friends with her? I guess our worlds were separated by just too much.

Now alone, I used the time before afternoon tea to write Laura and Hildegard.

Dear Laura:

Happy New Year! Hope you had a wonderful Christmas, and that your trip home was otherwise uneventful. My Christmas wasn't exactly what I had hoped for.

I had an automobile accident in East Berlin on December 23, coming back from the opera with a university friend. The car skidded in the rain and I injured my shoulder and wrist. Don't worry, I'm okay, but I'm writing this from a hospital. I expect to be released by at least the second week in January, and then you can reach me at my new address. The hospital can't release me from here if I live alone, so I'm moving to Kreuzberg to stay with Christine, a woman whom I met recently at a university function. When she came to see me in the hospital, I explained the situation, and she offered to put me up for a while in her loft apartment – she's an artist and has lots of space.

Drop a line when you can – I know the semester begins on the sixth and when you get my mail, you'll be bracing for the onslaught.

Love,
Renita

Dear Hildie:

I appreciated your Christmas card, and I'm glad to know you received yours together with your present. Isn't *Die Schöne Müllerin* just superb? I knew you would like it.

Just before Christmas Eve, I slipped on the ice, broke my wrist and elbow, and landed in the hospital. They operated on me, and set my left forearm in a cast. Don't worry, I'm fine, and look forward to the outside world in ten days. The doctors tell me I'll need physical therapy for at least six weeks.

The hospital won't release me without someone to take care of me, so Christine, a friend, has offered to let me stay at her apartment, where I won't have to shop or cook for a while. I hate to be a burden to anyone, but I appreciate her kindness. I wish you a Happy New Year, and hope this holiday finds you in good spirits.

Love,
Reni

I put my stationery away and decided to ask Christine to mail the letters for me. In this joint, by the looks of things, it might have taken days before they'd even got around to it.

The nurse came in to remove my head bandage. "Your forehead looks fine. It's the first stage in your recovery."

I paced the floor – couldn't wait to get out of here. Patience is a virtue, granted, but I was tired of virtue. I sat down at the desk and looked out onto a green mossy area near the River Spree. I remembered a family party when we rang in 1938, the year when I'd finally attend kindergarten. Our relatives brought balloons, horns and noisemakers – all of which I tried out early. I helped Mama set the table for the buffet, and of course Papi arranged to have waltzing and festive music. I wished I could relive that night. It was so much fun to dance with Papi!

New Year's Eve – in the floor lounge
Christine showed up tonight dressed to the teeth, She brought spar-
kling apple juice, which she called our "replacement bubbly." I was
touched that she had skipped the first part of the Panther party for
me. Just as well – no way you could have dragged me there. These
Germans are unable to celebrate without loud music and smoke.
Under different circumstances, Christine probably would have been
unhappy if I had wanted to stay home. Anyway, there will be
enough time for us to party. When Christine walked down the hall
waving over her shoulder, my heart ached that we couldn't kiss un-
der the mistletoe at midnight together.

Had Frau Nippe been here, she'd have noticed my swollen eyes. Even with her gone, there was nothing else to do but turn out the light. Happy New Year, Ren!

*   *   *

After the holiday hoo-hahs, Christine wasn't able to visit often, making me all the more impatient to get out of the Urban. In spite of my encumbered left arm I was in good spirits and actually looked forward to resuming work on my dissertation.

In readiness for my scheduled release, I resolved to get as much exercise as possible. I slipped a sling over my shoulder and went down to the ground floor. At the main entrance, I stepped outside, for the first time since I'd arrived. No one seemed to take notice. How crisp it smelled! All too soon, a nurse came along and motioned for me to come inside.

As I turned, I noticed a historical marker on the brick wall next to the door. To my horror, it commemorated the forced sterilizations and abortions carried out between 1933 and 1945 – in the Urban –

on an estimated 400,000 people with communicable diseases, (I learned later the forced procedures were based on a Nazi law enacted in 1933, referred to as the Prevention of Genetically Diseased Offspring.)

I was being treated in the same hospital where thousands had awaited cruel sterilization or abortion? My stomach turned queasy at the thought. I took the elevator up to my now single room, lay down, and tried to sleep.

January 4, 1964 – evening,
What a rude awakening that hospital sign was! A nap helped me through my nausea, but not my dark thoughts. Try as I might, I can't seem to avoid exposure to subterfuge, atrocities and cruelty in the Third Reich – and the GDR, for that matter. What made me feel I would be immune to them? I should ask Robert for his take on those two regimes after I've recovered from my wrist therapy (six weeks seems like an awfully long time). He's the sociologist. Does he feel the same way?

How do you spend the first year of the rest of your life without your mother? Mama would surely tell me "Halt Dich munter" – stay cheerful. But I remember her saying at Grandma Ruthie's memorial service, "When your mother goes, she takes a huge slice of your heart with you."

Mama never would have imagined the person I've turned out to be in this year abroad. Maybe it's better that way.

I prayed for guidance, and for a Solveig to believe in me.

34

After two weeks, I was dressed and in my own clothes. No more dumpy hospital garb! My bags were packed. All I needed was my release papers, and I was chomping at the bit. There was just one more appointment to get through. Who were these "authorities," and why did they want to see me before my dismissal?

My muscles tensed as I heard the door open.

"Yes?"

"Hello, Miss Seiler." A uniformed man with a row of shiny medals and polished black shoes stepped in. "I'm Lieutenant Dave Armstrong."

"Hello, Lieutenant."

Armstrong remained at attention. "Two gentlemen would like to speak to you in private. Would you follow me, please, ma'am? I've notified the staff about our location."

We came to a conference room that I'd always noticed closed and the blinds on the door shut. Armstrong opened the door. Two men, dressed in dark business suits, with close-clipped hair and black-rimmed glasses, pushed their briefcases aside and stood up.

"Hello, Miss Seiler. Please be seated. I'm George Jackson. My associate here is Ralph Stuart. We're from the United States Information Agency. We understand the hospital is about to release you, and we'd like to ask you a few questions."

I sat down across from them.

Stuart took a notepad out of his briefcase. "How are you doing?"

"I'm fine – and glad to be leaving today."

"As a matter of your security, we'd like to know where we might reach you." Jackson said, handing me a sheet from his leather notepad, along with a pen.

I wrote down Christine's address, and returned the pen and sheet.

"What are your plans for the future? Jackson asked, while looking at my address.

"To finish my dissertation."

"Do you intend to visit East Berlin again?"

"I don't know. Why?"

"We advise you to avoid travel there." Stuart removed his glasses to wipe them with a handkerchief from his breast pocket. "Ma'am, by now, it's a good bet the East Germans have found out who you are. You could be kidnapped."

"Kidnapped?"

"That's how the East operates."

"I think East Berlin won't be a problem. I finished my research over there in mid December."

"But you intend to remain in West Berlin?"

"I'm here on a grant till the end of July. Can you tell me what this is all about?"

Jackson conferred with Stuart, who jotted a few words on a legal pad.

"Miss Seiler," Jackson said, "we are impressed with your courage and poise in Mr. Jacobi's escape. You've given one fortunate man a new lease on life in the West."

"If I knew then what I know now, I'd be somewhere else other than here today."

"How's that, ma'am?"

"I didn't figure ending up on sandbags at Checkpoint Charlie." I gave him a rueful smile.

"We do appreciate your cooperation, Miss Seiler. For your safety, please inform us if your travel plans change." Jackson handed me his business card.

I said good-bye, tucked the card into my purse and hurried down the hall to call Christine. "I'm ready – get me out of this joint!"

"Take it easy. I'll be there as soon as I can."

While I sat by the window, I tried to imagine myself in Christine's place. What would it be like? The move would mean an adjustment for me – I'd never lived with another person before, except in college. The next few months were neatly plotted out in terms of my physical recovery – but as for the emotional part . . . where was I headed with my life? Was the academic route all I imagined for the future? With Mama gone, was the US still home? And what about my relationship with Christine? I wondered whether this arrangement would work out over time. All these questions put me on edge.

*   *   *

After supper, I sat on Christine's couch, hospital materials spread out on the tea table. A nurse had removed my large shoulder bandage and left a smaller one to be changed daily. With my wrist and lower arm in a cast, I couldn't manage on my own.

During my hospitalization, I'd spent time working on some credible story to tell Christine – I had lost control of the car in the rain near the border, or maybe the East Germans had been trigger-happy? Nothing sounded plausible. I'd decided that, come what might, I was going to tell the truth.

"Let's have a look. I've had some practice with Mutti's leg." She removed my dressing. "How did you get this injury? I thought you maybe tore a muscle. This looks nasty." She unpacked a box of bandages.

I tried to keep my voice as steady as possible. "It's a bullet wound."

"What? How come you didn't mention this?"

"I wanted to wait until I got to your place."

"Unbelievable. What else have you got up your sleeve?"

"Nothing, I promise."

Christine daubed antiseptic on the spot with gauze, applied a new bandage and helped me on with my nightshirt.

In bed, I told her a Lutheran pastor in West Berlin had contacted me, saying he was helping a man escape to West Berlin after a planned attempt with a contact at the East German border proved too dangerous. The past November, a couple and their child had been arrested after the contact leaked the escape.

The pastor explained he had arranged to have the church fund Martin's rescue. Christine stood up and paced the floor. "Renate, what were you thinking? How long has this deal been going on? You told me you had tickets to the opera on the twenty-third with your dissertation person. But instead you drove some guy over the border?"

"Christine, calm down. The way they worked out the escape sounded doable."

"Clergy were involved in this? I should've known. Then who is this guy you taxied over?"

"I understand he's already left for West Germany. I'm sorry I caused you so much distress and worry."

"What other stories have you got for me?"

"I promise, Christine, I'll be up front with you from now on. I've got no plans for further escapades." I stood up. "Come, don't let this incident stand between us."

I reached out to give Christine a hug. Her muscles tensed.

She never mentioned my misadventure again, but I knew she had put me on notice.

*   *   *

First thing the next morning, Christine got up early to move her desk – and my manuscript and typewriter – to a corner of the living room where I would be able to work with a pleasant view of the rooftops and church steeple – and plenty of strong coffee to help get over my hangover.

Mug and diary at hand, I sat down on the couch to survey the scene.

Kreuzberg, January 10 – at Christine's
So this is my new home – what a transition from the hospital room
to Christine's apartment! (Glad she didn't threaten to throw me

out!) I feared that by moving here, I'd lose my autonomy and my freedom, but instead, it looks like Christine – in spite of my faux pas from yesterday –is prepared to accommodate me right from the get-go.

I wonder how Dieter is. I haven't thought about him since the hospital. Does he ever think about me?

* * *

In spite of my best intentions, the ordeal in the hospital had taken more out of me than I anticipated. It took almost a week for me to bring myself to do any work. More than ever, rest and sleep seemed to be the name of the game. Christine was busy with work, her show, cooking detail and weekend shopping.

January 17 – at my desk
This injury had turned me into a kind of homebody. I'm not yet confident enough to maneuver through pedestrians as they zip by in their determined German way. Of course I can't tell Howard or Dr. Blume about my accident. It won't alter anything about my deadline or his picky eye anyway. The professor is used to the various tricks we advisees use – the most favorite being the death of a grandmother. When it happened once too often, the professor demanded proof of her death. "Oh Pein, hätte ich nur den Totenschein." (Oh woe, if only I had a death certificate), as Gretchen's neighbor lamented in Faust *about her husband who was listed as missing in battle, leaving her up s*** creek. Art imitates life.*

Okay, that's it, no more sick bay. I've got to get cracking on the diss. How long has it been since I wrote my last word?

I looked at the last page I had typed. My god, it was dated December 19 – an eternity ago – and this before Blume got his hands on it! 'What the eye doesn't see, the heart doesn't grieve over,' he liked to say about our once pristine seminar term papers, as he handed them back covered with red ink. How much red will he come up with this time? A chill ran down my spine as I contemplated my challenge for the next several months: to be there for Christine – plus work with a handicap – and meet my next deadline at Easter. Groan. I assembled some pens and placed them next to a notebook Chris had bought me.

My first real handwritten attempt at the diss felt good. After I'd completed several pages, I tapped away at the typed version with my right hand. Arduous as it was, I was happy to be productive. My brain often raced ahead of me. Thank heavens for corrective tape!

35

Snow blanketed the trees, sparkling in the sun like a diamond dress. Traffic was minimal – just those people who really had to be out and about. My life at Christine's had settled into a comfortable routine with me the Penelope, and Christine Odysseus.

As usual on a Monday, Christine had left work early to practice with her accompanist, and then was going on to the club. I didn't relish showing up at the Panther with a cast on, and carting me along to the accompanist didn't seem very practical, either. The rest of the workweek, I listened for her footsteps on the stairs around six thirty.

January 22 – at home
Christine is uncomplicated and direct; what you see is what you get.
She has introduced me to a simple life, where the basics are what
matters. I'm learning life offers you a lot if you're open to its cornu-
copia.

After supper, we sit together, drink wine, snuggle or work puz-
zles and games. Even as a one-armed bandit, I manage the games
rather well, and most often, I win. I've come to appreciate certain
silly features in magazines, like "Original and Fake," where you try
to spot the differences between two paintings. The fake has certain
items missing, and the goal is to spot as many of the changes from
the original as you can in two minutes. Christine usually wins this
one.

On Saturdays after breakfast, Christine goes shopping before the stores close, and I straighten up the apartment as best I can with my one available hand and arm. After depositing the groceries, Chris leaves for her weekend rehearsal. Sometimes she brings home new songs, which she sings to me later in the afternoon over wine. I look forward to those serenades, and then join her afterwards if I know the song – or borrow her sheet music to follow along. Now and then I offer feedback on her delivery, which she tokes graciously. She's even complimented me on my singing: "Hey you've got a sweet voice there!" she commented last weekend. I was touched, but somehow sad when she said it. I guess it reminds me of Mrs. Mueller in Bloomington. My shared musical time with Christine helps me bridge that loss.

For Sundays, I've requested American style brunch since we rarely pile out of bed earlier than ten anyway. (I taught her how to prepare eggs over easy for me.) After cleaning up the kitchen, Christine types from my handwritten manuscript for an hour or two, and I relish the respite from my tedious pace. Sunday afternoons remain open for a film, a cuddle, or when the weather permits, I get to enjoy short walks together with me hanging onto her left arm. In bed, on strolls or while making supper, we talk about stuff from A to Z, drink her beloved Alsatian and explore each other's bodies, with me on Christine's side of the bed to protect my arm – and her on the "wrong" i.e. femme side, as she likes to call it. The days blur into one another like a slide projector moving too fast. I don't want to think about summer yet. Do you suppose someone is going to read this diary forty years from now?

*   *   *

One night, as Christine and I were reading on the couch, I had a sudden desire to hear the first movement from *Vergnügte Ruh', beliebte Seelenlust* (Delightful Rest, Beloved Soul's Desire) from a Bach cantata for solo alto. Before the escape, I'd stopped into Bote und Bock to look for Christmas records, and had been struck by that very album title. *Seelenlust*, "soul's desire" – what a lovely German word it was. I understood its component parts, but noticed the combined word didn't appear in the German dictionary. Apparently, *Seelenlust* was a word unique to this cantata and the poem used as its text. I snapped up the album as an early gift to myself.

Back at the pension, I'd listened to alto Elisabeth Hölger's beautiful and moving voice, but it didn't prepare me for how I would experience her interpretation of *Vergnügte Ruh* with Christine. What had been a lovely piece now lit up with her presence.

I walked over to my desk, pulled out the record from a side shelf and handed it to her. We repaired to the bedroom and Christine put the record on. I figured she didn't know the cantata, and I was right. As Hölger's voice flowed with Bach's slow triple meter, she beckoned to me to stand up.

As I rested my cast on her shoulder, Christine placed her right arm around my waist, my right hand cupped in her left. When the music began, I sang the opening measures of the aria sotto voce into her ear, whereupon she pressed her cheek next to mine.

> *Vergnügte Ruh, beliebte Seelenlust . . .*
> *Du stärkst allein die schwache Brust.*
> *Drum sollen lauter Tugendgaben*
> *In meinem Herzen Wohnung haben.*

> Delightful rest, beloved soul's desire . . .
> You alone strengthen the weak breast.
> Therefore the pure gifts of virtue
> shall dwell in my heart.

We ended our sensual dance exactly at the conclusion of the aria.

"It blows me away, this *Seelenlust* aria, and your singing along as well! I've got goose bumps. May I play it once more, Ren?"

"Please."

Christine set the needle back to the beginning and lay down next to me on the bed. Her hand inched down from my breast to my belly, and paused to caress it before she penetrated my vagina. It was a transcendent moment, as my growing passion for her mingled with the soul's rapture.

For the first time I understood what love meant: how, when you're open to it, love changes the connection between two people. Goethe described this kind of chemistry as an irresistible attraction to a kindred spirit – with no need to explain – and no way to break it.

I reached in the dark to caress her head. "I love you, Chris."

She remained silent a few moments. "*Ach, Schatz,* I've waited for you to tell me that. When I looked into your eyes at the Panther, I experienced this *Seelenlust.*"

January 28 - at home
I'm still relishing our dance together. My relationship with Chris has already aroused such deep emotions that my trepidations are unfounded. Even Ryan College and course preparations have little sense of reality for me. I'm in love with her – a simple fact – like the Eichendorff poem I'd worked on:

> *'Dein Bildnis wunderselig*
> *Hab' ich im Herzensgrund,*
> *Das sieht so frisch und fröhlich*
> *Mich an zu jeder Stund.'*

> Deep in my heart.
> I have a wonderful image of you
> It smiles at me so openly and happily
> Every single hour.

January 31 – at my desk in Kreuzberg
Finally a break from my typewriter! It's a sunny day, high pressure and a steel blue sky. Maybe winter has decided to give up. In the courtyard a neighborhood cat is slinking its way across the backyard in hopes of additional morsels. Two kids have set up a pen where they let their rabbits out for a run. They nibble on pieces of lettuce

stashed in the kids' coat pockets. Cute! The other day the apartment manager curtailed their fun and shooed them inside. "Against the house rules," he barked at them. Curmudgeon, that guy – I'm glad they sneaked back!

February 5 – in the kitchen
With a vengeance, February has come roaring back. Outside it looks terrible! Cold Chicago-like winds are whipping through the trees in the garden, and I hardly hear any of the usual traffic sounds. I can't wait to get this damned itchy-ugly mess off my arm. Now, I'll be able to hug Chris properly and sleep on my side! Each itch reminds me of the escape. Fie on my foolish attempt to be nice and help someone I didn't even know! But, one bright spot consoles me: this month my cast comes off. Hoorah!

*   *   *

"*Toi, toi, toi!*" Chris patted my shoulder for good luck, as I got ready for the Urban Hospital outpatient clinic. "Hey, now you'll be able to do the housework and maybe a couple of other goodies!" She chuckled.

"Ready to go?" she asked, helping me on with my coat.

"Sure am."

Chris accompanied me on the streetcar to make sure I got to the correct place on time. The plan was for me to take a taxi back home, if I needed to. Chris couldn't afford to skip any more days at work. As it was, she'd be late, since we made the appointment for mid morning to circumvent the rush hour.

"I'll be pulling for you, so to speak" Chris laughed.

"We'll have to celebrate tonight."

"I've got Crément in the fridge, *Schatz.*"

Feb. 7 – at home
When the technician at the hospital clinic walked into the orthopedic room with his tools, I almost fainted. He took an electric saw, and with a piercing noise I never want to hear again, pried open

the cast. A shriveled and sallow arm emerged. It reminded me of horror movies with people who return from the dead. Glad Chris didn't stay on. There was no need for her to witness that gory sight – it might also have triggered questions I didn't want to answer. The tech cleaned up my arm while we waited for the Herr Doktor surgeon to check me out. Lucky thing I have German student insurance – and that no one asked how the accident happened.

After my dismissal, the doc marched me over to the physical therapy department to make an appointment *tout suite*. Now I've discovered what real pain is like. I've gotten – and practiced – a zillion exercises each competing with the next for masochism. I never knew how excruciating it could be just to move my wrist in any direction, or hold an object. At first, I could barely lift a pencil, let alone a wine glass.

When the exercises were over, whatever energy I had left over got funneled into just being. I discovered that before this year, I'd rarely if ever taken the time for taking in the world around me. Now I did it with relish.

Time alone with a recuperating arm gave me a lot of opportunity for contemplation. I would sit in front of the living room window and look out onto the wintry scene in the garden. The subtle changes intrigued me especially. A hard snow followed by cold winds gave everything a crusty white exterior. It reminded me of banana cream pie I once made for Mama. When I took it out of the oven to cool, the meringue looked so beautifully stiff like the snow on the bushes outside. Then, on a rare and welcomed sunny day, the snow would recede, and in the morning, crystal formations on the posts and dried vegetation would yield to something akin to drippings from a candle.

Thank heavens I had gotten quite a bit done in October and November, and that I had wrapped things up with Bautsch. Perhaps I had a premonition that a delay might crop up in my neatly planned-out life. Was there a lesson for me in this?

February 25 – at home

I've been tempted these past couple of weeks to cheat on the time I spend on these stupid exercises. Alas, they test us each session. <u>Especially</u> charming is counting against the second hand of the physical therapist's watch. I'm the world's expert on going from one to ten in <u>exactly</u> ten seconds! Chris watches me go through my routines, although I try to complete most of them while she is away. After each set – (three a day, each with seven parts and ten repetitions!), I'm so exhausted I have to rest, or go to bed early. Poor Chris often has to make do with a book or phone call to one of her buddies.

All I've been able to muster up to now is read up for my next chapters on post-romantic theory. I've about had it with books and research! They're not exactly my style anymore. I'd rather be out and about.

By now, I can tell that Chris, although patient and polite, has about reached her limits with dishwashing, cooking and shopping for two. Did her other partners handle those tasks? I didn't ask her about those previous amours – except Rosie – although I was tempted. I got the impression she didn't have women friends over much. Whatever transpired within her relationships seemed to have happened at someone else's place. Maybe that's why the place was so unkempt when I first came here. I'm no neatness fanatic, but Mama always expected me to make my bed and keep my room straightened. I often wondered: what if I had had a sister or brother?

*   *   *

By the second week in March, thanks to my conscientious exercise program, I regained full strength in my left wrist. The doc gave me a clean bill of health, and no one would have known about the surgery from looking at me. Finally I was able to wash the dishes – the warm water soothed my hand, and Chris seemed happy about the uncluttered kitchen.

Chris didn't look so pleased, however, that I made arrangements to venture out on my own to have lunch with Robert. Since coming to stay, I had spent – and wanted to spend – every spare minute with her.

"What's on your docket?" she asked one morning. My response: "aamd" – short for "work on my dissertation" in German – but not today, as I explained.

"I'd like to catch the Käthe Kollwitz prints at Gallerie Zehlendorf, and see Robert afterwards at the Free University in Dahlem."

"Robert?"

"You know, the guy who took me to the Panther."

Silence is golden, except with Chris. I'd better be here when she gets home tonight.

* * *

It was nice to be on a campus, where a mild break in the weather had prompted a few snowdrops to bud on the spacious lawn. I walked across the university commons and saw Robert standing at the entrance.

"Hello, Renate. Good to see you after so long." We entered a hall whose high walls were lined with rows of *Wappen* – coats of arms from historic German royal houses. Thin, brainy types with long hair, disheveled shirts and glasses chatted over lunch or read newspapers.

"A far cry from the Black Panther, wouldn't you say?" Robert helped me with my seat.

"More like a university chapel."

"So you had an accident and spent some time in the hospital? Gosh, that's too bad. I was surprised to hear you'd left the Pension Schulz. How come you moved?"

"The hospital wouldn't release me unless I had someone who'd be there to help me."

"So whom did you get for the honors?"

"Christine."

"Are you serious?"

"It's true."

"So do you plan to stay on?"

"I live there now."

"So you've snagged the biggest catch this side of Seattle!"

"You're surprised?"

Frank entered the lounge and came over to our table.

"Sorry I'm late. Mind if I join you?"

"Not at all. Nice to see you again, Frank."

Frank squeezed Robert's arm and sat down.

"And now it's my turn to spill the beans." Robert grinned.

* * *

I had some time before Chris got off work, so I stopped at a café and ordered their house specialty: rum cake, and pulled out my diary.

March 12 – Café Kreuzberg,

So Robert is a homosexual. Why did he insist he wasn't, at the pub? Now that he knows about Christine and me, perhaps he feels it's easier to reveal it? Or maybe it took Frank for him to figure it out.

So I guess now in his eyes I'm officially a – lesbian woman? Talks like a duck, walks like a duck, they say.

I wonder if normal folks have to go through self-reflection about their sexuality. Being different, I guess, gives you that advantage over an unexamined life. Or am I too pompous? I'm not taking any credit; instead, I'd say fate has given me the opportunity to see myself in a different light.

36

March 19 – out on the balcony
The first indication of spring is here, and I have someone I love to
share it with! It's wonderful to see the crocuses below peek through
the damp soil after so many grungy winter days. I'm looking for-
ward to our next outing, which Chris PROMISED we'd go on
even if she had to reschedule her rehearsal.

In West Berlin, you didn't have to go far for an outing. After an early Saturday breakfast and shopping spree, we went first to the Teufelsberg, or Devil's Mountain, a recreation area created from war rubble. People strolled – jackets zipped halfway down – or huddled outside at cafés. Everyone looked happy, but the area soon became too crowded and noisy.

Grunewald looked inviting with its fuzzy new undergrowth. We kept a safe distance from wild boars proudly trotting out their families, while flocks of birds soared by on their way north. Marvelous day! The next morning, a walk along the lovely Spree River with the fortified Wall glaring at us on the other side gripped us with its sad irony.

Two further outings proved to be more problematic. Christine decided to introduce me to the scene at her old haunt, Les Biens – or the LB – a women's bar, where she and I could dance.

I was curious but nervous. Chris said she hadn't gone to the LB for over a year – didn't want to run into old friends of Rosie's after their breakup. But Rosie and Chris themselves seemed to be on good terms, to judge by the Panther. I guessed the scene differed from the straight married couples I knew of who had split and said good-bye.

I soon learned what these women went through to meet each other. Chris and I got off the U-Bahn, walked about ten minutes and turned in utter darkness down a smelly back alley to a steel door.

The LB was a place behind lock and key, where a hefty bouncer stood outside. She checked IDs and took the cover charge. When we arrived, the place was jammed. Tough-looking women in leather hung out around the bar. One of them poked her neighbor as she spotted Chris and me. My first impulse was to run.

Chris managed to find a seat at a table near the dance floor. She told me to sit down and went to the bar, returning with two bottles. She handed me one, and I sat on her lap. I could feel her breasts press against my back.

Halfway through her beer, Chris saw a couple of women come in – buddies of hers, she told me – picked up her bottle and moved in their direction. She'd be only a few minutes, she said. *Charming – I came to nurse a beer?*

By now, everyone was either crowded around the bar or leaning against whatever available wall they could find. At my table, two women were engrossed in one another –a "new item," as Chris called each new starry-eyed couple at the Panther.

I couldn't talk over the din and decided to join in the bar's favorite sport: voyeurism. I was fascinated by the row of women along the wall, each with one leg bent, shoe propped up, wallet attached to their back pockets with a chain. Most had shirts rolled up with cigarette packs tucked in the fold.

Flashing an occasional thumbs-up, the onlookers scrutinized new arrivals; after approval from the group, someone would ask the new woman to dance. Their brash behavior seemed unrepentant. I guess they'd passed muster at the door and were part of the tribe. But where, I wondered, did I fit in?

What if someone wanted to dance with me? I didn't know how Chris would react, or how I should respond. Out of the corner of my eye, I saw her check me out now and then. Imagine my surprise when she invited one of the ladies at the bar to dance. I felt hurt and abandoned.

After a couple of fast DJ numbers, Chris beckoned me to the dance floor.

It must have been five or so minutes later when a heavyset woman in a greased hairdo, suit, tie and polished winged tips walked up. With a scowl, she tapped Chris on the shoulder.

"Sorry, Sam, she's booked."

"Hey, I'm not your property," I said.

Christine took my hand and whispered, "Don't worry, it's just an act."

We went to our table. No sooner had Chris sat down with me on her lap, than we saw Sam sidle up to the girly types in fancy dresses and spiked heels surveying the scene. She engaged a petite blond with coiffed hair in conversation until a masculine type from the pool table came over and tapped Sam on the shoulder with her cue. Sam turned around, made a fist against the player's chest and a scuffle ensued between them. As the group of ladies cheered "Atta girl, Thea!" the bouncer settled things by ushering Sam to the door.

Almost on cue, the DJ turned up the volume and booming bass.

Thea, a bit scuffed up, sauntered by our table, winked and returned to the pool table where her buddies waited.

"Is Thea all right?" I asked.

"None the worse for wear."

"What was that all about?"

"Just horseplay."

Not my idea of fun. The smoke got thicker; I could hardly breathe and asked Chris if we could go. I knew she was disappointed, but she didn't put up a fuss.

Arm in arm, we walked down the putrid alleyway. When we reached the street, her arm slipped out from mine.

*　　*　　*

"Is the LB always like tonight?" I asked that night in bed.

"Like what – you mean aggressive and smoky?"

"Yes, and loud. How does anyone communicate with each other?"

"It happens afterwards, *Schatz*. You've got to understand, this is a way for us women to let off steam and be ourselves. If you want it quiet, go on a weekday afternoon, when it's usually pretty empty."

March 22 – morning, in bed

Chris has just slipped out for bread and rolls. (I can almost smell them – they remind me of Mama's cookies at Easter!) She'll be gone long enough for me to get some thoughts down, at any rate.

So I've been exposed to the so-called Life at the LB: clandestine, smoke-filled, with a thumping bass. Not so gay, as some people might phrase it. More like dismal. From my limited exposure to the Panther and the LB, the nightlife here requires cigarettes, booze, muscles and blaring music. At the Panther, at least, I knew what the rules were – well, sort of. But last night I felt disoriented, disturbed. Whatever rules existed, I was too scared or green to figure them out. In a way the scene reminded me of the reception in that posh home in Chicago. I didn't know how to hold my cup of coffee and was clueless on makeup, and hightailed it to IU, where I felt safe and knew pretty much how to act. But the LB rules mystified me.

The sad part for me is seeing how fearful and tough the LB's atmosphere is. Women gather, and for a few hours only, they're allowed to be themselves. Once they're out the door, the rules change. Even Chris acted different outside the bar. We didn't hold hands, and walked as if we were only friends. I was shocked, even though Robert said everyone knew about her. Do I want to play such a secretive game? I don't know if I really want to show my face there again.

Come to think of it, I have my own secretive self to deal with: a persona who pretends to be someone she's not, and risks life and limb. Is this any way to live? I'd have to double the ante in Chris's world. Would Laura recognize me now?

*   *   *

A week later, for Chris's birthday, I invited her out to dinner. Afterwards, we went to a local art cinema, the Film Haus Berlin, to see the German art film *The Blue Angel*. Chris had seen the clip of Dietrich's famous song "Falling in Love Again," but I was surprised to learn, not the entire film.

"What's the plot?"

"In Heinrich Mann's novella, a working-class chanteuse named Lola seduces a local high school teacher named Professor Unrat."

"You mean Mann gave him a name that means garbage?"

"Mann liked to use descriptive names to describe his characters. And yeah, she treats him just like garbage. Little by little, Lola plays with her clueless lover like a cat does with a mouse, and eventually . . . he goes insane and dies."

"Whew! I guess the line from the lead song about men getting burnt takes on a new meaning."

"Right. Lola's not responsible, and she doesn't care, either."

On the way home, as we strolled through the balmy night, Chris was silent.

"What did you think of the film?"

"You know Ren, it makes me think of us."

"What do you mean?"

"For starters, you'll soon be the professor, and I'm already the cabaret singer, right?"

"Sure, but do you think those characters have something in common with us? Chris! Do you think it's about seduction, enslavement, and naiveté?"

"No, that's not what I meant. But the professor and the working-class chanteuse – we've got the same class difference."

"C'mon, Chris, am I that different from you?"

"Well . . . "

"What are you driving at, Chris?"

"You're educated and I'm not. Your life is the university and scholarship. Mine is much more mundane."

"Does that matter, Chris. Has it created a chasm between us?"

"No. I guess what bothers me is that if you were still a German, or if I were an American, there'd be no problem staying together. Either you'd live here or I'd follow you to the US."

Boy, she'd managed to leap right over into the forbidden topic, and one I had avoided for so long. Ice ran through my veins.

"Let's just take it one step at a time. Neither you nor I can predict the future. In the meantime, let's enjoy what we've got."

*   *   *

After we got back, Chris showered and went to bed without a word.

I sat on the couch and watched the moonlight flood the rooftops. For several months now, Christine and I had observed its cycle together, but in a few months, summer would be upon us – and in my other life, I had made plans to meet Laura in Spain.

March 29 – after seeing The Blue Angel *with Chris*
Okay, it was my big fat idea to go. I think Chris liked the movie, but she stunned me when she said the film had triggered her concerns about the future of our relationship. Chris feels we live in different worlds. Maybe she's right.

I haven't paid attention to that reality. Over the past months, I've lived in an eternal spring like a stopped clock on a public square. But is it real? A static season paradoxically carries the seeds of its own extinction. As Faust says to the devil, "You can have my soul when I say to any moment, 'Tarry, thou art so beautiful.'" I've acted as if there were no tomorrow, and now I can't figure out that tomorrow.

And what is my real identity? Chris didn't go into the lesbian dynamic. What would it mean to choose one side and not the other – a choice even Dietrich can't seem to pull off in her world – which still has some semblance of normalcy when compared to the women at the LB.

If I embrace the Life, I'll face some tough decisions. Should I live here with Chris, or should she come with me to Ryan? Do I even want her to? If I sided with her, would it alter my relationship with Laura or my colleagues? How would they react at campus functions or parties? Do I want to live as I choose or as society dictates? Lola doesn't give a damn, but I wonder if I can say that about myself.

The first draft of my dissertation is done; my time here will end soon. How different those two approaching closures feel. The one leads to a PhD and a ticket to advancement, the other means the end of my relationship with Chris, and would break my heart.

I slipped in between the sheets to a body turned the other way, fast asleep.

37

For days I had trouble rebounding from my *Blue Angel* discussion with Chris. To add to my upset, sober reality moved in. My contract for the academic year 1964/65 at Ryan had just arrived in the mail, forwarded from Schulz. A mere formality, the administration indicated – just sign and date at the bottom, and return before April 15 – and today was April 8! Did the staff know it took a week for mail to travel between Germany and the US?

I looked at the envelope, its upper left-hand corner emblazoned with the school mascot, a lion dancing on his hind paws. "The Ryan Lion!" fans would roar defiantly at football games. Just the thought that I should sign this thing took me to bed. I lay down and cried, my hands clutching the sheets Christine and I shared. What did Ryan know about my life since I'd come to Europe? If they knew, would they offer a contract to someone like me?

To clear my head, I took a train to the Tiergarten and walked in the forest. I felt like I was in a bad dream. How had I changed so much, so quickly? I supposed being in a foreign country could make you act in ways you wouldn't ordinarily – there was no one from Ryan to gossip about my relationship with Christine. Here I was free to break the rules, while the US would surely demand I adhere to them.

I returned to the apartment and sat down at the desk, the open letter on my stack of mail. The last pickup in the area was 3:45 P.M. I recalled

Schumann's song "In der Ferne" (Far Away), in which the alienated singer thinks about home – parents dead, he doesn't know a soul – and describes the emotion as *Waldeinsamkeit*, "loneliness of the woods."

I shared the same emptiness. And, like him, I didn't know what home was now. Was the Renate Seiler whose name was on the contract really me? Would I be able to continue life as usual if I stayed here? Could I bear to part from Christine?

I tossed a coin. Heads, Ryan, tails, Berlin. It was heads. I didn't wait another minute to talk myself out of it, just signed the damned thing and slipped it into the postbox. I returned to crash in bed.

When the phone rang at five thirty, I was in no mood to answer in my groggy state. It was probably Herr Schwarz, the owner of the Panther, who tried to track Christine's every move.

This morning at breakfast, Christine had told me she'd have to stay late at the office. I picked up the receiver, ready to brush Schwarz off.

"Hello, Miss Seiler, this is Mr. Stuart – you remember – from the hospital? Have you got a minute to talk?"

"Oh . . . uh, yes, of course."

"Fine, ma'am. How are you?" Stuart asked.

"I'm doing well. I finished my physical therapy a week ago."

"Glad to hear it."

I didn't think they were going to contact me again.

"Mr. Stuart, would you mind my asking the reason for your call?"

"Mr. Jackson and I thought that it would be nice to invite you to a steak dinner at the Hilton, now that you're out and about."

I'm not going to turn down their Hilton invite, but what's up with them anyway?

"That would be fine."

"We can pick you up if you like," Stuart said.

"I plan to be downtown tomorrow anyway. I could meet you at the hotel."

"Okay, we'll see you there. How about 1 P.M.?"

"Fine."

I spent the evening alone. My return to Ryan cycled through my head like a slide show: my dusty office, colleagues asking about my trip, the interminable rounds of faculty commitments, and a new apartment, alone. Nothing I could do or say would ever explain away my anguish, or the hurt I was about to cause. My subterfuge stunned and baffled me.

* * *

The Hilton was just down from the Memorial Church, a stone's throw away on the Budapester Strasse. A ten-story rectangular structure with a characteristic checkerboard pattern on the sides, the hotel was visible in both the West and East parts of Berlin, and, as I read, its design intended to show off American capitalist superiority.

I looked around in the spacious lobby and found Stuart and Jackson in the lounge. They rose from their chairs to greet me.

"Hello, Miss Seiler. Nice to see you again," Stuart said. "We'll go upstairs to the penthouse." He opened the elevator door and pressed P.

Why not? I'm still in the dumps from last night, so how about the top to compensate?

We entered the penthouse restaurant. Spacious windows offered a spectacular view of West Berlin's downtown.

"Shall we sit by the window? You can get a glimpse of beautiful East Berlin and that ugly Wall."

"Thanks, but I can do without the eastern half of town." I took a seat facing the restaurant.

Jackson nodded and seated me between Stuart and himself.

"Glad you could meet us so promptly." Stuart unfolded his napkin with a snap. "I imagine your dissertation takes up a lot of your day now."

"I welcome diversions."

The waiter brought our menus. American food abounded: steaks, chops, Caesar salad, burgers and fries, apple pie à la mode, and even a peanut butter sandwich. I had forgotten how much I missed American cuts of beef, and ordered a T-bone steak and a Caesar salad. Both men went for a Texas-style broiled filet with fries, tossed salad and Coke.

An assistant rolled a stainless steel cart with salad fixings over and tossed my Caesar.

What a treat! The salad has croutons and Parmesan cheese – just the way I like it.

"And you gentlemen?"

"I'll have Thousand Island, please – just dump 'er on the top," Stuart said.

"Same for me," Jackson said.

The waiter ladled the dressing onto their salads.

Jackson paused until the waiter had moved on. "We wanted to ask you, Miss Seiler. Did you know Mr. Jacobi before you agreed to help him?"

"No. I delivered some medicine to a gentleman in Friedrichshagen, and Herr Jacobi – Dieter – was present at my contact's apartment."

"We found out he belonged to the Young Pioneers. Were you aware of that, Miss Seiler?"

"No, Mr. Jackson, but Dieter told me that he wouldn't have been permitted to study at the university if he hadn't attended party meetings. He didn't impress me as pro-GDR."

"No doubt. Nevertheless, we investigated whether Mr. Jacobi might be an agent of the East German regime. He didn't show up on any official lists."

"I'm sure you didn't invite me to lunch at the Hilton to discuss Herr Jacobi."

"We're curious what motivated you to drive him to freedom," Stuart said.

I brushed an errant crouton crumb onto my napkin.

"I think it was his medical situation. After he finished his eye treatment in Berlin, he was to be sent back to Leipzig and any escape to the West would've been impossible."

"You have to admit your mission was a big risk for someone you barely knew."

"In retrospect, I probably acted hastily. But it all seemed so well thought out."

The headwaiter returned balancing a large tray with our piping hot entrees.

Stuart and Jackson slathered BBQ sauce on their steaks, while chitchatting about college football and good restaurants in Berlin.

I savored the only steak I'd probably get in Germany.

"How about coffee and apple pie à la mode?" Jackson asked as the waiter cleared away our dishes.

"Sounds great."

Over dessert, the men asked politely about my research in Berlin.

"When will you complete your PhD?" Stuart asked.

"I scheduled my defense for early September in Chicago, before the semester begins. After that it's a formality."

"We wish you good luck in advance."

"How long do you intend to remain in Berlin?" Jackson asked.

My throat tightened. "Until the end of July or so."

"I must say again how impressed we were with your desire to help Mr. Jacobi."

"Does that include my unintended stay at the hospital?"

"Even with a hitch at the end, the execution took a lot of courage and intelligence."

I looked at my watch. "Gentlemen, it's been a wonderful meal, but I need to get back to work. Did you want to contact me again for any reason?"

"Miss Seiler," Agent Stuart looked me pointedly. "We'd like to continue our relationship."

"What exactly does that mean?"

"With your proficiency in German, you could be of great assistance to our operations." Stuart leaned forward. "We figure you'd have an opportunity to serve your country, and earn some extra cash. A brand new PhD won't exactly leave you rolling in money, correct?"

"I've got a secure future – a college professor with tenure around the corner."

"What we've got in mind won't interfere with any of your plans." Jackson said. "We just want to know if you're open to the idea. Someone would contact you with details."

"And by these "details" do you mean in the States, or Germany?"

"It depends. There's no rush. You can ask questions when they contact you."

"I should be flattered, but this frankly takes me by surprise."

"Just think about it."

If I took them up on it, does that involve trading my PhD for a trench coat?

"May we give you a ride to your apartment?" Jackson asked, as we stood outside the revolving entrance door.

"Thank you, I'd like a walk. The weather's so pleasant."

"All the best to you, then."

We shook hands. The two men walked down the underground ramp and disappeared into the garage.

The agents' proposal sent my mind whirled with conflicting thoughts and reactions. I had to find a place to think.

Before getting off the bus, I remembered seeing what had looked like a local park and retraced the general direction of the bus route. A few minutes turned into half an hour's walk through a residential area and a shopping district. Damn, had I missed it? Down the road was a bus stop with the sign *"Am Bürgerpark"* – that had to be it.

I turned onto a grass-lined walkway and heard children at play. A few youngsters frolicked in a sandbox, supervised from a bench by a parent or nanny who looked up at me over her half glasses. Down the path, freshly planted pansies lined one side of an open grassy area. Spring had returned – and with it, I hoped, a better mood.

38

April 8 – in a children's park

Today I had a surprise lunch invitation from the two Americans, S & J. Two clean-cut guys add a new wrinkle to my already crumpled agenda – has Germany become a possibility after all? I don't know whether to believe them. And am I happy about that possibility? Fate enters when you don't consider options. Of course, it would solve all our problems – I'd have a job and Chris and I could stay together. Then what? Any way you worked it, nothing sounds like an ideal solution to the dilemma we face.

If I hadn't injured my arm, would I have moved in with Chris? Necessity and providence always trump any hesitancy and doubt. As I found out, you always get a lot of baggage when you hook up with another person. And that baggage – the homosexual baggage – can be heavy.

Still plagued by Christine's question about how we can make things work . . . I've never thought about the need to "work on" a relationship. What does that mean? My fantasy is that you agree to do things together, talk, have fights, make up etc. But Christine seems to be into probes with deep questions. I can't come up with anything profound, except that I have to leave. I need a miracle revelation before my talk with Chris.

I put down my pen. Children laughed in the distance, the trees were in bud all around me – but none of it could prevent my tears. Earlier today, a return to my life at Ryan had seemed the simple and easy way out of my dilemma. Had that been a mistake? I looked at my watch – 3:20 P.M. Maybe I should run to the mailbox at Savignyplatz and wait for the postman, beg him: "Please, I need that piece of mail. I retract it all!"

No. I've signed the contract; the die is cast.

* * *

The air had turned cool. I stashed my diary in my handbag and buttoned my coat. *Think fast, Ren; you'll have to put some cards on the table.* What's more, Christine expected me to be there when she got off work.

The LB came suddenly to mind. It wasn't far off my route, as I remembered. Maybe I'd feel more relaxed if I stopped in for a drink.

After a twenty-minute walk, I reached the U-Bahn station where Christine and I had detrained. I walked to the far entrance and recognized the liquor store where Christine had popped in for cigarettes. Maybe they could give me directions.

I paid the clerk a mark for chewing gum. "Is – um– there a bar named Les Biens near here?"

"Never heard of it." He wiped a speck of dust on the counter without a glance up at me.

I walked in the same direction Chris and I had taken, looking down each side street. Was this a wild goose chase, I wondered?

Up ahead, two women dressed in jeans and lumber jackets turned the corner across the street. *Tough numbers, I'll bet my last dollar they're on the way to the LB.* At the light, I zipped across, but they had disappeared. The club had to be somewhere close by. The second alleyway was lined with smelly garbage containers – impossible to forget the odor.

At least half a block down the alley I recognized the LB door, black and solid except for a peephole. A woman in a work shirt and jeans opened it a crack. When I reached into my wallet to pay, she waved her hand back and forth. "I'm not a bouncer – just helpin' out – the cover's on weekends. Name's Lisa." She motioned me in and pointed to the bar. "Dorle, our daytime gal, will help you out with your order."

Chris was right: business was slow at this time. The only other patrons were two pool players – the well-built women I had seen on the street.

A lone exhaust fan behind the bar whined on the wall. No wonder it had been so smoky that Saturday. A woman in a leather vest was chatting with Dorle. I didn't remember her from the night I'd come with Christine, and the woman didn't seem to recognize me, either.

"Hi there." I put my handbag on the counter.

"Hello." The woman in leather studied my black slacks, pea jacket and silk blouse; she motioned to Dorle for another drink.

"Comin' up, Elaine." Dorle handed her a bottle. "You know, they always leave me to clean up their crap from the night before. Nothing ever changes around here. Now, then," Dorle turned to me. "What'll it be?"

"A Pils, please – from the tap."

"You from out of town?" She took a glass out of the sink and washed it.

"A friend of mine mentioned your place."

"I asked 'cause we don't advertise." After drying the glass, Dorle laid her towel on the countertop. "We like to keep to ourselves" – she poured the Pils and slipped a coaster around the stem – "and gotta slip the police somethin' for protection."

Robert had mentioned payoffs to the cops at the pub he'd visited in Indiana. Here, these women seemed to be involved with bribes too. Not a good situation, I'd wager.

One of the pool players came to the bar and ordered a beer. I took my Pils and went to a table across the room. For about ten minutes, I watched the pool players while Elaine chatted on with Dorle.

The buzzer rang. Lisa got up from her station and let in three young women who plopped themselves on barstools. *Good. I won't have to make conversation with Elaine when Dorle gets busy.*

The buzzer rang again. Lisa jumped up and hugged two women – one with a checkered flannel shirt, jeans and a James Dean hairdo, and the other in slacks, a long-sleeved blouse, vest and fringed leather jacket. Greta and Ulli from the Black Panther were here! Our eyes met and my stomach sank. They ordered beers and sauntered over with their bottles.

"Hey – aren't you the gal we talked to at Christine's show?" Greta said. "Renate, right?"

"Yes."

"Mind if we join you?"

"Take a seat."

Greta threw her leather jacket down on an empty chair, and Ulli adjusted her long sleeves and leather vest. They sat down on either side of me.

"So what brings you to the LB?" Greta said.

"I had a bit of cabin fever."

"Cabin fever?"

"I broke my wrist and the doc removed my cast a few weeks ago."

"So you came here to be unencumbered?" Ulli asked.

"I hadn't thought of it that way."

"Nice outfit," Greta said. "Most of us dress a little different from the outside world when we come here. What do you do, if I may ask?"

"I'm a high school teacher."

"Ooh, all those budding teenagers."

"I'm not exa–"

"Open about who you are, you mean?"

"Not at my school, at any rate."

And not anywhere else, either, Greta. Hope that's the end of the personal questions.

"My grade school gym teacher was a butch if I ever saw one," Greta said. "Her hair was short and smoothed back. We all wanted to be the one she picked to demonstrate somersaults in gymnastics class."

"All right, enough about gym class." Ulli smiled. "May we treat you to another beer?"

I looked at my watch: it was nearly five o'clock. "I can only stay a short while, though."

"C'mon, the evening is still young." Greta reached out for my hand. "Wanna dance?"

We walked to the jukebox and Greta selected a slow song. On the floor, she took the lead, drawing me close to her breasts.

"So where do you teach? At our local high school?"

I winced. No way to avoid fibs. "Actually, no – at a private school in – Zehlendorf."

"With the rich folks. Right?"

"Maybe they are. I'm not. They needed an English teacher."

"Are you from Berlin? I can't place your accent."

Ulli came up from behind and placed her hand on Greta's shoulder. "May I have a whirl with the lady, too?"

"Don't worry, Renate," Ulli said, once Greta had left the dance floor. "My friend likes to ask new women to dance. But she's not going to mess with Christine's woman."

So she knows. Small world – this alternative bunch in Berlin.

When Ulli and I returned to the table, I found a new bottle of Pils and a small shot glass of clear liquid at my place.

"Is that vodka or what?"

"You bet. I told Dorle to throw in a chaser as well. It'll remove whatever you need to get rid of."

"Prost." Greta held up her glass.

"Prost." I took a sip from mine and winced. It tasted like the smell of rubbing alcohol.

"Vodka at the LB is not for the faint of heart," Ulli laughed.

"Now my turn. So what do you both do when you're not at the LB?" I asked.

"I work at City General Hospital as a nurse, and Greta has a construction site job – okay if I spill the beans on you, Greta?"

"No problem. I may work in the office, but I can lift weights the guys can't. They'd never let me do 'men's work,' though."

"Does everybody know about you at work, Ulli?" I asked.

"If they found out at the hospital I was a homo, I'd be out on my ear. Even in Berlin a lot of us don't talk about who we are in public."

"You see, Ulli, that's the difference between you and me. You keep quiet about it – but if they haven't figured it out about you at the hospital by now, they'd have to be blind."

"Well, I've been lucky so far. I haven't forgotten the masculine-looking woman who was beat up after leaving here one night. They messed up her face something awful. She had to have stitches and missed work for two weeks."

"Really? That's horrible! Didn't anyone call the police?"

"So they could join in the fun and take a few pokes as well?"

"I had no idea!"

"Welcome to the Life," Greta said.

"Would you mind if I asked you how you both became – romantically interested in women?"

"More like when did we realize we were lusting after them?" Greta chuckled.

Was that what I meant?

For the better part of an hour, over snacks and beer (and additional chasers from Greta), I listened as she and Ulli described their girlhood infatuations, coming to terms with their feelings, fear of societal rejection and parental disapproval, loves and loves lost, and heterosexuals who'd put the make on them – or vice versa.

"What's the um – toughest part of being the way you are?" I asked.

"Hmm." Ulli took a sip of beer. "When you can't ever be honest about *who* you are in public or with your family. It has consequences for everything you do."

"Can you give an example?"

Ulli paused, and Greta said, "Tell Renate your operatic story. It's true. I'll check out the scene with Dorle at the bar."

I turned to Ulli. "You're an opera singer? My goodness!"

"More like I wanted to be one. I've got the voice and the build for grand opera, like Wagner's Ring – you know, those tall, big-chested and strong women."

Her stature did remind me of Madame Manski.

"What happened? Didn't you get encouragement from your parents?"

"Absolutely. My mother's a church musician. She gave me voice lessons starting when I was fifteen, and accompanied me on the organ for Sunday solos. We also sang lieder together. Mom thought I should apply to the conservatory to study voice, and helped me prep for my audition. I was in top form that day and was admitted on the spot. But, a couple of years into my studies, I realized I couldn't continue with my dream of being on stage – let alone of becoming a diva – when I got older."

"Why not?"

"For starters, my voice teacher made it clear you had to identify with your character's emotional intent. In the dramatic soprano roles, I'd have to convince myself – let alone the entire audience – that I was in love with a man."

"What about Mozart and his character Cherubino in the *Marriage of Figaro*? That's a role for a woman who sings to another woman."

"Sure. But in trouser roles like that one – not the kind my voice type would usually get – the woman is actually playing a boy or young man."

"But Ulli, couldn't you have pretended you were singing to a woman when you were on stage with a man? Who would have known?"

"Play mental gymnastics? No."

"How about later, Ulli, after the conservatory? Aren't there more suitable roles available out in the real world?"

"Can you name some, Renate?"

"No, none that I can think of immediately."

"Exactly my point. At least not enough to keep me employed full time."

"Hmm. I never thought about a lesbian having issues with classical vocal literature. So what did you do, then?"

"A lot of soul searching. I decided to focus on lieder and church music, and see if that plan could work out."

"Sounds reasonable."

"As I discovered, where my identification problems hurt me the most was in singing lieder. Are you perhaps familiar with Franz Schubert's cycle *Die Schöne Müllerin?*"

"Yes. I heard it at school – the journeyman who falls in love with the pretty miller's daughter – but can't marry her because of his lowly station. Such a tragic story, and beautiful music."

Greta returned to the table with fresh beers from the tap for Ulli and me. *"Schöne Müllerin?"* she said. "Don't let me interrupt."

Oh, boy, I must have hit a nerve here.

"One day," Ulli said, "I brought the cycle to my voice professor at the conservatory and opened the album to the first song, 'Das Wandern ist des Müllers Lust" – (Wandering is the Miller's Joy) – and placed it in front of him at the piano. Dr. Baum closed the album, frowned and said in the most disparaging of tones, 'You know what kind of woman would perform this work!' I was humiliated and afraid. So I decided to play the game. For my conservatory graduation recital, I picked Schumann's *Frauenliebe und –leben*," a cycle of eight *Lieder* written for a woman, and quite dramatic in places."

"Sounds perfect for you, Ulli."

"You'd think."

"What's are the songs about?"

"They trace a woman's life from her engagement to her fiancé, through marriage, child bearing, and finally to her husband's tragic death. I actually performed the song cycle at school recital to see if I could pass muster. As I stood on stage portraying a woman about to get married, who refers to herself as a "'lowly maiden,' gushes over her 'marvelous man,' her 'tiny gold wedding band,' and her dream for a child who would be "her husband's spitting image"? When was I ever going to experience marriage or motherhood? Did I want to, from that frame of reference? I couldn't conjure up enough 'me' to make a performance to ring true for myself. Even though my jury was enthusiastic, I felt like an impersonator. And so, in the end, I gave up my dream, and left school. It hurt to the core."

"How did your parents respond to your change of heart?"

"My mother was shocked when I quit the conservatory and got a temporary job with the phone company. I think my father probably figured I didn't want a career as a singer, and let that sleeping dog lie. Had he known I left because I was a 'homo,' as he called us women on the masculine side, he'd have thrown me out of the house."

*　　*　　*

The bar patronage had begun to pick up. A half-dozen women in sweatshirts, jeans and jackets swaggered in, eyeing four women in high heels and dresses at a table near the bar.

Greta and Ulli turned around and exchanged nods with two of them.

"You know, it's a good question, what's the toughest part of our life," Greta said. "For me the scariest is the brawls and fights. Once, a woman asked me to her place, and when we got there she locked the door behind me. I had to slam her against the wall to get the key. Another time, a woman at a bar asked me to get in a scuffle with her over her girlie lover, and I said no. I didn't exactly want to appear at work with a busted jaw."

"So then . . . I guess I'm wondering – why would either of you want to go for women – romantically?"

Ulli motioned to Greta with her outstretched hand.

"Good question," Greta said.

This heavy topic was exhausting me. I glanced at my watch. It was just after six.

Oh, my God, I need to go!

"Table the question, Greta. I'm sure we'll connect again. Thanks for the conversation and drinks."

"Don't mention it."

I stood up and leaned on the chair.

Greta came around the table to me. "You're a bit wobbly. Just take my arm." She turned to Ulli. "I'll hail a taxi and you follow with Renate."

"Right."

Lisa buzzed Ulli and me out the door. We made our way down the alley. As we passed the smelly garbage containers, my stomach turned queasy.

Greta stood at the taxi. "What's the address?"

I managed to say it before I retched on the curb.

Greta passed Christine's address on to the driver, then wiped my face with a handkerchief and helped me into the taxi. "Hi to Christine."

They waved goodbye.

It seemed like a long trip home.

39

The taxi pulled up in front of Christine's apartment house. The sun had slipped beneath the rooftops across the street. *Damn, the light at the entranceway is on the fritz again.* I fumbled in my purse for the fare and said to the driver, "Would you please press the button on the top – Kaufmann – and tell my friend I need help up the stairs?"

The man buzzed at the door.

"Yes?"

"City Cab Service here, ma'am. I brought–" he turned to me – "what's your name?"

"Seiler."

"I brought Fräulein Seiler to your address. Can you meet her at the entrance?"

"Is everything all right?"

"Your friend wants you to come down. Look, I've got rides to pick up."

The cabbie helped me to the entranceway. "You don't have to stay. I'll be fine." I gave him a tip.

He drove off shaking his head.

The door opened. Christine stood in the entranceway. "Man, do you smell of booze and smoke." She gave me a daggerous look. "Where the hell have you been? I've been really worried."

"Let's wait until we get upstairs, and I'll explain."

She steadied me with her arm as we climbed the stairs. "What you say had better be good, because I'm hungry, and I thought we'd arranged to eat out. By the looks of you, that's out of the question."

Christine looked up. "Shhh. Frau Strohmeyer is on the landing above."

As she passed by, Frau Strohmeyer looked us up and down.

"I'm sure we'll be the talk of the house tomorrow," Christine said, barely controlling her anger.

She opened the door, and I staggered straight for the bathroom.

"I suppose you're going to puke. Nice."

When I emerged, Christine had lit a cigarette.

I sat down at the other end of the couch.

"Okay, out with it: where have you been, and why didn't you phone me?"

"I need a couple of minutes, please."

"Ren, you can't tell me? Is it so bad?"

"No, it's not that."

"What is it, then? I'd planned just where to go to dinner. Can you imagine how disappointed I am?"

"I'm awfully sorry."

"I'll make you some coffee." Christine went into the kitchen and returned with a mug. "Here, sober up."

While I sipped my coffee, Christine went over to the window and propped her elbows on the sill. "Well, had enough time?" she said, after I set my mug on the tea table.

"Okay. I finished a chapter of my dissertation this afternoon and went out to get some fresh air. On my walk, I decided to have a drink. The LB was nearby and I stopped in."

"Nearby? You walked the equivalent of three U-Bahn stops and just 'stopped in'?"

"It was spontaneous."

"Didn't you think I might be concerned when I walked in the door and discovered you weren't here? Maybe you were enjoying yourself, or what?"

"The LB was practically empty."

"So you sat and drank yourself silly all by yourself?" She stubbed her cigarette out, lit another cigarette and tossed the match onto the tea table.

"At first I was alone. Then Ulli and Greta walked in."

"You mean the women from the Panther?"

"Yes. And they asked if they could join me. Was it so awful?"

"So they bought you drinks, right?"

"Just as a friendly gesture, I guess."

"Some buddies those two are, Ren."

"They said to say hi to you."

"But you didn't think much of saying hi to *me* by phone."

"There's no phone at the bar."

"Oh, please. Here I wait on you hand and foot for some eight weeks or whatever, and now, when it comes to our dinner date, you can't get your butt out to the phone booth? Too much effort, I guess?"

"Chr–"

"Oh, shut up. Maybe you don't care about me after all."

"Of course I care about you. I just want to sort out . . . how I feel."

"Not sure about it all? I bet you'll be glad to be back among all your academic types this fall."

"I wouldn't exactly say Greta and Ulli were intellectual types, Chris, but I found it quite interesting what they had to say."

"About what?"

"I asked them some questions about their jobs and background. You know after listening to them, I'm not sure I'm ready to take on . . . the way you live. "

"Hate to tell you, *Schatz* – with me, you *are* living it." Chris got up and, cigarette in hand, paced the floor, moving tchotchkes up and down to different bookshelves. She turned around and faced me. "So in spite of our relationship you want to leave?"

"What do you expect me to do, resign from my job and live off your income? You barely make ends meet as it is."

"How about this idea, Renchen? You could get a position with a university here."

"That's not realistic, Chris. I don't even have my doctorate yet."

"I could move with you to the States."

"To Wisconsin?"

"Did you think it was Tahiti?"

"I don't understand your tone." I sat up on the couch. "I'm curious how this scenario with you in Ryan is supposed to work."

Chris walked over to the open window and blew out a puff of smoke, went to her desk and fished some brochures out of the top drawer. She walked over and handed them to me.

"I had these sent to me at work by the embassy in Frankfurt. They say a non-US citizen can get sponsored for residency in the States if their spouse is a US citizen. It only applies to married couples. But, you know, I have this friend, Anne, who went to Tennessee as an au pair, and met a woman she fell head over heels in love with. They were in the same boat as we are. Anne wanted to stay with her partner and found Zack, a queen fifteen years older, who said he would marry her for a thousand dollars."

"And then?" I put down the brochures.

Ugh does she have to put out that stinking cigarette right in front of me?

"It worked! They got hitched, and she moved in with Zack. There was a special interview for foreign nationals, which included 'intimate questions,' like Zack's toothpaste preferences, his favorite foods, and family members' names – even his moles. Anne sailed through the questions, got hitched, and then residency. Two years afterwards they divorced. She and Linda are now happy as clams. I could do the same – marry a guy, for example – and then divorce him."

"But we would live apart for two years?"

"If that's what it takes to be with you, then I'd be willing to do it. I plan to take English classes here, and then in the States I'd–"

"Do what, for example, in the meantime?"

"Housework for cash under the table. That's what Anne did when she was with Zack."

She really means business.

I put the brochures down. "Have you thought about your mom? You can't exactly visit her over a weekend when you're over four thousand miles away."

"I have to live my own life." She sat down next to me.

"Take it from me, Chris, it isn't easy to leave one's homeland. Plus, you have your career to think about."

"When you're out of sight, out of mind, do you think I'm going to sit around and wait for you to decide about me?" Chris sat down next to me, picked up the brochures on the table and thumbed through them.

I turned to face her. "For starters, let's live in the moment and savor the time we have."

"And how long is that?" Chris asked.

"I've decided to stay on until the middle of August."

"My boss just okayed three weeks' vacation for July, although I don't know how much of it I'll enjoy, knowing you'll be on your way to the US soon after that."

"Sweetie, can't we use the time apart in a constructive way to get perspective on our relationship and how to make it work? Rome wasn't built in a day, but it did get built. I just can't figure out how to manage things any other way. I've got to finish my PhD and fulfill my contract for the academic year."

"This is a nightmare." Chris cupped her head in her hands. "So you have your life figured out, but it doesn't look like it includes me, at least for now. If I knew we'd get married after two years under the same roof with some pansy, I could stand the separation, especially if we could see each other on weekends. But for me to be apart from you a whole year without some kind of certainty? I can't manage that."

"I love you, Chris, don't you know?"

At a loss to solve my dilemma, I took her arm and pulled her to me. The tears flowed between us as we embraced.

April 9 – at home alone mid morning
Wow! I can't remember tying one on like I did at the LB. My fears of an angry Chris proved all too true. I suppose she caught me in a vulnerable state, and really took me to the mat. But to threaten me that she wouldn't sit around and wait for me forever? That stings.

Maybe in secret, I assume she's crazy about me and would do just about anything to hold on to me. I just don't have a lot of experience to prepare me in how to deal with such spats. Mama and Papi rarely had a tiff. Well wait a minute. Once Papi did get angry with Mama when our Sunday dinner at 2 was not ready on time. His face got red and he sputtered, "Woman, you knew I'd be hungry and tired from a long service and a walk with Renlein!" I never heard him call Mama that ever again. Maybe she had a talk with him. He was on a rare leave from his post in Prague and seemed out of sorts. Maybe I hold things in like Papi. I rarely raise my voice, and I don't recall getting into any kind of shouting match with Carol or Laura. "Miss Nice," is what Larry Hartman, my high school classmate, wrote in my yearbook. He never could get my goat, no matter how many times he tried. Hah!

40

An embrace, of course, was at most a temporary solution. For a short while, the situation alternated between tense and torrid. Sometimes I was ecstatic, at other times in the pits. One peak made the inevitable nadir all the worse, like biking downhill only to skid on a gravel patch at the bottom.

To get some relief from the confines of Berlin and our emotional situation, we decided to take a long weekend to West Germany. Chris had wanted to go to Düsseldorf to visit an ex of hers named Gudrun – an ex she hadn't seen since their breakup in 1958.

At first I wasn't terribly eager to go along, but reconsidered once I weighed the advantages of being in the city where I could visit the Heine Archives and the Schumann Society. We got a special deal on a flight there, sparing me Chris's sermon on her dislike of traveling by train through the GDR.

Gudrun lived in Oberkassel, the artsy area of Düsseldorf directly on the Rhine, across the river from the old part of town. I didn't think I'd need any new material, since I had already finished my chapter on the town's famous gentlemen. No matter. I rode over on the streetcar and visited both locations, thereby giving Gudrun and Chris a chance to reconnect.

In the evening, I listened to the two women reminisce about their friends and trade lesbian breakup stories. First, you fight bitterly and one woman leaves. There follows a period of not talking to one another until the ice breaks and you reestablish contact. By then, it doesn't seem to matter if either had a partner – and you might even find yourself becoming friends with your ex's current (or ex) girlfriend.

Gudrun and I, for example, hit it off right away, since she had spent a year in Cincinnati with her parents when her father got a position there as an intern. She described her family excursions in Southern Ohio – and nearby Kentucky and Indiana – which made my ears perk up. Gudrun's American could still imitate the twang spoken in those regions. It sounded just like Bloomington – and made me homesick.

One evening, Gudrun took us around to the "scene," as she called the lesbian hangouts, which except for their size, resembled the LB in Berlin – hidden doors, dark, smoky (what else?), ear-splitting music, and women checking each other out.

*   *   *

All in all, the trip helped me further understand Chris and her past from a new angle. Lesbians, no matter what, stick to each other somehow, in spite of their splitting apart. Rosie was not the exception, but the rule, I found out. It also made me forget about Ryan.

But, when we returned to Berlin, reality set in fast. Dr. Blume had seen my latest work, and was pleased (as pleased as Dr. Blume would ever get), but recommended I include some sort of comparison of Third Reich reception of German romantic poetry with the GDR.

On Monday after Chris left for the office, I went as usual to the mailbox. Ryan had confirmed my signed contract. I had to force myself to read the letter, which dealt with faculty meetings, freshman week and department course schedules. I placed it among my correspondence and concentrated on the new Blume suggestion, until a surprise turn of events threw me off course.

Rumors had spread that Rick Hoyer, the club's star singer on weekends, had a new Canadian lover, but no one knew much more. All of a sudden Rick told Herr Schwarz that he planned to emigrate to Toronto, and May 15 would be his last night. In late April, Chris got the chance she had only hoped for: a solo night at the Panther. Management made a contractual offer to Chris for a solo debut on May 22, which she eagerly signed.

Suddenly, my cozy routine – work in the A.M., afternoon walks, then housework and evenings together with Chris – took an almost month-long digression.

While Chris fit extra rehearsals with the accompanist around her office schedule, I morphed into her stage manager. Nerve-racking, this stage production. I'd never realized how much work went into a solo show. With her instructions, I bought Chris makeup, helped with her wardrobe prep by finding a terrific store that specialized in theater gowns, and scrounged around for the furniture she'd need to use as props. On my own, I came up with flyer copy: "Thirsty for the thirties or fond of the forties? Come to the Black Panther for an all-new show, have a drink and bask in nostalgia with Christine."

As the date grew nearer I got more and more nervous. Would anyone show up? Had I gotten enough advance notice out to the papers? Was there anything I'd overlooked?

I sat in the darkened theater and listened from various spots to check the acoustics and let Chris know how her voice projected. No matter where I sat, she sounded terrific. She did need help with the schwa in English, just as I had in high school, to hear that the English "the" was pronounced "thuh" before a consonant. But she worked on it – occasionally to distraction – and finally mastered it.

On the night of the show the Panther was packed, mostly with women, some of whom I recognized from the LB. Greta and Ulli were there, of course, now with dates. They made a spiffy foursome, so I didn't have to bother with them. Chris didn't seem to mind, anyway, now that I'd worked myself into her good graces with help on the show.

Chris's interaction with the largely female audience was more intimate than I'd seen on nights with mostly male listeners. Dressed in a low-slung gown, she teased the women, drawing them into her spell, and released them only when she wanted to. Her renditions of Weill and Gershwin bewitched everyone.

Needless to say, the crowd clapped forever at the end, stamped their feet amidst catcalls, and generally let all their libidos hang out on the line. Chris returned for three encores. I was thrilled! After the show party we celebrated with Crément and made love, grateful Chris wouldn't have to get up early on Saturday. I told her how spectacular the show had been, but my euphoria was tinged with sadness at the thought of summer around the corner.

May 27 – after Chris's show

I finally have the serenity to process Chris's solo debut. I'm so proud of her that she pulled off this concert while working full time, and with so little lead time.

For the past month, that's all we have done – eat, drink and breathe this show. Did I let her agenda take first place and me get lost in the shuffle? (It wouldn't be the first time I've gotten involved in other people's business on this grant.) At times I thought about throwing in the towel, Chris came through with a dinner out, a weekend with lazy breakfasts, and a trip to the Peacock Island to celebrate our fourth month together. I just needed that reassurance, I guess, that I wasn't some lackey or other.

The time lost on the diss was more than worth it, though. What a spectacular performance, and with no voice teacher or coach telling her how to sing each word and vowel – except me of course – on the songs in English. I have to smile, thinking about Mrs. Mueller in Bloomington! When she urged me to study voice with Madame Manski, I said to myself no way, the thought of going on stage to perform would be worse than any of Dante's nine circles of hell. Luckily Mama wasn't around to sign on the dotted line for me.

At the reception afterwards, I leaned against the wall near the stage door waiting for Chris. At least a dozen women jockeyed for position in line, all gaga over her. They didn't seem to know who I was. Then this stylish broad in a red sequined dress asked me for Chris's phone number. Said her name was Carla. The nerve! Maybe she figured I was some sort of assistant. I told Carla I didn't know Chris's number. Anyway, she doesn't usually give out personal information. I didn't mention the encounter. Can I trust the incident doesn't matter anymore?

I hoped life would return to normal after the show. But no – Chris stopped by the theater after work yesterday and picked up a fistful of fan mail. I didn't know how to respond when she read them to me. Am I jealous? I have no reason to suspect she's interested in someone else. Nevertheless, I'm unsettled by all the attention she got – attention she obviously didn't mind.

The week after Chris's concert, the phone rang one Sunday after supper. Probably Irena – she usually checked in around 8 P.M.

"I'll get it on the extension," Chris shouted from the bedroom. A few minutes later, she emerged.

"Was that your mom?"

"Yes."

Chris joined me on the couch and looked down at the floor.

"*Schatz*, Mom asked me if I could get a few days off from work in June. She wants to schedule some doctor's appointments and get physical therapy for her knee."

"Doesn't she have any friends who can help?"

"Not really. Most of them are in worse shape than she is. And since you and I have gotten together, I haven't been so attentive to her. With Georg gone, I'm all she's got."

"How long must you be away?"

"I can scrape together five or so days of my sick leave to cover a workweek, and add a Friday and the weekends on either side. There's also a holiday on June 17, which would make one less day off to apply for. I reckon my stay would last about ten to twelve days total. What d'you think? Of course, I'd miss you, *Schatz*."

"And I'll miss you, too."

Would Chris take this trip as an opportunity to think about our relationship? For myself, I had to admit, time on my own might help me get some perspective, too.

"Maybe you can get a bit of rest. I worried about our late nights in May when you needed to be out of the sack early in the morning."

"The show did really take its toll on me. All that work for just one night!"

Tell me about it!

"Management still hasn't got back to me about whether they want more solo evenings. Now, with the club closing for renovations, and no shows for a couple of months, they might forget me."

"Come on, relax, attend to your mom and put Panther politics aside for now. You said it yourself, you won't miss any gig opportunities."

"You're right." Chris sighed. "Now . . . I have to tell you that when I'm at Mom's, I won't be able to contact you as often as I'd like."

"You don't need to explain it. I can read between the lines. Your mother might not be comfortable when you phone me."

"The thing is, the only telephone is in her living room, where she spends her day."

"Okay." My throat tightened. Shortly after I moved in, I'd overheard a phone conversation between Chris and her mother, in which she'd referred to me as "an American doctoral student" who was rooming with her after an automobile accident. "Fräulein Seiler is not allowed to stay on her own until her PT is done – doctor's orders."

Do men and women have to make up such stories?

June 8, at home on the couch

After we both worked so hard on Chris's solo show, I'm relieved the Panther plans a major redo and will be dark for a couple of months. I'm sad, tho, that she'll be away so long. We've never been separated for even an overnight since I moved in. Maybe the message is, I've got to learn to live in the present: enjoy my alone time and make the most of it. With Chris away soon, I won't have to straighten up my papers. Plus, I can sleep late without being awakened by her loud alarm clock and the local AM station with its hectic ads for local supermarkets, cosmetics and car dealers – and dumb German jokes.

I guess the fast talk blaring at her is the only way Chris can get herself mobilized for work.

Speaking of work . . . I've got to finish Jewish political issues in early nineteenth-century Germany so I can work Heine back into the text with the attention he deserves. Once I've done with that subject, I can discuss Schumann's treatment of Romantic irony – the tasty bit.

I returned to the desk and finished off that Jewish piece in one fell swoop. Hooray!

41

Chris waved from the taxi. She'd managed to get an extra family day and take off early on Thursday the eleventh. By the looks of it, she had taken along enough for a month or more: a large suitcase full of summer clothes, a second suitcase with comfort goodies – snacks, chocolate, her favorite thirties records – and the inevitable carton of cigarettes. Luckily her mom's place was only about twenty minutes away by taxi, so the fare didn't cost her a fortune.

I trudged up the stairs and opened the door. The apartment felt empty without her. Even the plants on the windowsill couldn't cheer me up. I walked to the bedroom. Chris's lavender pillow and stuffed teddy bear were gone. My pillow sported a new pastel cover, with a bar of my favorite dark chocolate propped on it. She must have put on the new sheets and the duvet while I bought fresh rolls for breakfast at the bakery.

I stretched out diagonally on the bed, pulled away the spread and buried my face in the sheets, so fresh from the outside air. I wonder if Frau Peters had groused when she saw Chris put a load of wash out to dry on Saturday afternoon, even if it was the first real sun we had enjoyed for days.

Tired of the noise from traffic, I pulled myself up and went to the kitchen to make a pot of herbal tea – my routine after Chris left for work. Funny, one cup seemed strange now, like a preview of tonight's glass of wine alone.

I sat down to look at the typed pages of my diss. No surprises there. I had only completed a partial chapter in May. I had stopped in midstream with a discussion of the young Robert Schumann's visit to Heine in 1828. Was it Schumann's intuition to sit at the feet of the master poet Heine before more racial and political unrest broke out in Germany?

"So what's new for a Jew?" I'd scribbled in the margin.

*   *   *

The next morning was cloudy, and the fog hadn't yet lifted when I sat down to work – June gloom, as they would say in the Midwest. The sound of a light rain on the tile roof added to my melancholy, like a Verlaine poem: "It rains in the city like it rains in my heart." More in the mood to write a brief entry in my diary, I left the unfinished page in the typewriter, moved over to the couch and propped up my legs on the tea table, a no-no when Chris was around.

The telephone rang. I pounced on it.

"Hello, dearest."

"Hi, *Schatz*, good to hear your voice."

"I'm so glad it's you! Are you settled in okay?"

"It's hard for Mom to walk much. She needs my arm for support. On the bright side, after we finished at the osteopath's, I treated her to a late lunch at the Piccola Italia around the corner yesterday. She ordered her favorite dish, *fagioli con cotechino.*"

I laughed. "Sounds wicked. What is it?"

"White beans with sausage."

"What did you order, Chris?"

"Oh the usual – you know me."

"Spaghetti bolognese?"

"Right on the money, darlin'."

"I bet your mom feels a lot better just having you there."

"Yes, she'll do stuff for herself, finally. Right now she's having a long soak in the bathtub."

I heard Chris light a cigarette and take a long drag. "Ren, the doc says she might need to have her knee operated on in the fall."

"It's bad, huh?"

"Let's wait and see."

"What's on for the rest of the day?"

"I might take a nap. Too bad it'll be alone."

"Yes, I know what you mean. By the way, I forgot to thank you for the chocolate and the clean sheets."

"I really raced to get the job done before you returned. Look, um, I thought maybe you'd like to come over to us for *Kaffee und Kuchen*, say at 4 P.M. on Sunday. Does that work for you?"

"Sure. What can I bring?"

"Just you, *Schatz*. I miss you a lot."

"Ditto. I just rattle around here without you."

Chris gave me directions to her mother's place, and for the subway.

"Chrissi!"

"Be right there, Mutti! Sorry, Ren, I really must go. Bye, love."

"Take care of yourself."

June 12 – at my desk after a phone call from Chris

So Irena's knee might require surgery. Hmm. This news puts a new wrinkle in our dilemma. If Irena is operated on, that would keep Chris stuck in Berlin and narrow her options. Why can't things be neat and tidy? I don't know if I can bear up under the stress of choosing between Chris and my career. And even if I decided to go back with the idea of returning sometime later? I'd feel like a traitor to Mama, Mrs. Foote, to Laura – and most of all to myself.

What if I stayed on now and scrapped the PhD, how will Laura react? Spain would be out, and a broken contract with Ryan – and for sure a broken relationship with Laura the result. Could I ask for an extension of my leave? Frieda would love that – it would probably be her last chance to replace me, unless I resign. But then, I'd have to scramble for a job in Germany from afar – hard enough when you live in the same country. I feel like I'm in the middle of a tug of war being yanked this way and then that. Maybe it's better not to fall in love – it can give such grief.

The world is closing in on me, and my time here is about to run out. It tears me up just to imagine saying goodbye. Do I have to

*part from my hometown and sweetheart, as the folk song goes? I
wish someone would come along and make the decision for me.
When I couldn't make up my mind, I could run to Papi. He always
had a perfect solution for his little* Schatz.

I clenched my teeth in frustration, shut my diary and stormed into the kitchen for a glass of Chris's Gewürztraminer. Until I met
Laura, I had never really drunk much. She'd introduced me to Spanish reds you only just dream about. Stepping out onto the balcony for
a few sips, I gazed out at the stars, bright and twinkly this June night,
when a pang hit me in the gut. *Laura, I could really use a let-your-hair-
down session with you! Even just to hear your voice would lift my spirits.
How to explain the charges on Chris's phone bill? "Screw it, I'm gonna do
it," as Carol used to say when she took a break from cramming for finals.*

I curled up on the couch and reached for the phone. Laura had
only one class on Friday afternoon, and would surely have hightailed
it home by now. No answer. "Damn!" I shouted, and pounded on a
pillow. What else could I do?

*   *   *

The next day, I caught up on an overdue letter to Howard, describing
my progress with the dissertation and setting an approximate date for
my arrival at Ryan mid to late August. I planned to break up my return flight to Chicago with a trip to Spain. Had Laura mentioned to
him she was flying there in August? Howard certainly wasn't dumb.
He could put two and two together, surely.

I took a coffee break, and turned to a more difficult letter.

Dear Hildegard:

I'm so sorry to hear about your recent illness and hip problems, and hope you're recovering well. I was disappointed we
couldn't celebrate Easter together. Do you remember we discussed
seeing each other in the summer? I wonder if you still intend to
see your friend Berta in Arizona, instead of taking your usual spa

sojourn in mid August. If so, would July be acceptable for a visit to Vogelweide?

As far as my life here is concerned, the peace and quiet at Christine's have been a godsend – which shows the truth of those comforting words on your mantelpiece, "everything happens as God wishes."

I would like to repay Christine's kindness to me. She hasn't got much money and is exhausted from a heavy work schedule, which this past winter included me, along with her mother Irena, who walks with a cane.

Would you be able to extend your invitation to her as well? She is a low-key person, unobtrusive, and could help out with repairs around the house.

By the way, did your neighbor come and fix the property line fence? You were worried an occasional wolf would stray onto the farm. I know you like your *Ordnung*, and a broken fence is, as you say, a *Schandfleck* – an eyesore – that needs to be fixed.

At Vogelweide, I'll need to work on my dissertation, and Christine needs some rest, so we won't interfere with your daily routine. I know there's only one guest room, but I'm sure she and I can share the bed. We'd fly to Hanover, since Christine can't bear the dreadful trip through the GDR. I remember the airport is in the southwest of Hanover, and much closer to you than the train station.

Your loving niece,
Reni

By late morning, the weather had broken. The sound of songbirds twittering in the courtyard and the smell of trees in full bloom signaled the approaching summer. I hadn't heard from Laura in a while, not that I'd always returned her letters promptly. But with August not far off, I was anxious to know how her plans for Spain had developed.

Should I come clean with Chris about Spain? No matter what I chose to do, it was fraught with problems and complications. I had to get this in the mail before 1:10 P.M., the latest pickup today.

My dear Laura,

I'm at my desk with your diary next to my notepad. It has been, as they say, the gift that keeps on giving. How grateful I've been for the nudge to write in it these past nine months!

The weather is turning milder. Somehow or other the change in June from gloom to bloom triggers thoughts of Lake Michigan, Ryan, and Wisconsin. Do you remember when the electricity gave out at my apartment house during an ice storm in my first year at Ryan? I stayed at your place and we sat for three days as tree limbs broke off with startling cracks all around us. (Such are the perks of life in Wisconsin! Half the year is cold and frozen, and the other half hot and humid. Ha!)

The most fun part: we traded poetry. You'd read a selection in Spanish, I remember "Arbolé, Arbolé" from Garcia Lorca – about the girl picking olives from the tree – then translate it into English and give a little interpretation. Then I'd do the same – with Heine, I recall. Somewhere in all my storage space are the notes from those magical days. (Alas, I didn't own a diary then.)

A propos June, actually, I'm reaching (yay!) the conclusion of the first draft of my diss. You said I'd probably get it done way ahead of schedule, and you were right – even with the accident. Now I can catch up with people I haven't seen much, like Robert and my aunt's friend Eberhardt, who has been away in Australia, and of course Hildegard.

Re: Lorca, where are you at with Spain? I don't want to pressure you. All I need is a little advance notice. An approximate itinerary is okay, too. I can change my flight day without any problem.

In any case, I won't have to worry about a shuttle to Milwaukee and one of those wretched buses to Ryan on my own.

Love as always,

Renita

Sunday, and time to get ready for K&K with Chris and her mom. I put on a casual light cotton blouse with matching jacket and trousers – gifts from Chris. Not excessive, but enough to pass muster.

After all, it would be my first real face-to-face with Chris's mom. Before I caught the train, I removed the flowers that I'd put in a vase the day before and wrapped them in plastic.

Three fifty-eight. I paused for two minutes in front of Irena's apartment house before ringing, and put the flowers behind my back.

Chris buzzed me in and met me at the end of the corridor.

"Hi there. Great to see you." She squeezed my arm.

"Good to be here." I showed her the flowers.

"What a surprise and sweet idea." she said, grinning. "Follow me."

We entered a large foyer.

Chris took my things, and motioned me through an open door into a spacious living room.

Irena, a portly woman with salt-and-pepper hair, was seated on a couch, her foot propped on an ottoman. A thick bandage around her knee protruded from underneath a long skirt.

"*Guten Tag*, Fräulein Seiler." She groped for a cane propped against the sofa.

"*Guten Tag*, Frau Kaufmann. No need to get up." I went around and gave her the flowers.

She held them to her face. "*Ach*, freesias, my absolute June favorites! Such a marvelous fragrance they have, *nicht wahr? Danke schön*, Frau Seiler."

"I'm glad you like them."

"Sit here, won't you?" Chris said, and pulled over a chair for me near the end of the couch.

"Chrissi, would you please fetch a vase from the cabinet in the hallway?" Irena said.

"Already on it, Mutti." Chris went off with the flowers and returned with them arranged in a vase, which she placed on the dining room table next to an assortment of pastries and three plates. "There," she positioned one flower a bit higher. "I think that'll do it."

"The arrangement is lovely," I said.

"Christine has talents when it comes to plants. I always thought a florist's shop would be better than an accountant's office, but it doesn't pay as well."

"That's my mom! She looks after my financial welfare."

"We'll have the coffee ready shortly," Irena said.

"Notice how Mutti uses the royal we," Chris said, coming over to her and putting her hand on Irena's shoulder.

A wall behind the couch was filled with mementos, knickknacks and numerous paperback books in a tall mahogany bookcase.

"You might be interested in snapshots of Christine in her younger years." Irena motioned to a mantelpiece on the right wall, lined with photos. "I've placed them in chronological order," she said.

On the left stood a picture of a handsome young man with a baby in his arms, followed by a portrait of a girl with a single curl on her head, and a framed picture of a toddler and a boy of kindergarten age.

Prominent in the middle was a photograph of Chris as a young- ster, posed in a white confirmation dress in front of a church.

"Wasn't she a lovely child?" Irena said.

I picked up the photo for closer inspection. Chris's curls, adorned with a white posy, cascaded down her shoulders.

So beautiful, her soft face and those innocent dark eyes.

I was reminded of the first line from a Hugo von Hofmannsthal poem: *"Und Kinder wachsen auf mit tiefen Augen, die von Nichts Wissen"* (And children grow up with depth in their eyes, which are not yet aware of anything.)

"What year was this taken, Frau Kaufmann?"

"Nineteen thirty-three."

The later photos on the right were mostly of Chris's brother Georg. In one of them, brother and sister stood erect, with Georg holding a diploma in his outstretched arms.

"That photo is from a couple of years ago at Georg's graduation from the Saarland University in Saarbrücken. I was so proud of him! I just had to grab my camera."

Chris had had her hair cut short in the picture. Was it after she'd separated from Rosie? The women in Ibsen's plays often changed their hairstyles after a breakup or before a new amour.

"We're all set, Ren, come join us."

I returned to the table. Chris lit a candle, set the coffeepot on a warmer and helped her mother into a chair opposite me.

"So, Fräulein Seiler, may I use your first name?" Irena asked.

"I'd be honored. My name is Renate. And may I call you Irena?"

"Of course."

We still used the formal *Sie* for "you," but the switch to our first names helped break the ice.

"Chrissi sounds happy to have you as a roommate while you stay in Berlin."

At least I've graduated to roommate.

I looked over at Chris, sitting beside her mother, and then at Irena. "I'm grateful your daughter took me in. The hospital wouldn't allow me to live alone during my convalescence."

"*Ja*, it's difficult enough to be injured in Germany, but abroad – well, I can't imagine what that would be like for me."

"I'm grateful that your daughter helped me out at such a tough time."

Chris brought over our cups and poured the coffee, then fetched a tray of pastry for Irena and me to select from. *Mmm . . . Black forest cake!*

"Yes, Chrissi is certainly a big help to me. On my own, I don't get out much anymore. This knee gets sore after a walk."

"I'm sorry. What did the doctor recommend to help your soreness?"

"Physical therapy and warm baths," Irena said. "But let's not dwell on me. I'd rather hear a little more about you. I'm impressed with your excellent German! Most Americans over here – the soldiers especially – don't try to learn the language."

"Actually, Mutti, Renate was born in Berlin and then emigrated to the States with her mother after the war."

"Yes, a lot of German women left for the US after the war. It had gotten very hard to survive in this town without a man around. Renate, I lost my husband in 1941 in the Battle of Stalingrad. And with two children, well . . . it wasn't easy to snag a GI."

"My mother did exactly that – figuring it was her only way to get us out of Germany."

"So are you now an American citizen?"

"Yes, Mama and I got our residency when I turned eighteen."

"So when do you plan to return to the US?"

"Renate, would you care for any more *Kuchen*?" Chris said.

"No, thank you. Black Forest cake is my favorite, but two pieces are my limit. Otherwise I won't be able to fit into these slacks again."

We laughed.

"Do you mind if we go to the couch? It's comfier with my foot up," Irena said.

"Surely."

Chris offered her mother an arm for support.

"You're a *Goldstück* – really precious, Chrissi. I don't know how I'd manage without you." Firmly seated on the couch, Irena took a cigarette out of her handbag. "Do you mind?"

"Of course not."

Irena lit up a Gauloise. "Sorry to say," she sighed, "the last time Georg visited, he tapped his foot if he had to sit still for more than a minute. To get that boy of mine to do the least little bit is a struggle."

We chatted some about Irena's husband – the handsome man in the photo. It was clear from her voice that Irena still grieved over his death in the war.

"When I first met my husband, I was struck by his beautiful dark eyes. It's a comfort to me they were passed on to Chrissi." She ran her hand down Chris's cheek. "When I look at my daughter, I think of my sainted Roland."

Yes, her mother's right. Chris's eyes are one in a million.

Irena reached into her purse for a hanky.

When Chris tilted her head toward the door, I knew the time was up.

I reached for my purse. "Thank you both for the *Kaffee und Kuchen*. I've had a wonderful afternoon."

"We enjoyed having you this afternoon, Renate." Irena smiled. *"Kommen Sie gut nach Hause."*

"Good-bye, Irena."

Chris accompanied me to the front door of the apartment and whispered, "Don't be angry. I could tell my mom was getting tired."

"Oh silly, I understand."

"Loved seeing, you, *Schatz*. I can't wait to get back."

"I've got the bubbly on alert."

At home in bed, I contemplated being with family, and what that might mean for me in the future.

My only real blood relative now is Hildegard. I hope she replies about the July visit. In-laws, friends, blood family or mate? Who comes first when you love a woman?

June 15 – sitting outside in the garden
What a beautiful day, there's a fresh breeze, the birds are singing and feeding their young. Still I feel a certain melancholy. Sorry Chris can't be here to enjoy it with me. It's quiet during the workday. Why don't I come out here more often? Too exposed, maybe.

The visit to Irena's on Sunday was enlightening. I think I passed muster, and feel she liked me. I tried to do all the right things, after all – bought flowers, arrived on time, didn't stay too late, asking the right questions, and not showing too much interest in her daughter – that was the hard part.

Her mother's knee doesn't look good at all – swollen, disfigured, sores on it. Not a pretty sight. I can see not having Chris around would be devastating to Irena. I try to imagine the scenario: I come with Chris into the living room and announce she and I are moving to Ryan. How could we pull that one off? For that matter, how could I have left Ryan knowing Mama was frail and on medication? It might have worked if Papi had been there, or someone like Hildegard, but alone? Let's face it, Hildegard didn't want to leave Detlev, either. Who wants to be the last person left behind?

When your parents are gone, does it get any easier?

42

At my desk, I checked footnotes, quotations, and the bibliography of my dissertation. Dr. Blume was a stickler for details, I knew. Even a misplaced comma amounted to a deadly sin.

The phone rang.

"Hello, Renate. Eberhardt Westerheim here. I called you at the pension, and Herr Schulz was kind enough to give me a contact number for you."

"Hello, Eberhardt, how nice to hear from you. Yes, I've moved since we talked."

"It's been a while, hasn't it?" he said. "How did you survive the winter in our fair city?"

"The dissertation and the German State Library have kept me busy."

"I can imagine."

"And how was your trip to Australia and beyond?"

"The adventure of a lifetime! When I realized how much there was to see, I extended my visit. An old friend from the war who immigrated to New Zealand invited me to stay at his house there. I was fascinated by a country populated with more sheep than people!"

"It sounds like you had a wonderful visit."

"Renate, I wondered if we might spend an afternoon together, perhaps for a stroll. The weather's supposed to be pleasant the next few days."

Do I want to see him again? Will it bring up all that pain about Papi?
"Shall we say two o'clock on Thursday?"
Chris will be gone till Sunday. The timing's perfect.
"Yes, that's good for me."
"How about I pick you up in my car?"
"Wonderful. My address is 31 Wertherstrasse in Kreuzberg. I'll meet you out front."
"I look forward to it."

*   *   *

At the stroke of two on Thursday, a dark green MG convertible pulled up in front of Chris's building. I settled into a spiffy beige leather seat. It felt peculiar sitting where I normally would drive.

Westerheim went around the front of the Morris and got in on the right. "As you can see, Renate, I'm a bit of an Anglophile. I bought this beauty from a British soldier stationed in Charlottenburg. He was heading home to England after his tour of duty, and I think the chap overestimated how much one could afford on a soldier's pay. He probably bought it to impress German girls." He started the ignition and pulled out from the curb. "So where would you like to go for our walk?"

"Your pick, please."

"All right. My favorite is the Tierpark – especially in June."

As long as I don't have to use the pay phone!

"So you live in Kreuzberg now?"

I winced. "A colleague at the university offered to rent me space at her place."

"Oh, I see."

"I've got the day to myself. Christine, my roommate, is gone most of the day. She's a botanist and works nights at the university library as well."

"I guess her schedule works out for you, then."

Passing the Brandenburg Gate, Westerheim turned into the Strasse des 17. Juni. At the Tiergarten, he slowed down to pull onto the middle strip. He looked up at the brilliant blue sky. "Even in Berlin, the top can safely stay down."

Soon after we entered the forest grounds, a path lined with peonies came into view.

"The grounds people do tend their brood with great care. We Berliners know there isn't much beautiful public space this side of town."

"How long have you actually lived in Berlin, Eberhardt?"

"I moved here in 1951." He stopped to inspect a pinkish-white flower. "Lovely hues these peonies have. Such short-lived beauties. One gust of heavy wind or rain and they're done for."

"Gone with the wind, like so much in life," I said.

"Right you are. I suggest we head now for something legendary in this park – and hardier than our frail friends, here."

A short walk brought us to a sea of pastel-colored rhododendrons.

"Fabulous! I can see why you like the Tiergarten."

We found a bench opposite a three-tiered stone fountain. Westerheim looked down, creating a circle on the sandy path with the tip of his shoe.

"Renate, I must tell you that I moving from Berlin at the end of June."

"Moving? Where to?"

"I'm emigrating to Australia."

Someone who is almost family just ups and leaves? Why must I experience so much loss?

"Eberhardt, why so far away?"

"Australia has always been on my mind. Berlin was only a way station. I no longer want to live in a country associated with the Second World War or the atom bomb. At one point, I considered Switzerland or Sweden because of their neutrality, or even Israel." Westerheim tossed a coin into the fountain and paused to watch it sink to the bottom. "But, I need to be even farther away from Germany."

"Would you come to visit me in Wisconsin?"

"No, unfortunately. But I'd certainly be glad to show you around the outback, Renate."

"Yes, I'd love to come." *Would that offer also extend to anyone else close to me?*

We watched the water shoot upward and flow down from one tier to another.

"Is there anything the matter?" Westerheim asked.

This is my last chance to talk to him about my father.

"You know, your revelation about Papi in November . . . I don't know how to put it exactly . . ."

"Put what, Renate?"

"I'm ashamed and distraught about what he did, and simply can't shake it."

"That's why I debated whether to reveal everything to you. The truth doesn't always set a person free."

"It's all right. You kept your promise to Papi. But it disturbs me that he couldn't find another way to solve his dilemma. I mean, why didn't my father recognize Hitler's evil intentions and flee with his family before it was too late?"

"Don't be so hard on Kurt – and on yourself. He did the best under the circumstances. If you had been in his position, wouldn't you have done the same? We all live in a gray zone between good and evil, and struggle with morality on a day-by-day basis. A witness at the Eichmann trial in Israel fainted when he realized if one human being could commit such evil deeds, then anyone would be capable of them."

"Do you feel guilty about your participation in the war, Eberhardt?"

"Of course. As a German, how could I not? Most Germans I'm sure carry a burden of guilt about the war. Some might choose to repress, some try to expiate with redemptive acts, and some learn to live with their guilt, as I do, for example."

"How so?"

"When you came to my apartment, I told you about Kurt, but it didn't seem appropriate to add my own story. You asked me when I moved to Berlin, and I said in 1951, six years after the war ended."

"So where did you spend those six years?"

"In 1943, the Reich recalled me and other scientists from the Russian front. I was assigned to duty at a secret research center for atomic weaponry located in the tunnels of the Harz Mountains. We were given orders to research and then to supply data for the development of the V-2 Bomb project relocated from Peenemünde on the Baltic Sea."

"What became of the project?"

"By the time the Peenemünde scientists had gotten the Harz facility off the ground, the Allies were landing in Normandy. The V-1 had been launched on London, but the damage to England never had the intended effect of bringing the Brits to their knees. As war intensified, we knew that the Russian army would soon capture us if we didn't flee to an American occupied area in Bavaria, where we scattered to a number of villages to find refuge."

"Were any of your colleagues members of the Nazi Party?"

"A good percentage of them were, but I was not. I'd worked on the research for rocket development, although I didn't participate in the launching of any of them toward the enemy. And, as I discovered when we decided to surrender to the American military, they were more interested in what we could do for the US weaponry programs than in our past."

"I don't quite understand. What about justice being served for war crimes?"

"The US government feared if the Russians got hold of our knowledge it would be a great security risk for their country. I was sent as a POW to a secret military operation called PO Box 1142, in Fort Hunt, Virginia. There, I was questioned about Nazi rocket projects, notably the V-2."

"But didn't anyone know about your past?"

"No. Under a code name called Project Paperclip we were provided with altered biographies by the American military and were not subject to indictment. President Truman apparently didn't know about the cover-up."

I can't believe it. Known Nazis in the service of the US military?

Westerheim pulled out a silver coin from his wallet and placed it in the palm of my hand. "Make a wish, Renate."

Please, good fairy, help me resolve my ambivalence about Papi.

I threw the fifty-pfennig piece into the water and watched as it swayed to the bottom.

"Good luck with your wish." Westerheim smiled. "Shall we stroll on, and see some more of the park?"

Westerheim involved in research on bombs? I'm not letting go of this topic just yet.

"What did you do after Virginia?"

"I was sent to a base in the Rockies with other scientists to conduct further research on rocketry."

That explains his book on the Rockies, with all the hard to read signatures.

"German scientists in POW camps. Was this public knowledge?"

"No. The work of German POWs was kept under wraps. Most civilians were unaware of our presence or our work. By the time I was released, I'd had more than enough. As a physicist, I learned that we humans achieve technological advancements that go far beyond our moral capacity to handle them. Just because a person can create something, it doesn't mean he should. You could say I was in the wrong place at the wrong time, and that will plague me the rest of my life."

"What about the other Germans you worked with. Did they feel like you?"

"I don't know. As POW's, we were no longer officers. There was a tacit agreement not to talk about the past, so no one knew exactly what anyone had done.

"In 1950, many of the German scientists were moved to Huntsville, Alabama, to work on the Redstone rocket, a direct descendant of the German V-2 rocket. But, after my POW time in Colorado was completed, I wanted to get on with my life. The authorities sent me to England for almost a year before I was released back to Germany."

"How have you managed life here for the past twelve years?"

"For me, the return to Germany has been like a descent into purgatory, where I've had to deal with my actions. After Kurt's death, and the separation from my colleagues before and after the war, I've lived a largely isolated life."

"I'm so sorry your path has been so difficult."

"I did get a good-paying position in Berlin. It gave me the opportunity to sort out these heavy issues while I waited for early pension. My retirement became official the first of this month. Now, I want to spend my remaining days in peace and contemplation. If I were Catholic, I'd have considered becoming a monk. Instead, I look forward to Australia, and perhaps someday I'll muster the courage to write about my experiences."

We sat for a while in silence. I didn't know what to say in my dazed state.

"I'm grateful I could reveal my past to you, Renate. For years now, I've prayed for a trusted person to hear my story. How wonderful that it turns out to be you, the daughter of my closest friend."

Over *Kaffee und Kuchen*, I picked at my pastry and listened to Westerheim's stories about the outback. It was hard to summon enthusiasm for the adventures he had experienced on the other side of the world when my own world was about to be torn apart. Who or what was left for me?

43

Westerheim pulled up outside Chris's apartment house. He went around and opened my door.

"Renate, I'm proud to have known Kurt and Edda, and to see how you've blossomed as a young woman. Your intelligence, your probing mind, and your respect for moral responsibility are remarkable. I hope you'll stay in touch. You *will* come to visit me, *nicht wahr?*"

I searched for an answer. "Of course."

"You'd be most welcome to stay at my place, wherever it may end up being."

"Thank you, I'm touched by your offer."

"Could you give me your mailing address?"

I wrote down my office address and phone number on a slip of paper from my purse. "Godspeed, Eberhardt."

"Yes, right you are. I wish you the same, Renate." He got into the MG, drove to the corner, turned right at the intersection and waved goodbye.

Upstairs, overwhelmed and exhausted, I struggled to absorb what I'd heard, snuggled under a coverlet on the couch. Finally I lit a candle and pulled out my diary.

June 16 – after my visit with Westerheim
For several hours I've been pondering Eberhardt's personal confes-
sion, as I guess you could call it. It felt like a double blow – not

only Papi's involvement – but also Eberhardt's, and I feel left to pick up the pieces and emotional wreckage. So he was involved with the development of the V-1 rocket in Germany. If you consider the repercussions of his work, does a rocket seem worse than my father's espionage for the Nazis? At the very least, it's fair to say it puts Papi's spy operation against the Czechs into a different light.

It seems to me, guilt must be seen as a relative matter: Do two wrongful deaths equal the killing of thousands with bombs? Papi took responsibility for the demise of two innocent people in order to save his wife and daughter (me). Does this desperate deed cancel a wrong one? Did Papi expiate the deaths of two Czechs by his participation in the Stauffenburg plot?

Papi ended his evil deed, as he put it, with suicide. Can that deed committed to save others be considered an evil deed? And if so, did the evil really end there, as Papi and Schiller think? The world I know thinks Germans bear a measure of guilt. Am I guilty, too – even if my passport says I'm an American? Can I, or should I find a way to expiate it? The war has torn so many of us Germans apart. What fond memories do we have to cherish? My heart is heavy with the pain of my German heritage and the deeds of our forbearers that we, their children, should also atone for. Does this mean my life will no longer be what I'd envisioned for myself? Two burdens lie now in my breast: Papi's legacy, and implications of my love for Chris. What destiny will they create for me?

By now the late night traffic had dwindled to a few faint sounds. I drank a glass of warm milk and lay in bed thinking, before I finally turned out the light at 3 A.M.

*   *   *

Friday, I heard from Hildegard. Her prompt postcard reply was just what I had hoped for.

Dear Reni:

Thank you for your letter. You know I lead a very private life, and do not tolerate strangers much anymore. Nevertheless, I understand your situation – you were cared for by Frau Kaufmann for so long, a kindness not everyone would show. I am sure your roommate Christine will not be an intrusion, and, as you said, I could use some help around here. Repairs have accumulated, as you might suppose. I can pick you up at the airport and will park next to the second lamppost from the entrance to lot C. Neighbors tell me it's never full.

Fond regards,
Hildegard

Thank heavens Hildie said yes! I was so afraid she might turn me down, or at least Chris, and I couldn't have visited Hildie without her.

Saturday brought another hoped-for letter. Usually I prayed Laura's missives would arrive on weekdays, when Chris was at work. On Saturdays, however, she liked to buy rolls and pick up our mail on the way back. I skipped the rolls, dashed upstairs and tore open the letter.

Dear Renate,

Sorry I haven't written you anything about Spain before now. The reason is – there's a new development in my life. You remember last October I mentioned Phil Bates, the new instructor at Ryan, and our day trip together to the Wisconsin Dells. So much of the outing reminded me of our camping days. I'll not forget them ever.

Maybe it upset you I mentioned a guy, even though the trip was pretty much as I wrote: a chance to escape encountering our students everywhere we went. When I said goodbye to you at O'Hare, I suggested Spain for this summer, and when I said it, I had every intention to come over and meet you.

But, as we've often told each other, fate intervenes when you're making other plans. The truth is, I've fallen in love with Phil. He proposed to me last week! I wanted to wait until you return to be my Maid of Honor. Phil and I would like to get married in August, so we can find a house to rent before the grind. Let me know so we can coordinate our ceremony with your schedule. I'm sorry, Ren – I was looking forward to Spain with you – my best travel partner ever!

My folks are excited about their new son-in-law to be, and especially that he's from the East Coast. I know you'll like Phil when you meet him. He's got a great sense of humor, loves classical music, and is a wonderful cook, by the way. Only you could appreciate what that means to me! You're invited to our house for dinner!

Of course, you and I can still meet for our wine and chats – maybe now we can meet at your place! I've already told Phil how important you are to me, and he understands. Hope the diss is about through, and that you'll be able to visit your Aunt Hildegard again before you leave.

As always,
Laura Bates – oops, Sanchez!

Laura's rosy pink stationery slipped out of my hands and fell to the floor; her name engraved across the top, "Laura Sanchez, MA," stared up at me. Was I imagining this, or having a bad dream? I stared in front of me, listening to the birds, and summoned strength to read the letter again. Yes, it was all true. I hadn't even considered the possibility of Laura with a guy – and only a pro forma apology! How about "Sorry, Renita, I didn't let you know earlier"... "I know how you must feel"... "I know it must come as a shock that the trip to Spain is off" – or similar?

The tears began to flow. Was this the Laura I had trusted and confided in, whose company I looked forward to, whom I'd taken to visit my mother – the one I'd laughed and shared my innermost fears with – and then THIS?

I reached down for the letter, shredded all of it into the tiniest of pieces and tossed them up in the air. Then I pulled out my diary, its dedication signed with Laura's beautiful handwriting and took my pen – Laura's pen – and threw both across the room. In bed I cried myself to sleep and didn't give a damn if anyone heard me.

Later in the afternoon, I stumbled into the living room to view the damage and lay down on the floor amidst Laura's toxic confetti.

The diary lay in a corner on its spine, the pen nowhere visible. I finally got up and retrieved it from under the couch, along with candy wrappers consumed after dissertation snags.

June 22 – on the couch
So Laura is getting hitched to a man. Why am I surprised? Get
married and that will solve all your problems. That's what hetero-
sexuals do, right? Say goodbye to the Peace Corps, Laura! We've
come to a fork in the road – you've got someone else in your life now.
When I arrived in Chicago I had counted on you to greet me, hug
me, to be there. You go your way, but where am I headed?

For an hour, I continued to pour out my fear, rage and sorrow. I put down my diary, rubbed my aching wrist, and looked at my watch. My God, Chris was due back in less than twenty-four hours! I replaced the white wine with a Spanish Cava from the pantry, picked up all the pieces of the letter and wadded them into a paper bag.

After leftovers from the fridge, I took a bath and finished off the remaining wine. The next thing I knew, it was 9 A.M. I was still obsessed with questions: *Why did Laura wait until the last minute to let me know? What will life be like in Ryan without her support? Do I even want to teach at Ryan if she's no longer there?*

I made some strong coffee and sat down to reread my journal entry from the night before. *God how angry it sounds! This is no condition to be in when Chris arrives tonight.* Fresh air would be the best thing to get clarity.

Outside, the world had begun its daily rituals, oblivious to my pain and hurt. Steeple bells across the street tolled their 10 A.M. invitation to worship while a few elderly women – hymnals in hand – entered the neighborhood church. Chris had been confirmed there; I recognized the entranceway from the photo at Irena's.

Like so many Germans, Chris had fallen away from any formal practice of her catechism vows. We never talked about religion much, and I didn't bring up the *Gretchenfrage*, for fear we might get into a tangle with one another. I wasn't sure what she might say, since I wasn't a regular churchgoer, either. Nevertheless, Sunday mornings without church always seemed a bit foreign and empty – even now.

I sat down on a bench and tried to let my sadness wash over me. When I was a child, my parents and I used to attend church every Sunday, until Papi left for Prague. Mama marinated the beef *roulade* for our Sunday dinner, got me all dressed up and helped adjust Papi's cravat. After breakfast, she made sure we all were supplied with hymnals and coins for the collection.

When the service ended, Papi and I took the streetcar for a stroll in the Charlottenburg castle grounds, while Mama prepared our dinner for 2 P.M. on the dot. Without Papi those Sunday rituals were never the same.

By now the town was awake with people headed to neighborhood cafés and restaurants. As I walked home, I wondered who would listen for my footsteps on the stairs. Who would greet me when I walked through the door at Ryan? Questions, for which I had no answers.

Still agitated from my walk, I paced from the kitchen to the bedroom and back, pausing to deposit wineglasses and supper dishes in the sink.

Face the facts, Ren. Laura's marriage plan changes a lot. Maid of honor! I can just picture me in a taffeta dress fighting my tears.

"*Scheisse!*" I yelled at the top of my lungs.

Collapsing onto the bed, I capitulated to my sane self. After all, Chris didn't even *know* about Spain and Laura. I'd kept my little secret all nicely tucked away in the closet.

Ren, what a hypocrite you are! You used Laura as a hedge in case your relationship with Chris didn't work out! And Laura's not supposed to have a life of her own? And did you clue her in about YOUR love life? And what if Chris were to come and visit me in the US? Would I be torn and uncomfortable with her there? Confused? Resentful that she was taking me away from time with Laura?

One consolation: with Spain out of the picture I wouldn't have to use any further subterfuge with Chris.

44

I heard the door click. Before I could stumble out of bed, there Chris stood in front of me.

"Hi, *Schatz.*" She gave me a hug and kiss. "I just couldn't bear to be away any longer. I wanted to spend at least part of Sunday with you before tomorrow." She threw off her coat and lay down beside me.

I hope I don't look the wreck I feel. "I'm not doing so well, it might be the flu."

"Oh, dear, Ren, one of those twenty-four-hour summer deallies? I'll bring you some chicken soup. That should do the trick."

I knew Chris must have been disappointed, but she didn't say a word. Our evening fizzled into her taking care of me. I may not have had the flu, but I did feel lousy.

By the next evening, as we were in the kitchen washing up after supper, I had enough clarity for a discussion. "Chris, I wanted to ask about our three-week vacation in July. Did your boss approve it?" I handed her a skillet to dry.

"Yes."

"Why didn't you tell me?"

"I just got approval at work today." She put the skillet in the oven.

"Where would you like to go?"

"Shall we talk about it over some bubbly?"

"Okay." I took two flutes from the cupboard and set them on the table.

Chris brought out the chilled Spanish Cava from the fridge. Holding the dishtowel over the cork with one hand, she unhinged the wire with the other until the cork popped, and filled both flutes.

"Cheers."

We toasted to our reunion.

"Now to your question," Chris said after taking another sip. "I'd like to see the Adriatic Coast of Italy, southern France, or even Madrid."

I groaned inside.

"Just kidding. I don't really have enough money to travel far. My budget won't cover a hotel for more than a few nights."

"You remember I've told you about Aunt Hildegard and her farm near Hanover."

"Yes." Chris put down her flute.

"While you were away, I wrote her and asked if we could visit in July."

"Who did you say I was?"

"Uh, a good friend."

Chris jiggled some coins she kept on the table.

"Hildegard just replied she'd be glad to put us up."

"Hmm."

"I thought you could get some rest and putter around on the farm. And besides, I think it would be wonderful to visit a place from my childhood with you."

"A country visit sounds tempting. Let me sleep on it."

45

"**O**h shit!" Chris said. "I left my cosmetics case on the plane"
"That kind of language around my aunt won't endear
you to her!"

"I'll go check at the lost and found." Chris returned all smiles
with her case. "Don't worry, *Schatz*, I promise to behave myself and
refrain for the next three weeks."

No sign of Hildegard yet at the lamppost. At least we'd managed
to arrive first, as I knew Hildie hated to wait. A black Opel stopped
at the ticket booth, and a woman's hand reached out for a ticket.

"Chris, Hildie's arrived."

*   *   *

At the farmhouse, Hildegard laid pastries out on the table and made
coffee.

"Frau Rehburg, the cake was marvelous," Chris said, while
fighting off a yawn.

It didn't escape Hildegard. "Why don't you girls have a rest? We
can take a walk later."

In our room, Chris said, "I'm so sorry, Ren, I just couldn't keep
awake. Hope I don't make a fool of myself on this visit."

"Take a nap, sweetie, I'll keep Hildegard company." With that, she
fell sound asleep.

I went downstairs and found Hildegard studying a broken hinge on the back door.

"Look, it doesn't close properly," she said, rummaging in Detlev's toolbox. "What will our guest think?"

"Why don't you wait until Christine has a look at it?"

"All right." She sighed. "I try to keep up with it all, but as you know, it's a struggle with my legs and hip. My doctor wants to see me the day after tomorrow. Would you be able to accompany me then?"

"Yes, of course, Auntie."

"Good."

I decided to table any questions about Hildie's health until I'd heard from her doctor in person.

After Chris had rested for a day, she busied herself with the broken hinge. In a matter of half an hour, she had replaced the culprit, much to Hildegard's delight.

"The door closes like new!"

"It only required a couple of screws and a few scraps of wood and glue, really," Chris told me later that night while we cuddled.

After Hildegard saw how handy Chris was with repairs, she promptly made a list on the blackboard Detlev had used for decades to note chores and tasks to be done. That very same evening at supper, she lifted her glass and looked toward Chris. "My friend, you are a second Detlev. Please, let us say *Du* to one another."

With that I heaved a sigh of relief inside.

Hildegard and I left Chris to her own devices while I drove her to Doctor Laurenz, her internist.

"Hmmm," Dr. Laurenz said, after listening to her heart. He felt her hands and feet. "Your limbs are cold – I don't like it."

Dr. Laurenz seemed concerned about Hildegard's overall fitness, especially in light of her desire to fly to Arizona. He warned Hildegard that the combination of a heart condition, poor circulation and swelling in her legs did not portend well for a long flight. He admonished her to rest, keep off her feet and "avoid strenuous activities." Then he wrote her a prescription for high blood pressure and rushed out to a new patient.

On our drive to the farm, Hildie sloughed off the doctor's fears with a shrug. "They think they're God, these doctors." What could I do given this outburst? Hildegard was a strong-willed woman. No matter what I said, she'd do as she saw fit.

* * *

By now at Vogelweide, a routine had carved itself out like a Michelangelo figure emerging from marble. We followed Hildegard's rhythm: sleep late, go to bed early.

Most days I sat with Hildegard while she reminisced about Detlev, or about her and Mama when they were young. Some stories got repeated, but I never tired of hearing them – like the one about stealing apples from the neighbor's orchard and getting caught in the act. Grandpa Theo reprimanded Hildie for egging Edda on at the age of three – preparing her younger sister, he thundered, "for a life of crime." Hildegard was eight years older than Mama and should have known better, he reasoned. Hildie said he'd slapped her so hard on the behind that she couldn't sit for a couple of days. We laughed until we cried.

After supper, Chris joined us for cards, or we sang a folk song or two (Hildie knew scads of them by heart). Sometimes, when Auntie was tired, we chatted over bedtime tea in the parlor.

One day I was reading on the living room sofa when Hildegard entered the room and went to her Steinweg. Chris followed her and ran her hands over the piano. "Beautiful mahogany, isn't it? Do you play?"

"I used to," Hildegard said, wiping the keys with a dust cloth she kept on a stack of music.

"What kind of music?"

"Oh, a lot of Bach in my youth, and then, when my sister got engaged to Kurt, Reni's father, I began to play songs by Schumann, Schubert and Brahms, and *Volkslieder*."

Hildegard set the dust cloth on the windowsill and slipped her half rim glasses from a case on the piano. Seated at the instrument, she thumbed through a well-worn song album.

The rumble of cascading chords followed by a doleful echo in the soprano – all were unmistakably Schubert.

To my surprise, Chris said, "That's 'Am Brunnen vor dem Tore.'"

"You know the song?" Hildegard stopped and peered over her glasses at Chris.

"We sang it in school."

"Would you care to try it now?"

"If you like, Hildegard. I don't remember all the words, but . . ."

"Come and sit next to me on the piano bench – there's room," Hildie said, moving a few inches to the side.

I slipped off to the kitchen to make dinner, but was not prepared for what I heard.

"Am Brunnen vor dem Tore da steht ein Lindenbaum. Ich träumt' in seinen Schatten so manchen süü-ss-en Traum." (At the well outside the town gate, there stands a linden tree. I dreamt in its shadows many a sweet dream.) Chris's mellow voice dwelled on the descending melisma "sweeeet dream," revealing a hidden musical depth that left me breathless.

As she sang, I could feel the peace the poet longed for – serenity at the babbling brook and the mighty linden tree outside the town walls.

Through Schubert's jewel, we three – each with our own history – were drawn together into the tree's magical spell. *"Nun bin ich manche Stunde, entfernt von jenem Ort, und immer hör' ich's rauschen, du fändest Ruhe dort."* (I've been separated from this place for many an hour. And I hear the fountain murmur again and again: you would find rest here.)

Hildegard let the last few notes fade into nothingness before lifting her hands off the keys.

"Christine, you understood the song just right. I must say your voice is lovely."

"Thank you, Hildegard, for the sensitive accompaniment." Chris stood up and walked to the stack of music. "Got any other gems in here?"

"Please pick one out."

"How about 'Im wunderschönen Monat Mai'?" Chris handed Hildegard a Schumann album.

"Heinrich Heine." Hildegard ran her thumb along the crease of the spine. "We had to do without him in the war. I remember this poem – so sad, so full of pathos – in May, when everyone was supposed to be happy."

After the atmospheric piano introduction, Chris entered softly. "In the wonderful month of May when all the birds were singing, love arose in my heart." Suddenly, she stopped, tears falling down her cheeks. "I'm sorry. I heard my grandma sing this when my parents and I visited her before the war." She dabbed at her face with a handkerchief from her pocket.

Hildegard put her hands on her lap.

"Shall we continue? Or ... "

"Yes, please, from the top." This time, Chris sang with tenderness I had only experienced when we were in bed.

"My goodness, it's been a while since I've tackled anything on the piano." From memory, Hildegard played the chorale "Brich' an du schönes Morgenlicht" (Break, oh break, thou light of day) from Bach's *Christmas Oratorio*.

The grandfather clock in the corner, however, insisted that it was five o'clock.

"I need to take my heart medication now." Hildegard set her glasses on the piano.

That night, I told Chris how moved I'd been by her singing.

I would miss her voice terribly.

July 17 – at Hildegard's, on the front porch
It's hard to believe we've been at the farm for a week! I've never seen Chris so relaxed and happy. At the first peep of a bird at dawn, she jumps out of bed with unbounded energy, makes herself coffee and "moseys around," as she puts it, "to find whatever to mend before the summer heat takes over." In a storm of activity, she's already pumped up the wheelbarrow tire, torn down the chicken coop, spackled cracks above the house doors, replaced a couple of

broken tiles in the kitchen and painted Hildegard's small bedroom a creamy off-white (Detlev never did like pastels, Auntie told me). To top off her regimen, Chris takes an afternoon nap – for which I (heh-heh) conveniently join her, claiming I'm tired.

Vogelweide has finally become a home away from home – a respite from the pressure to compete, complete or compare – and also from my hurt about Laura and decisions about my departure.

Hildegard seems genuinely happy that I'm here. She's also overcome some of her initial aloofness about Chris.

We did some touring through the countryside using Hildie's car (so generous!) and attended a concert in the cloister ruins near Hildesheim. We also tried out dinner at a country inn famous for its delicious Zander *caught from the local lake. Hildegard always declines our invitations to come along. Perhaps she senses we need to share some time together. I suspect she also welcomes the chance to take it easy while we're gone.*

In spite of Hildegard's frail condition, she likes to prepare Kaffee und Kuchen *on late afternoons, or what I enjoy even more – sipping her fruit concoctions with white wine on the front porch. Chris usually spends time out in the back, giving Hildie and me space alone for a chat.*

The big surprise for me was when I heard Chris sing Schubert and Schumann. What a combination of diva and divine! She told me the album just seemed to fall open to "Der Lindenbaum." Providence? And the intensity she brought to the May song by Schumann took me back twenty-five years to the same room at Vogelweide, where my father performed it with Hildegard.

We celebrated my birthday a few days before we left – a bittersweet occasion, me turning thirty, and about to leave Hildegard, Chris, Berlin, and home. I kept my feelings under wraps, and accepted Hildegard's gift of a picture book on Lower Saxony. Chris told me in our room she was reserving her present for when we got home. Hildegard didn't seem to notice Chris hadn't given me anything.

The night before our scheduled departure, Hildegard suggested we christen a new fire pit Chris had created. "For the occasion, a bottle of French champagne is in order."

I washed and put away the supper dishes, and Hildegard fetched a bottle from the fridge. We repaired to the fire pit, now surrounded with chairs Chris had rustled up from a storage shed. On a small table, Chris set out a bowl of pistachios, bought at our last supermarket visit, and Hildegard's beloved cut glass flutes.

I helped Hildegard to her chair and fetched a blanket to place over her shoulders.

"Would you do the honors, please? I'll pour."

"Certainly." Chris looked at the label. "Wow, Veuve Clicquot. What a treat!"

Hildegard tilted each glass at just the proper angle. "I don't get to use these beauties much anymore. They were a wedding present from Edda and Kurt."

I ran a fingertip down the stem. "Aunt Hildegard . . . a toast to your health and noble spirit."

"Thank you, and to yours, Reni – and Christine's."

As the sky dimmed, we sipped our bubbly. A crescent moon appeared over the horizon through the linden trees lining the property.

Hildegard turned to Chris. "How is it you didn't study voice at the conservatory?"

"After the war, music study was impossible," Chris, said, tending the fire. "As Renate knows, I lost my father in the war. We eked out an existence, and there was no money. By age sixteen I had to get a job."

"Yes, Reni, I often wondered how you might have fared in Germany if your mother hadn't decided to go to America."

I didn't know how to respond. "Where does fate take us? What would have happened to us all if there hadn't been a war, Aunt Hildie? Would we three be communing over a lovely fire now?"

"I admit, we must take life in whatever form it comes," Hildegard sighed. "Were it not for the Depression, I might never have met Detlev. Our marriage was the best thing that happened to me."

Do I dare take this chance to talk about Chris and me? Maybe I shouldn't risk it –being candid might spoil the evening. Ren, she's your only living relative. Ach, I hate this duplicity. Out with it!

"Auntie, do you remember what you said to Chris after she repaired your fence?"

"Something about . . . she was my second Detlev, as I recall. Why?"

"What did you mean by that?"

"That . . . Christine was like my husband."

"So Christine feels like a husband?" I asked.

"I didn't mean *that*, exactly." Hildegard adjusted her shawl. "No doubt it sounded a bit strange, *nicht wahr?*"

"No, it didn't sound that way at all."

"It didn't? Whatever do you mean?"

"You see, Auntie, Christine is for me like Detlev was for you."

"I don't understand, Reni. How could Christine be like my husband?"

"Hildegard, we're . . ."

"Lovers," Chris said. She touched my arm for the first time with Hildegard present.

We stared into the fire, and Hildegard poured more champagne.

"So you and Reni share the apartment now?" Hildegard asked, handing us our flutes.

"Yes."

"So what does this mean for you, Reni, when you head home again?"

I saw the pain in Chris's face. "I don't know. For me, Chris – that's what I call her –means home. That's the difficult challenge ahead. We still have to work some logistics out. It won't be easy."

"I suppose not. As I said, I couldn't have imagined emigrating without Detlev." Hildegard finished the last drop of her flute. "I'm getting cold. There's more in the bottle – don't waste it, you girls."

She got up. "I want to say my goodbyes now. I like to perform this ritual the day before my guests depart. So often over the years, I've had to bid farewell to loved ones. It's less painful if I can say *Auf Wiedersehen* and still see their faces again the next morning."

Leaning on her cane, she put her free arm around me. "Reni, I love you and wish you Godspeed."

Hildegard grazed Chris's hand. "I appreciate your help around the farm. I meant what I said about your being my second Detlev, Christine. Perhaps I should have expressed it another way – you are like my Detlev."

"On the contrary, Hildegard, I was touched. Thanks for making me feel at home these past three weeks."

"Reni and Christine, please stay by the fire if you'd like. I'll find my way back."

"Nonsense. I'll accompany you, Auntie." I followed Hildegard and whispered to Chris, "Stay here, I'll be just a few minutes."

She nodded.

"This damp air really doesn't do much for my bones," Hildegard said on our way to the house. "Berta says the air is dry in Arizona and would be good for me. But I don't know; it seems so foolish, in my condition, to visit her."

We reached her bedroom door. Up to now, I had put thoughts of Berlin on hold. My goodbye to Hildegard reminded me of sad farewells to come. "So sleep well, Aunt Hildie." I gave her a kiss on the cheek.

"Good night, Reni."

Six months later, I received a letter from Hildegard's attorney, stating that Hildegard had suffered a stroke and did not live long thereafter.

Detlev's nephew and wife inherited the farm and all of my aunt's possessions – but she had willed me her music. When I told Chris about Hildie's passing, I didn't mention the fate of the farm or the piano – and Chris never asked.

46

The moment I stepped off the plane in Berlin, my heart felt heavy. I had pushed aside thoughts about leaving at Vogelweide, but now the clock ticked with Kantian precision. Only a miracle could change the appointed day of my flight in early August.

Back to her normal routine, Chris returned home around six thirty in the evening. Over wine and chips, we debriefed the day. After dinner and more wine, the discussion turned to a rehash of our dilemma.

"Why can't you stay on here in Berlin?"

"It's not possible, Chris. I've got a contract to fulfill and a PhD to complete. For residency in Germany, I need a job. Please, let's just let the future take care of itself."

But it didn't end there. We continued to toss around options: move to another country together; go underground in the American West, maybe California or Nevada; Chris pursues a career on Broadway. On it went into the night: plan A, B, C, D, ad infinitum – each suggestion a desperate attempt to avert the inevitable, with frustration, recriminations and despair.

Each talk seemed to deepen the wounds and drive another nail in the chances for our relationship to survive. We considered every possibility, except Stuart and Jackson's offer, which I hadn't yet mentioned. How could I raise false hopes when their offer might be unacceptable or unrealistic – or might never even materialize? Furthermore, if I didn't admit it in so many words to Chris, my job security came first. The doctorate was my safety net. How could I prepare for her coming to live with me – and possibly even support her – without the security of a PhD?

The whole next day while Chris was at work, I mused on the theme of parting in poetry – often to the unknown, a different town or state – or even to another continent. I was reminded, too, of the irreversible parting in a contemporary song Anna Magdalena Bach had entered into her notebook back in the eighteenth century: "Bist du bei mir, geh ich mit Freuden" (If you are with me, then I can go gladly). This moving song shows the singer's fervent wish, as she departed for her final destination, to have her beloved at her deathbed.

> If you are with me, then I will go gladly
> to death and to my rest.
> Ah, how pleasant the end will be for me,
> if your dear hands be the last I see,
> closing shut my faithful eyes to rest!

I thought of the hospital, where Christine's first efforts to see me had been denied. What if I had lain there dying? Suddenly, all the fears I had about being different came flooding into my consciousness. The denial of our shared existence, whether at death or in any other context, hit me with full force: such denial was the epitome of political and societal cruelty. All I could do was to stand and watch our time run out. The reality of our ostracization left me collapsed on the bed in a stupor.

*   *   *

That night, I had just fallen asleep when I heard a rustle and felt Chris's hand cupped around my little finger.

"You awake?" she asked, with a barely audible voice.

"Yes."

"I want to tell you something. I've been lying here awake pondering. I left work early today and took a long walk in the Tiergarten."

"And?"

She shifted around in bed and stroked my head.

"*Schatz*, I'm tired of causing or feeling the hurt. The only sensible thing is to deal with what is. I have my mother to take care of, at least for now. And I've got to figure out my career, and you say you need to finish your degree and return to teaching. Sure, it would be better if we could be at each other's side, but realistically, each of us can only solve our individual issues for herself. Am I right?"

"Yes," I said and clenched my pillow.

"I know you need to go back for now. Well, you have my blessing."

I burst into tears. That was what I'd wanted – her okay, and now I had it. My relief coupled with the sadness of leaving tore me apart.

We hugged and lay back down. I reached out for her hand – a hand I'd recognize anywhere blindfolded.

Mercifully, sound sleep overtook me for the first time in days.

*   *   *

Now a glimmer of hope emerged that we could bridge the many months apart, get clarity, and find a way to live together that worked for both of us. No guarantees, but no false assurances, either.

Our lovemaking, while still genuine, began to take on an "Is this the last time?" quality. We clasped one another for dear life, as if to engrave each other's feel, smell, sound, taste and look in our memories.

With my departure accepted as a shared sorrow and not a guilty secret, I had enough emotional space to put the final touches on my dissertation and mail it off to Professor Blume in Chicago. What a relief, so rare, like sun in November.

I began to sort through my things, and cleaned out the desk. Last of all, I packed my clothes. Each time I heard Chris come toward the bedroom, I folded another shirt onto a stack. Chris would retreat down the hall and pretend to straighten up. Since my first dinner with her, the place had never been so neat.

47

Today ended our rituals. I was scheduled to fly at 11:15 A.M. to Frankfurt, where I would transfer to New York and on to Chicago.

The front door opened; the latch fell into place. Chris jiggled the keys against the inside of her hand. These were the sounds I always listened for. Now they seemed heavy, inevitable, melancholy.

Moments before, I had stuffed the last few items into my carry-on case and returned to the living room.

Chris stood in the hallway with her raincoat on. "I've ordered the taxi for eight forty-five. Is that all right?"

"Yes, my love. What's the weather like outside?"

"It's sunny, with some clouds. Does it matter?"

Chris removed her coat and walked toward me.

We embraced and kissed.

"I love you, Chris."

"I love you, too, Ren."

"Come with me to the sofa," I said, taking her hand.

I pressed her head close to me and caressed the fuzzy curls on her hairline that never seemed to grow out. Such gorgeous hair she had, so thick and silky black – now tinged with smoke from a clandestine cigarette. I rocked her in my arms; her muscles, usually so supple, felt like piano wires stretched tightly over their pegs.

A steady stream of trucks and old jalopies you could count on like the sunrise, rain in Berlin – or early morning hot rolls – rumbled by.

But all I heard was her heart.

Chris sat up. "Please stay a few days longer. You could change the flight to next week. Who's going to tell me if my mascara's on right?"

My stomach knotted up. Nothing I could say made sense.

"My God, Ren, I've said goodbye to women before – but usually after we'd had a fight and one of us moved out. Once a girlfriend started in with a guy. I got ticked. Couldn't get her packed up fast enough. I've sung so many farewell songs – but now this story is for real: I meet a wonderful woman, fall in love, and – this is the biggie – have to say *Auf Wiedersehen* to her."

My well-kept gates opened to burst the dam. "Chris!" I grabbed her by the shoulders. "Believe me, if there is a way to make our bond with each other work, we can make it happen. We're two resourceful, brave women, and no one can separate us unless we allow it."

"If you were here on Sunday we could go out to Grunewald for a walk." Chris's eyes searched for any sign of a "yes" in me.

"I'm sad – so utterly sad to be the one to go."

Chris got up and went over to the slanted window near the sofa, leaned forward on the sill and peered out at the multicolored clouds. "Tiepolo sky, you always said, right?"

"Yes."

"Before you came into my life, I used to spend a lot of hours staring out this window." Chris beckoned me to join her and put her arm around me. "I like the day's passages: early morning, when you can barely see the trees for the fog and cold, or noontime – if by chance a bit of sun hits the copper steeple." She pointed to the faint outline of a church tower through the mist. "And then, toward evening, women's heels clack on the pavement as they hurry to shop before the stores close. Most of all I like the night and the quiet she gives me. I'll look for a star or two over the top of the red brick building across the way, or watch the moon progress from a thin sliver to big and full. But now . . ." Chris turned to me, arms akimbo. "You know, Ren, I'll save money to visit you the earliest date we can agree on. She brushed off a fleck of dust from the tea table. "I'll pick up some travel books about Chicago and the Midwest. I know there'll be all sorts of fun things we can do."

"Just surprise me."

The church bells rang eight thirty.

I tugged at Chris's sleeve. "It's time to get going."

"Hey," she whirled around, "maybe I could get one of those sex-change operations I heard about. Wasn't it Christine Jorgensen who did it a few years ago? My name's Christine, too. Think that would work? Then we could get married!" She laughed and hummed the wedding march from *Lohengrin*.

"Send me a tape of your next show. Promise?"

Chris nodded. "I'll save a seat for you."

I stemmed my tears, and went down the hall to collect the suit-cases. Chris stayed behind. I listened to her sobbing from the bathroom. My heart ached with helpless grief. She was the deserted one, left with the lingering pain and remembrances, and I the leave-taker.

In the living room, I set down my bags and paused to look once more at Chris's playful arrangement of the living room. Her cute desk with shelves on either side – bills and magazines sharing space with a Chianti bottle candleholder.

New were the fruit bowl and stuffed dog I had picked out for her birthday in April. *Why do things look so beautiful just before you leave – like fireworks on the Fourth of July that flare and then die away?*

The first time I'd come to Chris's apartment I'd felt uneasy, like a turtle that sticks its head out of a shell and then withdraws for cover. But Chris's love and devotion, especially after my hospitalization, had removed any doubt as to her intentions. She had given me a space full of love in spite of my reservations. I wouldn't find this kind of harbor anywhere else, and I knew that. A chill ran down my spine – the chill of leaving the womb – and entering the world.

*   *   *

Chris emerged with a pair of sunglasses propped in her hair. Unlike Aunt Hildegard, I couldn't have managed a rehearsal of this performance.

"It's time, my love. The old duffel bag, you know the one with all the toggles and stickers you teased me about? I left it for you to bring."

Chris sang the first few bars of the Marlene Dietrich number she had performed my first night at the Panther. Up to now, she had declined to sing it at home, even when I asked her to. "Not today," she would say. "I need the proper mood."

We helped each other on with our coats.

"I remember when you first came here as if it were yesterday," Chris said. "I made room for your jacket on the rack."

Bags in hand, we walked down the creaky stairs past the faded sign on the lower landing: "Caution! Freshly waxed!"

"They'll never take it down. The manager wants us to think the place is in tip-top shape."

At a nearby taxi stand, a row of black Mercedes waited in line to whisk people away in luxury. The first cab lurched forward and stopped just behind us.

"I guess this one's ours." Chris put on her sunglasses.

The driver grabbed my bags and opened the door for us. He tapped on the meter as we set off.

"Templehof Airport, please," I said from the back. The cabbie nodded.

"You'll be okay on the U-Bahn by yourself?"

"Do it every day, Ren."

"No way to get across town now because of the damned Wall," the cabbie said over his shoulder. He rattled on about traffic and the foreign tourists with their inflated exchange rates.

"You goin' anywhere nice, Miss?" He wouldn't keep quiet.

"Just off on a little trip."

Chris's hand nudged my finger.

"And your buddy's seein' you off."

The cabby continued in his Berlin accent, "Now that's a real pal. You get to see a lot of stiffs in this taxi. People in fights on the way to their flights – hah! Or pickin' someone up they ain't seen in a while. But you don't often see a friend goin' along for the ride. You must be some special kinda lady."

My finger dropped to my lap. Chris grabbed it back.

So this is goodbye to Berlin: endless rows of apartment buildings, Hausfrauen rushing home carrying bags of groceries for the noon meal, and elderly window shoppers stopped in front of displays of drapes, shoes or apothecary specials. In less than two days, I'd be in sleepy Ryan, looking for an apartment, but trying to imagine what Chris was doing. My sore chest cried for some relief, but I could give it none.

Chris clutched my hand as the massive concrete buildings and the Hunger Fork Memorial in front of the Templehof Airport came into view. The entranceway was lined with travelers – probably tourists – climbing in taxis for the start of an exciting visit to the divided city.

The cabbie pulled up to the curb. I reached for my purse.

"All right, ladies, the tab will be . . ."

" . . . I'll get it," Chris said. She paid and took the larger suitcase. I carried a smaller one and my carry-on.

We walked up to the ticket counter. Chris glanced up at the departures panel. "Hey, the plane to Frankfurt is twenty minutes late! How about some coffee?"

"I don't want you to be late to work on account of me."

She shrugged. "The office is used to me by now. My women pals knew something was up when I began to invent sick days."

I checked my luggage. We walked to a nearby snack bar and ordered coffee. Was it just shy of a year ago Laura had taken me to O'Hare? It seemed like eons had passed since then.

Chris traced the rim of her cup. "I hate Templehof. I flew around the city from here for a club promotion and tossed out balloons for the grand opening. The police were furious because we did it without a permit. We even strayed into East Berlin before the Wall went up. Zipped back once the pilot noticed it. I almost lost my breakfast! That time's the closest I'll ever get to that awful prison."

"Last call for Lufthansa Flight 181 to Frankfurt. All passengers please proceed to Gate 22."

"When do you arrive? I want to set my clock to yours."

"It takes about fifteen hours total. I'll arrive the middle of the night here and be seven hours behind you."

"I need to get to the office early anyway – got work to finish before payday."

She patted my carry-on bag. "I put a little present in there earlier. Don't open it until you're in the air."

My stomach was in knots as we made our way to the gate. I'd never parted from a lover before. Waves of guilt overcame me for showing up in her life, only to disappear.

"Do you have plans to visit Irena this weekend?"

"No, nothing definite. I'll probably spend the weekend alone and get the apartment in shape, buy groceries or read." She tossed her hair away from her face and pushed her shoulders back. "Please get your PhD done soon, so I can send you a bouquet of roses. I'll say they're from a secret admirer."

All around us people dodged us as they hurried by. We stepped to the side.

Chris laid her head on my shoulder. "I'll watch you take off from the observation deck."

My little trooper.

"I love you, Ren. Keep me close to your heart."

"You're already in there."

We reached the gate.

"Phone me when you get there, okay?"

I nodded. "I'll follow it up with a letter as soon as I can."

My fingertips slid out from her hand as I reached for my carry-on bag.

So this was it. Words like "next Monday," "in a week," "tomorrow" – or even "tonight" would no longer be a part of our common vocabulary. I approached the boarding ramp in a numbed state – helpless to shout all my past months' frustration, anger, and hurt feelings into the terminal. Instead, I handed my ticket and passport to the ground attendant and turned around. With a stricken smile, Chris crossed her arm over her heart, and waved.

EPILOGUE

The short hop to Frankfurt gave me only enough time to down my sandwich. It was an unusually hot and sultry day for Frankfurt. After transferring to the new Terminal Two I sat in a sterile, crowded hall amidst sweating passengers for the several hour's layover.

Clashing and vying for my attention, a melee of past, present and future scenes whirled through my mind. What a difference a year's circumstances can create. In the States, I had looked forward to my trip to Germany. Although sad to leave Laura, my spirits were buoyed by the prospect of a rendezvous in Spain with her at the end of my grant.

A year later, on the other hand, I was stuck in the slow molasses of the now, with Spain no longer an option, Chris staying behind in Germany, and my future in the US unclear.

A few days before I left Chris in Berlin, I flashed on my last words with Hildegard. I figured she'd be okay with hearing from me by phone, even if my Aunt had made clear she didn't care for any further adieus.

"Hello Hildie, this is Reni. I'm calling from Berlin."

"My dear, I thought you'd long left the country."

"Not yet, Auntie, but I'm flying the day after tomorrow."

"I wish you all the best, then, and my greetings to Christine."

*　　*　　*

I paged through some of my diary entries – the Rhine castles, green pastures of Vogelweide, Hildegard's frail health, but indomitable pluck, the ghost-like train trip through the East, good old Schulz and his Eduscho coffee, the grime of the East offset by Dieter's eyes, the fabulous performance of Wachet Auf, collision with Mama's and Papi's past – and Westerheim and his revelations.

But my fateful encounter with Chris, my siren, Lorelei, and angel with her sensuous song, had set this year off from no other in my life. I laid down my diary and thought about my departure from her this morning – light years away it felt: Chris leaning on my shoulder, and me powerless to change the inevitable.

And when the plane angled sharply over the Wall between West Berlin from East Germany, and I saw the border guards, like ants moving on a forest path, I knew that the trip, now beginning, was actually drawing to a close.

Only once, when the pilot announced we were passing over Magdeburg – a city off limits to the West – did I peer out the window as the massive towers of her proud Cathedral appeared, only to fade into the distance like the sails of a ship at sea.

I looked up and saw that our plane to New York had just arrived from London. *Two more hours to kill.* I pulled out Laura's pen and diary from my purse.

August 20 – Frankfurt airport
All round me American tourists – on their way home – are engaged in animated conversation. I don't share their happy mood, having just left my home with Chris to return to a void.

Eichendorff's poem "Far Away," describes Heimat (home) as a place off in the distance, behind the approaching storm clouds and lightning, where his parents were buried – and where he had lived – and been forgotten.

And when I return to what was home, who would be there for me, I thought. My father lay somewhere in Bohemia, and Mama wherever the medical school had disposed of her. This year had shown me that Heimat is a complex, multilayered, often illusive

*feeling. Like Goethe's Faust, there were two souls in my breast –
one in Germany – the other a "Wahlheimat," Mama's choice of
home. But had it been mine?*

The passengers started to stir. I was tempted to rush to a phone
booth and talk to Chris one last time. No, she'd have been at work.
Better, as Hildegard believed, to let good-bye be good-byes.

I hadn't spoken much English for the year. In Frankfurt, I found
myself already missing the Berlin flavored German with its incorrect
grammar and humor. I could not have orchestrated this year's scenario
if you had asked me. So this had been my romantic poem: I had fallen
in love, then left – my Nunc Dimittis – the departing of this servant to
elsewhere. Circumstances had led me down the path I needed to go
rather than the one I'd imagined, a prelude to letting go of Mama,
Laura – or even perhaps my aspiration to be a Professor of German.

A ground crew member announced our boarding for New York.

I'll be back darling Chris. Stick with me. We can make it happen.

*   *   *

After stowing my carry-on, I squeezed into my window seat. *Thank
heavens only two seats together this side of the aisle.*

"Guess this must be row 32, right?" a young woman with dark
curly hair and smelling faintly of aftershave, said to me in English.

"Oh – yes it is."

She stashed her leather coat in the overhead bin and sat down.

After take-off, an American- speaking stewardess came around to
serve drinks and snacks. Her perky smile helped.

Amidst peanuts and wine, my neighbor and I started chatting.

"You by any chance from the States?" she asked.

"Yes."

"Been touring Europe before reality sets in?"

"No. I spent a year in Berlin."

"As a secret agent?" She laughed. "When I visited Berlin, I could've
sworn there were spies lurking everywhere. Every time I noticed some-

one slip a paper bag in a trashcan, I thought it had to contain top-secret photos taken with a hidden camera. Cool!"

"Actually, I was on a DAAD – a German government grant."

"Impressive."

"I wanted to wrap up my PhD before tenure. Hard to do when you have a heavy workload. My name's Renate, by the way."

"I'm Eva. Nice to meet you."

"So what's your diss. topic?"

"The Reception of German Romantic literature in the Third Reich."

"High brow material – music and German poetry. I don't know too much about either – except the Third Reich part."

That latter part was not a pretty example of German history, we both agreed.

"Did you get over to East Berlin?"

I nodded. "And you, Eva?"

"Yeah. I went a couple of times to a huge sport festival and checked out the East German swimmers. Now those are bodies – muscular, powerful, and they swim like a bat out of hell – if you'll pardon my French."

*   *   *

The plane passed over Land's End in England – far and wide, nothing to see but the ocean with an orange-red sun low on the horizon. I started to set my watch to New York time, but stopped, as grief welled up in throat like one of the breakers crashing on the rocks below.

Good-bye dearest, I hope you get through this day. I miss the smell of your body next to mine and can't imagine how you'll feel when you came home to an empty apartment.

The stewards came by with dinner and drinks. I took a small bottle of a complimentary California red and my neighbor ordered herself a cocktail.

After dinner, the crew announced the movie for the evening: Rock Hudson and Paula Prentiss playing in "Man's Favorite Sport."

378

"Interested in the flick, Renate?" Eva asked. "It was released last winter, but I haven't yet seen it – too busy with school."

"I haven't seen any of Rock Hudson's films, but I'm game."

It sure beats making further conversation when I feel so down.

The lights were dimmed and the cabin quieted down.

In this film Hudson played the all-American hunk, unable to do anything most males supposedly could: fish, swim, run or anything athletic, in spite of his masculine build. I wouldn't have enjoyed the film so much if Eva hadn't guffawed throughout.

"What's the verdict?" Eva asked while the credits ran.

"The love scenes seemed a little weird. Nothing much happened."

"Can't tell a book by its cover."

What on earth is she talking about – is this some kind of hint?

I folded my tray and stood up. "Care for anything from the galley?" I asked her.

"Oh no, I'm fine, thank you."

"It must be the time difference. I'm hungry at night – must be supper time in Berlin."

"Yes, it takes time to get over the time change. They say at least a day for every hour's difference."

It will take me a lot longer than that.

When I returned, Eva got up again. I couldn't help brushing by her as I took my seat. I felt a sudden twinge in my abdomen. "I'm kind of tired, Eva, so I'll catch you later."

"Ok," Eva said, "I'm going to read – My own thesis will put me to sleep." She chuckled.

I reached for my blanket.

"Thesis?" I puffed up my pillow and hoped to forget my troubles – or my curiosity – for several hours.

* * *

Eva was still reading when I awoke.

I wanted to open my present from Chris, but thought better of it. Maybe on the leg to Chicago.

The cabin crew came by with final snacks and sandwiches. My throat felt raw and dry.

"So you've taken your thesis with you to Europe? Doesn't sound much like a relaxed trip."

"Yes and no," Eva said. She shuffled the manuscript in front of her into a neat pile. "I'm interested in the 1936 Olympics. My topic focuses on the Reich's treatment of Negro athletes."

"So that's why you went to Berlin, right?"

"Yes. I wanted to see the stadium where Jesse Owens won four gold medals, and pay my respects to a great athlete. I conducted interviews throughout the summer with Germans who had actually attended, or participated in the Olympics. I'm basing my research on these interviews."

"Sounds like a great method for your topic."

"Man, have you seen footage from the Leni Riefenstahl's film which shows Owens winning the 110 yard sprint? Hitler looked furious. *The Festival of the Nations*, and *The Festival of Beauty* were both a milestone in filmmaking, although I had problems with Riefenstahl's friendship with the Führer," Eva said.

She talked on about Germany's racial politics, and how it affected sports, and particularly the Olympics. Germans were the inheritors of the Greek ideal of physical perfection, to which the Nazis added white supremacy and racial purity, all of which Owen's four gold medals called into question.

Fascinating what Eva knows about that period of history, even if I am aware of the Nazi myth of Aryan superiority.

"So you speak German?" I asked her.

"Yes, how'd you know?"

"By the way you pronounced 'Führer.'"

"I hail from Milwaukee. Both grandparents came over from the old country after World War 1. Guess they spoke enough of the language that it rubbed off on my parents. So I was predestined to study it at the university. I wound up majoring in history, with a focus on sports."

"What about the US? Did they do any better with blacks in 1936?"

Eva's voice became animated. "Funny you should ask. President Roosevelt never sent Jesse a telegram of congratulations or invited him to come to the White House. In those days, his race didn't quite make it with the Anglos in power."

Owens was not the only category of person who wouldn't have been invited, even in 1964.

*   *   *

The pilot announced our descent to JFK.

"It's going to be tough to get back to my hotbed of rest." Eva said, gathering her manuscript together into her briefcase.

"Did you get to any of the bars near the Memorial Church?"

What bars was she referring to? I'd rather leave this topic alone.

"No I stuck pretty much to the straight and narrow – went to plays and concerts – that sort of thing."

"They don't have anything at U. of Wisconsin to match them."

Wisconsin?

"Small world. I teach German at Ryan College on the Lake."

"My last name's Steinberg by the way. What's yours?"

"Seiler."

"Are you taking the afternoon leg to O'Hare, Renate?"

"Yes, and you?"

"No. I'm hanging out with friends in Manhattan."

I couldn't suppress a feeling of disappointment.

We exchanged addresses.

"Perhaps you'd like to visit Ryan sometime," I said.

"The Ryan Lion – "

"All hail to her we roar," we said in unison.

It felt good to laugh again.

ABOUT THE AUTHOR

Author, educator, singer, lecturer and composer Naomi Stephan was born and raised in Bloomington, Indiana, and has lived in Germany and the US. Holder of numerous grants, scholarships, commissions and awards, she earned a PhD in German and Music from Indiana University and BA in Voice as a Fulbright scholar in Berlin. The author of *Finding Your Life Mission* and *Fulfill Your Soul's Purpose*, Naomi turns to her first novel, *Duplicity's Daughter*, inspired by her experiences in Cold War Berlin, love of German poetry, song, and cultural history, and romantic liaisons. Currently, she resides in a rural village in the former GDR with her British partner Julie, and their two dogs Diesel and Brandy-Bandit. She continues to craft words and music.

Naomi can be reached at femcomposer@naomimusic.com, www.lifemissionassociates.com and on Facebook.

www.ingramcontent.com/pod-product-compliance
Lightning Source LLC
Chambersburg PA
CBHW060345260626
47160CB00006B/2204